THE
SECRET
CHORD

By Geraldine Brooks

THE
SECRET
CHORD

GERALDINE BROOKS

Little, Brown

LITTLE, BROWN

First published in Great Britain in 2015 by Little, Brown

1 3 4 5 7 9 10 8 6 4 2

Copyright © 2015 by Geraldine Brooks
Published by arrangement with Viking, a member of Penguin Random House Group (US)

Map copyright © 2015 by Laura Hartman Maestro

The moral right of the author has been asserted.

A CIP catalogue record for this book
is available from the British Library.

Hardback ISBN 978-1-4087-0451-6
C Format ISBN 978-1-4087-0593-3

Printed and bound in Great Britain by
Clays Ltd, St Ives plc

Papers used by Little, Brown are from well-managed forests
and other responsible sources.

MIX
Paper from
responsible sources
FSC® C104740

Little, Brown
An imprint of
Little, Brown Book Group
Carmelite House
50 Victoria Embankment
London EC4Y 0DZ

An Hachette UK Company
www.hachette.co.uk

www.littlebrown.co.uk

To Nathaniel . . .

". . . the isle is full of noises,
Sounds and sweet airs that give delight and hurt not."

"Now the acts of David the king, first and last, behold, they are written in the words of Samuel the seer, and in the words of Nathan the prophet . . ."

I Chronicles 29

"Now the rest of the acts of Solomon, first and last, are they not written in the history of Nathan the prophet . . ."

2 Chronicles 9:29

A Note on Names

Throughout the novel I have used personal and place-names in their transliteration from the Hebrew of the Tanakh: Shaul, Shmuel and Shlomo, for example, rather than the perhaps more familiar Saul, Samuel and Solomon.

The Names

Nizevet, David's mother according to the Talmud
Yishai (Jesse), David's father

David's Brothers and Sisters
Eliav
Avinadav
Shammah
Raddai
Natanel
Zeruiah
Avigal

David's Wives
Mikhal, daughter of King Shaul, first wife of David
Ahinoam, second wife of David
Avigail of Carmel (Abigail), third wife of David
Maacah of Geshur
Hagit
Eglah
Avital
Batsheva

David's Nephews
Yoav (Joab), David's general, son of Zeruiah
Avishai, Yoav's warrior brother

Asahel, Yoav's warrior brother
Amasa, son of Avigal
Yonadav, son of Shammah

David's Children

Amnon, son of Ahinoam
Daniel, son of Avigail
Avshalom, son of Maacah
Tamar, daughter of Maacah
Adoniyah, son of Hagit
Yitraam, son of Eglah
Shefatiah, son of Avital
Shlomo, son of Batsheva
Natan, son of Batsheva

Others

Shmuel (Samuel)
Avner (Abner), Shaul's general
Moshe (Moses)
Yehoshua (Joshua)
Avram (Abraham)

THE
SECRET
CHORD

*T*here was an almond blossom, yesterday. It had opened its pale petals on a twig of the bough that curls and twists up to my windowsill. This morning, the blossom is gone; the paleness upon the twig is snow. It does one no good, in these hills, to set store by the earth's steady warming.

My body is as bent as that bough. The cold is an ache in my bones. I am sure that this year's reaping will be the last that I see. I hope only for one more season of summer fruit, for the ease of the hot sun on my back, for ripe figs, warm from the tree, spilling their sweet nectar through these splayed fingers. I have come to love this plain house, here among the groves. I have laid my head down in many places—on greasy sheepskins at the edge of battlefields, under the black expanse of goat hair tents, on the cold stone of caves and on the scented linens of palaces. But this is the only home that has been my own.

They are at work, already, on Har Moriah. From across the wadi, I can hear the thin squeal of the planes scraping upon the logs. Hard work to get these trees here; felled in the forests of the Lebanon, lashed together into rafts, floated south on the sea, dragged up from the coast by oxen. Now the tang of cut cedar perfumes the air. Soon, the king will come, as he does every morning, to inspect the progress of the work. I know when he arrives by the cheers of the men. Even conscripted workers and slaves call out in praise of him, because he treats them fairly and honors their skill.

I close my eyes, and imagine how it will be, when the walls have risen from the foundations of dressed stone: the vast pillars carved with lilies and pomegranates, sunlight glinting on cladding of gold . . .

It is the only way I will ever see it: these pictures in my mind's eye. I will not live to make the ascent up the broad stairs, to stand within the gilded precincts as the scent of burning fat and incense rises to the sky. It is well. I would not wish to go without him. I thought, at one time, that we would go together. I can still see his eyes, bright with the joy of creation, as he chose and planned what materials, what embellishments, pacing the floor, throwing his arms up and shaping the pillars as he envisioned them, his long fingers carving the air. But that was before I had to tell him that he would never build the temple. Before I had to tell him that all his killing—the very blood that, one might say, slakes the mortar of those foundation stones—had stained him too deeply. Strange words, you might think, to come from the selfsame source that had required these killings of him.

Hard words, like blows. The blast from heaven, issuing from my mouth. Words born of thoughts I had not had, delivered with anger I did not feel, spilling out in a voice I did not even know for my own. Words whose reason no human heart could fathom. Civilization is built upon the backs of men like him, whose blood and sweat make it possible. But comes the peace, and the civil world has scant place for such men. It fell to me to tell him so.

And like all such words that have formed upon my lips, these have become true in fact. It has come to be just as the voice said it would: this one dear ambition denied him. A bequest, instead, to his heir.

In this, I am more fortunate than he. I have lived to complete my life's great work. I have rolled and tied the scrolls with my own hands, sealed them with wax, secured them in clay vessels, and seen to their placement in the high, dry caves where I played as a child. In the nights, which have become so long for me, I think of those scrolls, and I feel a measure of peace. I remember it all so clearly, that day, at the turn of the year, the month when kings go out to battle. How warily I broached the matter. It might seem odd to say so, as my whole life in his service had been bent to this purpose: the speaking of truth, welcome or no. But it is one thing to transmit the divine through a blasting storm of holy noise, another thing entirely to write a history forged from human voices, imperfect memories, self-interested accounts.

I have set it all down, first and last, the light and the dark. Because of my work, he will live. And not just as a legend lives, a safe tale for the fireside, fit for the ears of the young. Nothing about him ever was safe. Because of me, he will live in death as he did in life: a man who dwelt in the searing glance of the divine, but who sweated and stank, rutted without restraint, butchered the innocent, betrayed those most loyal to him.

Who loved hugely, and was kind; who listened to brutal truth and honored the truth teller; who flayed himself for his wrongdoing; who built a nation, made music that pleased heaven and left poems in our mouths that will be spoken by people yet unborn.

I have had a great length of days, and been many things. A reluctant warrior. A servant, a counselor. Sometimes, perhaps, his friend. And this, also, have I been: a hollow reed through which the breath of truth sounded its discordant notes.

Words. Words upon the wind. What will endure, perhaps, is what I have written. If so, it is enough.

I

A man alone in a room. Not such an extraordinary thing. Yet as I stepped into the chamber I had a sense of something out of place. My eye traveled around the space, the woven pillows, the low tables set with sweating ewers of cool water . . . all was in order, yet something was not right. Then I grasped it. It had been a while since I had found him in a room by himself. For a long time, it seemed, he had moved in a press of people: members of his household, the men of his army, his sons, servants, sycophants.

He stood by the open window, his back to me. From my place by the door I could not see what he saw, but the sounds made plain enough what held his gaze: the snap of banners in the breeze, the stamp of hooves, the wince and grind of iron on stone. And woven among these, like a bright thread through homespun, the sudden excited shouts of little boys. For them, born in the years of victory, muster for war was cause for uncomplicated joy. I knew that giddy thrill. I had been such a boy myself, once. When he, little more than a youth, led the band that sacked my village.

His fists, balled tight, were planted on the wide sill of the window embrasure, his arms encircled by polished copper cuffs. His hair, the same color as the copper, was undressed, and fell in a dense mane against the fine black wool of his mantle. The cuffs glinted in the low slant of early light as his arm muscles flexed. He was clenched from head to foot.

I am not a coward. Being in his service does not allow for it. My life, at certain times, has required me to draw upon deep wells of courage, and I am glad to say that I have never yet come up dry. But as I have resolved to set down a full account here, so I must begin with an honest accounting of myself. That morning, I was afraid. I had been summoned from my bed when it was still full dark, and though my slave, when he called me, had thought to bring a tray of warm bread fresh from the ovens, I had not touched it. Now, my empty stomach churned. Sound carries, at that hour, and as I waited in the anteroom, even the heavy cedar door could not muffle the angry voices within.

When Yoav exited the room, he burst through the door so abruptly that the young guard barely had time to come to attention, the butt of his spear striking the stone floor a few seconds after his general had already swept past him. Yoav's lips were drawn thin as a sheet of linen, his skin as pallid. He paused for a moment, fiddling with a strap on his greaves. His hand, which I saw was trembling slightly, could not manage the buckle. I have known Yoav since I was a child and he a youth thinking to kill me. I have seen him outnumbered on the battlefield and watched him run a man through at close quarters. I have seen him stand accused of murder, awaiting a death sentence. But never before had I seen his hand shake. He saw that I noticed, and he scowled. "Go in," he said tersely. "He wants you." Then, as I edged past him: "Take care. He is in a rage. His mood is foul."

The guard opened the door for me, looking to neither right nor left as I passed from the anteroom to the inner chamber. I stood, just inside, waiting for acknowledgment. After a time, unsure if he knew that I was there, I cleared my throat. Still he did not turn. I held myself motionless, my gaze on the yellow shaft of sunlight widening upon the flagstones. Although it was early, the room was warming. Soon enough, it would be hot. I felt a bead of sweat forming on my brow.

Suddenly, he opened his fists, reached for the shutters, and slammed them shut. He turned, his light mantle swinging. I, who had served him for years, was used to that face, its grave beauty, the bright glance that could kindle love or fear. But the expression was not the one I had expected. Yoav was son of the king's older sister; they had become men together. He knew David as well as anyone alive. Yoav had said anger, and anger was there, but I could tell he had not read his uncle in full. Anger was there, but not anger only. The tense set of David's body showed will at work, containing wrath, but also grief. The glint in his eye was, I believe, a tear.

"What is the profit of being an anointed king, Natan, if I am to be confined here like a prisoner?"

"Your generals act only out of love for you—"

His hand spliced the air. "They act out of fear." He had never been a man for platitude. "Love?" He spat the word. "There is no love in this. This is fear and mistrust. And for what? The lapse of a moment, merely. How many wars have we made together? You have been at my side, time and again, when we fought the Plishtim. You were with me in the south when we crushed the Moavites, and in the north against the Arameans. And you know well—who better?—I was a warrior for years before that. In all those battles, when did I ever flinch? Tell me. Tell me a time I faltered." The voice had steadied now, and was rising.

That voice. So familiar to me. So familiar to all of us. *The sweet singer of Israel.* So the people called him, long before he was king. I had heard that singer's voice fill a hall, and bring tears to the cheeks of seasoned warriors. But I had heard it also on the battlefield, fierce and wild, carrying over the clash of arms and the cries of the dying.

"Never," I answered him. This was not flattery, but unburnished truth. In my mind, the visions crowded, one layered upon the other, each of them with the unnatural vividness of memories forged at moments when one's life is at risk. I could see bright hair flying from beneath the iron helmet as he sprinted before us into a clatter of arrows, the faceted muscles of his calves as he led the swarm up a siege ladder, the sinews of his back, taut with the strain of the pulled bow as he braced himself in the *merkava*. Every memory I had of him was a view from behind. Simply because, at the deadly moment, he was always in the forefront.

I had been trailing after him, as ever, at the end of that most recent campaign, of which he now spoke. We had been fighting for more than a week, the advantage now theirs, now ours. The day was hot, windless. The air was thick with lingering smoke from the night's death pyres, still smoldering. The stench of charred bone met the stink of rot and vomit, shit and sweat. I have never loved war, as some men love it. I have fought of necessity, as has every man my age with two legs, two arms and wit enough to follow a simple order. It is what the times, and the Land, have required of us.

It was nearing sunset on the eighth day. We'd fought since dawn. I had reached that point beyond exhaustion, where every muscle quivers and my mind could not hold a thought beyond the next step, and the one after, the next breath, and the one after. We went forward through sheer will—his will, that force that could goad a man to do what was beyond him. Finally, in the long shadows of the late afternoon, the Plishtim began to fall back from the plain. Their retreat was toward the foothills. Another general would have let them go and been glad of it. But he saw that if they secured that high ground they might regroup and come at us again, this time with their archers positioned to advantage. So he called us to ranks with a curdling cry. I glimpsed his face through the crowd of men. It was bloodied, dirt-streaked, avid. Then he turned, fist to the sky, and sprinted. He set the pace for the fleetest of his runners, youths who could give him a decade. Even uphill, he seemed to fly over the loose stones that slid out from underfoot and left me skidding and swearing.

I fell behind, and lost sight of him. Others—younger men, better fighters—overtook me, swarming to him, compelled by his courage. When I finally glimpsed him again, he was above me on a long, slender ridge, in the thick of fierce fighting. Trying to narrow the distance between us, I lost my footing entirely on the uncertain ground. I slipped. Metal, leather and flesh scraped against rough limestone that bit like snaggleteeth. I could not control my fall until I planted my foot into something that gave softly under my weight. The man had been attempting to crawl away, dragging himself with his remaining hand while a slime of blood pulsed from the stump of his sword arm. My boot, mashing his neck flat into stone, had put an end to that. When I lifted my foot, the man gave a wet gargle, and was still. I scraped the mess off my boot onto the nearest rock and went on.

When I reached the ridge, the king was making an end of another fighter. He was up close, eye to eye. His sword had entered just above the man's groin. He drew it upward, in a long, slow, arcing slash. As he pulled the blade back—slick, dripping—long tubes of bowel came tumbling after. I could see the dying man's eyes, wide with horror, his hands gripping for his guts, trying to push them back into the gaping hole in his belly. The king's own eyes were blank—all the warmth swallowed by the black stain of widening pupils. David reached out an arm and pushed the man hard in the chest. He fell backward off the narrow ledge and rolled down the slope, his entrails unfurling after him like a glossy ribband.

I was engaged myself then, by a bullnecked spearman who required all my flagging strength. He was bigger than me, but clumsy, and I used his size against him, so that as I feinted one way, he lunged with his spear, overbalanced and fell right onto the dagger that I held close and short at my side. I felt the metal grating against the bone of his rib, and then I mustered enough force to thrust the tip sharply upward, the blade's full length inside him, in the direction of his heart. I felt the warm wetness of his insides closing about my fist. It was intimate as a rape.

When I made an end of it and could look up, the king had advanced again, to a higher ledge, and stood atop another fleeing adversary. Legs astride the body, he raised his dagger arm. The air throbbed then, the skirl of wings. A carrion bird. Reflexively, my eye followed it. That is how I saw the spearman. The setting sun had been hidden in a purple flounce of cloud, but just then a throbbing yellow crescent of fire broke the edge, and in the beam of sudden light, I caught a glint from behind the cover of an outcrop—a spear, poised for the cast. The spear thrower was above and to the right of the king. His legs were well braced, his line perfect. The bronze shaft sailed out of his hand. It would have been a lethal throw, if Yoav's younger brother Avishai had not risked his own life to deflect it.

Avishai leaped between the king and the spear, his head back, howling. He expected to die. Every man on that ridge turned to witness it. At the deadly second, some warrior instinct caused him to adjust his stance by a hairbreadth and raise his bow. The spear tip caught on the edge of it, splintering the wood, skittering harmlessly across the rocky ledge. It was the kind of thing we'd seen David do. Now a younger man had done it for him.

We all cheered, of course. Someone slew the spearman, and then the fighting resumed in the exhilarated frenzy that comes from catastrophe averted.

But the king did not wish to hear of this from me. Not today. So I buried the image of his near death and said: "Every man who has served with you knows how you have prevailed. Every one of us knows what you are."

"'Are'? Say, rather, 'were.' That is what Yoav means: 'You *were* a mighty soldier, but now we must fight your battles for you.' I tell you, when Avishai leaped before that spear, I knew how it would be seen. I had to laud Avishai before the men. It was his due. But the words were gall in my mouth. And even though he is my sister's son and the brother of my general, I tell you this, Natan: I wanted to strike him dead. I wanted to grasp the end of that shattered shaft and plunge it through his side. I have lived most of my life in soldiers' camps. I know what they saw. I know how they think. Their confidence sours as sudden as curdled milk."

"Not so. You may think you know the mind of the common soldier, but with respect—you are not one, and have not been for some time. The men know this, even if you do not. Times have changed, and you, King, have changed them. You are not that petty chieftain who led scattered bands of outlaws to skirmishes in the hills. Why do we not cower in the wastes, hiding amid thorns and rocks as we used to do every time a sortie out of Mitzrayim marched across our land? Why do we not huddle trapped in the highlands while the Plishtim garrison the passes to the fertile plains? It is not so long since we had to grovel to them for enough iron even to make farm tools, much less weapons. Now we push them to the coast and pursue them to the very gates of their towns. Now the very best of their fighters come and offer their sword hilts in your service. You know they would not bend the knee to any other man. Not they, nor the Hittites, nor the Yebusites, nor any other of the strangers who serve you. Do not tell me you would put all this at risk—after all it cost to bring it about— for some warrior-pride. You, who have nothing to prove to anyone about valor or skill at arms. You have taught our enemies to fear us. You are the lamp of Israel. Would you chance to quench it?"

I had thought what I said would stoke his vanity. Instead, he glared at me. His eyes, that amber gaze that I was used to feel warm with affection, had turned cold. "Spare me, Natan. I have had an earful of this womanly keening, these empty pieties. From you, at least, I expect to hear the truth. The truth is, I have made this army. It's I who drove them, I who gave them confidence. Too much, it seems. They think they can do without me, set me aside like some heathen's war-god idol, set up in a temple to bring good luck." He turned away, back to the window. He flung open one of the shutters. A few minutes, and Yoav's voice rose, giving the order to move out.

"Will you not go down? It would put heart into the troops."

"'Go down'?" He mimicked my solicitous tone in a voice oily with contempt. "To remind my men that I stay behind? That for the first time in memory I do not lead them? Are you mad? Of course I will not go down."

A great cheer rose as the runners set off. The foot soldiers first—spears, archers, slings. This was followed by a clatter of hoof-beats and the squeal of metal wheels as fifty merkavot—a full half of all we had then—pulled out behind them. Dust motes rose from the street and drifted into the room, sparkling. He turned from the window, crossed the room and laid his fingers lightly upon the neck of his harp. There was always one near to hand; every servant knew to see to that. A small one hung by the window in his bedchamber. He said that when a night wind stirred the strings, it was a welcome awakening. He would rise from his bed and pray to the Name, who had blessed him so greatly. The instrument he reached for now was one of his favorites, a fine tall harp from Mitzrayim, the slender curve of its soundboard a smooth and perfect arc such as that land's craftsmen know how to fashion. But, like all his harps, this one had been adapted to his use, the number of its strings doubled to allow for strange tunings, with half and quarter tones that gave his music its unique, complex sound.

"You know, I suppose, why Yoav sent you." I was unsure how to answer this. I did not want him to think that Yoav and I had been discussing ways to handle him, even though this was the truth. But it seemed he did not expect an answer. He snorted, and gave a smile that had no joy in it. "I know what Yoav has in his mind: he sees me sitting here with you, picking at the skein of my deeds like a woman at her weaving basket. He wants to give me occupation while he usurps my place and marches my men to war. You, I suppose, support him in this."

"No, I do not."

"No?" He looked up. "What's this? You are at odds with Yoav?"

"I do not think a recitation of your victories is worthy of your time." I took a breath and dived deep. "Nor mine."

"Is that so? My victories are an unworthy subject for your talents?"

Have a care, Natan, I told myself. It is one thing to speak hard truths to a king in that strange voice that rises up unbidden from the earth and echoes with the power of the heavens. It is another thing entirely to speak frankly to him as one man to another, especially as I am a man in his service. *Eved hamalek.* The servant of the king. But, then, what service could I offer, if not this: speaking, where other men held a prudent peace. Whatever the risk, I had him now. His anger was shifting, away from Yoav and toward me. I had drawn the boar. Now I had to stick him.

"Any half-skilled graver can etch a stela that says in this or that place the king did vanquish this or that people. I am sure the great king of the Two Rivers and your neighbor the pharaoh, each of them, has a legion of gravers at work this very moment, making fine monuments."

"And why should they not?"

"Because the rubble of a hundred such stelae lines the walls of our sheep folds. And the dust of a thousand more blows about the Land, ground down to sand."

He gave me a glance that, if not warm, was no longer a shard of cold stone. He returned his gaze to the harp, running a finger up and down the silken grain of the wood. "Go on."

"In our wine store at home, there was a graved stone, holding up the lintel. Basalt, I think, finely dressed. It stood out among the common limestone, so that was why I noticed it, I suppose, when I was a boy. There were just a few words of an inscription, very worn. I was excited when I found it—it is the kind of thing that fires the mind of a child—and I showed my father." I remembered the cool dark cavern carved deep into the rock, the tall, sweating rows of pithoi, the biscuit scent of the clay, the rich aroma of fermentation. My father's large hand, stained from many pressings, fingering the hollows etched into the stone. I remember that he turned to me, and smiled, and commended me for noticing it. "He was an unlettered man, but he guessed the writing might be in the style of the Hittites. No doubt it lauded the victory of some important leader. I would look at those words and wonder, Who was he? What manner of man? What sort of boy? Which people helped him to power? Which hindered him . . ." I paused, uncertain whether to continue. But David's gaze was on me now, arrested. So I plowed on.

"Whoever he was, he was gone. His story, however glorious, lost, and so thoroughly forgotten that his monument had been broken up into building stones and set to use in a humble vintner's storeroom." Here we came to the nub of it. My own voice had risen as I spoke. I took a breath, and lowered it. "You know my first prophecy." Even as I said the words, I felt sickness rise at my own memory of it. When one becomes a sounding brass for the voice of the unseen, there is a price to be paid: the throbbing head, the darkening vision, the rasping breath, the falling fits and spasms. And when it happens to you on a day when you have lost everything, a wicked day of death and butchery, it is hard, indeed, to revisit the moment. I had begun to breathe unevenly, just bringing it to mind.

"Of course I know. I have built all this"—he swept his arm in a wide, expansive gesture meant to encompass more than a fine room in a well-built palace—"on the foundation of those words. Every man alive knows what you said that day."

"It was not I who said it," I murmured, but he shrugged off my correction.

"What has that to do with this matter?"

"Your line will not fail. You know this. Yet memory surely will. Your sons—what will they remember? Or their sons, after? When all who knew you in life are but bleached bone and dust, your descendants, your people, will crave to understand what manner of man you were when you did these deeds, first and last. Not just the deeds. The man."

He gazed at me for a long moment. His face was unreadable. He picked up a low carved stool then, and when I moved to take it from him, he waved me off. He carried it to the harp and settled himself to play. As an afterthought, he motioned me to sit, so I sank gratefully upon the pillows and let out the breath I had not even realized I was holding. He tilted the tall harp, settling it against his shoulder gently, as a woman settles her infant. His fingers rolled a few idle triplets, but his gaze was fixed on the distant view of hills, the olive trees silver in the sunlight.

"It is true, what you say." All the anger was gone from his voice. "When I was a youth, learning war, I often thought of it. We hear of men like Shalmanezer or Sargon, who won great battles. Of Ramses, who built the mighty temples on the backs of our ancestors, or of Hammurabi, who, they say, ruled with wise laws. But these are names only. It would be something, to know their nature. To know them as men." He paused, his eyes still distant. "To be known as a man." His fingertips pressed harder against the strings. His hands were strong, but the fingers were slender, moving swiftly through the tall strings, weaving sound from the filaments.

It was as if the harp were a loom, the notes he drew from it a bright thread forming a splendid pattern. He played this way often, even interrupting meetings with his generals. He said that the music—its order and precision—helped him find the patterns in things—the way through the confusion of events and opinions to direction, to order, and beyond, to inspiration.

He played for some time. I do not know if he was improvising or playing from memory. The melody was sweet, intricate and soothing. You could read his mind through his music, always. I felt the tension in my body easing. I had been braced against his anger and his grief, but the music revealed a mellowing of his mood. Finally, he brought it to an end, in a graceful run of notes, and set the harp back upright. He turned his eyes on me. They were not cold now, but the expression remained opaque. "Catch a true likeness, see a plain reflection in the water of the well, you will not like the flaws revealed in the face that stares back at you."

I struggled to suppress a smile. I could not imagine that his own reflection had ever given him much grief. The golden shimmer of his youth had been tempered like worked metal in his adult years so that even now, in middle age, he gleamed. Years had brought only distinction to a beauty that had proved irresistible to men and women alike. But he was serious, deep in consideration of what I had said. I thought it best to add nothing further, to let the line of his thought lead him to his own conclusions. He commenced to play again, but after a time, his fingers paused and hovered above the strings. He turned his face to me.

"Perhaps I can prove myself brave in this, at least. I will consider it. Now go."

As the young guards' spears hit the floor and the door closed behind me, he started to play in earnest. His large, strong hands could draw forth a breadth of sound that one did not generally associate with the gentle harp. He could make it speak with a thousand voices, soft or stormy. He did so now. And then, that other instrument over which he had full mastery—his voice. It was an old song; I recognized it. He had sung it at his coronation.

> *. . . in the day of thy power,*
> *in the beauties of holiness*
> *from the womb of the morning:*
> *thou hast the dew of thy youth. . . .*

Good, I thought. Already he has turned his mind from the gnarled present to the shimmering past.

The next day, he sent word that I might make the history if I wished to do so. I assumed he would call for me when he was ready to begin. Awaiting his summons, I busied myself with the pumice, scraping calfskin. This work I would not trust to fragile clay. I have yet to train a servant who can bring a hide to my standard, and the scrolls to record the life of a king had to be free of all blemish.

But instead of the call to audience, what came from him instead that afternoon was a clay tablet with a list of three names upon it. Seraiah, his scribe, had graven it, apparently in some haste. I had to carry the tablet to the light to make sense of his hand. At first, I did not understand what David meant by it, but then I grasped his purpose. It was very like him. He was sending me to talk to those who had known him in childhood and as a youth, before I came into his service. At the end of the short list of names, Seraiah had added a note: *The king says: after these, you know the story as well as any and may set down what you see fit.* I smiled when I saw what he intended. It seemed he did not plan to give his own account at all. The work here would fall all to me, to gather and record these testimonies, to write my own account. I ran a finger over the names. *Mikhal.* That one name, alone, showed that he did not depend upon the emergence of a flattering portrait. Mikhal, for whom his very name was bile. Well, I thought. *That* will be a challenging encounter. She had been his first wife and, in name, a wife she remained, although to my knowledge she and David had not seen each other nor exchanged words in years. But as she remained part of his household, if the king bade her speak to me she would be obliged, at least, to receive me.

For a seer, I was remarkably obtuse. I know this now; I did not know it then. Yoav and I had conspired to find some occupation that, while worthwhile in itself, would serve to distract a restless and unhappy king. Instead, he had found a way to distract *me*, to get me out of his way. A man will silence the voice of his conscience when it suits him to commit sin. But if your "conscience" walks and breathes as a living man in your service, you might have to go to some additional lengths. I did not see this. I did not see that a proud and vital man who feared his manhood waning might take any reckless step to prove to himself it wasn't so. In the service of my gift, I have had to forgo much that makes a man in full. I know now that this sacrifice has left me blind to certain things. I can see what others cannot see, but sometimes I miss what is apparent to the dimmest simpleton.

At the time, I was caught up in the project, and interested in the names upon the list. One was unknown to me, and yet it was the very first he had set down. Seraiah the scribe had underscored it heavily, and written a note: *The king says, This one, before all others.* The next name, *Shammah,* I knew well enough. Shammah was one of David's older brothers. There had been seven of them, but Shammah was the last still living. He had been with us in the outlaw years, when Shaul the king turned on David and sought his death. There had been little love lost between David and his brothers. But Shaul's hatred of David had spread like a stain upon his close kin. They had been obliged to go into hiding with him in those years, because the alternative was imprisonment or execution. Now Shammah kept a household on the outskirts of Beit Lehem and administered that settlement in the king's name. According to the tablet, the unfamiliar name, *Nizevet bat Adael*, was a woman who was part of Shammah's household.

It was too late that day to set out, so I sent word to the stable to bespeak a mule for the following morning, and to the kitchens for provision. I left at first light.

II

There was a time, not long since, when no man would have traveled alone on the road from Yebus, as Ir David was then named, to Beit Lehem. It is easy enough to forget how it was in the Land, now that the trade roads are in good repair, the borders mostly respected and the bandits under the foot of the king's forces. Of course, he understood very well what was necessary when he came to power because he had spent so many years himself as a bandit and a marauder, living on fines exacted from unlucky travelers and swift attacks on ill-defended villages like my own.

I was ten when I first saw him. My father hated idleness, so when the pressing was done and before the time for pruning, he would send me with the goats to find better grazing beside the streams that cut a path through the mountains rising steep above our village. I did not mind this. I liked to be off by myself, away from the eyes of adults who always had some task or errand to demand of an unoccupied child. In those sun-blasted hills, I could lie prone on a rock and scan the bright hillside, doing little but casting a stone from time to time to redirect a goat that wandered too far from the flock. A boy could let his thoughts unspool in those idle hours, dreaming of a hundred things, or of nothing. Sometimes, through the dense air that hung like mist over the Salty Sea, I would gaze across at the bare hills of Moav, and wonder if there was a boy like me lazing by a spring, and what his life was like, and what his thoughts were. But that day, the heat defeated me. I lay there and felt it press down upon me, like a great furred beast, smothering even the desire for thought. I fell into a heavy doze. The sting of a pebble roused me.

"Better wake up, little shepherd, or your flock will be halfway to Beersheva." The voice, amused, came from above and behind me. I scrambled to my feet and turned, blinking. He was on the next ridge, the sun behind him, its rays dancing like flames in his bright hair. He jumped lightly from the ledge and moved toward me. I raised my hand to shade my eyes and saw that he was a young man, perhaps twenty, and armed. Dismay must have shown in my face. My fear was not caused by his short sword or his bow. It was the thought that I might have lost the flock. To lose even one goat was a whipping offense.

He smiled, reached out a hand and tousled my hair as an affectionate older brother might have done. "Well met, little shepherd. Good thing I found you. When your flock wandered into my camp, yonder, the men started sharpening their knives. There was talk of goat stew this night."

"Please, no! My father . . ."

"Don't concern yourself. Your flock is safe. I was a shepherd myself, not so long since. I do not take without asking. You are from the village below?" I nodded. "You know the head man?"

"My father is the head man."

"Well met indeed, then. Give your father my greetings, and tell him that my band will be camped here for some days. We are armed fighters, two score of men, and some few of us have families. We would be glad of provisions. Tell your father that David, son of Yishai the Beit Lehemite, makes this request."

My eyes grew wide. "You? You are the one that killed the giant of Gath?" I fingered the side of my head where the pebble had grazed it. A stone not so much larger had turned the tide for us at the famous battle in the Wadi Elah. Every boy in the Land knew that story.

He smiled. "So they called him. He was big enough, but no giant. He was slow, I was quicker. He underestimated me. That is all.

Sometimes, it is good to be small. Remember that. Use it while you still can." He eyed me, a summing look, as a buyer might cast over a lamb on the hoof. "I see from your hands and feet that you will grow to be a tall man. Is your father tall? Then you favor him. Now come and fetch your goats."

I followed him across the wadi and through the date palms into the clearing where he had made his encampment. It was a spare, well-organized and clean affair of four or five large goat hair tents. The kind of camp a military unit might pitch, that can be hastily struck and easily transported. They had herded my goats into their own makeshift thorn break, and as I was sorting mine from theirs, I noticed one of the women regarding me. She had her mantle drawn across the lower part of her face, but her eyes were the same deep green as the balsam fir that shaded her where she sat, and I found myself returning her glance. She lifted a fold of her mantle off a slim wrist, and turned her hand. It was a subtle gesture, but clear enough. She wanted me to approach her.

As I did, she stood—she was very tall, for a woman—and stepped back, deeper into the shade, out of sight of the main encampment. I followed her, as she clearly purposed. "Did my husband charge you with a message?" Her voice was low and quick. For a moment, I was confused. I did not think that by "husband" she could mean David. This woman was very handsome, but she was some years older than the youth I had just met. In my village, a commonplace thing was for the wife to be much younger than her husband, never the reverse.

She seemed to understand my confusion. She dropped her veil so that I could see her face. A slight smile played about her lips, which were very full, but already scored with the fine lines of her maturity. Her skin, a pale olive, was gently weathered like my mother's from many summers in the unforgiving dryness of the Land. But her wide green eyes had a level, intelligent gaze, and the lines that framed them seemed to me more likely etched by amusement than by hardship. "I am Avigail of Carmel, third wife of our leader, David. I am his wife because my first husband, Navaal, who was a drunkard and a fool, refused to send supplies for David's men when he requested them of us. We could afford it—we had three thousand sheep. I knew what the cost of that denial would be to us, so I saw to it myself, and met David on the road with the supplies before he and his band reached our village. Tell your father this: David is no ordinary outlaw, no ordinary man. When my husband died, I came to be his wife, even though I left behind a rich household to live as you see me here, among outlaws, begging for supplies. Boy, tell your father this is no small thing. Don't let him make the same mistake my foolish husband made. If he does, you—"

But she did not finish the message I was to bring, for David called for her then, and she cast her veil across her shoulder and left me alone in the shadows. I waited there a moment or so, and then made quick work of sorting and gathering my goats. I almost ran them down the hill to home, bursting with my news. By the time I reached the house, I had shaped the story so as to omit any mention of my putting the flock at risk. Still, when my father heard what I had to say, his brow creased.

That night, all the important men of the village gathered at our house. My mother sent me to pour the wine for them. One must not think ours was an insular community, distant though we were from other settlements. Because of the balsam resin we produced, and the sought-after fragrances we knew how to make from it, our village was well-known in the Land, and prosperous, too; the trade route was well traveled by all classes and kinds of men. So when our leaders gathered to deliberate, they were well informed. Our neighbor Shem, a resin maker, and therefore an important man, was speaking. "I say we pay him what he asks. His men do some service when they are camped in the wadi. They are a wall to us, and keep the young herders, such as your own boy there, safe from wild beasts or passing brigands. They are disciplined; they have not stolen livestock or plundered the date trees—"

"They are debtors and malcontents and troublemakers." My father, usually civil, cut Shem off in midsentence. "He that leads them has set himself against our king, who has made it plain enough that he wishes the man dead. If we pay him, we are abetting an outlaw, a condemned man. Do you want to incur the anger of Shaul?"

"I would risk that before I risk angering *him,* camped upon our dooryard." It was my uncle Barack who spoke, tossing his head in the direction of the hills. "The king is far away in Geba. What will he know of a dozen wineskins and a few bushels from our grain store? It was a good harvest, a good vintage. We can spare these things."

"And if we spare them to the outlaw son of Yishai the Beit Lehemite, what rabble next will we have at our door, demanding the food from our children's mouths and the fruits earned by our laborers' hands? Slaves run away from their masters every day, but we are not obliged to abet them. This brigand is no better than they. Worse, I say. There are rumors he serves the Plishtim *seren*, Achish of Gath. You would help him, and abet our worst enemy? I say we send him nothing."

"This 'brigand,' as you call him—when he was a mere boy he put the Plishtim to flight at the battle of Wadi Elah. The king did not think him a brigand then. Nor when he took him on as armor bearer, or married him to his daughter, or raised him up as leader of his fighters. You know how he fought in those days. How we all thought he had the blessing of the Name upon him, so many victories he won. Kings are fickle. You know that, brother. They say Shaul threw a spear at the boy, in his own hall, at meat, for no reason. Who would not flee, in such a case?"

"Who would not flee? A man who is innocent. A man who is honorable. It is not for us to question the judgments of our king. You would have us put food in a traitor's mouth?"

"I would put it there, yes. Rather than have him bring his men to take it."

"If that traitor and his rabble come here, we will fight them. Some few of us know how to fight." My father did not often speak of it, but he and his brother had borne arms against the Ammonites in their youth.

I loved my father, and I believe he loved me in his turn. I do not think it entered his mind that the denial of goods would put lives at risk. But when I left the room to replenish the emptied wine jug, I bumped into my mother, listening an ear in the passageway. I saw her face, before she had the chance to arrange it. There was dread in her expression, and also anger. She turned on her heel and led the way to the wine store. As she lifted the lid from the pithos, her hands were trembling.

"What is it?" I whispered. She shook her head and compressed her lips and would not speak. I reached for the dipper and took it from her. Her hands were too unsteady to fill the jug without spilling the wine. "You think Father errs in denying these outlaws?"

"It is not my place to say he errs," she hissed tersely. "Neither is it yours to think it. Go, serve and be silent."

"But I met a woman in his camp. One of his wives. She warned me that it would be risky to refuse him. Her husband did, she said, and she defied him, and brought the goods herself. That is how she—"

"Shhh." My mother raised her hand and laid her fingers on my lips. They were rough fingers, work worn from the hundred tasks she knew how to perform. But they were gentle fingers, too, always ready with a caress. "Your father heads this household. Leads this village. It is not for us to doubt him. I am no slut like this woman, who threw herself at the feet of a stranger and defied her husband's will."

"But she did it to save—"

"Hush, I said. You will obey me, and you will obey your father. Go now. They are waiting for their wine. Serve and be silent as I bid you."

A dozen wineskins and a few bushels of dates. It would have been a small price, and I might have lived a different life. I might have stayed in that village lit by the glare of the Salty Sea. Grown to manhood the beloved son of a prosperous house, learning to become a winemaker at my father's side. Feeling the weight of the warm grapes fall into my hands as each long summer ripened, plying the pruning knife with skill till the long rows of old vines held their balled fists up to the winter sky. By now, the vineyards would be mine to tend, and I would be teaching my sons in their turn. Or so I like to think. But perhaps this other destiny could not have been gainsaid. I do not know. All I do know is that no supplies were delivered, and I was instructed to take the goats by the southern wadi rather than the stream that ran to the north. Two days later, David sent to ask again. One of his men—a youth, really, no older than David himself—presented himself in the village asking for my father. He was received, and put his requests—or I should say, demands—rather more urgently than David had put them to me. My father became angry. I heard him say hard words: "traitor," "brigand," "thief." The young man became angry then in his turn. He raised his voice even louder than my father's, so that I could hear every word he said as if I were in the room.

"You dare to speak so of a man whose spittle you are not fit to wipe. David son of Yishai is the rightful leader of our people, the best leader—the best man—any of us has ever served. The king in Geba knew that, once. Did he not make David his son-in-law before madness seized him? Now he hates David for his very qualities, which are a reproach to his own failures. You should ask Shaul's son Yonatan, if you doubt me. It is well-known where *his* heart lies. Were it not for the command to honor the father he would be with us now, not propping up a demented, drooling . . ."

My father cut in then—loud, angry—saying that he would not have such disloyal words uttered in his house. He was not a stupid man: he could see the danger by then, I am sure. Yet he did have a stubborn streak, and a regard for his own opinions. Small flaws, maybe, to cost such a price as he paid for them. But he could not unbreak the eggshell. A few moments later, the tall young stranger pushed past me, thrusting me against the wall so hard that the stone bit into the bare skin of my upper arm. When he looked me in the face, I saw naked anger. For perhaps a thousand men, that look has been the last thing they ever saw. David's messenger to my father was Yoav, who would become our mighty general, though on that day I did not yet know his name.

At dawn I walked through my father's blood and stood face-to-face with his killer. David had come in the dark, swift and silent. He slew my father and my uncle Barack with the dispatch of a slaughter man attending to his trade. As I approached David, I could hear my mother screaming. Her voice was horrible—a ragged rasp. Stay back, she cried. Run. Hide yourself.

But I had done with obeying. I could no more heed her than stop my own heartbeat. I walked up to David. He looked down at me, puzzled. I imagine he saw a tear-streaked child, too touched or stupid to fear the blood-flecked murderer who stood before him.

"Did you not hear me, little shepherd? Did I not say I would kill all of his kin that can piss against a wall?"

Yoav lifted his spear, but I just stood there. David raised his hand wearily. "The boy's simple," he muttered. "Let him be." He shrugged and turned aside.

Then I spoke. Later, others had to tell me what I said. I knew that my lips and tongue were moving, but I could not hear my own words because my head was ringing like a stone under the blows of an iron mallet, blows that beat the blood behind my eyes. I stood there, in the crimson-misted ruins of my own life, and the words poured out. Through the red blur, I saw the faces of his fighters distort with wonder. Yoav lowered his weapon and gaped. David's own face creased, confused. Then it changed. His look became greedy. He spoke, but I could not make out his words through the thunder in my head. I saw him reach out to me, and then I fell.

When I came to myself, I was in his tent. The woman Avigail was leaning over me, swabbing my forehead with a cool cloth. David himself was sitting on the edge of my pallet. When he saw my eyes flicker, he nodded to Avigail, who went to the water jar and filled a cup. He reached and took it from her, caressing her hand as he did so, and offering her thanks even for so small a task. Even in my pain, I noted it. My father had never treated my mother with such distinction. David helped me into a sitting position, and then raised the cup to my lips. At first, I recoiled from his touch, but he clasped my shoulder with a gentle authority. "Drink," he said. When the water touched my lips, I realized I was parched. "Slowly," he cautioned, taking back the cup and setting it down.

He had washed off my father's blood and was wearing a fresh tunic of fine wool. To my complete astonishment, he grasped the neck of that tunic and rent it. He stood then and walked to the fire pit, stooped for a handful of cold ashes, and rubbed them into his bright hair. "I want you to understand. I regret these deaths. I mourn your kin. But what I did was necessary. These men—my fighters and their families—have put their trust in me. I have to do whatever it takes to sustain them. Know that I did not kill your father and your uncle for a few bushels of dates. I killed your father because if his refusal of my request had been allowed to stand, word of it would have spread, and I would not be able to feed my people—people who have risked everything for me. I can't allow that. It's the bargain I have made. They would die for me, so I must live for them. And kill for them, when I have to. Your uncle I had to kill to forestall blood vengeance. For that reason I should have killed you, too. You know that. But here you are. You will see how it is, now that you are one of us."

And I did see. And heard, and smelled. In my dreams, even now, I hear the screams of the enemy's stumbling warhorses, after he ordered their tendons cut. I smell the reek from the leaking bowels of the terrified Moavite captives, lined up in rows upon the ground as David's men ran the measuring cord alongside their squirming bodies, measuring life as one might measure out cloth, marking out a quantity to live and sentencing those beyond the cord's end to be butchered where they lay.

Whatever it takes. What was necessary.

These words might well have been the graven mottoes of his house. What was necessary, and no more. He spared a hundred of the Aramean horses—they are the ones that pull our merkavot today. He spared what he deemed to be a safe number of the Moavites, who pay tribute to us now and trouble us in war no longer. And he spared me, also, to be the pebble in his sandal and the goad in his hide. For he took me into his service that day and since then I have rarely left his side.

It might seem strange, that a boy would so easily desert all that he knew to serve his father's killer. It seemed strange to me, too. But as I lay there, my grief raw and my mind addled, I was not confused about where I now belonged. I knew, in some deep place, even then at the very beginning of things, that the heart of a prophet is not his own to bestow. I had to go with David whether I would or no. And not just because he willed it. Had he beaten me, thrown me out and left me dying by the side of the road, I would have crawled after him, shouting the words he needed to hear. Later, had he exiled me (as he might well have done, after some of my pronouncements) to some dry scab of white crystal in the middle of the Salty Sea, I would have waded back to him. But I have not needed to do any of those things. Until now, he has kept me close, even when my words have blistered him. I think he learned from what passed between Shaul and *his* prophet, Shmuel. He saw that the kingship of a people such as ours could not be fashioned after the kingships of other nations. It is, instead, a fragile and mysterious gift, and what is given by such a mighty hand can be snatched back in less than an eyeblink.

The remarkable thing is that he recognized me, even then, for what I was. It would be several seasons before I spoke again in that strange voice, and when I did, the message I gave was by no means as welcome as the first. Yet his faith in me never wavered. It has been allowed to me to see many things—bright shards of vision that sometimes foretell events as they will unfold, and other times are waking dreams that come and go with less effect than mist in the valley or the smoke about an altar. Some of these words have become famous; some have been for his ears alone. Some bear my name, some are remembered now as if they came to him directly from the mouth of the divine. It matters not, to me. In fact, it is better—truer—that men think so. For they are not my words. Often, as it was that first time, others have had to tell me what I have uttered.

He did not speak to me, that first day in his tent, of what I had said. He did not then realize that I did not know. I gleaned the content of my words from the men around him. It was easy enough to do so, for the whole camp was abuzz over what they already called Natan's oracle.

I had promised David a throne. More than that: the voice that used my mouth foretold for him an empire and a line that would never fail throughout the generations. Now, when the first two of those promises have come to pass, it is hard to recall how outlandish such words seemed. David, then, was an outlaw. A wanted man, declared a traitor. And the Land, this narrow notch, riven and divided by jagged lines of hills, was hardly the country likely to usher forth an empire. Our tribes were a frayed and flimsy alliance, fragmented by enmity, led by a king whose own anointing prophet, Shmuel, had disavowed him, whose behavior was erratic, if not mad. We were squeezed between the Sea People on the coast, Pharaoh's armies to the southwest, and the mighty peoples of the Two Rivers to the east. Our chief and nearest enemy, the Sea People, or Plishtim, as they called themselves, controlled access to iron so completely that we were obliged to use wooden boards for our plowshares. Tin and copper, such as we had, were no match for their forged arms. We could not pass freely even in the territory we claimed, that scant strip from Dan to Beersheva. But David believed the words I uttered that day, and so therefore did his followers. They took strength from that belief, and events surged rapidly forward on the tide of their confidence. By the time the seasons turned through four more reapings, he had been crowned king of

Yudah. By the time I was counted a man, he had added the crown of the kingdom of Israel and made the tribes of the Name one people at last.

The day my father died, I left childish things behind me. Even though I remained a mere boy in the reckoning of the world, never again was I treated as one. If I took orders, it was from David, as a man willingly in service to his leader. The tribe of my birth meant nothing to me now. I was neither Benyaminite nor Levite, Yudaite nor Ephraimite, but simply David's man. No one else had charge of me, or claim upon me. No one else nagged me about what chores to do or when I might come or go. From then on, I walked my own road, always at his side.

I left behind all my close kindred. I left my widowed mother and my infant sister. My mother returned to her father's household. Had my uncle been spared, he would have been charged with her care, but as things stood, she had no choice. Our last meeting was bitter. She did not give me her blessing when I left to follow David—how could she?—but she certainly did not press me to stay at her side. She did not like uncanny things, and the voice that had spoken through me had frightened her as she stood there, the screams dying on her lips as I walked forward toward what she thought would be my end.

I felt, in her shunning, the first of many such turnings-away. It was hard for a child to feel that ebbing love, to sense an estrangement that I could do nothing to gainsay. For my part, I still loved her as much as I had the moment before my mouth opened and the words poured out of me. But like the leper when the first lesion darkens and pits his skin, I was marked in her eyes, blemished, unlovable. I grieved to leave her, and wished I had the power to make her understand that I was still the boy she had carried and suckled, not some strange, tarnished, foreign thing. When she died, of a sudden fever, David was not yet king, so she did not live to know the worth of my gift, to see the words I had spoken become true in fact.

Given that my place with David made me into an outlaw in the world's eyes, my grandfather sanctioned no contact with my infant sister. By the time my status changed, she was a betrothed maiden and I, a stranger to her, had no part in her life. I regret this, but as I have set down, I had no choice.

I knew all this, even then, a boy of ten years. No other human noise was to come between that mysterious voice and me. Accordingly, when the season came to take a wife, I did not do so. I knew that the simple joys and intimacies of a common life were not for me. And in any case, who would want someone like me? The truth is, the people abide my kind, but no one loves us. There is awe, but no affection. We grow used to the turned shoulder, the retreating back, the bright conversation that sputters to a murmur when we enter a room, the sigh of relief when we leave it.

David alone understood what I was to him, and why he needed me by his side. And that has been my life, twinned with his. Since I joined him, I have known him as well as any man alive.

But what I did not know—what I would need to learn from several others in order to set down a full and true accounting of his life—was who he had been until that hot, dry, deadly day brought me to his side. I had heard the stories, of course. There is not a person now living in the Land who has not. But the stories that grow up around a king are strong vines with a fierce grip. They pull life from whatever surfaces they cling to, while the roots, maybe, wither and rot until you cannot find the place from which the seed of the vine has truly sprung. That was my task: to uncover those earliest roots. And he had directed me to the seedbed.

III

The Sheep Gate was not yet open when I set out. The captain of the guard, recognizing me, quickly gave the necessary orders and I urged the mule on. I never tire of the view from that gate, where the land slopes steeply away from the city walls and the light silvers the leaves of the olive groves that cling so tenaciously to the thin soils. Below, the valley was already a wash of swaying green. Families, early to work in the cool of the morning, bent their backs in their plots of flax and barley, somehow coaxing plenty out of crusty earth that seems more stone than tilth. A man plied his goad on a pair of oxen, prodding them forward ahead of his plow. Nearby, his sons did battle with the sprouting thistles and thorn bushes that threatened the young plantings. That is the only battle they now must do, thanks to the king. Common folk are no longer called away from their fields. Our standing army, trained and organized, is sufficient for such skirmishes as still trouble our borders.

The road to Beit Lehem is through the hill country and soon enough, the land began to rise again. I let the mule set her own surefooted pace as we began to climb. Farmland slowly ceded to the fir forests that lie between the settled areas. By the time we passed into the dense emerald stands, the sun had risen high enough to make me glad of the fragrant shade.

When I reached the outskirts of Beit Lehem I stopped at the well to ask direction. The women drew their mantles about themselves as I approached, but were easily able to point the way to a property on a gentle rise to the east of the town. It was a tidy compound set behind high walls. Within, three small, pillared houses shared a large courtyard. This was divided into two parts by a grape arbor. The noisome things—the kine pens, the dun cakes drying in the sun—occupied the downwind side, while a table and the hive-shaped *tannur* sat beneath a large old citron on the other. The tree was in blossom, so the tang of citrus mingled with the lingering scent of the morning's baking.

It was here that David's brother Shammah received me. And not with good grace. He had been pacing. The courtyard was etched across with a raw line of yellow earth stamped with the marks of his heavy tread. He was a big man who had let his large frame run to fat in the years since he had left the army and taken up the role of local judge. He looked nothing like his brother. Not simply because he was a decade older. The two were different in build, coloring, voice, manner, gait.

There was a table set in the shade of the citron trees, but Shammah did not invite me to sit. So I stood while a boy—Shammah's nephew or grandson, it was not clear—barred the wooden door behind me and took charge of my mule, leading her to the kine pens. Shammah strode up to me and stood, toe to toe. I am tall enough, but he was taller, and his massive neck and shoulders blocked out the light. "What in the name of a she-ass's cunt is my brother playing at now? 'Tell Natan everything.' What shit is this?"

I was taken aback by Shammah's tone, but even more by the implication of his words, his knowledge that I was coming, and my reasons for being there. For word to reach Shammah ahead of me, the king must have dispatched a royal messenger directly after our meeting, even before he sent me the list of names. I must have shown surprise.

"Did you not know he commanded that I receive you? You think I would have agreed to admit you here on this mad errand had he not? He sent word last night, set my son Yonadav to ride here, in the dark—could have broken his neck—and on Prince Amnon's own mule, no less, so that he could make good time. My mother's been locked up in her chamber weeping, ever since Yonadav told her she's required to speak to you."

Nizevet, the name I had not known. The one I must speak to first of all. So she was their mother. All the time I had known David, I had never heard her name. There might be two reasons for a man to hold his mother in such obscurity. He could wish to shield a woman's honor by seeing that she was not spoken of, or he might be in some way ashamed of his begetting. Shammah gave no clue as to which might be the case, but he continued to vent his displeasure. "I don't like it, and she likes it even less." He turned aside and spat into the dust. "I warn you, if you cause her any further distress . . ." He did not finish his threat, for she had appeared in the doorway of the smallest dwelling, leaning heavily on the arm of a young girl.

"It's all right, Shammah." A voice with a quaver that betrayed age, yet a lilting, melodious voice. David's voice, in female form. "If the king wants this, so be it. He must have reasons that seem good to him."

"Reasons? What reasons? Picking at old scars till they bleed—what good can possibly come of it? But you always favored him. Do what you will."

Shammah shrugged his immense shoulders and turned away. He lifted the heavy door bar as if it were a straw stalk, flung back the door and strode through, walking at an agitated pace down the hill toward the town. Nizevet raised her head and looked after him, until the boy who had taken my mule ran across the courtyard and drew the door closed. She turned her eyes on me then. They were the king's eyes: the same luminous amber that seemed to entrap light and shadow. Though hers were swathed in folds of tired flesh, they were set wide and deep, like his, with strong brows defining them.

"Forgive Shammah. He, too, has his reasons for his actions. And they seem good to him. You will know why, presently, I dare say." She moved with some effort toward the table, and we sat, the blown blossoms falling upon us like snowflakes. There were bowls of hyacinths about our feet.

The girl set a pillow behind Nizevet's frail shoulders and poured watered wine, and then withdrew into the shadow of the portico. You couldn't see her, but I could hear the scrape of her hand mill, the coarse basalt rider passing over the slab of the saddle, crushing the last season's wheat. Perhaps Shammah had instructed her to stay close and lend an ear to what was said.

I set out the reed pens and the phial of ink I had blended, and waited. When the old woman began to speak, her voice had a slight rattle, like a breeze through dry grass. She spoke in low tones, so that I had to strain to hear her.

"'Tell Natan everything.' That was the king's message. His order." Her mouth thinned as she said this. There was an awkward silence between us.

"The message did not please Shammah. It does not please you."

"Please me? How should it please me? I have lived very quiet all these years. The story of the king has never included me, and for good reason. I never thought he would want anyone to hear what I have buried so long in silence. You will have to be patient with me, therefore. These things that he suddenly bids told are not easy things. After all the good that has come to him, I cannot think why he wants to probe these old wounds. 'Tell Natan,' my son says. As if it were nothing. Well. Maybe it is, to him, now . . ."

Her voice trailed off, and she looked away from me, her eyes welling. The girl was at her side in a moment, offering a bowl of rosewater and a cool cloth. Nizevet took it, and pressed it to her brow for a moment. Her face was scored all over with lines, but the skin was delicate and unblemished, and the bones beneath the aged flesh were very fine. I saw that there had been great beauty, once. I would have wagered a talent that beneath her linen headdress, the silver hair was still streaked through with fading tongues of fire. When she started to speak again her voice was low and full of emotion. I could see the strain in her face as she tried to command herself.

"The name I gave him. Beloved. It was my act of defiance, you see.

He was the only one of my sons I named. Their father had been quick to give names to all the others. But to this one, he would give nothing. Not even a glance. He hated the very sight of him. Had the infant died, Yishai would have rejoiced."

What she said shocked me so that I stopped writing and stared at her. She gazed back, a hint of amusement in her troubled eyes.

"I see in your face that you doubt me. You will know why, presently. The older boys took their lead from their father. They treated their youngest brother as if he were an unwelcome stranger. Even Natanel—the closest in age, the kindest of them—ignored him. That was the best of the treatment he received at their hands. The older brothers put vinegar in his drink and gall in his food. They beat him and accused him of thefts for which he was blameless. No one knows these things that I am telling you. No one outside the family. And— before this odd command of his, if you had asked Shammah or any of the others, they would have denied it."

I had known her sons, most of them, but not well. None was close to the king, not one of them part of his inner circle. While she lived, his sister, Zeruiah, stood close in his affection and confidence, and her three sons, most especially Yoav, were prominent men. David's brothers, by contrast, had enjoyed lesser places at court. Yet in all my time at the king's side, there had been no hint of enmity. Nizevet seemed to read these thoughts as they passed through my mind. She smiled slightly.

"No one wants to remember how it was. The king, perhaps, least of all. But I remember. How could I not? When he was barely six years old, his father ordered that he be sent away from the *beit av*—the family home—to tend the sheep up in the hills. He was to live in a little hut of stone and branches, and come home only to get supplies. It was to get him away from the house, you see, so that Yishai would not have to look upon him. And this, too: the hills were full of lions then—not like now, when one rarely hears of an attack. How was a six-year-old supposed to survive out there alone? I believe Yishai hoped for his death. I wept the day he left, the crook—too large for him—threaded over his narrow shoulders, his slender wrists draped over the cane. He had the cheeses, olives and dried grapes I had packed for him tied in a cloth on his back. He looked small, and helpless, and lonely. My heart ached over it. I was in agony for him. But now I think that it was a good thing he got away from his brothers' persecutions and his father's open hatred. Those years in the hills taught him many things. You could say that they made him the man he became. For better . . ." she paused and drew a deep breath. "And yes, perhaps, for worse. Should a mother say such a thing?" She gave a swift, wan smile. "'Tell everything,' so he said. And so. Everything."

As she spoke, my pen scritched across the parchment and my mind filled with memories of David at our first meeting on the high hills above my village. I imagined him as that small shepherd boy, living in the long silences broken only by the baaing of the ewes and the clatter of stones shifting as the herd moved over them. I imagined the sharp scent of thyme crushed under the hooves, and the calls of the little birds in the thorn bushes.

He must have found ways to fill the long days and the silences. In those silences, perhaps, he discovered the consolations of music. I interrupted to ask her this, and she told how he fashioned his first harp. He had heard a harpist only once, when some itinerant musician had come to play in Beit Lehem. But out there in that hut, from ram's horn and sinew, by trial and error, he fashioned a crude instrument of his own, and learned how to draw prodigious sound from it.

He found his voice there, she said. There, where he could sing as loud and as long as he wanted with no one to complain of it.

As I wrote down her words, it came to me that there was something else he must have found there. Something that a boy who lives all his life in a busy household or a crowded town might never find. He found the ability to hear. In those endless days and in the still nights, I believe he learned what it means to really listen, a skill I had seen him wield to great effect. Men love the sound of their own voices,

and David knew how to let them speak. I had seen taciturn fighters
and oily-tongued emissaries alike undone by David's ability to draw
them out. He was not afraid of silence, which most of us will rush
to fill.

And this, too: our holiest men have always gone into the wilderness
to hear the voice of the Name. Avram was in the far desert under a star-
encrusted sky when the Name promised him descendants as numberless
as those stars. Moshe was in the distant hills, and also a shepherd, when
Yah spoke to him in the crackling fire. David heard some echo of the
divine voice out there, too, I am sure of it. For when the time came for
him to speak in the world, his words carried the roar of holy fire. How
else to account for his poetry, those words that fill our mouths and
hearts and give us voice to praise, lament, beseech and atone.

Struck by this realization, I had let my thoughts drift from Nizevet, who was recounting the more practical details of their lives at that
time. "I was his only contact," she said. "When he came down to the
house for provisions, all the others shunned him. But I would steal
hours with him. I would bathe him, cut his hair, dress him in the
warm things I had woven for him. I tried to feed him enough love to
make up for the way his father starved him. But it was never enough.
How could it be?"

I nodded as I set down her words. I understood then that I had
witnessed his long search for that missing love. That need is, you
could say, his great strength and his grave weakness. Then she said
something that made me shift in my seat.

"Yishai was a good man." She saw my involuntary movement and
turned her hand over and tilted her head in a gesture that seemed to
ask me to attend more closely to what she was about to say. "I see,
after what I have just told you, that you doubt me. But it is true. He
was an upright man, who sacrificed often and kept the law, in letter
and in spirit. He was known for it. People looked to him for guidance.
I was just a child when I married him, so to me he was like father and
husband both. Kind, gentle, generous. He inherited a middling flock

and built it into the largest in all of Beit Lehem. Our house, too, he expanded, over time. Not this place—" She waved a dismissive hand at the pleasant yet modest buildings surrounding us. "Our *beit av* was made of dressed stone and cedar, very fine. It went to my eldest, Eliav, of course, when Yishai died, and now has passed down to Eliav's son in his turn. But in those days I had a wing of my own, just for my servants and me, with a chamber for the looms so that we could work sheltered from the weather. I bore Yishai strong sons and modest daughters, and he honored me for that. What more should a woman expect in her life? I know well that most receive much less.

"But you are a man; you must know how it is. When a woman has borne a man so many children, even if she is still young, she is no longer the bride he once desired."

I did not interrupt her. I did not, as she assumed, know how it was. How could I?

"It is a common story," she continued. "But for a man of Yishai's character, it is not an easy thing to give way to lust as a lesser man might do. He could have taken other wives, but he had promised me, in the early heat of our union, that he would never do so. And he was a man of his word.

"Still, I began to see his eyes drift elsewhere. I knew he struggled. And then came my new maidservant, a Knaanit. She looked so much like me. It was an uncanny thing. Younger, of course. I think that is why, in truth, he hired her, even if he was not aware of what he did. He could not take his eyes from her. She was a good girl, from a decent family, who had sent her to our service because of Yishai's upright name. If she had been a willing slut, I might have acted differently. I might have turned my face away and let it unfold. But I could see how she drew her mantle higher when he walked into the room, how she hurried to complete her tasks and get away from him. How she contrived, as best she could, to avoid finding herself alone with him. His attentions frightened her. She wanted what any girl wants, honorable marriage and sons of her own. She knew that Yishai's lust, if satisfied upon her, would put all that at risk. But I knew it would happen one day. She could not hide from him indefinitely. So I sent her away to my daughter Zeruiah's house, on a pretext, as my daughter had recently been brought to bed with her third son. In doing so, I angered Yishai, even if he could not say so. She was my servant, supposedly, to dispose of as I liked. So his resentment festered, and he began to turn on me. In any case, that was when he started to rake over the matter of his ancestry, to try to cast doubt on the legitimacy of our union.

"I have said already that Yishai was ardent in his observation of the laws. And you will know that it has been the law since Moshe that the Ivrim must not marry from among the Moavites, as they were the tribe who denied passage through their lands when the Ivrim fled Mitzrayim. You know also that my husband's grandmother was the Moavite Ruth, who lay with Boaz just before he died. Some doubted that Yishai's father, who resulted from that union, was the legitimate issue of Boaz, and there were whispers at that time. This was all finished long before our wedding, and no one raised any question but that Yishai did me honor in choosing me to marry.

"But as his illicit desire burned him, so he turned to this old gossip about his grandmother Ruth. He flailed at himself, saying our marriage was unfit, that he, grandson of a Moavite, had not had the right to marry an Israelite of pure lineage, and that our marriage was unclean and we must separate. You can imagine how hard it was for me to hear it. Harder still when he refused to lie with me, infrequent as that had become since his passion for my servant took hold of him. Daily, he became more obsessed with the imagined uncleanness he had engaged in. He refused to take a dish from my hand, a cloth to wipe his brow. In the end, he put me by, and I returned, ashamed, to my father's house.

"Still, even with me gone from the house, he did not act on his lust immediately. I believe he wrestled with himself, knowing in his heart that desire had twisted his soul. But finally his baseness overpowered him, and he sent to our daughter ordering that she return the Knaanit maid to our home. The girl came to me, in secret, weeping, saying Yishai had made demands that she could no longer gainsay, and that he intended to have her that night.

"I have said she looked like me. And since the misery of my situation, I had fasted and lost the flesh that comes after childbearing. I had also thrown myself into physical tasks, to take my mind off my sorrows. My own sister had, not long since, taken my face in her hand and reflected, in some surprise, that my misery became me most excellently, and had returned to me my youthful form, even as it had extinguished all my joy. This remark of hers, I think, put the notion in my mind. I told my maid to go back to Yishai, to pour his wine that night unwatered, and as much as he would take. When the time came and he insisted on retiring with her, to claim a maiden's right to modesty and ask that the lamps be extinguished. At that time, I promised her, I would take her place. Together, we went to the market and purchased some balsam scent. She would wear it that evening, and so would I, when I took her place."

Nizevet stopped speaking then. A pale flush had crept up the wattled skin of her throat, and she pulled at her mantle to hide it. I looked away from her, to ease her shame. As the silence persisted, I said, softly, taking care to keep my eyes only on the parchment under my hand: "And so Yishai's unlawful lusts were answered in the body of his lawful wife?"

"Yes," she whispered.

From the corner of my eye, I could see her hands working, one washing against the other in her agitation. Then she gathered herself, and went on in a great rush.

"For all my contrivance—I used an egg white to feign a young girl's juiciness, and smeared the bed with drops of chicken blood—I did not have to play a part. I wept, just as that innocent girl might have wept, and my tears incited him. His lust seemed to feed on the idea of my helpless despair and his own power over me, and when he took me it was with the hard hands of a stranger. Wife or no, I felt defiled. When he fell off me into a drunken sleep, I got up to creep away. The moon had risen by then. As I opened the door, he raised his head and stared at me. I was sure, in that moment, that my deception would be plain to him. I was afraid. But he was still drunk of course, and half asleep, and gave no sign that he recognized me. But neither did he call me back. In the morning, he sent for the maid and dismissed her, blaming her, unfairly, as the cause of his sin. He came to me, begging me to return to him. I did. I longed for my home and to be once again a proper mother to my sons. But between Yishai and me, much had been ravaged, and even though I assured him he was forgiven, when he lay with me, he was no longer able to perform as a man. By then, truly, I did not care. My affections had been so trammeled, I no longer hungered for bodily love from him. But it became a problem soon enough, when I could not hide the fact that I was with child. This was in the fifth month since he had lain with me unknowingly. He, of course, bereft of any other explanation, believed that the child I carried was begotten adulterously during our separation. I could not tell him the truth for fear of what price he might exact, in his humiliation, on the maid. Not even when he tried to beat it out of me."

I looked up. Her eyes met mine, steady now.

"Oh, yes. He stooped to that. Only once, when he was drunk. But the fact that it happened at all only confirmed my fears of what he might be capable of, and so I sealed my mouth and kept the secret. That is how the baby—my last child—was, in the eyes of his father, a *mamzer*."

She seemed to gag on the word, and no wonder. That word, whose roots dig down into rot, corruption, defect, the unwelcome other, the despised alien.

"The child I called David—Beloved—was, as Yishai thought, an outcast from the congregation of Israel unto the tenth generation, according to the law of Moshe. Contrary to our law, and, I must say, contrary to his own nature, Yishai did not speak his mind on this to anyone. He should, of course, have gone to the gathering at the gate where he sat with his fellow elders, and disowned us both—me and the child I carried. I do not know if he held his peace out of some lingering regard for me, as the mother of his other sons, or to protect himself lest I, accused, accuse him in my turn. In any case, to the world, we appeared like many another family where regard has waned between a man and wife, and a father takes a set against a particular one of his children for reasons that are his own and of no public concern. I deluded myself that things would change. In the best of times, men have little regard for infants, no matter how comely. But when the child begins to walk and speak, to look like them in gesture or feature, ofttimes their hearts soften and their interest swells. I have seen this, with Yishai and many other men. And David was a beautiful child, of the sort that draws eyes. He was forward, too, in walking and in speaking, a lively child with a curious nature and a sweet temperament. But all these blessings just seemed to goad Yishai all the more. It did not help that David, of all my children, favored me, without any one feature of Yishai's plain in his face. If the child ran to him, he would push him away or answer his gesture with a cuff of the hand. Soon enough, David learned better than to try for his father's notice, and would keep out of Yishai's way."

I could not restrain myself. It seemed impossible to me that a mother would keep a secret that proved so costly to her son. So I put it to her directly: "Even after some years had passed, you did not feel you could tell Yishai that David was his son?"

She drew a trembling hand across her brow. "Oh, I did tell him, in the end. I had to. It became so painful, watching him torment that child. The maid was beyond his reach by then, married honorably to a young man in another village, and I—I did not care what became of me. Better I should bear his anger than my son bear it. But it did no good. He still hated David because he reminded him of that night of weakness, and because, once he knew the truth, he felt humiliated, made the fool."

She sighed. Her frail body quivered. But then she drew a breath and went on.

"Not all was misery in our home. The older sons, Eliav, Avinadav, Shammah and the others, gave us joy and pride, growing into honorable manhood. The girls we had married in good season to suitable husbands. Eliav won early distinction as a soldier in Shaul's army. Shaul's general, Avner, saw his quality and promoted him to head a unit in the field. In time, he became one of Avner's principal officers. I think that you are too young to remember those years, when Shaul himself was young, and had been drafted reluctantly to the kingship. You have known hard fighting in your time, I am sure of it. But most of what you have experienced of war was as a victor. That was not the way of it then."

I did not interrupt her to assure her that I did know. I had made it my business to study those times, to learn every detail I could of Shmuel and his relationship with Shaul. I had seen Shaul once only— briefly, in the half-light of dawn. I was still a boy then, gripped by fear, in the fog between two moments of prophecy. That huge man, our king and our pursuer, asleep, his fate in David's hands. But Shmuel I had never seen at all. He died when I was just beginning to realize that I shared his gift, or his burden. I would have given much to have sat with him and had his counsel. There are not many men who have stood as I do at a king's side and said to him what must be said, whether the words be welcome or no. So I had done what I could to learn about Shmuel, questioning every man who had known him. Their memories were of the times when each tribe held on in its own scattered hamlet, constantly called to this skirmish or that one. We were hill shepherds from small settlements, always threatened by the Plishtim in their wealthy cities on the coast, where they worshipped their many gods, forged their iron, made their handsome pots of red and black, and wove rich cloths, the likes of which we, in our sheepskins and homespun, seldom saw. They were organized and united under their *serens*. But we did not fight as one people in those days, and so we were weak.

And then the day came when the Plishtim routed us completely, penetrating deep into our territory, killing thousands and capturing the ark of the Name. They carried it away deep behind their lines to their chief city, Ashdod. The ark, the very soul of our people for five hundred years. Yah himself had instructed Moshe in its design, and the artist Bezalel had crafted it—the acacia wood lined and clad with purest gold; the hammered figures of the cherubim, cunningly wrought of one piece with the cover, their raised golden wings out-spread, sheltering the tablets of the Word that lay within. It was our chief treasure: precious and beautiful, sacred and powerful. When our priests carried it onto the field of battle, the tips of the golden wings caught the very light of the sun, and sent up such a blaze as struck awe into our enemies and gave heart and strength to our own fighters. It worked for us then, as it does now, as a mighty weapon. We look at it, and remember who we are: the people of the One, the children of the great Breath of Life. We recall that the ground on which we fight has been promised to us, and always a new frenzy boils in our blood. The power of the idea swells like a great wave—you can feel it pulse within you, around you. The army becomes one with this idea, and then we break upon the enemy with mighty force.

But that one time, the force was not enough, and the very ark itself was lost. The woe of it sucked the heart out of us. When a messenger brought the news to our high priest and chieftain, Eli, he fell back in his chair and died on the spot. All glory seemed gone with the ark fallen to our enemies and housed, as we heard, in their heathen temple beside their idol, the grain god Dagon, as if it were just any other trophy of war.

That was when the talk began that we must have a king, as other nations had, to lead us in battle. It was talk born out of a heartsick desperation, the fruit of utter despair. Shmuel warned the people against it. He said that a king would be a yoke upon freedom and a charge upon our purses. He, of course, was famed for taking nothing from the people, not so much as a sandal strap or a sheepskin. But as he grew old, and his sons began to take over some of his tasks, they proved corrupt. And so the clamor for a king grew. Moshe's law had allowed for the possibility of a king, and in the end, Shmuel gave way. He found Shaul, tall and handsome, and anointed him, just as the people demanded. Shaul, at first unwilling, accepted his destiny and grasped it with a hard hand. He united the people with threats, butchering oxen and sending the pieces to each of the tribes, saying that if they did not join him and fight, they would be butchered just so, in their turn.

Shmuel, perhaps still not reconciled with the very idea of kingship, drove Shaul hard. It seemed he could do nothing right; Shmuel held him to measure with a harsh rod, and neither Shaul's worship nor his warfare met Shmuel's mark. Even the victories against the Plishtim did not satisfy. Instead, Shmuel proclaimed that the Lord of Armies commanded total war be made on the Amalekites, in retribution for ancient grievances. Nothing was to be spared. So, Shaul made war, and routed them, and captured their king. But in the aftermath of battle, when the soldiers were used to take spoils, Shaul wavered. He feared rebellion from his troops if he denied the accustomed rewards after such hard combat. So he allowed them to keep the best of the flocks for themselves. When Shmuel arrived and heard sheep bleating in the pens, he castigated Shaul for disobeying. "As you have rejected the command of the Name, so he has rejected you as king," he declared, and turned to leave. The king, pleading for forgiveness, reached out and grasped Shmuel's robe. It tore in his hand. "So has the Name torn kingship from you," said Shmuel. He withdrew to his own lands at Ramah, and never saw Shaul again as a living man. This estrangement sat heavily upon Shaul. Some say it drove him mad.

As Nizevet had lived through these times, and I had not, I let her tell all this in her own way, waiting patiently for the thread of her account to stitch up once again to her personal story. Which it did, at last, on a day sometime not so very long after that final estrangement, when Shmuel arrived unexpectedly in Beit Lehem, seeking out Yishai.

"I did not know how to feel that day," she said. "I dreaded Yishai involving himself in intrigues against the king, especially with our elder sons serving at his side. Shmuel made pretense that he had come only to sacrifice, and had brought his servant leading a heifer for that purpose. Yishai and all the elders went up to the altar and did the rites in the presence of the townsfolk. Yishai had told me to make everything ready to receive Shmuel after the rites, and so I did. I had asked the servants to take out the mats from the upper chamber and give them a good beating. I was overseeing their replacement, and ordering in the braziers—it was winter, and very cold—when Yishai and Shmuel arrived. I saw the look on Yishai's face and it surprised me. He was lit like a torch with pleasure and anticipation. I could not think what could come from Shmuel to affect him in such a way. Shmuel had nothing to give that Yishai could possibly want. The old judge was famous for the austerity of his ways, the simplicity of his household in Ramah. Nor was an evening with him an occasion for levity. He was a stern man who thought only of his duty. Yet here was Yishai, beaming like a man who has just been gifted a pair of oxen.

"I decided the only way to get to the root of it was to be in that room, so in the guise of doing our judge a particular honor I took the tray from the servant and said that I would carry in the meat myself. Yishai gave me a look when I entered the chamber—I did not usually show myself there when guests were present—but he was too preoccupied to spare me more than a second's thought. When I had handed around the dishes I took up a place in the corner, half hidden by a pillar.

"I saw Shmuel's head turn sharply as our eldest son, Eliav, entered the room. Shmuel rose and took several steps toward Eliav, who uttered the proper salutations. The old man's face was creased with lines of concentration as he studied my son. I could see him noting with approval the young man's height and soldierly bearing, his handsome face, his clear, direct address. I admit it, I was proud as I observed this. Eliav had grown into a fine young man, sober, dutiful, the kind other men readily follow. Shmuel gazed at him a long time, then closed his eyes and raised his hands to heaven. A sour expression passed across his face. He opened his eyes, shook his head and turned back to Yishai. 'This is not the one.' Eliav looked startled at this curt response to his courtly greeting. He turned to his father, the confusion clear in his face. Yishai, in turn, looked at Shmuel in bafflement. Shmuel shrugged. 'Not as man sees does Yah see. Yah sees beyond what is visible. He sees into the heart.'

"Yishai laid a consoling hand on Eliav's shoulder and said softly, 'Send Avinadav in to us.' Avinadav was just a little more than a year younger than Eliav, and had lived in his shadow, imitating him in all ways. He, too, was an upright young man, and handsome. But Shmuel waved him off. 'Yah has not chosen this one either.' So it went on with all our sons, until even young Natanel, not much more than a boy, had been called for and dismissed in turn.

"'Are these all the sons you have?' Shmuel demanded. 'Is there no other?' Yishai looked down, not meeting Shmuel's gaze. I saw him about to shake his head—for him, after all, there was no other son he fully counted as his own. But he must have sensed my eyes boring into him, or else I made an involuntary movement of which I was not even aware, for he looked over then to where I was. I had risen to my knees in a kind of supplication. He met my gaze and I saw him flinch. I did not know what Shmuel wanted with one of our sons, but clearly it was something important, something Yishai very much desired. And if he deemed it— whatever honor or position it might be—good for Eliav or any of the others, then my David must also have his chance. 'There is one other,' Yishai muttered. 'But he is a boy, merely. He is away, tending the sheep.'

"'Then fetch him. For we will not quit this place until he comes.' I slipped out then and went downstairs to the beasts' stalls. I did not know who Yishai would send to summon David but I wanted to be sure whoever it was went well mounted. I told the boy to saddle the mule, not to make do with a donkey. Finally, Raddai appeared, wearing a heavy cloak and a sullen expression, affronted that he had been chosen to fetch his despised younger sibling, and would have to abide a cold night with the flock in his stead.

"The hour was late when I heard the mule returning. I had sent the servants to their beds, content to sit a lonely vigil. When I heard the clop of hooves on the still air, I kindled an oil lamp and went out. David looked, as I expected, unkempt and filthy. His hair was a tangle, with bits of twig and lichen knotted into it, his skin ingrained with dirt, and to complete the picture of neglect and wildness, he had draped himself in the skin of the lion he had slain, which he had somehow roughly cured and fashioned into an outlandish kind of cloak. I had water ready, and fresh clothes of Natanel's laid out, but Shmuel appeared at the head of the outdoor staircase, and called out to bring the boy straight up to him. Yishai had fallen asleep, sprawled out upon the cushions. Shmuel had not even dozed. He was alert and agitated. He waited by the door, the lamp held high in his hand. As David climbed up the stairs toward him, that hard old face softened. His eyes filled. 'Bring the oil,' he said softly. Yishai was roused now, on his feet, his mouth open, eyes wide. Shmuel's servant rifled through his pack and pulled out a twisted ram's horn stoppered with wax. He approached Shmuel, knelt, unstopped the horn and held it up to him. Shmuel took the vessel and raised it above David's head. A thin spiral of golden, viscous liquid dribbled down upon David's dusty hair. David showed no surprise or confusion. His face, tilted upward to Shmuel, was calm and grave, his eyes wide. It was as if he could see right through the walls, into the future that awaited him. 'Behold!' said Shmuel. 'The anointed of the Name.' Then he knelt. I followed. Out of the corner of my eye, I saw Yishai, going down on his knees before the son he had spurned.

"Shmuel gestured to David then, and the two of them walked out together, down the stairs, into the cold night. I do not know, to this day, what was said. But when they came in, Shmuel went straight to his rest and David allowed me to help him bathe and change into a clean night robe. We did not speak much, and nothing at all to the purpose of the strange events of the night. He answered me when I spoke to him, but he was off in the distance somewhere, far beyond my reach. I steered him to Raddai's empty pallet, in the room where four of his brothers slept on, oblivious.

"In the morning, Shmuel and his servant left for Ramah, and David went back to the sheep, and it was as if the whole uncanny business had never taken place. I did not speak of it to my other sons, and when I asked Yishai if they knew what had occurred he said that if they did, they knew better than to own to it, and urged me to put it out of my mind also. He said that Shaul was still our king, and while that was so it did no good to speak, or even think, about David's anointing.

"But of course, not a day passed when I did not think about it, and wonder. And then, soon enough, we were at war again with the Plishtim, and my older sons were called by General Avner to join the king, in battle, in the Wadi Elah . . ."

IV

Her voice trailed off. She reached for her wine cup, but found it empty. She waved for Shammah's girl, but there was no need. The girl had been tending to the making of a small cook fire and had set a large pot on a tripod of three stones. But as soon as she sensed her grandmother stir, she was at her elbow, filling our cups. She placed the pitcher, which was beaded with moisture in the afternoon heat, on the table between us. It had grown late as we talked. The twisted shadows of the citron boughs elongated in dark knots upon the ground. Nizevet put her cup down and lifted her hand to her brow.

"I have tired you," I said. "I am sorry."

"No, I am not tired. It is not that. It is just that it is difficult for me to speak of things that I have kept close to me for so long. I see you writing down my words, and I—and I—I feel such shame, such shame—"

I started to speak, to reassure her, but she hushed me with a wave of her hand. "I know my son has sanctioned this, for reasons that must seem wise to him. But the common people know his story so differently. Their story begins with that radiant boy who suddenly appeared from the hills. Do they need, I wonder, to know what came before?" She was not looking at me, but at her hands.

"That will rest with the king," I said. "He will decide what will be recorded, and what will be left out."

"Very well," she said. Then she signaled again to the girl, and began to rise.

"Is that all?" I said, rather more sharply than I intended. "I was hoping you might go on."

"Go on? Why should I go on? Shammah can better tell about the Wadi Elah. Shammah, and others who were there. My part in the story is of no significance beyond what I have told you. Be content."

I stood then, and bowed. The girl came and gave Nizevet her arm. The two disappeared into the house and I was left alone to gather my writing materials. The girl returned to tend to the pot. Pungent aromas—onions, cumin, coriander—wafted from her pot. My mouth watered and I realized I was very hungry. Just before sunset a noisy pair of youths returned to the compound, herding their animals before them. The younger boy, who had been dozing in a corner, rushed to spread straw in the lower stable rooms, a chore I sensed should have been done sometime earlier.

The girl brought me a basket of flatbread, a tray heaped high with the fragrant, spiced grains, and a dish of yogurt to blend with it. It was clear I was not to dine with the rest of the family, as they had all withdrawn to an upstairs room in the larger of the three houses. I ate the food, glad of my solitude. My thoughts were occupied with the remarkable words that lay bound in my parchment, and with Nizevet's parting advice. She was wise. It was best to speak only to those who were there when events unfolded. David's life already was the stuff of wild elaborations. Men always make myths around their kings. I needed to be wary of such men.

When I had done with the food, the girl was there again, at my side, holding a bowl of rosewater so that I might wash my fingers. "If you are ready, I will show you to your place." So I was to stay. I had not been sure if Shammah would offer me a roof, or whether I should have to bespeak some dubious shelter in the town.

"I think I will sit for a while," I told her. And so I did, counting the stars as they twinkled alight until the sky was glittering. When a boy came with a torch to lead me to my room, it was very late. Shammah had not returned. A pale light was already seeping through the shutters when I woke from a restless sleep to hear him come in, drunk, stumbling and cursing. I heard the king's name, and my own, interspersed with references to donkey's balls and camel dung. I rolled over and went back to sleep, reasoning that it would be many hours before Shammah might be ready to speak with me.

The house stirred to life not long after. I dozed through the sounds of morning tasks, the animals being let out of their stalls, the men and boys leaving for pasture and field. When finally I rose, only two women were left in the courtyard, baking the day's bread in the tannur. The one I had met the day before worked beside an older woman whom I assumed to be Shammah's wife. She looked up for a moment from working dough, and nodded a brief acknowledgment before turning her attention to the bread. The girl peeled a hot round from the curved wall of the tannur and brought it to me, steaming, along with a handful of olives. I asked after Nizevet, as I did not see her in the courtyard. The girl replied that she was resting. She was very tired from the prior day's long talk, the girl said, with an air of rebuke. By the time I had consumed my morning morsel, the women had finished the bread making and were preparing to milk the ewes and nannies pastured nearby. As they took up their bowls, I unrolled a hide to review what I had set down the day before.

The sun was high in the sky before Shammah came stomping across the courtyard. He snatched up a round of the fresh bread and threw himself down heavily into the chair opposite me, gnawing on it. He wiped his mouth with the back of a hand and fixed me with a glare of complete distaste. "I've never understood why my brother puts up with you," he blurted. "The things you say to him. It's a wonder he hasn't put a spear right through you."

There was no answer to this, so I gave none. I carefully rolled up the skin I had been reading and drew out a blank one. Shammah snorted. "So you wrung my mother out like a filthy rag and now you propose to begin on me, to see what more dirt you can squeeze?"

"Your brother . . ."

"Ah, yes, my brother wants it. My holy, miraculous, mighty brother, beloved of all—men, women—even Yah. He wants it. And he gets what he wants, always. Well, now you know that wasn't always how it was. Until that old man and his oil pitcher showed up here, that boy knew his place—and a dung-spattered, dusty place it was." He grinned to himself, a mean, private mirth. "I can still see the look on Eliav's face—and Avinadav's, for that matter . . ." He gave a throaty laugh, and then winced, and put a hand to his temple. The previous night's excess was claiming its usual price.

"Well, none of us believed what the old man said. How could David, that worthless little turd—don't look at me like that. It's how we thought of him; I know she told you that. But I'll bet she didn't tell you that he well earned his reputation. No. I bet she told you he was her perfect darling. Well, he wasn't perfect. He was a sly little shit. He'd learned to be. He knew how to keep an eye to the merest advantage and he did not scruple to take it, once it showed itself. He was like you in that way." He scowled at me, malice in his face. His mouth twisted into a grin. "You forget. I was there that day he killed your father. I saw your wonderful piece of playacting. It was well done, I have to give you credit. I thought at the time, that boy's got balls. How you came up with it—kingdom, crown, all that stuff—and had the front to put on that show with your father's blood up to your ankles. It won you your life, and now look at you. The king's prophet. A man to be reckoned with. Well, you might have suckered my brother but you don't fool me. I thought you were a clever little fraud that day you saved your skin, and I think you're a cunning charlatan now. But no one gives a shekel for what I think. I'm just the king's old drunkard of a brother. So I keep my mouth shut and stay out of my son's way so he can do what you've done, and be someone at court when Prince Amnon comes into his own." He picked up the bread and gnawed at it.

"I believe," I said, "that we were discussing your brother at Wadi Elah. Not your opinion of me, or your ambitions for Yonadav."

He gave a dramatic sigh. "All right. Let's get it done with, then." He mimicked my haughty tone: "My brother at Wadi Elah. The mean little *mamzer* making his name. To be fair. He had reason to be the way he was. He had cause, ample cause, as a beaten mule has cause to be sour and malicious, just looking for the chance to land a kick. We—all of us—would've done anything to earn our father's approval, and if he treated David like a mangy cur dog, then we would, too. We never showed that boy a cup of kindness. He had to use his wits to survive out there in the hills and he did, with no man's hand to guide him. So when he came to the Wadi Elah, he swooped in like a buzzard, looking to feed himself on the misery of that battlefield. And what a ripe corpse he found there, and what a meal he made of it."

I scribbled furiously to get these words down, words as sour as the gall ink in which I wrote them. As frank as Nizevet had been, this was another kind of truth telling entirely. Shammah had been restless in his seat, shifting his great bulk, working the knot in his shoulders. He got up and began to pace, wearing the same track in the yard that I had noted the day before. He pulled down a switch from the citron bough and beat it against his thigh as he walked.

"I suppose you have some picture in your mind of how it was that day. Who doesn't? The cloth of that story is threadbare with the telling. It has been an amusement to me, who was there, to have it told to me fashioned thus and so, restitched until I do not know that the events described are the ones I stood and watched with my own good eyes. Every time I hear it, the Plishtim champion has grown a cubit in height and my heroic little brother has lost a year in age. After all this time, I think I can see him as you see him on that day. You see a shining boy, don't you? Here he comes, dancing out of the ranks of common men. What a beautiful, brave boy you see. You can own to it. You are not alone. That is what everyone thinks. Well, for one thing, he was scarcely a boy. My brother had reached his fourteenth year. There were many of his age already in the ranks, battle tested, counted as men. And he'd grown as a cactus grows, bitter and prickly and tough enough to survive what came his way.

"But my brother has fed the other legend. Indeed, by feeding it in others, I think he has grown it within himself. Even he probably now believes the story of the glowing, blessed boy and the hideous, looming giant. Not true. That gloss and polish all came to him later, after Shaul and Yonatan took him up and made much of him. Gave him, to be frank, the love that we—his own family—had held back from him. Shaul's court was nothing much, in those days. No singing men and women, none of the finery that David fills his hall with these days. Shaul's was a simple chieftain's headquarters. Nothing more. There was none of this prideful pomp then. Most of the time he held counsel under a tree, like a soldier. But for a love-starved urchin from a mud-daubed sheepfold, Shaul's so-called court was the garden of paradise and, thanks to Yonatan's folly and excess, David flourished there. And was corrupted there, too. Oh, don't you give me that look. Not you. I've heard you say worse, and to his face. . . .

"In any case, there we were, our ragtag troops up on one hill and their forces across the valley on the other. Everyone makes out it was a massive standoff—two great armies—but that's not true. Never happened. It was just another skirmish in a long, boring season of skirmishes. They were always at us in fighting season, trying to pick off a village here, a hamlet there. Steal the livestock, disrupt the harvest. They were good at it, and they had better arms than we did. It had been going on for months, and we were all of us done in. Seemed like neither side wanted to sound the battle horns. And Shaul was canny, in those days. He knew that a standoff served us just as well as a victory. If the Plishtim fighters were pinned down in Wadi Elah, then they weren't running about the Shefala looting crops and raiding cattle. I think it suited him just fine to sit out the season until the villagers got their harvests in. Then the weather would change and we could all go home.

"But then they started taunting us with their champion from Gath. He was big; I'll give you that. And armed better than any of us. Better than Shaul. Better than anyone we'd ever seen, at that time. Not the usual Plishtim stuff, either—more the kind of thing that came from the island peoples far to the west. He had an odd-looking foreigner's bronze helmet and scale armor—I remember that, because it was uncommon then—and a great bronze breastplate and greaves. His spear was as big as a weaver's bar with a massive iron point set to it. There was a curved sword as well.

"I'll own to it, when he'd come down into the valley and yell his taunts, none of us felt like stepping forward to fight him. 'Get me a man!' he'd yell. And then he'd laugh when no one came forward. The trouble was this: any man who had a chance to defeat him was too valuable a man to lose. Shaul would not let Yonatan go, and his other sons, the younger princes, weren't up to it. Nor would he allow Avner to meet the challenge, and rightly so, because the defeat of such a one—the crown prince or the general—would have taken heart from the men and fed the battle lust of the enemy. But some of the hot young asses in the ranks grumbled about it, especially after the wine-skin had been passed a few times. They didn't like it, that Shaul just sat there and took the insults. They'd talk big at night. But I didn't see them so brave come the morning.

"So the three of us, Eliav, Avinadav and me, had been there in the wadi for weeks, and our father, back home, realized that our food would be running short. Somehow, David contrived to get himself entrusted with the resupply. Or maybe he wheedled the errand off some kitchen slave. In any case, there he was with the donkey, panniers laden with parched corn, loaves of bread and rounds of cheese. His charge was to bring the food and go back to his work with the flock. But did he do as he was bid? Of course not. Little shit was off in an eyeblink, looking out for himself. Eliav got word of him far beyond the baggage train, mingling with the troops, pestering them for infor-mation. Eliav was none too pleased, and sent me to fetch him. I got up behind him before he knew it. He was bragging away when I caught him, belittling the real fighters who had borne the battle while he was dozing in the hills, or sticking his little cock in some unwary ewe . . . "

"Don't," I interjected. I couldn't help myself. No one spoke of the Lamp of Israel in such a way. But Shammah just glanced at me, sneering.

"*'Don't.'*" He pitched his voice into a high whine. "Don't what? Don't tell the truth? But you said you wanted the truth. I'm giving it to you. *Do* you want it or not? Well, then. Shut up and write." He threw down the citron switch, rubbed his two flat, square thumbs into his eye sockets, inspected the thread of rheum he extracted and smeared it on his tunic. "So, there he is, big-mouthing, pointing over to where the Plishtim champion stood in the valley. 'See how slow he is?' he was saying. 'Did you see him stumble coming down the hill? All that armor is probably weighing him down. Yes, he's got the height, and he's well armed, but you could attack him from a distance, you don't have to meet him hand to hand, on his terms. If you don't give him a chance to even . . .' I cut him off there, grabbed him by the ear. I dragged him back to Eliav. I can still hear his whiny little voice—'What have I done now? I was only asking.' But Eliav had his measure. He chided him for his black-hearted scheming and his pompous bragging and told him to get on home to his work. But it was too late. Someone had told Shaul about David's empty boasting, and a messenger came up to say David was wanted in the king's tent. Eliav thought it would teach David a lesson, and sent him off with a smirk.

"All right. I'll confess: We all of us wanted to see him put back in his place. And we all of us underestimated him. David saw his chance and he took it. I think he reckoned that he might not get another one, and that any risk was worth taking to change his miserable little life."

Shammah stopped pacing and sat again, heavily, in the chair opposite me. He propped his elbows upon the table and let his chin rest on his hands. I looked up, waiting for him to continue, and found him glaring back at me. I thought, for a moment, that his disgust for me, and for this undertaking, had mastered him, and that he was about to put an end to it. But the story he was telling seemed to have caught him up, despite himself.

"We all followed behind David to the king's tent. We thought it a great joke, and so at first did Shaul. When David repeated his boasting right to the king's own face, Shaul just laughed. How could a shepherd lad untrained to arms fight a professional soldier? Then David launched into a preposterous tale of how he'd slain a lion, grabbed it by the beard and wrenched a stolen sheep out of its jaws. Well, it was true he did have a lion skin, but I'd always assumed he found some dead beast and skinned it and made up all the rest. But it seemed that the king was taken in by the whole thing. David was certainly giving it all he had: 'The Name saved me from the lion and he will save me from the man,' he said. I don't know if Shaul was already a bit touched, or if he was desperate, or if he just didn't give a shit what happened to my braggart brother. Maybe he thought, if the big man slays him, so what? The slaughter of an unknown shepherd boy would be no great loss to us and no great boast to him who slew him. But Shaul did offer my brother his own armor, so I suppose he thought the lad brave, at least. We had to stifle a laugh, I have to tell you, watching David try to walk in Shaul's breastplate, which hung down past his skinny knees. When he unstrapped the gear and set it aside, I thought he might use that as an excuse to back out, but no. He took up his shepherd's staff and went off to the wadi. He picked up a few stones, weighing them in his hand, looking for the densest ones, and skipped off with his leather sling in his hand. The king watched him go. He turned to his commander. 'Whose son is that boy, Avner?' Avner shrugged. He said he had no idea. Eliav, Avinadav and I didn't speak up. We didn't claim our brother, because we were sure that when Goliath turned up, David would get himself smeared into the sand.

"So it went on as it usually did. The Plishtim archers lined up, and so did we, with the usual shield banging and insults. Goliath stepped out and called for his man. And there goes little brother, prancing in and out of the line, brandishing his staff. When Goliath saw him, he threw back his massive head and laughed. Well, why wouldn't he? Does a gnat worry a bear? He yelled out to David, 'Am I a dog that you come against me with sticks?' He'd only seen the staff, at that point. He hadn't noticed the sling. David ran forward, farther out of the line, but still well clear of spear distance. He loaded up a stone and let it fly. It missed, of course. He was too far back. The big man's voice got angrier then. 'Come here!' he yelled. 'I'll give your flesh to the birds of the sky and the beasts of the field!'

"And then David stunned the lot of us. He always had that voice; you've heard it, you know what I mean. He called back, as clear as a trumpet: 'You come against me with sword and spear and javelin, but I come against you in the name of *Hashem tzva'ot*—the lord of armies, the God of the ranks of Israel, whom you have defied.' We were raised in an observant household—we kept the feasts, we did the sacrifices, you know that—but this kind of holy talk, well, not even our father went around spouting out that kind of thing. None of us knew where he came by that style of speech. It was a bit uncanny, to be truthful. I started to feel the hair rise . . ." Shammah's hand drifted to the back of his neck, remembering. His face had lost its scowl as the memories possessed him. For a few moments, it was as though he'd left me behind in the courtyard. He was no longer sitting there under the citron, conversing unwillingly with a man he disliked. He was far away, a youth in the Wadi Elah, watching with disbelief as his youngest brother rushed headlong toward his destiny.

"So then the Plishtim started in on their own man. Goading him. 'Are you going to take that from a weedy boy?' He's getting taunted from both hills, and you can see he's getting more and more rattled. David slings another stone, and Goliath can feel the breeze as it passes. He dodges out of the way of it, and he's in all that armor, so he stumbles, and everyone laughs at him—his own and ours both. David's the only one not laughing. He's in some kind of a state, trumpeting away. . . . 'This very day the Name will deliver you into my hands'—and more of that style of thing—it just poured out of him— the kind of high-blown words your kind comes out with: 'All the Earth shall know there is a God in Israel . . .' Not the kind of thing you expect out of the mouth of a shepherd boy. If the Plishtim had hurled his javelin right then, things might have gone otherwise, but he was still standing there, feet planted, baffled that this loudmouthed little nobody was making a fool of him. He turned around to curse at the men in his own ranks, to shut them up. That's what did him in, I'm sure of it. The stone from the sling was airborne by the time he looked back toward David, and when he did, it was too late to avoid it. And I have to credit it, David's aim—or his luck—was perfect. The stone hit right in the forehead"—Shammah raised a beefy hand and laid two fingers on his own brow just between his eyes—"right here, just a hair below the edge of his big bronze helmet. You felt it, even from far off. It was as if you heard it. Smack."

He slapped his meaty hands together and tossed his head back, mimicking the instant of impact. "Rock. Bone. Crack. You should have seen his head snap. The helmet flew right off him. The big hulk dropped, just like that, right onto his knees. He groped for his sword. He couldn't see. The blood was pouring into his eyes—you've been to war, you know how scalp wounds bleed. And David hadn't stopped. Hadn't even checked his stride. He just kept sprinting forward after the stone, and the Plishtim archers are shooting, but missing him. And he cries out some other thing about *Hashem tzva'ot* being with us, and that's all it takes for our young hotheads to break ranks and charge in after him. I heard Avner trying to call them back, cussing and yelling, but it was no good, because they'd been spoiling for this fight for a long time.

"I ran myself then, following after David. I was catching up to him when he got Goliath. He grabbed the sword hilt right from under his hand. It was almost too heavy for him to lift. He staggered as he tried to raise it, and I thought he was finished. But he found his feet, and grasped the sword, two-fisted, like an ax. He still could barely lift the thing, and it fell under its own weight. Right on that thick neck. Must've been sharp, that sword, because the head came off clean. David picked it up by the hair and held it up, so that everyone could see it. Our men took heart then, and plowed through the enemy. That's how battles turn. The Plishtim scattered and fled, and we pursued them all the way back to the gates of their town, Ekron. When we got back, we looted their abandoned camp.

"I heard later that David had walked right up to the king with the head still dripping in his hand. He told him his name and whose son he was. Avner wasn't happy. How would he be? He'd lost control of his men to this little nobody. But of course, he didn't stay a nobody. Yonatan was all over him, praising his guts and his leadership. And so began all that folly between the two of them. I think that very night, if I had to lay a bet on it. Well, you know what it's like, when you take your first man. You're ready for sex—or, maybe, you don't know." He looked at me with a mixture of distaste and contempt. "Well, I can tell you this: a normal boy'll put it anywhere, after that first kill. Girl, hag, mule. And if a prince wants to suck your cock . . ."

He turned his head aside and spat into the dust.

"I will not speak of that. But there it was. The days of humble sheepherding were over. Yonatan wouldn't let him go home, and David surely wasn't clamoring to get back there. Next thing we knew, he's the king's armor bearer. And then someone mentioned that he played the harp. Shaul took to having him play anytime an evil mood seized him, and they say the music brought him relief, for a time. But I don't know much about all that. David had a gut full of malice toward us, and made sure we were not asked to Shaul's court. Well, it was no more than our due, I suppose. Later, when Shaul turned on him and made us all outlaws, it was a different story. We had no choice but to join forces with him or be cut down. My brothers and I went on the run with him; he arranged refuge for my mother and father off in Moav, across the Yarden, under the protection of the king there. Well, you know all that. You were with us soon enough. In the end, he saw to it that we survived, and we've all made shift to get along with each other through the years since. I don't say he hasn't been generous. Since he came to his throne he's made sure all of us got back what we'd lost on his account, and plenty more, too. But there. I'm sick of talking about him and I'm as parched as the dirt."

He called out for water and the boy came running. He did not wait for the boy to pour, but snatched the pitcher and lifted it, letting the cool water run into his mouth and down his chin. When his thirst was slaked he upended the pitcher and let the water spill over his head, then he shook himself like a dog. He laid his hands flat upon the table and pushed himself up. "Get this man his mule," he ordered the boy, and turned away. I had been dismissed.

V

It was an easy ride back in the cool of the evening. The mule was willing and sure-footed, so I sat her at my ease as the stones exhaled the day's heat and the soft cloak of the sky changed its hues from golden to pink to royal purple. It was late when I finally had to put some leg on her, to urge her up the last steep approach to the town gate. The moon had risen full, bathing the white stones in a cool, pearly luster. The gate was closed of course, and when one of the younger sentries challenged me, I heard his senior officer upbraid him in a low hiss: "Fool! Can't you see it's the prophet? Let him pass."

The metal of the bolts groaned, and in the dancing light of cressets I saw the youth's hand tremble as he held the heavy gate. I have never become used to it: the awe that common men have for my kind. I suppose it is because I feel no more than a common man myself. Even less, perhaps. No more than a tool in the hand of an unseen craftsman, something to be used as needed and then cast casually aside.

But I have come to accept this fearfulness and distance. My own slave, a Hittite boy named Muwat, in my service a full two years, still looks at me sideways. He is a capable youth, nonetheless, skilled not only in meeting my simple needs but also in reading the temper of the household. I have found that the common people, and even, on occasion, those who should know better, such as the king, nurse strange ideas about me. They do not understand that I am given to see only those matters that roil the heavens. They expect me to know everything. Muwat keeps me in credit in this way, his ears open to the gossip in the slaves' quarters, the stables and the kitchen, where one who knows how to listen can learn a great deal. Most useful of all, because he saw service as a child in the eastern kingdoms, he grew up among eunuchs and does not share the common aversion of most of our young men toward these unfortunates. He has befriended one or two, so from time to time I can learn from him even those private matters that pass in the women's quarters. As tired as I was that night, I could sense, as Muwat came and went with my bathing water and my bed robe, that he had news for me. He was a timid boy who had come to me from a hard service with a master who did not invite familiarity. I had learned that I would have to tease out his confidences. So when I was clean and robed and he had brought me some bread and dates and a cup of watered wine, I inclined my head toward a stool in the corner. "Sit, Muwat. Pour a drink for yourself and tell me what I need to know this night."

He sat, his eyes locked on the floor and his foot tapping nervously. He had not fetched himself a cup, so I got up and got one for him. At this, he shot me a look of confusion from under his long-lashed eyelids. "Come now, Muwat. We are alone here. There is no need to stand on ceremony with me." Still, he didn't speak. "What is it? Does it concern the king?" At this, he nodded.

"Well, perhaps. That is, they say so . . ."

"Who says so? What do they say?"

"They say the king is not himself—well, you know that, of course. But since you left him, the morning before the last, he has not slept. The servants of his bedchamber say he does not come to rest, but paces the corridors. Last night, he visited the concubines and asked for this one and then another and finally a third. But Gholagha—you know him, I think?—he's the youngest of the eunuchs—reports that he sent each one of them back without . . . well . . . you know . . ." He was blushing now, the flush a spreading stain under his fine skin. He had not lifted his cup, so I pushed it toward him. He took a long swallow. David had always been a sensualist. In the outlaw years, he'd made do with two wives. Ahinoam he'd taken because he was urgent to get an heir and she was a sturdy, uncomplaining girl who could bear the hardships of the outlaw life, and then Avigail, who was a love match. In Hevron, he'd added others. Most of them, like the Princess Maacah of Geshur, for well-founded diplomatic reasons, to seal an alliance, secure a border or bind a tribe. It was only after Avigail's death that he had, in my view, abandoned continence and embraced excess, adding and subtracting concubines simply because he could, to satiate the lusts of a day or a week.

"Today, they say, he has been sharp with everyone who has come near to him. He did no work and received no one—he would not even give an audience to Yoav's messenger from the battlefield. And in the kitchen they say he sent back all his food uneaten. As a result, the hands have had a miserable day of it, the chief cook all out of temper and looking for someone to blame."

I raked a hand through my hair. David's appetites—bedchamber and table—were well-known. As was his hunger for the merest scrap of news from any fighting when he had not been in the heat of it. Also, he was famed for his zealous attentiveness to governance. This kind of disengagement from life was unlike him, and worrisome. As tired as I was, I told Muwat to bring me a fresh tunic. I would go to the king's quarters. I would use the pretense of carrying greetings from Nizevet, even though no such message had in fact been sent. And even if he would not see me, I thought I might learn something of use there.

But when I arrived in the antechamber, the attendant said the king had not retired. He could not tell me where he was. "When he comes in, tell him I would speak with him at his pleasure, no matter how late the hour," I said. I took the long way back to my own quarters, wanting to bump into him, or to meet someone who might know where he was. But I could not stalk him all night long, so in the end I returned to my room and sat up, fully dressed, hoping for a summons. The candle guttered and I did not trouble to light another. My body ached from fatigue but my mind was restless. And then my boon companions, gut spasms and pounding head, arrived to join me in my vigil. For once, I welcomed them, these precursors of vision. The moon was full that night and bathed the room in a dim glow. But in the small hours it set, and the dark was so complete, my eyes might as well have been closed as open. I probed the dark, hoping that a sudden glare of vision would disrupt it. Throughout the night, my head throbbed and a weight of dread settled its great fist upon my heart. But no visions came. No bright shard of certainty arrived to tell me what I must do to help the king.

I now know why sight failed me that night. I have lived long enough to see the pattern whose first stitch was placed in those late hours. But for many years, I wondered. If only vision had led me to the roof, to where he stood in the soft air under the luminous moon, what sin, what folly and pain, might then have been prevented. And yet, if vision *had* led me there, what greatness might have remained unmade, a design unrealized, a future lost. Decades have passed now, and still I do not know how to fashion my thought on this matter. Still it gnaws at me. At the time, as I lived it, I stumbled through what followed like a clear-sighted man whose eyes are suddenly clouded, afraid of the next obstacle that would rise up and trip me.

Once, I would have known exactly whom to go to with my concerns. I would have laid the tangled skein of my thoughts in the lap of Avigail, and together we would have unraveled it. Avigail befriended me when I joined David's outlaws. David encouraged me to spend time with her—this was allowed as I was still young enough to have the liberty of the women's tent. "You can learn from her," he said. "She understands how to read men's hearts." And I did learn from her, most especially about him. She wanted me to understand him, and so she bared to me those private matters that men do not usually share one with another. "You are young to leave your mother," she said. "I do not say I can take her place. No one can do that. But if you ever feel lonely here, if you need a woman's care—" I remember my face reddening. She smiled kindly. "Do not look so dismayed. You'll be a man soon enough. But for now, you cannot be always underfoot among the fighters. David will call for you often enough, be assured of it. He uses every tool that comes into his hand."

That night, as I sat in my room in the silent palace, waiting to be used again in his service, I remembered Avigail's kindness to me in those outlaw days. I remembered how she had extended her long fingers and raised my chin so that I was obliged to look right into the deep green of her eyes. I was young then, and embarrassed by the intimacy of it. I am sure she knew that, but she wanted me to understand our kinship. "We are alike in some ways, you and I. We have each of us been sent to him, to help him according to our means."

At the time, boy that I was, I thought she spoke literally. Having no sons of Navaal, she had inherited a share of her former husband's wealth, and had brought it to David on their marriage. I knew they were bedmates, of course, but as I had yet to feel any stirrings of desire, that part of their relationship was obscure to me. Now, in hindsight, knowing about David's childhood, I can see more clearly and understand truths that eluded me then. The difference in their age meant that Avigail was more than a wife to David. She was like a sister and, in some measure, a mother also, giving him the affection that he had been severed from as an exiled child.

Directly after he sacked my village, David struck camp. He had looted ten times the supplies he had asked for. That was the way of it in those years. A temporary camp or a hideout in a set of caves. If supplies were not forthcoming, a punitive raid to secure them, and then on the move again, to keep ahead of Shaul, who hunted him constantly. Barely a week passed without the arrival of some new recruit, anxious to join us. Shaul's erratic behavior was driving many good men to desert him. Some who were in distress, and some who were burdened by debts and some who were generally discontented or dismayed by the direction of his leadership. Such men gathered to

David, and our numbers swelled. Sometimes, David would have me by him when a new man found his way to us. He would greet each of them, offer them honey cakes or wine, and draw out their stories. He lent a sympathetic ear, and made them know that he thought them patriots, not traitors. Avigail would be there, too, always, serving the food, unnoticed by the strangers. But I noticed her, and I noticed she missed nothing.

I was there one such evening, as she gathered the uneaten rinds and crusts from the meal David had shared with a man who had described himself as a trader from Shechem in the north, dealing in purple dye. As this was a risky trade, necessitating travel along the Derek Hayyam, the Way of the Sea, which passed through Plishtim territory, the man claimed also to be skilled with arms and had offered us his services as a fighter. When David asked why he had abandoned the dye trade, he said that the king's steward had reneged on payments, a large sum. When he tried to bring the matter before Shaul in person, the king had refused to see him. On the steward's word alone, the king banned him from doing further business with the court, which ruined him.

It had been an amiable meal: the merchant was a good storyteller, and kept the company amused by tales from his journeys. But now that the man had retired, David reached an arm out and drew Avigail down to sit with him. "What did you think?" he asked her.

"He had very white hands," she said. "I suppose a dye merchant need not handle his own product, and yet . . ." She let her voice trail off.

"What else?"

She tilted her head, considering. "He seemed a bit confused, for a dye merchant, between *tekelet* and *argaman*."

"What?" said David. "Is there a difference, then?"

"Oh, yes," Avigail replied. "One is a blue purple, the other a warmer, reddish purple. It's true, the distinction can be difficult to make"—she smiled—"though not if you're canny—one is much cheaper, and no capable wife in purse to afford the dye in the first place would let herself be misled. And if it is your trade and livelihood . . . and you say you sell to a king . . ."

She always fashioned her words in that way, opening a question rather than giving a certain answer, so that David might feel that he had come to the truth himself.

"Anything more?"

She paused. "Well, he said he traveled often by the Derek Hayyam, but it was clear when he spoke that he did not recall that the highway turns inland in the Carmel mountains to cross the plain of Yezreel at Megiddo."

David frowned. "Spy, do you think?"

"Perhaps not. Perhaps Shaul's spy would be more careful. More likely a brigand with a disreputable past, who does not want to own to it."

"In any case, I will send him on his way in the morning. I'll not take a chance on him."

Had it gone the other way, had Avigail found the man's tale convincing, he would have been embraced on her word. There would be a celebration to seal his joining the band—singing and dancing, the sharing of stories. Such nights were full of music and mirth and good feeling. That was how David drew men to him and made them his. He never forgot a man's story and could recall the names of his kin and all those who were dear to him, wept with him in loss, celebrated with him in joy. He learned which man enjoyed a ribald jest and which of them disapproved of bawdiness, and tailored his words accordingly. It was not that he played false in this. He had both elements in his nature, both the coarse and the refined. He could be a predator at noonday and a poet by dusk. And he exercised uncommon tact with his men, meeting them where they stood, rather than demanding that they always be the ones accommodating themselves. I have learned over time that this quality is rare in any man, even more so in a leader.

Those who knew or loved music found an instant bond with him. You cannot harmonize in song or play instruments together without listening one to the other, sensing when to be loud and when soft, when to take the lead and when to yield it. I think that few grasp the connection between waging war and making music, but in the long evenings, when the firelight flickered on the cave walls and the voices joined and rose with his, I learned the unity between the two.

Having had so little love from his own brothers, this adopted family was what he cherished, and they cherished him in return. But none came into this family without Avigail's scrutiny. I never knew her to judge wrong. So I came to rely on her to teach me how to read men. And women also. I enjoyed the hours that I spent in the women's tent. I liked the subtlety of the women's way with one another, the veiled indirection of their talk. Most men, you needed only to look into their faces to know their mood, and generally their speech would be the first thought that came into their minds uttered out of their mouths. Women, whose very lives, sometimes, might depend upon concealing their true feelings, spoke a more artful language, more difficult to understand.

David set me to learn other skills, too, in those days of restless waiting. Arms, I had to learn, as did every man and boy. I practiced with Yoav's younger brother, Avishai, who was just a few years my senior but already highly skilled in weaponry. At first, I was barely strong enough to pull a bowstring and clumsy at handling a blade. Lucky for me, Avishai was an enthusiastic and relentless trainer, hot-tempered, but good-humored, unlike his dour older brother, and he showed me how to make best use of my limited skills. I had no great talent in these things but I was young and healthy and growing into my height and, having seen my father slain before my eyes, I had an appetite to learn how to defend myself.

I had less appetite, at first, for the instruction of my other teacher. Seraiah was a slight youth who was not skilled to arms, but had worked as a scribe in Shaul's service. David tasked Seraiah to teach me my letters. As a vintner's son, I had not expected to need such learning, and unlike my schooling with weapons, at first I did not grasp the purpose in it. But David saw further than I did, and when I did not apply myself, he chided me. (He could not have known then that the best use of the skill would be the setting down of this—the chronicle of his life.) As I wanted his goodwill, I stopped resisting, and soon found that Seraiah, who loved his work, was a fine teacher. From him I came to understand that there was a great power in scratches upon skin or clay, from which one man might know the mind of another, even though distance or years divided them. He showed me that marks etched on a stone or inked upon a roll of hide could make a man live again, long after he had died. So for an hour or more each day I sat with him and drew figures in the dust, mouthing out the sounds that each scratch stood for, until one day the strange marks resolved themselves before my eyes. Before long, I could easily read any parchment or tablet that fell under my eyes, and make my own marks almost as skillfully as Seraiah.

Some dozens of David's men had brought their wives with them, and with them came a score or more of children. Daughters, of course, dwelt with their mothers in the tent. But there were sons also; infants mostly, and one or two beardless boys near to my own age. I did not become friends with them as I might have done in another season. I had moved on, and was a child no longer. So when I had liberty, I sat with Avigail, listening an ear to what she had to tell me, and watching for what could be imparted when no words were exchanged. A younger woman sat always by her, and she, too, was David's wife. Ahinoam was a quiet, solid peasant girl from the Yezreel valley. She deferred to Avigail despite the precedence that by right was hers by earlier marriage. Ahinoam had little to say. I remember chiefly her placid, bovine beauty. David treated her with proper kindness, and had her often by him in the night. But by day, it was Avigail he wanted by his side.

I knew—everyone knew—that these camp marriages were shadowed by another, earlier match. David's famous first wife, Mikhal, the daughter of King Shaul, was not with us. She had abetted David's flight from her father, and in reprisal Shaul had married her off to another man. "Do not speak of it," Avigail cautioned me. "It is a sore matter with David." It was a measure of how easy I felt with her that I was able to ask if this grieved her, that he cared still for this lost wife. She smiled. "You are very young," she said. "Too young, perhaps, to understand such things." She looked down and studied her hands in her lap. "If there is a child of Shaul's that excites jealousy in me," she said softly, "it is not Mikhal." She raised her chin and looked off into the distance. "No, not her. Not that poor girl."

VI

A few weeks after, I awoke suddenly from a dream—a confused dream peopled by strange beasts. I was at home again, in the hills of Ein Gedi, fighting off a lioness that had come for my goats. In the dream I was strangely strong, but just as I wrested the goat from the lion's jaws, she changed shape into a she-bear, and her claws grasped me and held me against her pelt so that I could not breathe. I woke then, heart pounding, glad to find my face pressed only into a greasy scrap of sheepskin. I was lying in the dark, waiting for my heart to slow, listening to a light rain tapping on the earth beyond the cave mouth. I lay there, breathing the scent of damp stone and wet live-stock as the men around me shifted and grunted in their sleep.

Then I became aware of another noise. The sucking sound of feet on wet earth. Someone was moving outside the cave entrance. I sat up, to listen more closely, and saw the shadow pass across the opening. There was always a watch set, so I was not at first uneasy. Men had to answer the call of nature, even at night. But these swift steps did not resemble the weary tread of a man making a drowsy path to the latrine. These steps were purposeful, and they were heading directly for David's cave. I stood, cast my dark mantle over my head and stepped out into the rain.

I caught sight of him just as he reached the cave where David slept. He was tall and broad, and even in the dark I could see that he wore the garb of Shaul's military. Killer. The hairs on my neck prickled with fear. The rational act would have been to cry out and rouse the guards—armed men who could actually be of use against a trained murderer. But I was far from rational thought. Some other faculty had me in hand, for I sprinted toward David's cave, my bare feet sliding on the rain-slicked ground. As I reached the entrance, my gut clenched. The bigger man already had David in a wrestler's lock, pinning him with one massive arm. Then the killer raised his other hand and grabbed a hank of David's bright hair, pulling his head back to expose his neck. I expected the flash of a blade. As David groaned—a deep, animal sound—I opened my mouth to scream.

The cry died in my throat. The tall stranger had no dagger. As he drew David's head toward him, he leaned forward, and the dark fall of his hair did not conceal the truth of this encounter. They kissed. There was violence in it, and power, like lightning reaching from sky to earth.

And this, as most of the world now knows, was the way of it between David and Yonatan. A love so strong that it flouted ancient rule, strained the bonds between father and son, and defied the will of a king. When I sat by David's side as he fought through his grief to compose the lament—"The Song of the Bow," which everyone now learns by heart as a matter of course—only then, I think, did I fully understand the power of the love they had, one for the other. And I knew what Avigail had known, what she had endured, and why she pitied Mikhal. But that night all I felt was confusion and embarrassment. I backed away from the cave and crept back to my bed, hoping that no one had seen me.

I did not sleep again that night, but tossed and turned, disturbed by what I had witnessed. I was still very young. Too young to understand the force of adult desire. I had only just felt the first brute stirrings of a boy's simple lusts; the hot, shameful swelling that came unbidden and provoked a mocking ribaldry if noticed by the older men. Eavesdropping once, at home, when my father was entertaining wine merchants from the coast, I overheard some talk about the strange practices of the Sea Peoples. The trader claimed that some among them extolled the love between man and man, even going so far as to field warrior units of couples pledged to each other. The man was saying that the unit so formed was greatly feared, as the warriors fought not only for their own honor but also for the honor of their beloved. I hadn't much credited any of this, placing it among other implausible travelers' tales of sea monsters and cities of gold. In our tribe, such alliances were viewed as undesirable, even unclean, and those who indulged them did so in some secrecy. I fretted for David, lest others in the camp should awaken and learn the truth.

When Yoav rose before first light, I scrambled from my own bed of sheepskins and followed him. He stopped to make his water, and then headed right for the king's cave. I cried out his name, and he turned.

"What?" he said impatiently.

"David," I stammered. "He is . . . he is not . . . perhaps you shouldn't . . ."

He raised a weary hand, as if to swat an irritating insect. "David's not alone? Is that what you are trying to say?"

My face turned as hot as an ember, and I nodded, looking at the ground.

"Foolish boy. It's the king's son Yonatan. He sent word last eve that he would be here." He grasped me by the shoulders and forced me to look him in the face. "Yonatan loves David. Every man in this camp knows that. More, he is loyal to him. How else do you think we elude Shaul's relentless hunting, as large a band as we are now become? If Yonatan didn't risk his neck to bring us word of the king's spies, we would never be able to keep ahead of the pursuit. Get about your business, and think of this no more."

Some months later, we were encamped on the table mountain at Horesh, in the wilderness of Ziph. Unknown to us, Shaul's spies had tracked us there. Acting on that intelligence, Shaul himself saw an opportunity to entrap us at last, and he set out himself, leading a large force. Yonatan appeared in the camp just in time to warn us. I was with David when he arrived, and he did not send me away, but presented me. To my surprise, Yonatan embraced me, and thanked me for my service. The meeting was brief: the danger was imminent and we all had tasks to do to strike camp and move off swiftly before we became encircled on the mountain. Yonatan and David clasped each other in a farewell embrace, not caring that I stood there as witness. When they separated, Yonatan took David's shoulders into his hands and held him at arm's length. "Don't be afraid," he said. "The hand of my father will never touch you. You are going to be king over Israel and I will be second to you, and even my father, Shaul, knows this is so."

As he finished speaking, a shard of ice shivered through me. I was aware of a terrible voice.

Red runs the sword in the hand of Shaul. The blood is royal.

I saw their faces turned to me. I saw the avidity of David, the awe of Yonatan.

Yonatan! Why come ye not to aid your king? Why linger ye in Yavesh, sleeping in the tamarisk shade?

Then all the breath went out of me and I fell to my knees. I could not hold my head up. It hit the rock floor with a crack. They had to carry me on a litter, still unconscious, when we broke camp. When I awoke, Yonatan was long gone, and every wise man and priest in David's band had been set to puzzling the meaning of my words.

He was waiting for me when I awoke, his face haggard. This time, he did not wipe my brow or offer a solicitous draft of water. He was pacing. In a low, affectless voice, he repeated to me the words as I had spoken them. Then he turned to me, glaring.

"What did you mean? Whose blood did you see on Shaul's sword? Was it mine? Was it Yonatan's?"

"I don't know."

"How can you not know? You said the words. You must know."

"It wasn't me speaking." I took a deep breath. Even that small effort made my head scream, and I winced.

David loomed over me, menacing. He kicked the earth, raising a spray of gravel. Then he picked up a rock from the floor of the cave. I flinched. His face registered my fear, and answered with a sneer of disgust. Then he turned and hurled the stone at the wall. "What good is it, then, this gift of yours? You speak—or words come—about those most dear to me—words of swords and blood. And yet no one can tell me what to make of them." He clenched his fists and then opened them heavenward in a gesture of supplication. "Why?" It was almost a wail.

"I don't know," I said. And tears rolled down my cheeks. In my weak state, I was powerless to stop them. I hated this feeling, that I was disappointing him. His question—What good is it?—seared me. Why had I left behind my family and come into his service if I could not serve him at his need?

"Get up," he said harshly. I rose, unsteady, to my feet. "I'm tired of being the hunted one. Tonight, I will hunt, and you will hunt with me. After dark, be ready."

I had no idea what he meant. I dressed warmly; the night was cold. Every movement cost me. I was tired beyond fatigue. I tried to hold my head still, as every movement sent pain pulsing through my jaw and brow as if my head were crunched in a vise. As I waited, the pain slowly ebbed, until I could drift into a fitful doze that must have turned to a deep sleep. When I woke, David's nephew Avishai, my weapons master, was shaking me. "Come," he said. "It's time." To my surprise, there were no others: just David, Avishai and me, moving through the dark, and at speed, across the table-topped hill. I felt empty and light, and to my surprise was able to keep the pace. On the other side of the hill, I knew, lay the track to the village of Yeshimon. "Where are we going?" I said, but Avishai hushed me with an urgent gesture. When we reached the cliff edge, the dark was graying into the approaching dawn. Below us, at the base of the hill, lay a military encampment, more than a hundred soldiers, all of them fast asleep. I peered through the half-light, looking for a picket line, for sentries on watch, but I could see none. Where were they? Was it a trap?

David and Avishai moved swift and low, running between bushes.

I followed, moving when they moved, stopping when they stopped. When we reached cover, I bent double, retching noiselessly, dry heaves that made the sweat bead on my brow. David stood, listening, waiting to see if any of the sleeping men stirred. Then we moved again, silent and swift, until we were right in among the sleeping forms. My heart was bursting in my chest from fear and exertion. We picked our way through that large force, men prone, men supine, men curled in their cloaks like infants. They lay as if in the grip of some powerful drug, and we moved through them with no more trace than a shadow, or a breeze. And then suddenly David was standing over a large man. He lay sprawled out in a dead sleep, his spear stuck in the ground at his head. A purple cloak covered his body. Although he was an older man his face, even slack-jawed in sleep, was handsome, his beard still full, fair and unsilvered. David looked down, his face a mask, un-readable. Avishai crept up beside him. *His* face I could read quite plainly. It was lit with the nervous triumph of a hunter who has cor-nered his prey at last. I knew then that the tall man must be Shaul, our king. Our foe. I began to tremble, violently. All the more so when Avishai spoke. His voice was an urgent whisper, brimming with anger and hate.

"Let me run him through right here and now, pin his carcass to the dirt." His eyes glittered. "I won't have to strike twice." But David shook his head. "No one can lay hands on the anointed."

I spoke then. *He will go down to battle and perish.*

David clapped a hand over my mouth. The voice of prophecy did not whisper. Yet none of the sleepers had stirred. Under his breath, David repeated to me what I had said. He gave me a hard look. "Noth-ing more?" I shook my head. Then he turned back to Avishai. "Take Shaul's spear. And give me that water jar also. Let's go."

I still, to this day, do not know how we got in and out of that camp unseen. How it was that I spoke prophecy aloud across the body of the sleeping king and yet did not wake him, and all those trained soldiers slept on as if drugged, or enchanted.

We climbed back up the hill and waited for the sunrise. We had a perfect view of the camp, and of the king where he lay sleeping. As the sky lightened, David pointed out Avner, the famous general, asleep in a sitting position, weathered and craggy as the rock that supported him. As the first rays struck the hilltop above us, David raised his powerful voice and shouted.

"Avner!"

The general sprang up with the reflexes of a seasoned fighter, grabbing his spear and his sword in a single fluid motion. "Who dares to raise his voice?" he cried.

David's reply dripped with a silky sarcasm. "There's no one like you in Israel." He tossed his head, and dropped the unctuous tone. His next words were loud and harsh: "Why don't you keep watch over your king? Look around! Where is the king's spear? Where's his water jar? You know it was right by his head."

Shaul scrambled to his feet, reaching in vain for his spear. He scanned the hillside, raising a trembling hand to shelter his eyes from the swiftly rising sun.

"Is that your voice, my son David?"

David stepped out from the shelter of the trees, so that Shaul might see him. "It is, my lord king." There was a catch in his voice. That one word, "son," had undone him. I saw that he struggled for self-mastery. Avishai moved forward, a soldier's reflex, to shield him—he was a plain target, there on the hilltop, with a hundred trained spearmen, alarmed and confused, gazing up at him. But David extended a firm arm and pushed him back.

"Why does my lord continue to pursue his servant? What have I done? What wrong am I guilty of, that the king of Israel should come out to seek a single flea? Here is your spear, my king. Let one of your men come up here and get it. For the Name delivered you to me this night, yet I would not raise a hand against you. Just as I valued your life, so may the Name value mine, and may he rescue me from all this strife."

Shaul cried out then. "I am in the wrong. I have been a fool. Come back, my son David . . ."

David's hands clenched at his side. "He is calling me his son." His voice sounded young and plaintive. I opened my mouth to say, "Go down to him. You wanted reconciliation, and now he offers it. Go down." But the words that formed in my mind were not the words that uttered from my lips. I could not force the breath to shape itself into my thought. Instead, my tongue lapped helplessly—sibilant and fricative sounds made against my will, carrying another message entirely.

Flee this land. Or surely you will perish at his hands.

David looked from me to the king, anguish on his face. A soldier of Shaul's guard was already climbing the hill, coming toward us to reclaim the king's possessions. Avishai grasped David's arm. "You brought the prophet with us," he hissed urgently. "Heed him." David raised the king's spear then, and hurled it, so that it stuck the earth just ahead of the young soldier. He left the water jar where it lay on the ground. Then he turned and ran, and we followed.

By midmorning, we were on the road to the coast, leaving the lands of Yudah. Whether it was the words I had uttered, or the voice of his own heart, David made his decision. He could not put his trust in Shaul, unstable as he had become. That left us only one place to seek refuge where Shaul could not pursue us. We were on our way to Gath, to offer service to Achish, the Plishtim *seren* of that city and its surrounding territories, who had been our bane and enemy.

Many blamed us, in those days. Some blame us still. But those same words that had cost my father his life still ruled David's actions: *Whatever it takes. What was necessary.*

And so we left the hill country, heading east into the flat lands of the Plishtim along the Great Sea. It was a weary, footsore journey. When I felt the hot sea breeze on my face, it recalled to me the briny scent of my childhood. My heart should have lifted, but instead a great gloom settled on me. No man—not even a hunted outlaw— walks willingly to become a vassal of his most bitter foe.

In return for David's promise of service, the *seren* of Gath allowed us to settle in an old fortress within the town of Ziklag. David and those others with wives and families all lived there, while single men were billeted with Plishtim families nearby. Though we took most of our meals together at the fortress, I lodged at night in the home of a prosperous ironsmith who supplied most of the *seren*'s weaponry. It is a hard lesson, to accept refuge in the home of those you have been raised to despise. Yet the family I lodged with was kindly, and the other single men grudgingly admitted the same. Though they could have no cause to welcome us—unkempt strangers—they showed us no ill will. In time, I became ashamed of the baseless hatred I had harbored for these people.

I found it most difficult, at first, to live among idolators, averting my eyes from the strange bird-headed statues that seemed to stare from every crevice and nook. To be sure, many of our own people kept the old house idols, even as they were castigated for it by the priests. But our people, I think, kept them as sentimental decorations, mementos of a past time. Few really believed they held any power. The Plishtim, on the other hand, revered these things. I saw this reverence plain when I went to their temple. One time only. I made myself go there. A man like me, held safe in the fist of a jealous God, has nothing to fear from idols and should understand their power over his foes. Or so I told myself.

To my surprise, I found myself strangely moved by their rituals. Are we not all of us thankful for the soft, soaking rains that bring the harvest, and for the golden ears of ripening grain? We all fear the power of the lightning that rends the heavens. If they call these things Dagon or Baal, what of it? *Elohim hayyim,* our one living God, who knows all, must know that the thanks and the awe belong to him. Can it matter so much to him that some people need a statue in order to pray? These questions troubled my sleep. I did not visit their temple again.

My room in the ironsmith's home was finer than any I had known, certainly better than the caves and tents of our fugitive years. The smith's young wife was very beautiful, once one got used to the strange artifices that were the fashion among them. She did not hide her hair, for instance, but wore it in a most unnatural arrangement: a shoulder-length fall of tight, tiny braids. Her eyes she painted with heavy lines of kohl and she dyed her lips a distracting red. You could tell where she was by the strong, flowery perfume she wore.

The main room of the house was a columned salon built around a pebble hearth where the smith's friends would gather for drinking parties. They preferred spirit liquor, which they drank in honor of their grain idol, Dagon. At first, I found the searing drink too harsh for the palate of a winemaker's son. But in time I came to crave—and require—the oblivion it brought me.

For these were bitter seasons of lies and killing, by which we earned our ignominious keep. Shaul did not pursue us into the Plishtim lands. He did not have the means to engage Achish on his home ground. So, in return for our safe haven, David made many raids in the name of the Plishtim *seren*. The raids were brutal and served no high purpose other than to ingratiate us with Achish, who supposed that we raided our own people. But David was too shrewd—and too loyal—to do that. Instead, he plundered the outlying settlements of the Amalekites and the Geshurites and lied to Achish about where the loot came from.

These lies had a cascade of ill consequences. To conceal our duplicity, David commanded that we leave no one alive in the sacked villages to tell what we had done. These were ugly, cruel, asymmetric fights. We were well-armed and seasoned soldiers; the villagers were simple herdsmen and farmers, often defending themselves only with scythes and hoes.

On one searing day I fought beside David as he cut down a man who had confronted him bravely—the village headman, so it seemed. There was something in the decisive, almost casual way that David slew him, something in the way the man fell, his face registering surprise rather than fear or panic—and then I saw the boy, struggling in the grip of his howling mother. A boy of the age I had been when David took my father's life with just the same detachment.

Bile rose in my throat. Despair, like a smothering fall of earth, crushed me. As David turned and moved toward the boy and his mother, I cried out.

"Don't do it!"

David turned for a moment, his expression perplexed, but then he moved like a lynx and in two sword thrusts dispatched the woman and her child. He turned back to me and lifted his shoulders. "It was necessary. We can't leave any alive. You know that." And then he turned away, moving off in search of his next kill.

I stood there in the swirling dust, staring at the body of the boy. He'd fallen against his mother, his hand open on the dirt as if reaching for her face. The sobs that convulsed me were unstoppable, a spring in spate. I could barely breathe. These were the tears I'd never shed for my own father, the grief that vision's fierce grip had torn away from me. I went and knelt by the boy, my hand on his head. Others of our band passed me. Some paused a moment to see if I was injured. After a summing look, they moved on to the chore of killing until everyone was dead.

It didn't take long. It never did. I made no move to rise when David, the spoils loaded, gave the command to move out. It was Avishai who raised me up and set me on a plundered mule at the rear of the baggage train. When we arrived at my billet, the armorer's servant waited, as always, with hot water, fresh clothing and a beautifully decorated pottery crater brimming with grain liquor.

I drank it down, and signaled for another. I drank that night till I lost myself, and with the Plishtim liquor, it did not take much. Soon, it became a habit. I would take a crater before we set out, to numb myself, and then on our return I would down as much as it took to secure oblivion. But the pain for my father's death stayed raw, as if the calendar on my mourning had started on that day, in that foreigners' village, far from my own home and kin.

Perhaps it was the dulling liquor that explains why, for all the injustices I witnessed—and, yes, had a part in—my inner voice never spoke up again against any of it. Not the old woman burned alive in her hut. Not the infant, dead with one of our warrior's boot prints mashed into his tender flesh. Sometimes, I would kneel in the blood and the smoke, exhausted and retching, hoping that the cramp in my gut was a prelude to vision. Hoping that the roar of heaven would issue from my mouth and decry what we had done, that divine wrath would cleave me apart and leave me there among the dismembered dead. But it never happened. It seemed that *Hashem tzva'ot*—the lord of armies—tolerated this butchery. *Whatever it takes. What was necessary.* I had no visions at all during that time, and I had begun to doubt my own oracle. I could not see any road ahead that would lead David from this shameful exile to the mighty throne and the glorious destiny I had foretold for him.

When David brought the spoil—the herds and trade goods we plundered—to Achish, he would tell the king that we had raided our own tribes in the Negev. In secret, though, he sent a portion of the spoil back to Yudah, to those he knew to be friends, to elders whose goodwill he hoped to earn and to all those places where our band had roamed and been furnished with supplies. Such was his cunning, and by year's end, Achish trusted him. As far as he knew, David's rift with his own people was total, and he had aroused their hatred. Achish believed that David would be his vassal forever.

Not everyone was fooled, however. Achish's chief generals, many of whom had fought David in the field, remained skeptical about his supposed new loyalty. When we mustered with them for what was to be a major assault on Shaul's forces, they objected. Unwilling to go forward with dissent in the ranks, Achish ordered us back to Ziklag.

Before we arrived there, a sour stink of burning reached us. We could see, in the distance, a pall of smoke rising over the town. We increased our pace, and arrived to find the town gates unmanned. We ran through the streets toward the plume of smoke, which we soon realized marked the site of David's fortress. The gates hung splintered on their hinges, and beyond the courtyard, the fort stood a smoldering ruin. David and his men ran heedlessly over the fallen timbers, calling the names of their wives and children. But no one answered.

Finally, Avishai beat down the shuttered door of a neighboring house and dragged out the reluctant householder. He was an old man. The young men of the town were all of them gone—they had mustered with us and were still on the march with Achish.

Avishai's face was black with rage. "Who did this? Speak!"

"Amalekites. My lord, they came in force. We who are left could do nothing."

It was a revenge raid. We had laid waste several of the Amalekites' settlements. They had bided their time, waiting until, as they thought, all our fighters had gone to war. They had killed the guard on the gate and then marched out the women and children, bound one to another at the neck, before they set fire to the fort.

David, standing behind Avishai, fell to his knees. His hand scrambled in the dirt, piling it on his head. He was crushed by the knowledge that this is what his tactics—all that killing, all those women and children dead—had brought upon us. Get up, I willed him. This is not the time to let guilt or grief rout you. Yoav, who had been searching in the ruin, came running across the courtyard. He spoke all in a rush, giving voice to my own thoughts.

"The Amalekites think we are heading north; they will not expect us to pursue them. We have to take that advantage and go. Now. Before they rape and kill them all."

But David did not get up. Instead, he fell prostrate in the dirt. I looked around at the faces, many of them also tear-streaked. But what I saw was not sympathy. It was anger. David had lost his wives, but they had lost their sons. At that moment, they did not want a leader in mourning: they wanted a cool-headed avenger.

I had not seen this before. David knew his men, knew their hearts, read their every mood. As the head and the hand work as one, so it had always been with David and his men. I often thought that he read them better than they read themselves. But there, in the square, as I blinked against the stinging embers and spat the dry ash from my mouth, I saw that the gift had deserted him.

One of the men picked up a rock from the ground. I have no idea what he intended, or even if he was aware, in his anger, that he had a stone in his fist. I waited for Yoav to restrain him, but he just stood there and locked eyes with the man, almost as though urging him on. Another then bent and took up a stone. Then a third. They began to advance upon David, crying out curses, as he lay oblivious, keening.

What madness was this? I stood at the edge of what was fast becoming a mob. Wifeless, childless, I was outside the frenzy. And then I took myself in hand. For what reason had I resolved to be celibate and barren if not this? To defend David from his own human entanglements, and the weakness they engendered. I pushed through the crowd, shoving aside men twice my size, until I stood between David and the sea of angry faces.

"Get back!" I bellowed. I had never heard my own voice so loud and resonant when not under the power of the Name. I drew my sword and swept it in front of me in a wide, glittering arc. My newfound ferocity must have worked on the men's natural awe and wariness of me, because they did step back, muttering and cursing.

I knew I did not have long, but in that moment of their uncertainty, I took the risk and turned my back on them. I reached down and grabbed David by the shoulders of his tunic and pulled him up. He was a dead weight in my hands, but somehow I found the strength to bring him to his feet. I was actually shaking him. I saw his face, a mask of grief, re-forming itself into bafflement.

Then I bellowed again. It was still my own voice, alone. I spoke without power. But no one but me knew that.

Pursue! I cried. *Pursue! For you shall overtake and you shall rescue!*

David's head snapped back as if I had struck him. The glazed look vanished from his eyes, as if his soul, departed, had reentered his body. He cried out and the men answered in a roar.

Others have written of that pursuit, of how David ran us till we dropped, all the way from Ziklag to Wadi Besor. A third of us, too spent to continue, we left behind there. The rest of us went on, rallied by David's will and my words. With luck, or divine guidance, we stumbled upon a half-dead Egyptian slave who had fallen ill and been left to die by his Amalekite master. We gave the man food and water, and he gave up the Amalekite position in return for his freedom. David pressed on through the night to mount a surprise raid at dawn.

I have already set down the details of some of the most notorious things we did. But at this skirmish we excelled ourselves in our brutality. Half crazed with grief and exhaustion, those whose wives and children had been taken fell on their enemies with a red frenzy. Corpses were hacked apart, severed heads kicked from man to man till the faces were mashed like ground meat. It took very little time. Any who stayed alive long enough to witness what became of the fallen turned and fled into the wild. We did not pursue them. David walked through the piles of defaced corpses, kicking aside body parts, his boots red to the calf, until he came to where the women and children were penned, roped together like beasts and lashed to pickets. He went to Avigail first, and slit the rope that bound her. Then he fell to his knees, his arms around her thighs, weeping. He was sticky with blood and brain matter but she did not regard it. Avigail wrapped her hands in his hair, raised him up and embraced him. Then she took his knife and severed the bonds on Ahinoam, who was tied up beside her. She took David's hand and placed it on Ahinoam's swollen belly. His face moved through a spectrum of expressions, from confusion to realization to joy. Ahinoam was carrying David's firstborn son, Amnon. He had had more to lose that day than he had even imagined. David drew Ahinoam into a grateful embrace. But when he drew back, I saw the bloody handprint on her robe, and I knew it for what it was. An ominous anointing.

VII

All these memories unspooled that night, as I sat my lonely vigil in David's house, in the city that now bore his name, the years of exile far behind us. I did not often choose to recall those ugly, bitter times. But remembering Avigail and yearning for her counsel had brought those months vividly before me. Had she lived, even now, when David's household boasted the loveliest and highest-born women of a half dozen nations, I believe he would have continued to rely on her affection and her wisdom. When she died, David mourned her fasting. But he sang for her no such gorgeous lament as he composed for Yonatan.

I did not even doze throughout the night, which is just as well. Who knows what dreams might come in such a state, poised on the edge of vision, yet unable to push through the reeking mire of doubt. Outside, dawn was still distant, but finally the blackness of full night began to lift so that I could make out, once again, the shape of the pitcher upon the table, the smooth expanse of my undisturbed sleeping couch. I rose from my chair, walked to the window and opened the shutters on the ebbing darkness. Muwat, on his low pallet in the alcove, stirred and uttered an involuntary groan. I heard him shuffling to the ewer, and water splashing into the basin. As he handed me the linen cloths, he stifled a yawn. I pressed the cold fabric to my face. My body ached, joint and sinew. I let my head drop to one shoulder and then the other, loosening the cables that knotted about my neck. Muwat shambled out, heading for the kitchens to await the first bread. I did not bother to tell him that I would not be able to eat it. The dread that bored a pit in my belly would not permit it.

I would go to the king as soon as I decently could. My chamber's window faced east. I stood there, gazing out toward the dark mass of the Har HaZeitim, the Mount of Olives, willing the sun to scale its curve. Finally, a sliver of light spilled over the brow of the mount and reached swiftly across the Wadi Kidron, wakening a rooster to crow to the dawn. I watched the shaft finger its way up the walls of the outer houses, crawling inch by inch across the rough mud, making a swift sprint across a flat roof, illuminating a servant emptying a pan of fouled water into the street below. Layer by layer, the light rose through the levels of the town, the winding streets and angled houses, until finally it leaped the gap between the citadel and the king's house and lapped against the ashlars at the base of the wall against which I leaned my exhausted body. I shook myself, straightened, pulled a mantle around my shoulders and went out.

I had barely taken a score of steps when Muwat rounded the corner, the bread platter in his hand and his eyes, almost as wide as the platter, staring wildly from his head. "Thank you, Muwat, but I won't—"

I was about to say I would not be taking anything to eat when he, most uncharacteristically, cut me off. He laid a tentative hand on the sleeve of my robe, and inclined his head back along the passageway in the direction of our room.

"So?" I said softly. Then in case we were overheard: "I think I will take a morsel, after all."

Inside the room, I closed the door. Muwat set the platter down. "You know that the king is not alone." It was a statement, delivered with the air that had become familiar to me: the ordinary man's assumption that as a prophet I knew everything. "You're aware that there is a woman with him."

Well, I thought, one didn't need to be a prophet to know that. And this hardly seemed cause for such a concerned expression as my servant now wore. I felt relief, in fact, that the king was acting more like his normal self.

"What of it?" I said, smiling. "When is there *not* a woman with the king?"

"It is not a woman of the household. It is the wife of Uriah."

"*Uriah?*"

Muwat nodded, looking surprised at my astonishment, and at the same time a little bit gratified that he had been able to tell me something I did not in fact know.

"Not Uriah the Hittite captain?"

Muwat nodded again. I breathed in sharply. What madness was this? Uriah was one of David's principal fighters, loyal and brave, known for his discipline and honor. He had gone to the siege with Yoav, leading his own company. I sat down. So this was the cause of my unease. David had his appetites, as I have said, but this kind of incontinent behavior was most unlike him. He did not abuse his power in this way. His bonds with his men were bonds of real love, of friendship and devotion. He was more apt to reward a good soldier like Uriah with the honor of a virgin from his own household than to cuckold him.

"Speak of this to no one," I said. Muwat gave me a look, which I deserved, telling me he was not such a dullard as to need that instruction. "Send to Yohoshaphat and ask him if I might have the morning's first audience—or the first after any urgent military matters have been dealt with." He turned to go, but I stopped him. "No. Forget that, Muwat. Better to go instead to the youth who attends the king's bedchamber, and see if you can get him to tell you when the king is again alone." It would be preferable, I thought, if I could confront him on this matter in his chamber, before the press of people crowded us. Even if he cleared the hall, and we met there with no other present, ears would be everywhere, and tongues wagging about what might or might not have passed between the king and his seer. Muwat nodded.

He was a subtle youth; he understood these things. He went out, and I paced. This matter would need to be covered up, and swiftly. It was the kind of thing that corrodes, like a drop of lye fallen upon linen. You don't see the effect at first, but in time the fibers weaken and fray, a hole widens, and the garment is spoiled. Only if the drop is washed away directly can the damage be gainsaid.

The sun had not traveled much higher in the sky when Muwat returned to tell me that the woman had been escorted from the palace, swathed from head to foot in mantle and veils. I went then and ascended to the king's chambers on the upper floor. The guard on the stair did not stop me and the chamber attendant looked only mildly vexed that I should ask to see the king at such an early hour. The rules that bound others in the king's house were understood not to apply to me.

He was standing by the window as I entered, just as he had been two days earlier. But this time, the face that turned to me was glowing and relaxed. "You're abroad early," he said. "Do you have news for me of my mother? How does she?"

"Your mother is in good health. Your brother, as ever, drinks too much. It was an interesting visit; we can speak of it later, if you like. But that is not why I am here." I tilted my head in the direction of the chamber attendants.

He raised a brow, but said nothing, and gave the sign to dismiss them. When the door closed, he passed to the table where a pitcher was set. "Have some laban," he said, pouring me a cup. "It is very good now. The goats like this season's grasses." I shook my head. Just the sight of the creamy liquid oozing into the cup aggravated my nausea. He shrugged, downing the laban in greedy gulps and wiping his mouth as unselfconsciously as a boy.

He was still smiling when he spoke again. "So what does bring you here, if you have no news and you will not take a morning morsel?" The amber eyes were fixed on me, wary now, despite the smile.

"What do you think you are doing with the wife of Uriah?"

There was a flash of anger. "That is an impertinent question, even from you." He put down the cup with a thump. "I might have known better than to expect some privacy in my bed—in my bed!—with a seer underfoot. Don't trouble yourself. It was an impulse of a moment and it's done with. Nothing will come of it. She is discreet. She has to be—she has most to lose in this, after all. Uriah will never know of it. But Natan—it was an uncanny thing—" His face softened, and his tone also. He was no longer curt and flip, but distant, almost dreamy. "I saw her quite by chance. I couldn't sleep. You know how I've been since the troops left. I was up on the roof, pacing, trying to quiet my mind, and there she was, on the roof of her own house—you know the one?—she and her maid. The maid was helping her to bathe. Oh, I know. I should have looked away as soon as I saw that she was undressing. I swear, I didn't know who she was, or I would have done so. You will say I should have resisted the temptation, no matter who she was. But I couldn't. The night before, I hadn't been able . . . with a girl . . . it doesn't happen to me like that, and it had been eating at me. What was I, if I couldn't fight and I couldn't fuck? Then I looked at her, and I felt alive—I felt like myself—for the first time since the troops left. There was something about the moonlight on her shoulders, the tumble of her hair . . ." His long fingers caressed the air, describing a picture in his mind, and he smiled. "I tell you, even you, Natan, for all your iron discipline—even you would have been overthrown."

Unlikely, I wanted to say. But I did not. "What's done is done, but I must tell you I think it most unwise. What makes you sure Uriah will not hear of this? Word reached me as swift as the deed. No, not in that way. Be assured, my visions do not reach into your bedchamber. I learned of it by normal human means. Servants' gossip." I did not tell him of my nightlong watch, the foreboding of some wretched, unclean thing. I tried to steady my breath. "Presumably you sent a servant to fetch her, so that is one mouth that must stay silent. The palace guards had to admit her, and to do that they would need to know who she was. Your chamber attendants—two? Three? They must be silent. So, let us tally it: so far, we have eight or ten or a dozen of us who know. Her maidservant, also. The porter at her house. So. How quickly we arrive at near to a score. What makes you think so many tongues will remain still? And if news comes to Uriah, what damage might it do, and he a loyal fighter, loved by his men. You do not need to risk such an enemy for the sake of a moment's spasm."

"And you, Natan, do not need to be such a sanctimonious doom-sayer. This is not a matter of high policy of the kind that concerns you. I needed it, and it was good. If you had a woman yourself from time to time you might know—" And then his tone changed. He rubbed a hand across his head and dropped his gaze like a chastened boy. "I'm sorry. I know you live as you do for my sake. I should be thanking you for the sacrifice, not goading you." I lifted a hand, waving this off.

"There can be no talk of sorry between you and me. I do not measure my words to you—indeed, I cannot. And I have no right or desire for you to weigh yours. Remember: I am *eved hamalek*, a man at your service, always." I allowed myself a small smile then. "Even if sometimes you'd rather I wasn't."

His face lightened. He stepped toward me and clapped me on the shoulder. "Truly, I don't think you need to concern yourself with this. I sent her off with a gift and I will not see her again. Yes, I sinned. I know you consider yourself the custodian of my character. But really, Natan, do you think Yah will punish me more than he will punish the hundred other men who committed adultery last night within a cock's crow of these walls?"

"You are not 'a hundred other men.' As you well know." That was all I said. I bowed then, and asked leave to go. He dismissed me with a wave of his hand. His good humor had been disrupted, but not much. As I closed the door I could hear him humming. By the time I reached the stair he was in full-throated song.

What he said was probably true. His servants loved him; they were handpicked, well treated and loyal. One could only hope hers were not similarly loyal to her husband, but would protect her secret, even if they did so only to guard Uriah from the pain of the insult to his honor. She, certainly, was hardly likely to tell her warrior husband that his king had whored her.

I went to the audience hall directly. I wanted to observe him. I took my usual place, among the counselors. While I did not always attend him there, it was understood that I might come and go from time to time. Sometimes, he would turn and seek my advice on this or that matter, but generally I was there as a silent observer.

As he dealt with dispatches and petitioners, I had to concede that the night's ill-judged folly seemed to have done him a power of good. He was alert and focused. To be sure, he was buoyed by good news from the front. The messenger brought word from Yoav. Our troops had devastated Ammon with small loss to our numbers. They proceeded on to Rabbah, where they drove the defenders back within the walls of the town and sat down in front to besiege them. Only once, when Uriah's name was mentioned in dispatches for valor, did I see the muscles of the king's face tense. But no one else in the hall would have noted it, and he soon smiled again as he spoke of the siege. "It is well done," he said, slapping his hands together and glancing warmly around the hall. "What time of year better favors the besieger? They will squint at us over their walls and watch their fields waving in the breeze. Let them grind the last of their hoarded grain and bake their mean loaves. Let them choke as they watch the barley ripening beyond their reach."

David was taking petitions, dealing with each case attentively and justly, when I rose and went out. So why was my heart still tight in my chest?

The moon had waned and waxed and waned again before I learned the reason for my unease. In those days and nights, I went about my appointed business heavily. It was, I suppose, because I felt so ill that I decided to see Mikhal at that time. I needed to see her. She held in her memory the missing piece I needed in my account: David's ascendant season as the favorite of Shaul, and how that season had become blighted, making David into the outlaw he was when I first met him. Mikhal—Shaul's daughter, Yonatan's sister, David's first wife. The most intimate witness to that time of any person living. And as I could barely expect the visit to be an easy one, better to get it done when my mood was already melancholy than save it to darken a brighter day.

VIII

She received me without warmth, but more civilly than I had expected. Her apartment was a small cell, dim and chilly, set off at the very edge of the women's quarters. There was a slit for a window, looking north, its view obstructed by the bulk of the barracks that loomed across a narrow lane, stealing what little light might otherwise have found its way to warm the stones. I pulled my mantle over my arms. In midwinter, I thought, this room must be frigid. Her handmaid, an ill-favored, hunchbacked crone, occupied a low alcove separated by a curtain. It was the quarters of one who has fallen from grace, more fit for an upper servant than the daughter of one king and the wife of another.

She had brightened the cramped space as best she could, with some good weavings, embroidered pillows and a nicely carved low table fashioned of olive wood. She gestured for me to sit, and as I arranged my writing things, she composed herself on the pillows opposite me. The years had not told on her in the usual ways—she remained tall and lithe, as I remembered her, and the shawl that she wore against the damp chill of the room revealed a glimpse of hair, still thick and lustrous. Her features were the image of her brother's cast into a gentler female mold. Both of them had their father's height, his high, intelligent brow, the chiseled chin and long, regal neck. I had not seen their mother, but since Shaul was fair, their coloring—the ebony hair and the light gray eyes rimmed with lush dark lashes—must have come from her. Mikhal and Yonatan might have been twins, as far as their appearance, even though eight years separated their births, and a sister, Merav, who was fair like Shaul, stood between them in birth order.

But if age had not ravaged her, life had. Her face was drawn, and her eyes, once lively and compelling, were as dead as a deep well in which the water had long ago been poisoned. The first time I saw her, she was exhausted and had been weeping. But even in her grief on that day, she retained the glow of a woman who is loved and desired. Not now. Not after all the years of estrangements: one that had been forced upon her, one that she had invited.

She had always been uncommonly direct for a woman and I soon discovered that this was still true.

"I loved him. You know that, I suppose?"

She had begun to speak even as I pared my quill. I set down the knife at once and began to write even though the tip was still imperfect.

"It is important that you know. I want you to set it down: 'Mikhal was in love with David.' Nobody ever writes that about a woman. It's always the man whose love is thought worthy of recording. Have you noticed that? In all the chronicles, they state it so. Well, you write down that it was I. I was the one who loved."

Her observation was quite true. Indeed, in most of our important histories, it's rare enough for wives to be named, never mind the state of their affections noted. So I set it down as she had requested. Then I paused, and looked up at her. "Surely it would not be untrue to write that David was in love with Mikhal? He did love you—once."

She tossed her head, and the shawl slipped to her shoulders. She did not trouble to replace it, but returned my gaze levelly.

"You want the truth, you say? The truth is, at that time, the other love consumed him. There was a little room for me—you know what he's like, he seeks love like food or warmth, and he doesn't turn it away. But David was at the height of his passion for my brother when he took me in marriage. When we made love, he made no pretense. He asked me to do things in the dark that recalled my brother to him."

She looked at me and her dead eyes flickered with a kind of angry light.

"Is this too much truth for you, Prophet?"

As a soldier I had seen everything that one body can do to another. In the aftermath of a battle, when women and boys alike are taken as spoils, soldiers in heat do not trouble to seek a private place for their debauching. But I had never had a woman speak to me so. I suppose the shock was plain in my expression. She tossed her head defiantly.

"Do you know what is funny about it? I didn't care. Because I adored him. I loved enough for both of us. People doubt it, who only know what happened between us after he was king. But before all that—before my father's hateful, vindictive act, before David rushed off to warm our marriage bed with the bodies of others—I would have taken him on any terms, been anything he wanted, done anything that roused his desire. All I cared was that I had him in my arms. Yes, of course, I would have liked it to be otherwise. What young girl would not wish to be loved for herself, and not as some pale, soft version of her brother? I would have liked to be allowed to be the shy, trembling virgin, who could lie in my lover's tender caress as he awakened my senses one by one, gently, patiently, until I was wet and ready. But do you know how he came to me on our wedding night? Hot from my brother, reeking of sweat. He made clear how it would have to be, if it were going to be at all . . ."

Her voice sank to a deep, throaty whisper. The thick lashes dropped low over glazed eyes, her lips glistened, her face flushed. I let my eyes shift to the stone of the wall behind her, trying to imagine its rough texture and cold chill as her intimate, insinuating voice continued to describe warm, slick declivities and how various digits and appendages had been deployed there. Finally, she interrupted herself.

"You're not writing this down. Why is that? Have I misunderstood? I thought you wanted the whole story of my accursed marriage.

The king's messenger was quite explicit: 'The king orders you to receive Natan, and tell him everything.' And here I am, trying, at last, to be an obedient wife. But wait. I had forgot. You're a voluntary gelding, aren't you? Celibate, they say. Am I arousing you? Is that even possible? Do you get hard, still? Or were you cut, like a foreign slave boy?"

There was real cruelty in her face now. The same cruel look that she had worn when she said the words that brought her marriage to David to an ugly, irrevocable estrangement. I suddenly understood, in a way I never had, how this had come about. Now the miracle of it to me was that he hadn't killed her. I knew what he was capable of, when his temper was roused. I wanted to strike her myself, even I, who prided myself on self-mastery. I closed my eyes and drew a deep breath, feeling my ribs expand in my chest and slide downward as I exhaled slowly.

"We were talking about love," I said coldly. "We seem to have strayed."

"Oh, yes. Love."

She tossed her hair forward, over her right shoulder, and ran a hand down its glossy length. A long-fingered hand, unblemished by work. You didn't see many women of her age with hands like that. It was a reminder that she was the first of her kind—an Israelite born royal.

"I wanted him. For a long time, before a marriage was even possible, I wanted him. But Father had promised David to Merav, my sister, the eldest, right at the beginning, when he still loved this brave young warrior who had sprung out of the sheepfolds to bring us a victory. David was unpolished and awkward then. Tentative. You'd see him at meat, watching to see how the rest of us got on. Merav found it funny and contemptible. I thought it sweet. And he picked it all up quickly, of course. It was no time at all before he carried himself like a born courtier. But when Father told Merav of the match, she wept and begged him to reconsider. When he ignored her, she raged and sulked and complained to anyone who would give her an ear. She deserved better, she whined, than a jumped-up shepherd boy four years her junior. She even took her complaint to Yonatan. To Yonatan! Who loved David, who would do anything for him. That's what a fool she was. Yonatan tried to reason with her, to show her that this was the best of all possible matches. But she wouldn't listen, and went on with her sighing and nagging. I was overjoyed when Father changed his mind and gave Merav to an older, richer man. I thought he was just looking for peace in his house. I didn't see the decision for what it was—the cooling of his regard, the birth of the envy and suspicion that would eat him alive. David, of course, pretended to be at peace with this decision—he was all modesty and duty then, when it came to my father. He said he had no business being a king's son-in-law in the first place. I thought he really felt that way, at the time. But you and I know—everyone knows, now—how it festered inside him, so that when he had the chance, and the power, he avenged the insult. Merav paid for it in the end, bitterly. I grieved for her in her loss. But not that much, to be honest. Not as much as I should have. I'm not saying she deserved it. No woman, no mother, deserves such a thing. But she was a vain, stupid, spoiled girl. You had to be very stupid not to see what David was, what he would become. That was Merav. He never forgot, nor forgave her. He's like that, isn't he? Unforgiving . . ."

The archness of her tone faltered then, and her hard gaze softened. She looked down and drew a sharp breath, and I thought she might be about to cry. But I underestimated her there. This was a woman raised in a turbulent house, who had learned early to master herself. Her next words seemed to follow my own thought. "It was no easy thing, to be part of that family." She looked up at me, searchingly. "*Why* did Shmuel choose my father to be king? How can a prophet make so vast a blunder? Can you tell me that, Natan? Doesn't it make you question yourself? When you speak in that way, so hard, so certain. Shmuel, the great seer. And yet he could not foresee my father's madness."

I made her no answer. I had none. The same question kept me
awake often enough. Shmuel had made Shaul a king against Shaul's
own will and inclination, indeed, dragged him from his hiding place
to anoint him. And then, when Shaul struggled to fulfill this unwelcome destiny, Shmuel withdrew his support and his counsel, cursed
him, undermined him, maybe even drove him mad. How had foresight failed him? The question burned me. But the question was about
Shmuel, not about the voice that spoke through me. Mikhal did not
understand—how could she? Though I could question the acts of
Shmuel, I could not question the voice that howled through my
own soul.

"Do you know what the greatest cruelty of madness is, Natan? It's
the power it has to blot out a person. After a man goes mad, you
struggle to remember him sane. The madness is so consuming, it eats
up everything else, even memory. As you deal with the madman, who
can recall the ordinary joys, the daily kindnesses, that came before? I
have to struggle to think of my father as he was, when I was small. I
can barely find a day, an hour, when I see him clearly: that big, powerful man, sweet and patient, intelligent and kind.

"David's music could bring that man back. I think the seeds of my
love were planted there, in the ground that my father's madness har-
rowed. We all of us—all of us who loved my father—would have
looked with affection on anyone who could do what David did. He
brought joy back into our household, for a brief time. When he first
came to us as my father's new armor bearer, the young hero of Wadi
Elah, we had no idea what a change he would bring. That first time,
he went and fetched his harp—a crude handmade thing he'd crafted
for himself—my father soon saw to it that the best craftsmen were
commissioned to fashion a better one. Nobody paid him much mind
when he plucked the first notes. But soon, every head turned to him.
None of us had ever heard the like."

I knew that she did not exaggerate. In my time, I have heard even
travelers from the court of the pharaoh—men speaking in private,

who had no need to offer flattery—say that in voice and in musician-ship, David has no peer. To me, even now, after so many years of hearing him play almost every day, it remains a marvel, that a man can draw forth such sounds from a piece of wood and some strands of gut. His overlapping harmonies, the way the plucked strings swell and ebb, swell and ebb, and every minute, every instant, he is overlaying new, fresh melodies as the old harmonies linger and resonate. Not only the ears feel the pleasure of it. You feel the vibration on your skin. The hairs rise on your arms. The pulse, the breath, the very heartbeat. It's a kind of sorcery, a possession of body and spirit. Yet a wholesome one. And there is one chord, one perfect assembly of notes that no other hand can play. The sound of it—pure, rinsing sound, void, so that your spirit seems to rush in to fill the space between the notes. So sublime that the priests asked David to offer it at the sacrifice . . . the music rising up to heaven with the sacred smoke. Every soul that hears it is refreshed and restored. So it was with Shaul.

I could see that Mikhal was remembering that music, the glorious shock of it, the first time. Her face was tilted upward, to catch a mea-ger shaft of light as it struggled briefly through the narrow slit. David would have noticed that lovely face—a girl's face, then—as he played the first time in court.

"I was scared for him, even though his singing and playing were so beautiful. Before he started to play, that first time, there had been tension in the hall. Everyone knew my father was cliff walking again. Well, that's what I called it, when the madness came. He would be like a man staggering along the rim of an abyss—which was his rage—and when the edge gave way or he missed his step, he might clutch at anyone within reach and drag that person with him over the precipice. We all of us had learned that it was not safe to try to reason with him, or even to distract him. Such a person was the likeliest to be pulled down into the dark. So when he needed us most, we with-drew. The talk would die into an awkward silence and my father would be left alone to wallow in his own grim thoughts. So when David fetched that harp, I feared for him. I feared that in his attempt to soothe my father, he would become the target of his rage. Then, he started to play. You could feel the strain in the room ease. The brilliance of his music lifted everyone. But for my father it was much more than that. For him, the music worked like soothing ointment on an open wound, or the binding that sets a broken bone back into its proper place. David sang and played, and drew my father's spirit away from that cliff edge. That's why I began to love him.

"It was a different thing with Yonatan. He didn't need a reason. He just loved. It was as if one soul had been sheared in half, breathed into two separate bodies and then cast adrift in the world, each half longing to find its other. That was how they came together, or so it seemed to me, young girl that I was. I think they became lovers the night after the battle of Wadi Elah. Even though their lives had been different in every respect, they could finish each other's sentences, they knew each other's thoughts. I had never seen my brother so light and so alive as he was after David came to us. And that fed my love, also. Because my brother had been sad and David made him happy. I'm not sure if you can imagine how hard Yonatan's life was, bearing the brunt of my father's fits, all the while trying to prop him up and provide the judgment and governance when the king wasn't capable. It was a great burden for any man to bear, and Yonatan took it up when still little more than a boy in the world's eyes. Until David came, Yonatan's loyalty to my father was absolute, but he felt his duty to our people also, and holding the balance between the two almost crushed him.

"And yet despite all that, despite all his cares, he was good to me, when I was a girl, and good to my younger brothers, too. He was more like a father than my father could be. I don't know how he did it, but he would find time to play with us, carving little toy horses out of olive wood, listening to our nonsense stories, teaching us songs."

Her eyes came alive as she spoke. Her voice, too, had become lighter and more animated. Poor girl, I thought, to have so few and such brief moments of joy—slender planks to cling to in her shipwreck of a life.

"I came of age knowing Yonatan would protect me. He would make sure that Father made a good marriage for me, and wouldn't merely use me as some token in a game of statecraft, or give me away in some mad fit. It was Yonatan who insisted that Father make the match for me with David, after Merav was married elsewhere. By then, of course, Father's affection for David had waned. He had come to agree with my vain sister that David was not good enough. Or at least that's what he told her, and she fed on the flattery. Father had begun to grow unpredictable in all matters, but most especially the matter of David. He would laud him one day and want him at his side. Another day, he would shun him, the suspicions eating at his addled mind. It took time, but Yonatan pressed the matter delicately enough, and so finally, our father gave way, or seemed to. He said that David could have me. But then he named my bride price: the foreskins of a hundred dead Plishtim.

"You remember, of course, that those were not the days of great battles with the Plishtim. They did not come against us in strength, but only harassed and raided our outer settlements. In such skirmishes, the enemy dead might number in the tens, never the hundreds. So Yonatan was dismayed. He knew what our father was about. It's one thing to kill a man like the Gath champion in single combat, or lead a unit to drive back a party of border raiders. Another to go against a seasoned army, which was the only way David could meet this grisly dowry. Father thought he was being clever, sending David off to die while placing the bloodguilt on the Plishtim. Yonatan fretted that he, in pressing the case for the marriage, would become the unwitting agent of David's death.

"But David laughed at Yonatan, and went off singing. He would do that, you know, sing as he marched. He said it kept the men in spirits. Yonatan and I kept vigil together, waiting for word. I was with Yonatan when the first messenger came, just a few days later, bearing news that David had set a trap for a Plishtim brigade just outside of Gaza, and killed at least the hundred required of him.

"My brother could not believe it. Gaza was a five-day march. My brother asked the messenger how such a thing could be possible—that David could have got his men to the outskirts of Gaza, done battle and sent word back to us, all in less than a week. The messenger replied that he had encouraged them to 'move fast.' My brother gave a great bark of a laugh at that. 'Encouraged you to fly, you mean?'" The messenger had described it all. How David never tired. How, every hour or so, he would run down the column and then back up, to his place in the vanguard, having a word for every man. How he sang to them to keep their spirits high.

"My brother smiled as the messenger went on, his face glowing with affection, pride and relief that the deadly task was done and over. But when he asked the messenger when we should expect David's return, he told us that he had pressed on, to continue the campaign with a raid on Ashdod. I couldn't restrain myself at that. I was not supposed to speak, when my brother received dispatches, but I burst out: 'You said he killed his hundred.'

"The messenger turned to me. 'He told us that to be son-in-law of the great Shaul should not be bought so cheap as that. He wants to double the bride price.'

"Yonatan looked grave. 'Wants to double it? That will be more than have fallen in all the skirmishes since the battle of Elah. He counts you quite a prize, sister.' Yonatan glanced at me, and I felt coldness, as if he blamed me for David's recklessness.

"Of course, my father had no choice but to let my marriage go ahead. It was hard on him, as he could not seem to be sour about such remarkable victories. But in the weeks of preparation for the marriage feast, you could feel the tension in him as he strove for the required good humor."

She rose, and walked to the narrow window. A great sigh escaped her. But when she turned and sat down again, her face had lightened. A hint of a smile lifted the corners of her lips.

"I was so happy, the day of the wedding feast. David entered the hall and stood, singing to me of the bridegroom's love for his bride. But even in my joy, I was not blind. I saw his gaze drift past me as he sang. I knew where he was looking. Yonatan sat right behind me on the dais. Yonatan had already given David everything he could: his royal clothes, his best weapons. Even, for a time, his place in our father's affections. I was just one more gift, laid down upon the altar of that great love. And I was grateful. It was joy enough for me, to share David with my brother. I was glad I could be a bond between them.

"Those were the years when David could do no wrong as a fighter. Most young brides fret when their husbands go to fight, but I did not. I knew he would prevail, and he did. Every time the Plishtim tried to eat away at our borders, seizing our threshing floors, pasturing their cattle on our lands, David was able to beat them back. Yonatan had taught David everything he knew of weaponry and raiding tactics. David took those lessons and added to them his own gifts for strategy, his own way of leading from within, never seeming to command, just expecting the men to be there when he ran forward. Soon enough, they were two captains together, and then David eclipsed even Yonatan. The men loved him, even though he commanded some twice his years. It helped that he was brave. He never asked a man to do more than he did himself. He always put himself in the forefront—well, you know that—you fought with him. So I do not need to tell you these things, who saw it all, when I only learned of it from tales told at meat. But there were many such tales. Yonatan came often to our house, and I would be there as they went over every battle. My younger brothers looked up to David, too. They were his own age, and younger, but even those close to him in years were still far from earning their own command. They might have been jealous, but they weren't. All of them worshipped Yonatan, of course, and took the lead from him in the deference they showed to David.

"At first, my father celebrated David's victories just as we all did, basking in the reflected glory of his young captain. And then, he changed. Suddenly, my father had had enough of it. Finally, he saw.

"I was with my father, waiting for the returning fighters. David's unit, victorious again. The women greeted him, as they always greeted the returning men, with their tambours and tambourines. One of them stepped out of the throng, and raised her voice—a good voice, clear and sweet, that carried—and she used the old words, the old poetry, where you sing of a thousand and ten thousand. Everyone's heard the rhymes, sung for this or that. The first number, the smaller, in the first line, the next line the number grows. She started with the king's name, naturally. One always starts with the king. She put David in the second line."

Mikhal raised her voice and sang the familiar couplet:

"'Shaul, Shaul has slain his thousands, and David, David his tens of thousands.' Soon, all the women had picked up the chant. My father stood there, and the blood left his face. I knew what he was thinking. I looked up and grasped his hand. 'It doesn't mean anything, Father. It's just an old rhyme.' But he wasn't listening to me. His face had turned to wood. He couldn't be rational. He heard that stale old phrase—a phrase he'd heard a hundred times—and his madness made him take it as a personal insult, that the women believed David a greater warrior, a greater man, than he was. I saw him look at David with hatred. And then I saw him look at Yonatan, saw him suddenly recognize what had been apparent to everyone else for many months. Yonatan was deferring to David as if David were the prince. David, in turn, was treating my brother as a beloved lieutenant. My father finally saw his throne—his house—at risk. And he saw that Yonatan didn't care. That Yonatan had willingly surrendered his birthright to this upstart. He saw truly, for once, despite the madness that so often distorted his sight. My brother had laid his life at David's feet; his every action proclaimed this.

"David marched out again the next month in a sally against the Plishtim and was, as always, the most successful of my father's officers. And every new victory drove my father deeper into his hate. He began to ask his closest aides to kill David. Then, mad as he was, he asked Yonatan to do it. A test of love, I suppose. And the greater love prevailed. Yonatan came to David right away to warn him. David made light of the threat. I suppose, having bathed in my father's affection, he felt secure in it. Or perhaps he believed in the worth of his own deeds; that his success would save him. He was weighing the matter as a rational mind weighs it, and Yonatan could not bring him to see that our father's mind no longer worked rationally. He grasped David by the arm and almost shook him. 'Come tomorrow morning. We are hunting, my father and I. There is a ruined croft near the place. Hide there. When we come, I will speak with him about you and you can hear for yourself and judge if there is a threat or no.'

"So they went, and Yonatan talked with our father about David's valor and good service. He begged him not to wrong a youth who had himself done no wrong. He warned that it would stain the kingship with bloodguilt. My father was himself that morning, and was able to hear Yonatan's plea. He swore an oath that he would not put David to death. So, for a time, all seemed well enough. David served my father as before, as musician and as fighter, as the times required.

"And then—well, you know what happened. David was playing harp after the meat, as he always did when he was home from the field. My father had been brooding all day. He'd allowed his wine cup to be refilled many times. He was sitting quietly, listening to the music, or so it seemed. His eyes were closed; he seemed at peace. We were all of us relieved that the evil mood of the day seemed to have lifted from him. And then, from nowhere, he leaped up, grasped a spear from the hand of the door guard and threw it right at David. David tried to make light of it, in the moment and then later, with me, at home, when he showed me the slash in his sleeve where the spear point had gone through it and pierced the wall. 'I told your father that if he disliked my singing, a simple "Enough!" would be sufficient next time.'

"'Don't make a trifle of this,' I warned him. 'Now that he has acted in this way, any of his captains, jealous of you and wanting to find his favor, might come after you. You cannot be forever on your guard. And next time he might not miss.' But he just smiled and shrugged the torn robe from his shoulders and kicked it across the floor. He held out his arms. 'If I have your love, and Yonatan's, and the people's, then what matter if he hates? I was hated my whole life by my own father and I survived that. I will survive this, too. Let him hate. But I do not think he does, in truth. It is his illness, merely. This fit will pass.' He pulled me down upon the bed and embraced me. He was tender that night. I remember it. I thought, if I am to conceive his child, let it be tonight. But of course there was no child . . ."

She looked down. I stopped writing. There was something in the abject tilt of her lovely head that filled me with pity. The earlier anger had passed. After a moment, she spoke again.

"He took my face between his hands, after we made love. 'I never thought to have this life,' he said. 'I feel like a beggar at a banquet that he has prepared for me. I owe your father for it. I will not forget that, no matter what he does.'

"I couldn't sleep that night. And that is, I think, what saved him. I'd risen from the bed, not wanting to wake him with my restlessness. I was by the window when I saw them coming: an armed unit, moving through the dark. I shook David awake. We both knew they were coming for him, and that if they took him, he might never see another morning. My hands shook as I tied the bedclothes together. 'Where will you go?' I said. 'Where can you be safe from my father?' 'I will go north, to Shmuel at Ramah,' he said. 'Shmuel will know what to do. No one knows your father better.' As far as I was concerned, Shmuel destroyed my father. But I could see the sense in the plan. Shmuel was the one person my father feared. If David were under his protection he might stay safe till the fit passed. I clutched for his hand and kissed it, then he jumped up on the sill and let himself down from the window using the crude rope we'd fashioned. I watched him melt away into the dark as I pulled the sheets back inside, untied the knots, smoothed the fabric as best I could and replaced them on the bed. Then I took the old house idol from its plinth in the corner—yes, we had one—it had belonged to my mother's family and I begged David to let me keep it, even though he wanted it broken. I laid it in the bed under the coverlet with some rufous goat hair from my maid's yarn basket arrayed on the pillow. When the leader of the detachment knocked upon the door I tried to sound as imperious as I could manage—I thought of Merav and how she would have sounded, had her rest been disturbed. I told the captain that David was ill and that I would by no means admit them; that he could not rise from his bed, and that he would attend upon the king later in the day, if he felt able.

"I heard the men at arms muttering together outside the door, arguing whether it would be all right to defy me and force the door. Had they done so, and exposed my deceit, David would not have had time to make his escape. I have my father's instability to thank for the fact that they did not, in the end, force their way into my chamber. They knew how his moods could change upon the moment, and none wanted to risk the blame of having invaded our bedchamber against my express command.

"So they reported to Shaul that David was too ill presently to attend him. My father was insane by then, probably, but he was no fool. The troops returned, of course, and he came with them. I had no choice but to admit him, and hope that David was now beyond reach. I was trembling when my father pushed me aside and strode into the room. He pulled the coverlet back and saw what I had done. His face was red with fury. He grasped my wrist and shook me, demanding to know why I had defied him.

"'I had to,' I lied. 'He threatened to kill me if I didn't help him escape.' He stared at me until I couldn't hold his gaze. 'Which direction did he take?' 'South. He means to make for Beit Lehem.' He lifted my chin roughly, so that I had to meet his eyes. He could read the lie in my face. In that moment, he knew he had lost me, too. He flung me upon the bed and threw back his head and gave a demented cry. It was awful. I can never forget the sound he made. Wounded.

"It took two days for his spies to bring word that David was in Ramah. He sent a party to seize him and bring him back. But David had made the right choice in going to Shmuel. There was a strange power in that man. The detachment returned without David, all of them raving ecstatically and calling upon Yah. So my father set out himself for Ramah. Even after their long estrangement, Shmuel still wielded the old sway over him. No one would ever tell me what really happened there. All I know is that Shmuel humbled my father completely and kept him naked and praying for a day and a night while David slipped away and came back here.

"It was Yonatan he wanted to see, of course, not me. But they met in our house and I was with them as they tried to decide what was the safest course to follow. The roles were reversed now. I think Shmuel had worked his influence on David, poured all his ugly thoughts about my father into his ears. In any case, it was David, at last, who was persuaded that Shaul meant to kill him, and Yonatan who could not bring himself to believe that our father was so lost. 'My father does nothing, great or small, without disclosing it to me. If he intended to kill you I would know of it.' I broke in there. 'Brother, don't be a fool. Do you think he's blind as well as mad? This affair of yours is part of the reason he wants David dead. Don't delude yourself. He *will* kill him, the moment he gets the chance.' Yonatan shook his head, but David grasped his arm and looked into his eyes.

"'Your sister'—that's what he said, 'your sister,' not 'my wife'; strange, that never struck me until now—'Your sister sees the truth. There is only a step between me and death.'

"'Tell me what to do,' Yonatan said, looking from one to the other of us. Then his eyes, full of love, rested on David. 'Whatever you want, I will do it for you.' David drew him into a deep embrace. I might not have even been there, so intimate it was between them. But I *was* there, and I feared, for a moment, what David might ask of my brother.

"'The day after tomorrow is the new moon. If the king returns from Ramah, there will be the customary festive meal. He invited me, before all this, to sit with him at the feast.'

"'You can't mean to go?' I interrupted, alarmed.

"'Of course not. But if he misses me, if he asks where I am, tell him I went to my family at Beit Lehem because my clan is gathering for its annual sacrifice. If he is content with that excuse, it will show that his feelings have softened, the fit has passed, and maybe he no longer means me any harm. In that case, I can come back here and we can try to go on as before. But if he rages, we'll know the opposite, and I will have to flee. Yonatan, you know I've only ever wanted to serve him. If you think I'm guilty of anything, kill me yourself, but don't make me go back to your father to be slain.'

"'Don't talk like that. If I think my father intends to kill you, of course I will warn you.'

"'But how will I know? Who will bring me the message? Who can we trust?' 'Trust me,' I said. They both looked at me then. I saw Yonatan searching my face. 'You need not involve yourself in this. Father is already enraged with you over the escape.' He turned to David. 'Let's go outside. We don't need to bring more wrath down upon Mikhal.'

"'I don't care!' I said. 'David is my husband.' I reached out and clasped his arm. 'I belong to you now. If you go into exile I want to come with you.'

"David looked down at me, his expression kind, yet already remote. 'I hope it will not come to that. But if it does, if I do have to flee your father, I will go quicker and safer alone. Taking you will only feed his rage and his resolve to hunt me down. But let's not talk of that now. Yonatan and I need to make a plan, and then, the day after tomorrow, we will see.'

"The two of them went out into the darkness. An hour later, Yonatan returned alone, his face haggard. His voice broke as he told me that they had made their plans and taken vows to protect each other's lives. To me, his wife, David had given no pledge. From me, he had taken no tender leave.

"The new moon came, and the king sat down to partake of the festive meal. He took his usual seat, back to the wall. Ever since his madness took hold, he had insisted on always sitting with his face to the door, so that he would be prepared for any enemy that might come upon him. Yonatan rose then, and gave up his seat so that Avner could sit by the king's right side. He came and sat by me, at one of the lower tables. But the seat to his left, David's place, remained empty. Father did not at first remark on it. Then he leaned over to Avner. He pointed to me. From my father's lewd gestures and Avner's awkward, forced laughter, I could tell the king was making some ribald joke about David's lack of continence. Because it was a ritual meal, impurity prevented participation. My father assumed that David was absent for the commonplace cause: an untimely emission of his seed.

"But by sundown, when the law states that purity is restored, David still had not come. My father looked with annoyance at David's vacant seat. 'Why hasn't the son of Yishai come to the meal?' he asked loudly. A hush fell over the room, the scraping of platters, the chatter all falling silent. Everyone sensed the change of mood. I caught my breath. That he would not speak David's name was a sign of ill temper. I opened my mouth to speak up, but Yonatan drew a brow to hush me. Instead, he raised his voice and addressed our father. 'David begged leave to go to Beit Lehem. He asked it as a particular favor: "Please let me go," he said, "for we are going to have a family feast and my eldest brother has summoned me to it. Let me slip away and see my kinsmen." So he said, and so I agreed. That is why he has not come to the king's table.'

"My father rose suddenly to his full, intimidating height, knocking his goblet to the floor. He strode across the room to where

Yonatan sat by me. Yonatan was scrambling to his feet but he wasn't
quick enough. The king pulled him up by his tunic. 'You son of a
faithless whore! I know you side with the son of Yishai—to your
shame, and the shame of the cunt that bore you. For as long as the son
of Yishai lives on earth, neither you nor your kingship will be secure.
Now, then, remember who you are. Have him brought to me, for he
is marked for death.'

"I was cowering, in fear for my brother. 'Don't answer him!' I
hissed. 'He's not in his right mind.' But Yonatan was too enraged to
hear me. His face was twisted and dark. Instead of pulling away from
my father he took a step toward him. 'Why should he be put to death?
What has he done?' The king grasped a spear then, and brought the
point upward, right beneath Yonatan's chin. 'Don't!' I cried, reaching
out to grab his spear arm. He did not even turn in my direction, but
he brought his arm back and slapped my face with such force I went
sprawling. I felt a sharp pain where my body hit the edge of the table.
I gulped for breath. The broken edge of a rib ground against flesh. I
slid to the floor. Yonatan stood there, eye to eye with our father, as
the fallen goblet rocked back and forth on its rim. You could feel their
rage like a solid form between them. No one else moved. Then, without taking his eyes off my father's face, Yonatan reached down and
pulled me to my feet. Grasping me firmly by the wrist, he strode from
the room, dragging me after him. He saw me safely to my house,
set two of his loyal men to guard me, and went off to the agreed meeting place, where he delivered to David the news that the rift with
our father was lethal. Later, when he told me about it, he said that
they kissed each other and wept together, and that David wept the
longer.

"My father took his revenge before Yonatan returned. The bruises
on my face were still purple and yellow when my father had me married off to Palti. It was a brilliant act of vengeance, designed to punish
me and humiliate David. I wept and keened all through the wedding,
and screamed all through the bedding that followed it, and not only

because Palti's hard body pounded on my broken rib. I didn't need to be put in physical agony to know I was being raped. Palti was drunk from the wedding feast and he apologized, after. He said he had consummated the marriage because the king ordered it done; he said he would not come to me again without my consent. I said I could never consent to be an adulteress, for so I thought myself.

"But in time, as you know, I changed toward him. We went off to live in his house in the hills, and he was kind and patient toward me, and saw to my comfort and kept his word. It was a peaceful house, such as I had never known. And when Yonatan finally came to see me, he was full of terrible news. You know what David did; I don't need to recite it to you. The lies, the betrayals . . ."

I knew that she was no longer talking only of personal matters. David's behavior when he left Shaul's court had been desperate and reprehensible. He committed theft, sacrilege and, maybe, even treachery. His actions and his lies brought death and terror upon innocent people.

"I didn't know what had happened till Yonatan finally saw fit to tell me," she said. "All I knew was that David had left me in the hands of my father when I was injured and defenseless. I knew he fled with no food and no weapon. To provision himself, Yonatan told me, David stopped at the shrine of Nov, which stood about halfway between our home and his family *beit av* in Beit Lehem. His great trophy, the sword of the giant of Gath, was kept at the shrine, wrapped in an oilcloth, concealed behind the ephod. He knew that, of course. That's probably why he risked stopping there. The priest greeted him, somewhat surprised to see Shaul's top captain traveling alone and unarmed. David lied, and told the priest that he was on a secret mission for the king, and that his troops were encamped nearby. He said they lacked supplies, and asked for the shrine's consecrated bread with which to feed his men. He took the sword of course. And you know what came of it . . ."

It was a heinous business. Shaul, in his madness, believed the priests of the shrine had betrayed him by feeding and arming David.

He would not accept the true account—that they had no knowledge that David was an outlaw; that they had no reason to doubt that he was serving the king as his son-in-law and most trusted servant. Shaul sentenced them all to die. But no soldier of the Land would carry out these sacrilegious murders. It fell to an Edomite, who followed other gods, to kill all of them. The refusal of his men to do his bidding further fueled Shaul's rage, and he ordered the whole town of Nov sacked. He put his soldiers in such fear for their own lives that this time, alas, the men obeyed him. They killed everyone in that town— women, babes, the frail elderly.

She had fallen silent, gazing blankly.

"Do you need wine?" I asked her. "You are very pale."

"Am I? So was Yonatan, that day, when he finally girded himself to come and face me in my misery. I was half mad with not knowing, full of hurt and anger that my brother—my protector—hadn't been with me, hadn't saved me. And then, when he came, at last, he was civil to Palti, but he could barely look at me. I could read the disgust in his eyes. I could see he was fighting himself to be just to me, not to blame me for the fact that I'd been whored, that I was dishonored."

"Surely not," I blurted. I thought of Yonatan as I had briefly known him; a man so loyal that he risked his life to bring David the intelligence that would ensure his safety. Such a man could not at the same time be disloyal to a beloved sister who had been wronged and was innocent.

She gave a grim laugh. "Even you, Natan, must know what men are, when it comes to matters of sex and honor. I was his sister, and what fouled my honor fouled his. So my father's sick revenge worked its poison, even between Yonatan and me.

"As distraught as I was at his coldness, I could tell from his face that dreadful things had happened. Finally, I demanded that he tell me what he knew. He unfolded the whole of it—the massacre at Nov, the flight to Gath, everything. And even as he spoke, I could see him struggling to cast it all in his own mind as necessary and forgivable, one more tragedy of our father's madness. Oh, yes. He laid it all there, on our father's wretched malady. I suppose he had to fashion it thus, so as to be able to forgive David, whose rash and selfish acts caused such mayhem. I suppose it was just one more offering to the great love they bore each other: that even such grave sins and acts of treachery could be forgiven. Of course, he told me that David greatly lamented the deaths, and took full blame. As if that were enough to absolve the butchery of holy men and their families, the ruined homes and the burned fields. Forgiveness aplenty, yet none for me. None for his sister, who was nothing but a victim.

"But I, who had been less loved, was less able to be forgiving. And of course he brought news of another betrayal. A more intimate one. I'm speaking of the marriage to Ahinoam. I'd been broken enough, but this news flayed me. Yonatan tried to explain it away, to give me a way to bear it. David cared nothing for this girl, he claimed. She was little more than a pretty simpleton, a healthy peasant girl who would go uncomplaining with him into the wilderness, tolerate hardship and make no demands upon him. It was simply necessary for him to get an heir. It was any man's duty to do this; much more so a man destined to be king. Furthermore, he could not wait until he was reunited with me, for no one could say when that might be. He had to get an heir while he was young enough to protect and raise the child. David's life was full of perils; I must not blame him for wanting to make a son. My own future son would of course take precedence over any child of this nobody Ahinoam, should she be brought to bed of a boy. Indeed, Yonatan assured me, David longed for me, for our reunion, for the chance for us to have our own son. So he spoke, and so I tried to believe, as I lay in my cold bed, while Palti knocked fruitlessly upon the door and I sent him, unsatisfied, away.

"And then, as you know well, David married Avigail of Carmel, the widow of Navaal. Palti made sure I heard of it. When finally I got a chance to confront Yonatan, he confessed the truth of it, and was honest enough to confirm what Palti had told me, that this time it was

a match of affection and mutual regard. I think my brother saw, by
then, that I was wasting away in Palti's house, pining for a future that
might never be, estranging myself from the one man who could give
me happiness in the present. So, in stages, my faith wavered. I began
to believe that David had not loved me at all. I began to look at Palti
for the man he was: a good man, kind and just. And as I looked at
him, I would see him looking at me hungrily, as if he really desired
me. Me. I had not been desired in that way before. In the end, I gave
way to it, and I fell in love with him. And then you all fled to Ziklag,
to the enemy king, or so we thought. Yonatan could no longer bring
me any news or word from David. I began to will myself to forget
him. There were days, weeks, when I did not think of him at all. And
when my children came, finally he became just a bitter memory, without, as I thought—wrongly, of course—any power to wound me at
all. Then when the news came from Har HaGilboa—"

She stopped. I glanced up from my writing. Her eyes brimmed and
her chin quivered. I looked at her, and what I saw was David's face,
grief-blasted, the day that same news came to us, in our Ziklag exile,
that the battle on the mountain of Gilboa had been lost. That Shaul
and Yonatan were among the many dead.

"No more," I said, putting down my reed. "No need."

She gave a ragged sigh. The tears were spilling down her face now.
She reached out a hand and laid it on my arm. "Thank you. You . . .
you are kind. I'm not used to it."

I blew on the parchments to dry the ink, then I rose. I bowed to
her and turned, reaching for the door latch.

"Natan—will you tell the king I did as he commanded?"

"I will," I said. "I will tell him you fulfilled his request in full
measure." As I stepped through the door, she spoke again.

"Natan?"

"Yes?"

"Will you—" Her voice broke. She took a breath, composing herself. "Will you remember me to him?"

I left her in that dismal little cell, and crept away. I had gone there expecting a difficult interrogation with a woman animated by hatred. I had prepared myself to deal with a refractory silence or to withstand an outpouring of bile. I had not expected to be overwhelmed with pity.

All women's lives are like that, I told myself, as I climbed the stair that led to the better-appointed rooms of the king's house. Which of them ever is mistress of her own destiny? Highborn or peasant, it makes no difference. At least David hadn't had her flogged or killed, as another king might have done.

But now that I had heard the tale of her life in her own words, my heart ached for her. I didn't need to make her relive the events that led to the rift with David. I knew all about it. I was there.

IX

I sat in the buttery light of the late evening, lingering over my wine. Outside, finches and larks tousled the trees, singing their frantic hymn to the waning day. Craving solitude, I sent Muwat out, offering him an evening of liberty. He went reluctantly, his young face anxious. I imagine I looked rather ill, if my outer self gave a true reflection of my low spirits. I poured more wine, letting the light find fire in the liquid as it streamed from the jar into the cup. It was good wine, from the king's own store. My father would have valued the skill of the winemaker. I thought of our vineyards, the green vines scribbling across the steep russet hills that sprang up from the flat white shore. I could recall every crevice and cave, every rough tree trunk, every dusty leaf, the sudden pulses of fresh springwater through tumbles of stone. I felt a stab of longing for the apricot-colored earth of those vineyards, for my father, rubbing it in his coarse hands, tasting it, assessing as it crumbled, not too sticky nor too fine, but just the correct tilth to support the roots and sustain the vines. All that skill, lost with the plunge of metal. His blood, soaking into the soil. Even in death, nourishing that earth he had loved and tended. Had his death really been necessary, as David had asserted, and I, a child, had so readily accepted? I pushed the thought away. Doubt was like rot. Excise it at the first speckling, the first stain, the first faint stench of decay. But then—I suppose because my mind was on the wine—I thought of that other kind of rot, the soft gray fungus that sometimes afflicts the late grape harvest if the air turns unexpectedly moist. That rot causes the grapes to yield up a heavy, viscous juice of stupendously rich flavor. The wine pressed from such grapes was the best of all. Maybe doubt was like that sometimes. Maybe it, too, could yield rich fruit. Perhaps, then, it was right to doubt. Perhaps I had a right to doubt.

But this line of thinking could bring me no ease. I did not want to collapse again, as I had that day, killing for Achish in the Amalekite village when thoughts of my father had overcome me. I had learned to live my life in the grip of an iron-fisted discipline. For a man like me, self-mastery was everything. I exercised that discipline, swilled the fine wine, and willed my thoughts elsewhere, to a part of the Land I had never seen.

Har HaGilboa, that spinelike ridge that looms over the Wadi Yez-reel. They say it is lovely there at this time of year, the wild iris all abloom, the thorn breaks full of the music of migrating birds, the cold white tip of Har Hermon visible in the distant north. We never got that far, of course. We marched out of Ziklag and joined with the forces of Achish, the army of Gath. Our men were in mixed spirits. Some, who had been ill treated by Shaul, carried a yearning for vengeance and were spoiling for this fight—a clean fight of army against army instead of the mean skirmishing that others as well as I found dishonorable. But for some of our men, the idea of joining forces against our people was gut-wrenching. Their enmity was toward Shaul himself, not toward our people as a whole, and only their loyalty to David drove them forward.

So, we marched under Achish's banners all the way from Gath north up to Shunem, which was the staging area for the Plishtim armies. It was dark when we arrived, but even so, it was clear that the forces mustering comprised a mighty host. We made a hasty camp, and David called me into his tent. Yoav and Avishai were already there. David had drawn a map of the dispositions, as he had understood them, in the dust at his feet. "It's clear what Shaul means to do," he said, tapping the point of his spear on the lines that represented the position of Shaul's forces across the wadi on Gilboa. "He means to attack head-on. He thinks having the high ground gives him an advantage. But he's underestimated the Plishtim forces. The only chance, against these numbers, is to let them overrun the Wadi Yezreel. Let them think they've won. Then surround them by night and sweep in from the rear, here"—he prodded the dirt—"and the flanks, here"—he swept the spear point in a wide arc. "What's wrong with him? He must have sent out spies to assess the forces, and if so he must know a frontal assault is madness."

"Well, you said it," Yoav rumbled. "As if we needed more proof of madness."

What I noticed was that David had used "them" to refer to the army of which we were purportedly members. It seemed a strange thing to me at the time. Between that, the hard ground and the normal wakefulness on the march to battle, I got little sleep that night.

I rose at first light, and made my way through the stirring camp. All the *serens* from the coastal cities had answered the call to arms, their diverse banners snapping in the stiff breeze. I walked up the rise to survey the totality of the encampment. I had never seen such an army.

By the time I returned to our tents, David was in conference with Achish and several other Plishtim leaders—*serens*, by their elaborate armor and the circlets on their helmets. Even from far off, I could see that the debate was heated. As I moved forward to hear better, one raised his voice and extended an accusing arm at David. "This man is our enemy. I will not go into battle with him, or with his men. They'll cut us down and betray us."

Achish answered in a low, steady voice, and from where I stood, I could not make out his words. Whatever he said, it must have been unconvincing. One of the *serens* pulled off his helmet and threw it at Achish's feet, cursing in his own tongue. I saw Achish turn to David, laying his hands on both his shoulders. After a few moments, David bowed, turned to each of the *serens* and saluted them, then turned away, calling out for Yoav.

Even to this day, I have no sure idea how David would have acted had we been allowed to march on. I believe he had some stratagem, some intrigue, that would have kept us from shedding the blood of our own. Part of me believes that the Plishtim *serens* saw correctly; that David had marched out intending to betray Achish—to sweep in behind the Plishtim, closing a lethal circle and mowing them down until, at last, he came face-to-face with Shaul, having proved his loyalty by delivering him victory. It's the kind of grand moment he would have fashioned for himself in the long days of exile. The kind of bold move he, perhaps alone, could have imagined and then made real. But I think that vision faltered when he saw the disposition of Shaul's forces, and the magnitude of the army massed against them. In any case, there was no such moment. No battlefield reconciliation. No victory.

As I have already set down, we were not there to witness the rout. As our people fell and bled on that battlefield, we were back in Ziklag, the women still bearing the red marks of rope burn on their necks and wrists, the deeper scars of terror in their eyes.

We worked together, cleaning up the debris of the burned fort, David pitching in, hands blackened like the rest of us, the rift with his men healed over, if not forgotten. The work went swiftly, I think because we all craved the distraction of hard physical tasks while we waited for scraps of news from the front. A day after our return, a messenger brought news that battle had been joined. After that, nothing, for two days. Then on the third day, a ragged fellow, a foreigner, staggered up to the gates of Ziklag claiming to have important news, hoping for reward. David was in counsel with Yoav and some others of his close advisers. The room bore the scent of curing plaster laid in over the smoke-damaged walls. I was there, sitting quietly to the side as had become my way during those days of exile when the voice did not speak and my vision of our future was misted by doubt.

"Bring him!" David said, his face alight. "If he seeks a reward, the news must be good." The man came in, giving off the ripe, familiar

stink of a battle-weary fighter—the unmistakable odor of days-old
fear-sweat dried into the fibers of his tunic, which was torn and
stained brown with blood. As soon as he identified which of us was
David, he threw himself upon the floor in prostration.

"Where are you coming from?" David asked.

"I have just escaped from the camp of Israel," he said, though his
accent was foreign.

"Get up," David commanded. "Someone, bring him a stool. Some
water."

The man sat, heavily, and drained the cup. When he was done,
David asked him to account for himself. He glanced up, warily. He
was, he said, an Amalekite mercenary. He flinched as he said it. Considering how things stood between the men of Yudah and the
Amalekites—our sworn enemy—I thought him either very brave or
very foolish to admit to it. And then he said he had been captured by
Yonatan's men early in the fighting.

"Yonatan?" David stood up abruptly, his face greedy for news. "So
they held you where? In Shaul's camp? What happened? Tell me!"

The exhausted fellow, unnerved by David's sudden urgency, stammered out an account of a battle gone hopelessly wrong, the Israelite
forces outmanned and overrun, the massive casualties and finally the
rout, as the survivors fled for their lives, leaving Shaul, Yonatan and
his brothers holding the ridge with only a handful of loyal men standing ground beside them.

A certain drawing back of the shoulders. The slightest tilt of the
head. I knew David well by then. I knew how to read his body. I saw
him adjust his stance as if to receive a great blow. The mercenary took
a ragged breath, and stated what I—and, I think, David—already
knew to be true. Shaul was dead, and Yonatan beside him.

David's shoulders sagged, his belly contracted. A sigh, no more
than that, escaped him. Then he took a step forward, bent down and
lifted the Amalekite up by the tunic, his voice a flat, hard whisper.
"How do you know this?"

The man glanced up into his face, and then quickly looked away, as if to avoid what he had seen there. His words came in a breathy rush.

"When the battle became a rout, our guards fled, and all the prisoners scattered. We were running for our lives, as you, lord, surely would understand. By chance I came over the ridge, and ran right into Shaul's own unit, and realized that he had made his stand there, on that very spot. You could see the signs that fighting had raged all around him. There were many dead. At his feet I saw one I knew—the body of his son Yonatan, gashed by many wounds."

The muscles beneath David's eyes worked. His words were a rasp. "You are sure of it? You knew him, you say?"

"My lord, I did. His unit was the one that captured us, and we were paraded before him. And there he was, not ten spans distant from where I stood."

David's voice was even lower now. He pulled the man closer. "You are sure he was dead? His wounds—they were mortal?"

"My lord, no man could have withstood them. He was laid open like a gutted buck."

David's eyes closed. The muscles of his throat worked. His hand clenched even more tightly on the Amalekite's stained tunic. The man went on, his words tumbling forth.

"The king alone was alive, save for a youth—a boy, merely—I think it was his armor bearer." David winced. He had been that boy, once. "The two of them, man and boy, were covered in blood. The king was leaning heavily upon his spear to keep himself upright. The enemy's archers had made a target of him. Their arrows had pierced his gut. You could see it cost him merely to stand. He was looking out to the plain, where the Plishtim merkavot were advancing. They were close; you could hear the grind of their wheels. And through the dust, you could make out the glint of their spears. They were almost to the foot of the ridge. In minutes they would dismount and swarm the mountain. I saw the king turn to the boy. His face—my lord—you could read the pain there. He knew well enough what the Plishtim would do with him—to him—if they got to him while he yet drew a breath. He could barely speak, but he managed to mouth an instruction. "Draw sword," he told the boy. "Run me through." But the boy couldn't do it. He fell to his knees, weeping, shaking his head, crying out that he could not raise a hand to the king he loved. Shaul lunged for his own sword. He braced the hilt against a rock, and fell forward onto it. He didn't even cry out. As he lay there, the sword right through him, I thought he was dead. But then he rolled onto his side and raised his hand, as if gesturing to the boy. The boy didn't see it, in his grief. He was on his face, tearing at his hair and weeping. So I crept forward, to help him, if I could. As I bent over him, his eyes fluttered. He looked right at me. My lord, he could barely lift a finger, but he gestured me to come even closer. I knelt down there in the dirt beside him—this is his blood, you see it, here on my tunic. He tried to speak. Blood bubbled up through his lips. I had to put my ear to his mouth to make out what he said. He asked who I was. I told him I was his Amalekite prisoner. 'Then finish me off. I'm in agony.' So I took the short dagger from his dead son's belt and cut his throat with it. He was barely alive when I did it. Then I took the circlet from his helmet and the amulet from his arm, and ran for my life. I have brought them here to you, my lord."

He made to reach into a small cloth sack that he wore cinched about his shoulders. I saw a glint of gold before David swatted his hand away. There was a clatter as the circlet fell back upon the amulet inside the bag.

David dropped his right hand from the Amalekite's tunic as if he had just noticed how foul it was. He pushed him away so hard that the man staggered. David's eyes were voids. I had seen it before. I knew what it meant.

"How dare you?" He spoke slowly, his voice low. "How dare you lift your hand and kill the Name's anointed? No one may take it upon himself to kill a king."

The Amalekite's voice became high and shrill. "My lord, I knew he would never rise from where he was lying. He was as good as dead. . . . He, he begged me. The Plishtim would have done terrible . . . I was not . . ."

I saw David's hand clench at his waist, where his sword would have rested had he been wearing one. He turned to Yoav, who was armed. "Strike him down." Yoav hesitated for only a second, his brow raised in interrogation. David answered with a curt nod. Yoav drew his sword and, with a step like a dancer's, ran at the man. With his right hand, he plunged the blade into the Amalekite's chest, and with his left he pounded the hilt, driving it home.

David reached for the neck of his own robe and ripped it, lifting his head and crying out such a lament as I have never heard before, and hope never to hear again. We all of us in that room rent our clothes and wept with him.

I know that David wept for Yonatan, whom he loved. I believe he also wept for the memory of Shaul as he had once been, and for the reconciliation that he might still have hoped for. Some in that room, I know, hated Shaul and envied Yonatan his special place with David. Yet they also wept. I suppose they mourned for our people and our ignominious defeat.

I wept for David. And I will own to it, I wept for the Amalekite. I can close my eyes and watch his blood, glossy and crimson, pooling on the gray of the flagstones, forming bright little runnels that fingered out along the joints in the stones. I believed his account, that he had dispatched a suffering man and saved him from torture at the hands of the Plishtim. I suppose he thought David would welcome the news of the death of his greatest persecutor. He expected a reward. Poor soul, he would have done better to make off with the crown and armband—worth more than he'd earn in a lifetime. One of the door guards picked up the pitiful corpse by the ankles and dragged it out of the room. I stared glassily at the snail trail of blood across the flags.

But even as I wept, I began to feel the world shift. These tears were cleansing. The murk in my mind lightened and lifted, a relief, as if the wind had freshened, blowing away a noxious smoke that had stung my eyes and fouled my nostrils. I could see, again, the road ahead of us. Our exile—the seasons of wanton murders and low deceits—was over. We would go up from this wretched, humid plain to the hills, into the crisp air and the clean sunlight. We would return to the Land, to our own people. We would go home.

But first, before any such plans were made or even spoken of, we mourned and fasted for the dead. David asked me to stay by him, and so I did. I sat in his chamber throughout the day, keeping a silent vigil, as he worked the harp strings, composing. In the evening, we rejoined the others in the hall where he sang, for the first time, "The Song of the Bow," which I shall set down here as I first heard it, even though every child now can give some version.

> *Your glory, Israel,*
> *Lies slain on your heights.*
> *How have the mighty fallen!*
> *Tell it not in Gath,*
> *Proclaim it not in the streets of Ashkelon,*
> *Lest the daughters of the Plishtim rejoice,*
> *Lest the daughters of the heathen exult.*
> *O hills of Gilboa—*
> *Let there be no dew or rain on you,*
> *Or springs or freshets,*
> *For there the shield of warriors lies rusting,*
> *The shield of Shaul,*
> *Polished with oil no more. . . .*
> *Daughters of Israel*
> *Weep over Shaul,*
> *Who clothed you in scarlet and silk,*
> *Who bejeweled you with gold.*
> *How have the mighty fallen*
> *In the thick of battle—*

Yonatan, slain on your heights!
I grieve for you,
My brother Yonatan,
You were most dear to me.
Your love was wonderful to me
More than the love of women.
How have the mighty fallen,
The weapons of war perished.

I have written here of his harp playing. I have not described his singing voice. It is hard to describe a sound without likening it to another
sound, and yet the timbre of David's voice was a thing apart. It had
the urgency of the shofar, and yet was not shrill. It could engender
awe, as a high wind howling dangerously through mighty branches, or
bring delight, as an unexpected trill of sweet birdsong. It could satisfy,
as the sound of running water rinses and slakes a thirsty spirit, or it
could bring unease, like a wild beast howling in distant hills. To describe the sound, I find myself turning to other senses—sight and
touch. The fall of fine silk through the hand; the rich warmth of
enveloping fur. Or a goldsmith beating out a foil, at the moment when
he lifts and turns the leaf; the sudden gleam, as if sunlight itself had
been captured. David's voice was that bright flare of shimmering gold.
It could transmit light and warmth. But not that only. Sometimes, the
voice could summon such a power that it recalled not sunlight but
lightning—something so fierce and magnificent that when it passed
through you, it left you stricken and hollowed.

That night, as he sang, his grief still raw, his voice did all these
things. None of us who heard it could be the same man, after. My
breath was still uneven when, after he set down his harp, he signaled
me to come and sit by him. He did not speak for some time, but I
could sense his mind, unrestful. I waited, silent, until he turned to me
at last. He spoke softly, so that others in the room could not hear
what was said. " *'Red runs the blade in the hand of Shaul. The blood is royal.'*

Those were your words, in the camp at Horesh. Shaul's own blood upon his blade, you meant. Still you tell me you did not know that he would end his life thus?"

"I knew he would perish in battle. That is all. I did not know it would happen as it did."

"And what about the rest? What did you mean about Yonatan, Yavesh, the tamarisk tree?"

I shook my head and stared at the floor. "I have no . . ."

I was about to say "I have no idea" but a great noise of cawing birds drowned out my words. There was a gust of foulness, a stench of rot. I raised my hands to fend them off. I was on my feet, shouting. I could see the others in the room, rising to their feet also.

Bodies, headless, black with buzzards, impaled to the wall. The birds' wings flapped as they fought one another to get at the meat. Each beat carried the stink to my nostrils. I ducked and waved my hands about my head as one swooped low, a strip of flesh dangling from its beak. At the base of the wall, foreign faces, twisted, laughing. Hurling stones at the poor broken torsos.

Fetch them down, oh men of Yavesh! I was crying out, running from one stranger to another, frantic. *Save your king from this dishonor!* Then the noisome vision cleared, and I was back in a room in Ziklag, face-to-face with David, his tunic grasped in my fist. I uncurled my hand and let it fall to my side. Yoav and the others had backed away. They stood against the far wall, fear in their faces. But David's face was calm, waiting. He reached out a hand. His thumb wiped the cold beads of sweat from my brow. Then he laid both hands upon my shoulders. "What must I do, Natan?"

Through the pounding in my head, I could not hear the words I shouted: *Go up to Hevron, King! Shaul is buried. The men of Yudah wait to anoint you.*

X

It was a lovely tree, old and wind sculpted. Its generous canopy had been pushed eastward by the hard, hot gusts from the western desert, so that its trunk curved out over the newly turned soil and extended its largest branches like a pair of sheltering arms. The fine sprays of foliage slid about in the afternoon breeze, amplifying each breath of air.

The four graves were small. They'd burned the noisome remains to clean ash before interment on this hilltop. For a long time, David stood gazing at the mounds of yellow earth and white stone. Finally, he sank down, resting his back against the tamarisk's rough trunk. We had made the long journey north and west because David said he wanted to see for himself the burial place that I had described in my vision. At first, I wondered if he doubted me. I was not unduly troubled. For I knew that we would find the place, just as I had seen it.

As the sun dipped into the western ridge, the oval pool of shade stretched and lengthened. I studied his face, gaunt from fasting, yet lit from within by some deep source of energy. He had one of the small harps—he had carried it up the hill himself, slung across his back. In the last golden light of that day, he set it between his knees and sang "The Song of the Bow." When he got to the verse of Yonatan, tears spilled down his cheeks. Yet his voice did not waver, and he held the last sweet note long and pure. Then he stood, and we walked back down through the gathering dusk to the town of Yavesh.

The men there had long memories. They remembered that Shaul fought his first great battle as king for them. Before madness, before Shmuel's rejection, at the dawn of his power, he saved their town from the tyrant who threatened to sack it and gouge out the right eye of each of its defenders. The men of Yavesh did not forget this. When they learned that the Plishtim had severed Shaul's head, and that of his sons—Yonatan and two of his younger brothers—and impaled the desecrated torsos on the walls of Beit She'an, they resolved to repay their debt. They went by night and reclaimed the rotting corpses and buried the cremated remains with honor under the tamarisk upon the hillside.

David entered Yavesh with a train of spoil from the Ziklag years. He bestowed it on the men of the town who had led the raid. "One day," he said to me, "when I can, I will bring the remains home to Shaul's own lands, and give them a royal burial." Then we went back south, crossed the Yarden River and traveled east to Hevron. The town opened its gates to David as to a long-expected, much-beloved son. They crowned him king of Yudah as soon as the mourning rites were completed. It was done with little ceremony, because we all of us knew there was little, as yet, to celebrate. We were ravaged by the losses at Gilboa, and as disunited as ever.

They gave us the best house in the city, and there we waited to learn how Avner would answer David's crowning. During those weeks, David's first son was born. On the eighth day, David held him in his arms as our priest, Aviathar, marked him with the sign of our covenant. The look on David's face as he held that tiny infant was something I had never witnessed before. His expression conveyed a range of emotions that I hadn't realized one man could feel all in the same instant. There was the wide-eyed avidity that I'd seen in the heat of battle, but coupled now with tenderness. There was, also, the transfiguring awe and wonder that I had glimpsed in his face when he prayed. His long, shapely hands cradled and caressed that child as if it were valuable as solid gold, yet fragile as a moth wing. As he held up the boy before the crowd, he was laughing and crying at the same time. I looked at the red, wrinkled, squalling infant, and tried to see what David saw, to feel what he felt. But it was no use. Those emotions were opaque to me. This, I thought, is what real love must be, and I will never feel it.

Being a father, having an heir, seemed to add an extra dimension to David. He had always been a vivid, animating presence in any room he entered. But now he would come from visiting the boy, whom he had named Amnon, crackling with even greater energy and force. He had been an engaged listener, ready to learn what any man might have to offer in discussion, but now there was an additional depth to his questions, a more far-reaching vision behind his decisions. He thought now beyond the span of years, and into a future that glittered ahead into centuries. It's one thing, I suppose, to have a prophet tell you that you will found a dynasty. Now, it seemed, he allowed himself to truly believe it.

The timing for this happy transformation was ripe, as the hard matter of Avner stood before us. Shaul's general had seen to his own survival on Har HaGilboa. No one seemed to know quite how he had escaped uninjured, or why he had not been at the side of his king at the battle's deadly climax. They did not whisper "treason"—perhaps they dared not. But by some craft or stratagem, that sinewy old trouper had saved his own skin and lived to gather the frayed threads of Shaul's defeated army into his own hands.

Avner had lived too long and become too canny to claim the crown of Israel for himself. Instead, he propped Shaul's last living son upon the throne, making clear enough that this was a gesture only. The Plishtim had killed all of Shaul's sons save this one, Ish Boshet. He had not been at the battle, because he was no warrior. From birth, Ish Boshet had seemed like a foundling among that family of tall, handsome boys and girls. He was slow-witted from some mishap in the birthing tent, or so the women said. He hovered at the edges of the family, never regarded with anything more than pity. When word came to us that Avner had taken Shaul's favorite concubine to bed, David was in counsel with Yoav. The two of them were incensed. "He might as well have set the crown upon his own head," David said, pounding his fist upon the arm of his chair. "That woman is Ish Boshet's, by law. Avner is brash, to throw down such an insult as that. Even Ish Boshet might have been moved to answer it."

"Ish Boshet?" Yoav said dismissively. "What has Ish Boshet? A name, and you can't wield a name. You think he would confront Avner? Avner would crush him if he moved a finger. Avner has the remnant army in his hand. And Avner does nothing lightly. He has done this to show that Ish Boshet is no more than his glorified hostage."

"Well, if Ish Boshet won't answer the insult, I will," David said. "I won't have the king's house belittled in this way." Yoav looked gratified. He had reason to wish ill to Avner, and any sign of David's disfavor in that direction brought him satisfaction.

We were braced for war, and war came. Not all-out war, as one people might wage who seek to expunge another. This was tribal in-fighting: a probing, to see where the power lay. I think Avner knew already that David would prevail. He knew David, and his gifts, better than anybody. He had relied upon him in war. He had pursued him fruitlessly as an outlaw. If he couldn't put an end to David when he was on the run and poorly armed, he could hardly expect to do so now, with all the men of Yudah rallied to his banner. I believed that Avner meant to position himself the better to negotiate terms from a place of strength. He was not willing to give up the dominance he enjoyed as Shaul's right hand. For David's part, he had no great personal enmity toward Avner, the man who led him from obscurity to greatness on the day he held Goliath's bleeding head in his fist. He knew that Avner's pursuit throughout the exile years was Shaul's doing. So the battles we fought were enacted in set-piece engagements. Our young warriors went off to these skirmishes high hearted, as if to contests rather than to mortal combat.

It might have been resolved with far less loss of life were it not for

Yoav. He and I had never been close. He was an earthy, practical man who distrusted what he could not touch or smell. He mistrusted my visions and deplored the fact that David set such store in them. Also, I believe, he was jealous of our intimacy, feeling perhaps that I usurped the intimacy that should have been his, as David's nephew and blood kin. For my part, I remembered the cold-eyed youth who had thrown me against the wall in the corridor of my father's house, and who had raised his spear at me the next day, ready to run me through. Yet I knew he loved David with a fighting man's intense, to-the-death affection and loyalty. And I believe he credited me with similar feelings. Moreover, he had seen the use in my predictions, and even though he set no store in uncanny things, he was soldier enough to value whatever weapon came to hand. So though there was no warmth between us, we dealt civilly enough with each other.

But I don't think he would have come to me in the matter of Avner were it not for his younger brother Avishai. Avishai was a hotheaded warrior to whom violence came as naturally as breath, but even so, we had forged an unlikely friendship. He had been my weapons instructor when I first joined David's band, and we were close in age. Avishai believed that my foresight had saved David the night we surprised Shaul in his encampment. It was Avishai who urged Yoav to come to me for counsel, hoping that he might enlist me to put his case to David.

But it came hard to Yoav to solicit my help. I was in my chamber, after meat, when Muwat, rather wide-eyed, said Yoav was at the door, seeking a word with me. Of course, I bade him enter, and set my servant to pour the wine. I invited Yoav to sit, but he paced instead between the window and the door as he gulped his wine in two long swallows. I nodded at the boy to pour more, then I inclined my head, indicating that he should leave us. Perhaps, I thought, Yoav would more readily speak his mind if the two of us were alone.

He was looking out the window when he finally spoke. The words poured out in a rush, without preamble. "My brother trusts you. He told me to seek your counsel. Once the two kingdoms of Yudah and

Israel reconcile and are united, there can be but one general in chief. Avner's claim is strong. He's led a great army, not merely a band of outlaws, and in war, not just raiding parties. He's got all Israel in his hand. If he delivers it, if he's the one to broker peace, David will be deep in his debt." He turned then, and stared at me, his brow compressed. "Will the king choose him over me?"

I spread my hands. "We have not spoken of it."

"But what do you think? What do you . . . see?"

"If you mean have I *fore*seen anything to the purpose, no, I have not. What I see, as an ordinary court observer, is that you are the king's nephew, and his trusted general. Furthermore, there is no one David relies on more, in military matters, than you and your brothers. And you're the only blood kin he cares for. He has told me that when he was a child, your mother was the only one of his siblings who showed him any affection or regard. Avishai is skilled at arms and fearless and Asahel is the swiftest runner in the army. David relies on all of you."

"But is it enough? Will it serve?" He was pacing again. "Avner has all Israel behind his banner."

"So he wishes us to think. But Avner is old," I said. "That is the obverse side to all his experience. He is old enough to be your father."

"He doesn't act so. He doesn't fight so."

"Really? Then why was he not at his king's side on Har HaGilboa?" I thought of Avner as I had seen him in the predawn gloom, asleep at his post as Avishai urged David to let him kill Shaul.

"You think his loyalty to Shaul was in doubt?" Yoav's brow unknotted, his eyebrows raised. He had not thought of this. Now I could see him savoring the idea. "Does David see it so?"

I lifted my shoulders and spread my hands. "I do not know. I do not counsel him in military matters." I allowed myself a wry smile. "Based on my fighting skills, I am hardly in a position to do so." Yoav returned my grin, picked up the wine jug and refilled his cup. "But I *will* counsel you, since you have asked," I said. "Go to David. Put this matter to him directly. Better, surely, to know his thoughts than to live with this festering unease."

"Perhaps," he said, running a finger around the rim of his cup. "Perhaps you're right."

But in the end, he did not do so. Instead, he continued to thresh the matter privately with his brothers Avishai and Asahel. To say these three were close does not do the matter justice. They had shared more than a womb. They were knit together by the rind of scar tissue that comes after long, bloody service. If battle makes men brothers, then these three were twice bound, each ingrained with the habit of vigilantly watching the backs of the others. And that, I believe, led to the events at the battle of the Pool of Givon.

It should have been another in the series of set-piece contests of arms in that season of feints between the men of Israel and the men of Yudah. As with all such encounters, the rules of engagement were agreed in advance. The youths went out to meet one another in even numbers. This time, there were to be just a dozen youths as combatants on each side. Any supporters who came with them—officers, armorers—understood that they were not to engage in the fight. Injuries were the common outcome of these things; one fought one's opponent to land a telling blow; one did not seek his death.

They began to fight with short swords, and then a cry went up: a youth had fallen dead. Someone called out that the youth had yielded, and that his opponent should have spared him. I do not know even today the truth of the matter, so lost was the spark in the conflagration that ensued. Both sides ignited, and the blood lust rose in all the young men, until they were laying into one another brutally and falling from lethal blows.

In the mayhem, I suppose Asahel saw his chance to do his brother service. That, or some crazed, incontinent rage seized him, and he set off to attack Avner. Avner had come to the pool to watch and direct his men, not to fight. He was both unarmed and unarmored. When he divined that a young warrior had singled him out and was bearing down upon him, he grabbed a spear from the hand of the nearest man, and ran. Asahel rounded the pool, easily closing the distance between them. Avner had an old leg injury that had knit awry, which made his gait ungainly. He knew that the youth would soon overtake him. He called out over his shoulder, saying he had no wish to fight. But Asahel kept coming, closing in. So Avner, with the wiles of a veteran, turned the younger man's own gift of speed against him. As Asahel, at a full sprint, closed the last few steps between them, Avner suddenly stopped dead. He braced the point of his spear hard into the ground before him, positioned at a low angle, and let Asahel's own momentum propel him into the hind end of the shaft. Asahel, unable to check his onrushing momentum, ran himself right through. He was stuck like a boar. Still, he reached out for Avner and kept coming on a last few steps. Avner took a step back, out of his reach. Asahel stood there for a long moment, before his knees buckled and he dropped.

Avner stared down at the body, truly distressed. "Must the sword devour us forever?" He raised his voice in a plaintive cry. "Yoav! Your brother lies fallen. End this. Now!"

Yoav, stricken, raised his horn and winded it. The men ceased their skirmishing and put up their weapons. They gathered around Yoav, silent, as he withdrew the spear and signed for Asahel's closest friends to lift the body. They marched all night. In the morning, they buried Asahel in their father's tomb in Beit Lehem.

That futile and unwanted death did more than end a battle. It marked the shift toward forging the peace. Avner sent a messenger to David: "To whom shall the land belong? Make a pact with me and I will bring all Israel over to your side." I was there when David received the message. I expected him to reach out and grasp the proffered crown. Instead, he made no reply at all. He lifted his chin and gazed across the crowded audience hall. As the silence stretched, there was a rustling, a clearing of throats. Men shifted their weight from foot to foot, uneasy. I noticed a bead of sweat developing on the messenger's brow. It was he, finally, who broke the silence. "My lord king," he said. "What reply would you have me bring to General Avner?"

David blinked and tossed his head, as if recalled from distant thoughts. He looked at the messenger as if trying to remember what errand might have brought the man before him. Then he spoke, in a clear, calm voice, the slightest hint of a smile playing at the corners of his mouth. "Give Avner these words: I will make a pact with you. But do not come before me unless you bring Mikhal, daughter of Shaul. Give me back my wife Mikhal."

I was stunned, as were many of those closest to him. None of us had heard a word from him of that old matter. Later, he called me to attend him in his rooms. "What did you think of my condition?" he asked.

"You have not spoken of her these past years. I did not know you thought of her. I was surprised. But I see it is a brilliant piece of statecraft."

"Statecraft?" He looked down into his wine cup. "How so?"

"You ascend the throne of Israel with Shaul's daughter at your side, you quiet the voices of Shaul's loyalists, and unite the northern and southern tribes at last."

"Yes, that is what Avigail said. It was her suggestion that I do this."

That woman's capacity for canny reckoning was a rare gift. It spoke to either a great selflessness or a great degree of security in her position. It had become apparent in recent weeks that Avigail was pregnant with the child that would be David's second born. For a woman, that is no small matter. But when Mikhal bore David a son, such a descendant would be twice royal, with a lineage that would outweigh birth order when it came time to consider the matter of succession.

I spoke the thought aloud: "Mikhal brings Shaul's blood to bind the dynasties."

He looked up sharply. "Shaul's blood?" An expression of distaste crossed his face. "I care not for Shaul's blood. Blood of defeat and madness. I would prefer my offspring *not* have that blood."

"Yonatan had that blood," I said quietly.

David's face softened, the creases in his brow smoothing. "So he did." He smiled, a sad, fond smile. "And remember how Mikhal favored him? But I forgot. You have not seen her. Well, you will see her soon enough. You, Natan, will go to Avner with the messenger, to make sure that my terms are understood, and that it is understood that they are not negotiable. Be sure to speak to Ish Boshet, also. It is proper to do so. He should be a party to what concerns his sister. In fact, to be seemly, the instruction to her should be couched as if it came from him. After you have secured his consent, I want you to go with those they send to fetch her."

I spoke carefully, looking down at my hands. "It is many years— ten, by my reckoning—since you have seen her. She was a young girl then. She is surely much changed. In appearance, certainly. And maybe in her heart, also. Have you considered that she may have formed bonds of affection with this man Palti, after so long as his wife? There are surely children. Have you inquired?"

He stood up abruptly, pushing back his chair so that the legs scraped across the stone. "That girl risked her life for me. You think she loved another, after?" He tossed his head and gave a kind of derisive snort. He had reason to be vain, I don't say otherwise. Still, it is not an attractive quality, even in a king. "In any case, what is that to me? I care not for Palti, nor for what may or may not stand between them. The match was a greivous insult. It should never have been made, and now I have the power to unmake it.

"Bring her to me, Natan. I will set watchers on the walls."

It was a hot, dusty journey from Hevron across the wadi of the Yarden to Avner's stronghold in Mahanaim. Avner received me civilly enough, as one might receive a favored page. He gave a great sigh of relief when the messenger reported that David had accepted his offer. "So the bloodletting between our tribes can end at last," he said. "I will bring this daughter of Shaul to him, and then I will go and rally my tribe the Benyaminites to accept David. The rest will fall into line behind us. As for this matter of the woman, Ish Boshet will not stand against it. I can answer for him."

"Nevertheless, it is my king's wish that I consult Ish Boshet, and so I will do."

Avner glared at me, scowling. "Will you so?" Then his frown lifted and he shrugged. "Go ahead, then. See him if you like. He will *not* stand against it."

Avner was right: Ish Boshet could not have stood against a gust of strong wind, so thoroughly had he been cowed. He muttered that he wished David joy of his sister and would be honored by the kinship.

I was surprised, therefore, the next morning, to see Avner mounted and a troop of twenty armed men ready to escort us to the house of Palti in Gallim. They were bringing an empty litter, with curtains. At noon, when we stopped to water the mules, I came up to Avner and asked, in a low voice, if the armed escort meant that he expected difficulty. He stood up, flexing his shoulders and rubbing at the base of his thick neck, where ropes of scars knotted the flesh of an old knife wound. He gave me a look that was just this side of hostile. I imagine he did not often feel called upon to explain himself to those he considered subordinate, especially a subordinate as young as I was.

"You're supposed to be the prophet. I thought you could tell me how it's likely to go." He made a sound somewhere between a laugh and a grunt. "When a kingdom rests on it, I always expect difficulty. Then, if there is none, no blame. But if there is, well. One is prepared." He walked off then, calling out for someone to bring him a crust of bread.

It was late afternoon when we came within sight of the township. Avner ordered that we make camp in the valley rather than proceed into the town at dusk. As the tents went up, he drew me aside. "You're to take the message to Palti," he said. "It's a delicate bit of business. You're quite the courtier, so I hear. You'll be able to manage it better than a rude old soldier like me." He gave the same derisive snort of laughter. "And if anyone's going to botch it, better it be David's own boy."

I had not been called "boy" in some time. I felt the heat rise into my face. To my chagrin, I was blushing. "I don't know why this falls to me," I said. "You were the hand of Shaul, who made this unholy, unjust match. Surely, then, it is the place of Shaul's man to undo it?"

"'Unholy,' 'unjust'—I don't know how you can stand the taste of the cant in your mouth!" He turned and spat, as if to reinforce the point. "This was about power then, it's about power now. You know about power, Natan. I know you do. No one rises from farmer boy to chief adviser—oh, yes, I know about you—it was my business to know who was stiffening the spine of my opponent and taking the heart out of my king. All that high talk of 'thrones' and 'crowns' and 'lines that would not fail.'" He had pitched his voice into a girlish register, in mockery of me. He dropped back into his own gruff rumble. He had a voice like a grindstone. "Powerful weapons, words like those, to wield against a man of ailing mind and waning spirit. Yes, I took the trouble to trace you to the source, to know if you were real or sham. I know all about your butchered father and your ransacked village. Must've been something to see, a child spouting all that. I know soldiers; they're a superstitious lot, always looking for signs and omens. But David's no fool. He would've smelled an obvious charlatan, so I know you must've put on quite a show. And I know this, too: no one sits, as you do, so close to a king, who does not begin to grasp how the levers of power work, and the cost of the oil that must grease them. Get you to Palti, and fetch this woman. Tell him I want her on the road an hour after sunup."

Eved hamalek, I thought to myself, as I toiled up the hill in the dusk. And the servant may not choose his tasks. Avner was right: better the message should come from me. I had no doubt Avner would use force, if force were needed. Better that the threat remains at a distance, in a tent in the valley, than comes barging through the front door dressed in military greaves.

Yet there is no courtly way to break news to a man that one has come to take his wife. Palti received me with curiosity. He was a well-made man, with dark hair and a sensuous mouth. If Mikhal favored her brother, as David said, they would be a handsome couple. Word had, of course, come to him that Avner was encamped in the valley. I think he expected that I had come to ask some service of him in the negotiations between the Benyaminites and David's Yudaite forces. I began by outlining to him the news that hostilities would soon be over, that Avner had sued for peace and that David had accepted it.

"Good," he said, pouring two cups of wine and handing me one. I took it, and drank deeply, looking for courage to say what I had to say. Palti, oblivious, was buoyed by my news. "It is time to put an end to this. Everyone knows that Ish Boshet is no king. The Benyaminites will welcome reconciliation, I am sure of it. The threats we face are become too great for one tribe alone. Gilboa showed that plain."

"Avner will be glad of your support, and David the king will welcome it also," I said. I drained my cup and drew a breath. "There was a condition."

"Oh?"

"Palti, he wants his wife back."

"Back? But he has his wives—the Carmelite widow, the Yezreelite, and we heard tell that he recently took another one, part of the treaty with the northerners, the daughter of the Geshurite king, wasn't it? But I don't see what that—"

And then, as my meaning penetrated, he put a hand out to steady himself against a pillar. "He cannot ask this. Not after ten years. What can she mean to him after all this time? We have children— the youngest is not five. All this time, and he never sent so much as a word to her. Even when her father and her brothers lay dead on the battlefield." He was pacing now, his voice rising. "Not a word to her in her mourning. He cannot have any feelings for her. This is pride, merely—"

"No, Palti," I said. "Not pride. Politics. He needs this. You ask what she means to him. That marriage was his invitation into Shaul's dynasty. Now that Shaul's house is reduced, he must reclaim that place. David will be king, not just of Yudah, but of Israel, too. Shmuel foretold it. You cannot stand in the way."

"If it is foretold, as you say, then it will come to pass whether he has Mikhal at his side or no."

I raised a hand. "Enough. Your marriage was not valid under any law but a king's fiat. That king is now dead. Another king has spoken. Now, go to Mikhal and prepare her. Avner means to ride for Hevron an hour past sunrise. I will return then with a litter for her transport. If you have found joy in these years, be glad of it. But accept that it is over. For it is over, Palti." I waited a beat. "One way or another."

I let the threat hang there between us, and then I turned to see myself out. As I lifted the door bar, I glanced back. Palti had sunk down against the pillar, his head in his hands. His shoulders shook. If he, a stern man, could be felled by this news, how would Mikhal be? I dreaded the morning. As the heavy door closed behind me, I leaned against it for a moment, breathing hard.

I slept fitfully that night, listening to the grinding snores of the troops around me. At first light, I walked out and woke the men detailed as litter bearers. When we approached the house, Palti came out, dressed for the road. Behind him, walking unsteadily, supported by two maidservants, came a tall, slender figure swathed in a traveling mantle. Before the door closed behind her, I saw a boy snatch up his sister, who was reaching her hands out and wailing. The boy's own face was tear streaked. When Palti had assisted Mikhal into the litter, I placed my hand on his shoulder. He turned.

"You can't mean to go with her, Palti."

"I mean to follow," he said. "I mean to see the king, and beg him . . ."

"It's fruitless," I said. "Stay here, and see to your children." I dropped my voice. "They need one parent, at least. If you remind David of your adultery, it won't go well for you."

"I have to try," he said.

I shrugged. This I would leave to Avner. He was the leader of the expedition. It was for him to order Palti to stay behind.

But Avner seemed unconcerned. "The heat will get him," he said. "Or the terrain will. He's not so young. He has no mule. I don't think he can keep up with soldiers trained to the march." Yet as the morning wore on, and the heat rose, Palti showed no sign of faltering. Every now and then he would cry out Mikhal's name, assuring her that he followed.

At noon I went to bring bread and water to Mikhal, handing the goatskin through the curtain. She accepted the water with a trembling hand but would not take the bread. I rode my mule back to the rear of the train, where Palti staggered on, his tunic soaked through with his own sweat, his face as purple as a grape. I leaned down to speak to him. "It's not fair to her, what you are doing. She needs to reconcile herself, to prepare to meet the king. How can she do that when she hears you crying out to her? All you do here is increase her grief."

He made me no answer but just kept trudging. So I threw a water-skin at his feet, booted my mule and rode on. When I drew abreast with Avner, he turned to me. "Someone better shut that howling dog up, or I will."

Not long after, when Palti cried out again, one of the younger soldiers—a good mimic—started echoing his calls in mockery. Another youth took up the game, answering in a high-pitched voice. Soon a band of them had taken up the call and response, adding ribald suggestions. I turned to Avner.

"You'd better stop this. It's not fit to have the king's wife referred to in this way."

"You're right." Avner turned his mule and rode back to Palti. Palti did not even glance at Avner, but just kept moving forward, though it was apparent his whole body shook from the effort. Avner steered his mule across Palti's path. "Enough! Turn around, get on home." Still, Palti ignored him. Without looking up, he stepped sideways, as if to pass in front of Avner's mule. Avner took the butt end of his spear then and thumped Palti hard just under his shoulder blade, so that he fell backward, raising a cloud of dust. Immediately he put his hand behind, to push himself back up onto his feet. Avner brought the spear butt around swiftly and laid it into the side of Palti's head, sending him sprawling in the dirt. Blood ran from the cut above his ear.

"I won't say it again. Turn around and walk away. The next time I use this spear, it'll be the blade end you feel."

Palti groaned and struggled to his feet. The train had stopped now. Every man in the detail was watching, waiting to see if Palti would turn or take another step forward and be slain.

Suddenly there was a movement. Mikhal had thrown aside the curtains of her litter and stepped out, blinking in the strong light. Her veil slid to her shoulders and her unbound hair streamed behind her as she ran to Palti. I think she would have run straight into his arms had Avner not kicked his mule in between them. She lifted her tear-streaked face. "Do as he says, Palti. Go back to our children. I will beseech the king. I will find a way to come home to you."

Palti's eyes searched her face. "Swear it," he said.

"I swear it."

Then Avner jumped from the mule and grabbed her arm. "Shame!" he cried. "You dishonor your husband the king! Be glad if word of this does not reach him."

He pulled her in front of him, her arm twisted up roughly at her back. Then he marched her to the litter and almost threw her back inside. He should have a care, I thought. She would remember this. Avner called out gruffly, giving the order to move off. I turned in my saddle and saw Palti, on his knees in the dust, keening. And I saw her pale hand, through the curtain of the litter, reaching out to him. Then we crested a small rise, and turned onto the Hevron road.

It was near dusk when we arrived at the city walls. Inside, I handed off my mule to the stable lad and went to the litter to fetch her. She had replaced her veils by then, but I could see her eyes. They were not sad anymore. All I could read there was fury. A serpent of anger, coiled up inside her.

When I brought word to David that she had arrived, he seemed in no hurry to see her. I was surprised—curiosity, at least, I thought, would have goaded him. But also I was glad. I did not want him to have her brought to him as she was, travel stained, tear streaked and weary to the point of exhaustion. He asked how Palti had taken the news.

"Badly," I said. "He walked behind us all the way to Bahurim."

"Did he so? I'm sorry for it. Have him sent a ram from those Ziklag sheep with the long-staple fleece such as everyone prizes, and a pair of oxen, and some other gifts as seem good to you. I don't need an enemy there, if I can avoid it. He should know that I do not blame him in this matter."

I hardly thought a gift of livestock likely to placate Palti, and I wondered that David could be so callous as to suggest it. It was not as if he were a man without experience of deep affection. Where, then, was his empathy? Buried, I supposed, beneath his self-regard. I waited, girded, for his next inquiry, as to how Mikhal had received the order. But he did not ask. Instead, his thoughts were all on Avner, and his outreach to the Benyaminites. This night, it seemed, he was a king before he was a man. At the time, this troubled me. Later, I would have cause to wish that it were always so.

"I plan to feast Avner and his men tonight. You may send to Mikhal that I don't expect her. I shouldn't think she will be minded to attend a soldiers' feast." He paused a beat. "After such a long journey."

And after being wrenched from her children and seeing her husband of ten years almost cut down in front of her, I thought. But what I said was: "Will Yoav and Avishai be at this feast?"

"By chance not. They are away. Raiding party."

"Just as well," I said. David nodded.

"You'll have to deal with it at some point. And soon."

"I know."

It was one of the more lavish feasts, the wine abundant, the air thick with the delicious aromas of fat lambs turning on the spits and succulent fowl roasting in the clay ovens. As dark gathered and the torches came in, the flames seemed to dance with extra brightness. The music, too, was remarkable. David had invited some players from Avner's own tribe, in his honor, which delighted him. There was not a song he called for that they did not know, often in some lively and original variation.

David was at his best in such settings, soldier enough to join the raucous jests, king enough to make it matter that he remembered some moment of bravery or sacrifice, and praised each man accordingly. To Avner, he was generous, standing on no precedence but offering instead the deference that a young man owes an elder. Everyone present in the hall was allowed to understand that this man was esteemed, even loved, by David. It was clear that the young king and the old soldier were ready to reconcile. Avner basked in the attention. I imagine his recent years at the side of Shaul, alert always for the signs of madness, could have offered few such pleasurable evenings. Late that night, Avner stood up in the hall. He was flushed and unsteady from the drinking, and more than one person looked sideways at his neighbor, wondering what was coming. Avner raised his cup, toasting David.

"We are your bone and flesh. In times past, you led us out and you brought us home. So let it be again. You are the one who will shepherd all our people. I promise you, the next time we meet, I will deliver all Israel to your banner."

The hall erupted in cheers, men thumping on the boards, as David rose and embraced him. More than one warrior dashed the back of his hand to his eyes at the sight of the graying general offering his love and loyalty to his new king.

Avner departed the next day at noon. Not an hour after, Yoav and his men rode in from the other direction, leading a long train of carts filled with plunder. David sent for Yoav to honor him for his successful raid, but by the time Yoav made his way to David's apartments he had already learned that Avner had come and gone. He had also likely heard, or gathered, that the tone of the feast had been more than congenial, and that Avner had been treated with distinction.

Yoav was a soldier, not a diplomat. He had never learned to school his face. He burst into David's room, and the expression written there was the same plain rage I had seen as a boy when he flung me against the wall of my father's house.

"You had the enemy's commander in your hands, and you let him go?" He did not pause for David's response, but blustered on. "How can you think to trust him? All this talk of uniting the kingdoms. You can't possibly believe he'll go through with it. He came here to study your dispositions and assess your strengths. He'll be back with an army behind him."

He turned on me then. "Natan, how could you not counsel the king on this? Surely you, at least, can see?"

"Yoav, what I see is a bereaved brother, who harbors a thirst for revenge. But remember, Asahel attacked Avner first."

"That has nothing to do with it!" Yoav was spitting now, his anger uncontained.

"If that's so," said David, "then this outburst of yours is unwarranted and offensive. You are a fighter, not a politician. Do not cross me in this. Avner knows that the tribes must unite, and he needs me to do it. He, at least, is able to put aside personal feelings, and see the broad strokes." David turned away to pour more wine. "Experience counts in these things."

Because he had turned, he didn't see the expression that crossed Yoav's face at the mention of the word "experience." It was not like David to misjudge a man. Later, I wondered if this remark was, in fact, the result of misjudgment or rather a calculated goad, to bring about just such a result as it did. But at the time, I thought only that he lacked tact. When David turned back with two cups of wine in his hand and proffered one to Yoav, Yoav, uncharacteristically, waved it off. "You're right," he said. "I'm too tired to discuss this now. Let me take my leave."

David shrugged, and passed the cup of wine to me instead. Later, he demanded to know why I did not see what would happen that night and the next morning: why I sat there and offered no warning. I could have asked the same of him. One didn't need to be a seer to understand Yoav's anger and jealousy, and to foretell that something grievous might come of it. Men raised in a culture of blood revenge do not change in a day.

In the morning, Avner lay dead, just inside the gates of Hevron. Yoav had gone straight from the king's chamber and dispatched a messenger, supposedly at the king's request, to find Avner where he had camped for the night at the cistern of Sirah. The message was that David desired him to return to Hevron. Avner, no doubt still basking in the good feelings of the previous evening, made haste to answer the summons. Yoav waited for him. No sooner had Avner entered the gate than Yoav took him by the arm, pulling him into the shadows, saying he must have a private word. The "word" was a dagger in the belly; a brother's blood debt repaid.

David called for me just after dawn, when the change of watch discovered the body. He was casting off his night robe and fidgeting as a servant strove to help him into a tunic. "Leave it, I can do it myself," he said impatiently, pulling at the fine fabric until it tore in his hand. "Never mind. I will have to rend it anyway." He turned on me then. "*How* can you not have foreseen this?"

I knew those blank, empty eyes. I knew what his anger looked like. I'd felt it before, in the caves of Horesh, the day I was unable to interpret the prophecy about Yonatan. Now I felt it again, hard and bright and searing. I struggled to make my own face a mask of composure, although inside I was roiling.

"I might put the same question to you, King. Yoav has been your loyal fighter at Adullam and in the wilderness of Ziph and in the stews of Ziklag. He's followed you in your exile, stood by you in your disgrace. Now, when everything you have fought for—together—is about to fall into your hands, he learns you've been feasting and embracing the man who hunted us. The man, moreover, who slew his brother.

Yoav knows you mean to make him underling to this man. And yet, when he came to you last night, instead of a kind word, a gesture of reassurance, instead of drawing him close, as his uncle and as his life-long friend, you insult him and push him away. So I ask you: how did *you* not foresee this?" I had never spoken to him like this, not in my own voice. I could see the vein throbbing in his temple, his hands clenching and unclenching at his sides. His eyes, wide with surprise at my words. I braced myself for an outburst.

Instead, he dropped his head. When he spoke, he was still angry, his lips compressed. But there was no eruption. His voice was low, contained, but he spat out his words as if they tasted bitter. "You, Natan, are the only one brave enough to speak the truth." He raised his head and gathered himself up. "Walk with me. I go to the gates to see to the body." He turned and I followed, sweating with relief.

"Is that wise?" I asked as we walked. "Should you not stand apart from this murder?"

"How can I? This reckless act of Yoav's puts all at risk. The Ben-yaminites will never join with us now, without Avner to persuade them. They will say I committed basest treachery." I struggled to keep up with him as he pounded through the hall.

"You're wrong. They will join you. The Name has said it. But you must act now. Make Yoav pay, and pay dearly, for this."

"But how can I?" he repeated. "I can't spare him. Not with Avner dead. You're right. You're always right. I *was* going to put Avner over him. It was necessary. But now Yoav is the only capable general I've got. Our wars won't end just because the tribes unite. *If* they unite, after this night's work. That will be but the beginning. I need a sea-soned general to send out against the Plishtim, and all the others who scent our weakness and covet this Land. I need Yoav."

"I don't say kill him. The Benyaminites, of all people, can be made to understand this, if you cast it as a blood debt. But you must stand aside from it. You must lament it. And you must find a way to punish Yoav and yet keep him in your service."

"Thank you, Natan." His voice dripped with sarcasm. "Thank you for laying out this clear and easy path for me."

It was a bright morning, and I blinked as we emerged into the square. The streets were crowded, the usual early bustle congealing into clots of people standing about, whispering news of the killing. David did not look right or left, nor greet any person, but continued his fast stride to the gate. There were guards around the body, holding back gawkers, but they parted as David approached.

Avner lay as he had fallen, his legs twisted one around the other. His head had shattered when it hit the ledge of stone, which now bit right into his skull. The fall had probably killed him before the slash in his gut had a chance to do its work.

David dropped his head for a moment and covered his eyes with a hand. He spoke quietly, so that only I could hear him. "Should Avner have died the death of a churl?" He crouched down beside the body, and took the shattered head between his hands. A clear yellow liquid spilled between his fingers, but he did not seem to mark it. "Look at you," he said to the corpse. "Your feet were not put in fetters, your hands were unbound. Yet you fell as one falls before treachery and betrayal."

He stood up, gathering the fabric of his tunic where he had accidentally torn it, and making a show of the rending. He had done a good job of working himself up. There was real grief, as well as wrath, in his eyes. He raised his voice. "Tear your garments! This man is a general of Israel. Pay him his due." He turned then to the men of the watch, standing, heads down, eyes averted. "Have Yoav brought here, and tell him he comes in sackcloth!" The soldiers looked at one another, and then at their feet. Not one of them, it seemed, wished to bring this message to his general. "Do it!" David cried. "Now!"

I leaned in closer. "Let me go. Better me."

David turned to me sharply, glaring. He might have accepted the fact that he, too, bore responsibility for this outcome, but he still brimmed with rage that I had not foreseen it. "Go, then." He pushed me, hard, almost a blow. "Be a messenger. That's at least a service you *can* perform."

Yoav was sitting in his quarters in the soldiers' barracks, Avishai standing behind him. He was still in his military dress.

"For the love of your life, Yoav, get out of that blood-stained tunic. David wants you."

He did not move. "Get up! Do you not hear me?"

"I hear you," he said quietly. "Why should I bestir myself to rush toward my execution?"

"Yoav," I said. "He does not intend to kill you. But do not press him. Put on penitent dress and get you to the gate." Yoav gazed at me, his eyes glassy, his body sagging, inert.

"Do it, man, if you want to live."

Avishai laid a hand on his brother's shoulder. "Trust Natan. Do as he says." Yoav looked up at his brother, and then stood, moving in a daze. Avishai took his arm and steered him toward the stores, where some kind of rough sacking could be found to serve as penitent garb.

Not long after, Yoav emerged from the barracks, clad in a loincloth and shawl torn hastily from a grain bag. As he made his way through the parting crowd, David stared at that battle-scarred, hairy body with a look that flayed. Then he turned his back on him and addressed the crowd.

"Know that a prince, a great man of Israel, is fallen this day. And today I am weak, even I, an anointed king. These sons of my sister Zeruiah are too savage for me. May they be requited for their wickedness."

He turned back to Yoav and pointed at the ground. "Lie down in the dirt and lament for Avner, son of Ner." Yoav slowly sank to his knees. He paused for a moment. I could tell it was costing him—he, a general, kinsman to the king. But the will to live is stronger even than pride. He lowered his face into the dust at David's feet.

David's countenance was flushed, his mouth a thin line. His pupils were huge and black, even in the brightness of the morning sun. He took a running step forward and kicked Yoav, hard, in the ribs. Yoav suppressed a grunt of pain. He raised his arms, instinctively, to protect his head.

"You and your house bear the guilt of this. May your house never be without one who suffers." He kicked him again. "May murderers hunt down your kin. May your offspring know hunger." It was a heavy curse, and Yoav writhed on the ground as the words and blows landed. But as the assault ended, I saw some tension leave his body. Words and kicks were one thing, the executioner's sword another. As the king released his rage in this torrent of cursing, Yoav withdrew his arms from around his head. He realized, as no further physical blows fell, that I had spoken truly, and that the king would let him live.

In the confusion of that day, David had no thought to spare for Mikhal. That evening, I belatedly remembered to inquire after her. The master of the household told me that David had made no particular provision for her, but that Avigail had sent her own attendants to see to her comfort. I went then to see how she did. But though the servant who opened the door was full of apologies, she would not admit me. "Mikhal says she is unwell, and wants to rest." When I turned to go, the girl, whom I knew to be quick-witted, put out a hand as if to restrain me, then quickly drew it back. "My lord, she eats nothing. She barely sips water. We—my mistress and I—we fear for her."

"Do you so? You do well to confide in me." I went then directly to Avigail. Between us, there was no need for small talk. The moment we were alone, she poured out her thoughts. "I know what you're going to say, Natan. Why did I press for this? Truly, I am asking myself the same question. Will you believe me if I tell you I did it for her?"

I must have looked doubtful. She was up, and pacing. She was round-bellied with the child she carried, and yet she was drawn in the face. I noticed that save for the thickness at her waist, she was very thin. The wasting disease already had its hand upon her. She winced as she paced. For an instant, a sharp pain stabbed between my eyes, and I saw her—laid out upon a bier, David holding her fleshless hand, a small boy weeping in the corner. It was the apparition of a moment. When I blinked it was gone. But I knew it for a true vision. A shard of grief pierced me. She was my confidante and my friend. "Sit," I said. I poured wine and handed her the cup. She drained it like a man, in one thirsty swallow, and held the cup out for more.

"Is the pain so bad as that?" I asked quietly.

"Sometimes. When I'm tired. At night it's worse."

"Avigail—"

She waved a hand, as if to dismiss the subject. "Don't. At my age, to be with child is a blessing. More than that. It is a miracle. I thought—because of Navaal, five years married and no child—I thought I was barren." She ran a hand over her swollen stomach. "I just want to live long enough to give life, that is all." She hadn't asked directly, but I heard the question hovering in the silence.

"You will," I said. "And beyond. Long enough for your son to know you."

She smiled. "A son? Good. And I will live to see him. Then that is more than I had hoped. I am satisfied. I can bear anything now . . ." She took another gulp of the wine, and gathered herself. "Natan, I'm glad you came, and not just for these sustaining words. I have been asking myself what I have done, what I can do, for Mikhal, now that she's here. I made a mistake. I truly thought she would want this. Yes, yes, I thought it would be good for David, for his house, to restore the link with Shaul, to silence future claims from that direction. But I also thought she was like me.

"I despised my husband Navaal. I despised his drunkenness and his folly, long before I ever saw David. But after . . . after I'd seen David—Natan, he looked beautiful that day, when I met him on the road. He was dressed for battle, the hair bound back, skin oiled. And angry—you know how he is, in anger. I could feel it. Feel the heat of it coming off him. The sense of purpose in him, the coil of it, how tightly he held himself in, but how ferocious he might be, unleashed. The self-command. And then, the way he softened to me, when he understood what I was doing. His kindness and his blessing as he sent me home. Home. Home to that stinking ass who had almost had us all killed. I had to go back to my house and sit with Navaal and endure one of his drunken feasts. Had to look at him, his beard crusty with food, wine and spittle staining his tunic. Had to listen to his foul, stupid jokes and watch him put his greasy hands all over the serving women. Listen to him boast that he'd stood up to the ragtag outlaws, knowing that if it weren't for me he'd be dead in his own blood. And wishing, in my heart, that he *was* dead.

"The next day, when he'd sobered up, I went to him and told him. Told him what I'd done, and what a fool he was. He got up, and staggered to the bowl and vomited. You know how violently a drunk vomits—his eyes were bloody when he'd done. And then he fell in a fit. They say I caused it with my words. It's not true. He caused it. He'd ruined his body. I am sure he would have had the selfsame fit that day from his excess whether I'd spoken truth to him or no.

"But I was glad. And gladder still when day following day, he did not wake up. Then, on the tenth day, he died, leaving David free to ask for me. I had to keep my countenance when they came to inquire whether I would or no. But the moment I was in private, I danced around my room for the joy of it. Truly, Natan, I thought Mikhal would feel the same way. How was I to know that she loved this man Palti?" She rubbed her hands over her face. "What can I do?"

"Nothing," I said. "Be kind to her, as you have been. You and I both know that David has a great gift for inspiring love. He had hers, once. He will know how to win her again, I am sure of it."

And I was sure of it then. But sure as a man is sure. Which is to say, as likely to be wrong as right. Avigail chose to think I meant sure in that other way, and took comfort in my words, which was something.

I cared for her and I didn't want her to punish herself. Not in the short time I knew she had left to her.

Word of Avner's death traveled quickly to his stronghold in Mahanaim. As David had predicted, everyone there assumed his hand was behind it. Shaul's son Ish Boshet, sure that he was next marked for death, took to his bed, paralyzed by fear. Two of David's company commanders, supposing Ish Boshet's assessment correct, decided to do David that service, thinking to ingratiate themselves with him. They broke into Ish Boshet's room and stabbed him to death. It did not take the two killers long to find they had misjudged matters. When they arrived at Hevron with Ish Boshet's head in a bloody bag, David had their hands and feet cut off, and hanged them by the pool of Hevron. I went with him to inspect the bleeding corpses, swinging from the scaffold. David looked up at them, his face blank. "Now, maybe," he said, "the people will understand that I want this killing between the tribes to stop and be done with."

Maybe, I thought to myself. And maybe they'll understand that you show no mercy to king slayers, even if the king is your enemy, as Shaul was, or a powerless puppet like Ish Boshet. But whatever the people might be brought to accept, I knew that once again, a murder had been done, and once again, the results only furthered David's ambitions. And perhaps some others also would see this coincidence, and find it suspect.

Whatever whispers passed in private, the public reaction was just as David wanted. In the next week, envoys came from each tribe of Israel, even from Avner's Benyaminites. There were parlays, and at each, much recollecting of the times before David's rift with Shaul, when he had led them so successfully in battle.

Sometime during all of this statecraft, David finally remembered Mikhal. "I suppose I should call upon her," he said, after a roomful of envoys had departed. "Come with me. We'll go now and see to it." His tone was of a man addressing a chore. I wondered at it. As full of vital matters as his days had been, I thought that curiosity—if not desire, if not plain kindness—might have led him to a greater zeal.

We found her sitting by the window in her apartment, gazing out into the square below. She was clad in the plainest of gray robes, her hair bound back beneath a severely tied head scarf. When she turned her face to us, even the drabness of her attire could not deaden her beauty. She was gaunt—I learned later that she'd eaten little in the two weeks that had passed since her arrival. But the hollows beneath her cheeks and the gray of her robe only served to emphasize the beauty of her eyes. I saw the tension go out of David's body and a wide smile light his face. Sensualist, I thought. He means to get an heir on her, and he's relieved she's not become a crone. But no such relief or joy animated her face. Indeed, she barely registered that we'd entered the room. David strode toward her, uttering words of welcome and extending his hand. Her own remained resolutely folded in her lap. If he noticed this, he did not falter, but reached down and grasped her shoulders, gently lifting her until they stood, eye to eye—she was very tall. Then he embraced her. Her body did not answer his, but seemed to shrink and stiffen. Standing behind him, I saw what he could not: her eyes, blank and opaque, staring unblinkingly into the distance. Her face cold, expressionless.

He disengaged from the embrace, still holding her shoulders, murmuring polite platitudes and questions as to how she did and whether she had all she needed. She remained passive in his arms, but as soon as he released his grip she immediately sat again, her gaze trained upon the floor. He fingered the coarse weave of her robe. "This won't do," he said. "I will see to it that some silks and linens are sent. You must choose what you would like. My new wife, Maacah—have you met her yet? Perhaps not . . . She is daughter to the king of Geshur and so has her own household outside the palace. Political marriage— you know how it is . . ." A flush had crept up his neck and was brightening his cheeks. He was perhaps aware this wasn't the best conversational gambit. I had rarely seen him clumsy in this way. I realized then that Mikhal's lack of response was unnerving him. "In any case, she brought a skillful seamstress with her. Very fine work. I will see to it that she's put at your disposal."

David's stream of talk stuttered to an awkward invitation to attend the evening's feast in honor of the latest emissaries. Still, she said nothing. And as we backed out of her apartment, she did not offer a farewell.

In the hallway, David shrugged. "We have time," he said. "Once all this—" He waved an arm. "Once things are settled . . ."

She did not come to the feast that night, and if he noticed her absence he did not remark on it. One week later, when he was anointed king of all Israel, she was there with the other wives. But while Avigail, Ahinoam and the new wife, the Geshurite princess Maacah, were brilliant in silks and jewels, Mikhal was conspicuous in the same joyless gray robe—almost a mourning dress. She did not join in the praise singing.

This time, the anointing was accompanied by full rites and ceremony. David was, at last, what I had foretold he would be: king of Yudah and Israel. We were a nation at last.

He had just turned thirty.

XI

It became clear soon enough that he would need to seek a new capital if we were truly to forge the tribes into one nation. The Israelites made it plain that they felt slighted by the king's location in Hevron, in the center of Yudah. But to move to Shaul's old capital in Geba was out of the question, since it would affront David's own tribe. And relations in that direction were unsettled enough. Inevitably, some of his most loyal men had been demoted, or felt as if they had been, as he incorporated the men of Benyamin into positions of authority.

David's mind became much occupied with the problem, but he had little time to act on it, amid the press of urgent affairs. These were years of bloodshed as all our enemies came against us, hoping to disrupt the new kingdom even as we strove to forge it. Yet they were also fruitful years, when David's family grew and expanded as befit a king. Avigail's son, Daniel, arrived soon after the anointing, another cause for feasting and rejoicing. Then Maacah, before a full year in the household, gave birth to a striking baby boy named Avshalom. Later, she bore David his first and only daughter, the radiant child Tamar. There were new wives, too: Hagit, who gave him a son named Adoniyah; Eglah, whose first child was named Yitraam; and Avital, whose boy was called Shefatiah.

I did not have occasion to get to know these later wives, who were acquired to bind the tribes. David made it clear enough that they were honored, and would be made in all ways comfortable, but once he had got an heir on them it seemed to me he paid them little mind. If he wanted a woman's company, it was still Avigail he sought out, even as her illness took her ever more firmly into its grip. He also spent time in Maacah's separate house, but it wasn't clear whether the attraction there was the beautiful Geshurite princess or her infants, or both.

I did go to the women's quarters, of course, when I had cause to. I went, as always, to visit and consult with Avigail, as far as her waning strength allowed it. And I went reluctantly, at David's request, about two months after the anointing, to speak on his behalf to Mikhal. He had invited her to his bed on a few occasions in that time, and was most unsatisfied with the outcome.

"She's changed, Natan," he confided, the morning after one such encounter. He had called me early, and his face was drawn as if he hadn't slept. The servants were still bustling about performing their morning duties. Before I replied, I tilted my head in their direction and gave David a look. He came to himself and dismissed them wearily.

"How not?" I said. "It's been ten years since you were man and wife. And she has been through a great deal—"

He cut me off with a sweep of his hand, not wanting, I think, to listen to a catalog of the grief and loss that his own behavior, in large part, had caused her. "She's cold. It's like lying down with a corpse. The first time, I thought, well, as you say, it's been a long time, she's suffered . . . I'm not going to force myself on her. I waited a week, two. But it was the same again, the next time, and the next. Limp, ungiving . . . I can't even get her to look at me, much less . . ." His voice trailed off and he glanced away, embarrassed. "I wouldn't turn to you, except that Avigail isn't well, since the birth, and I won't burden her. So I want you to go to Mikhal and see what she wants. I will give her anything. Short, of course, of . . ." Again, his voice trailed away. I had rarely seen him so awkward. "If it's her children, for instance—it could be that she misses them. I can see how that would be a heavy thing for a woman. The last thing I need is another man's children underfoot, resenting the young princes. I won't risk that kind of thing in my household. You'll have to be clear with her on that—if I bring her children here she'll have to have her own house outside the palace."

I fiddled with a scroll that was open on his table so that I would not have to meet his eyes. "I don't think it's that simple," I said.

"Is that so?" His tone changed. He was suddenly terse. "Well, let me simplify it. I'll give her a house. I'll get her children here. I'll do any reasonable thing. In return, I need her to act like my wife. I need you to find out what will make that happen. Is that simple enough?"

I looked up and held his eyes, which were angry now. I returned his gaze with my own hard stare. But, *eved hamelek*, after a few moments I dropped my head in a nod of compliance. "As you wish," I said, and waited for him to dismiss me.

She received me, as she was obliged to, but offered me the same silent passivity that the king had described. She looked resolutely at the floor as I launched into a big speech about how David cared for her welfare, was troubled by her apparent unhappiness, and was willing to do whatever it might require to make her content, given the current circumstances. I saw her eyebrow rise at the words "current circumstances." She made me no reply.

"He says you may send for your children, if you would like."

At that, she sprang to her feet and glared at me, her eyes narrow. "My children? *My* children? They are Palti's children, too, and he loves them. Do you think I would strip him of that last comfort, after he has been unmanned and debased? Do you think I would bring them here, to serve as attendants and sycophants to the king's mewling litter?" She shook her head violently and then drew herself inward, sitting down again and staring at the floor, compressing her lips as if to ensure that no more of her true feelings escaped.

"'Litter,' you call it," I said quietly. "Yet one of those young princes or princesses could be your own child. I know the king greatly desires it. Such a child would be the perfect heir—"

She looked up at me. "Still a herdsman at heart, is he, looking for the perfect ewe on which to get a fatling lamb?"

"Look," I said. "You're here, he's the king. This is your life now. These facts won't change. Why not make it easier on yourself? Let him give you those things that might provide you some solace. You can neither of you change the past, but you can change this day, and the one after—"

She cut me off with a strained laugh. "*That's* what passes for wisdom in this court? That's the best the king's great prophet can do?" She laughed again, but I could see her eyes fill. I realized then that the only kindness I could do for her was to leave, before her hard-wrought shell cracked open, and all her pain spilled forth.

I went from her room straight to Avigail, and gave her the gist of our exchange. "I don't know what to tell the king," I said.

"It's difficult," she agreed. "He's much too vain to grasp it."

I gave her a sharp look. She smiled. "You are not the only one, Natan, who is allowed to sometimes speak the truth. We may love him and yet not be blind to what he is. I've come to understand that he is what he is because of his faults."

I felt a sudden urge to embrace her. I had a painful premonition of all the empty years ahead, when I would not be able to turn to her for counsel. When I would be alone, with no wise ear to listen to my most private concerns about the king.

She seemed to sense my sadness, and reached for my hand. She took it in hers and patted it reassuringly. She was still mothering me, after all these years. I would miss that, too.

"I've observed Mikhal," she went on. "I no longer think as I did, even a month ago. I do not think David can win back her affections, even if he devoted himself to it. And he won't do that. It's not important enough to him. Perhaps that's all we can hope for—that other great matters will distract him so that he loses interest and lets the poor woman be."

Not many months later, Avigail lay dying, and I spent many hours at her side, talking, when she had the strength for it, of all the great things that had been done with her help and of the further greatness that lay ahead. One thing we did not speak of, and I was thankful she did not ask. I saw nothing in the future for her sweet young son, good-natured little Daniel, who was often at her side in those days and brought her much joy.

Sure enough, the boy did not live to see his sixth year. He was carried off by a flux. David mourned him grievously. He loved all his children deeply, but Daniel he especially cherished as the living reminder of Avigail. He had favored him after her death, asking for him whenever he had a few moments to spare.

As the small, linen-wrapped body was laid in the earth beside his mother, David's shoulders shook with sobs. He leaned on the priest Aviathar for support. I remember the oldest boys, Amnon and Avshalom, standing with their father, shifting their weight restlessly from foot to foot. Their eyes were dry. Amnon, who was nearly seven then, looked sullen, angry that he was not the center of attention. Avshalom, Maacah's son, born just a few months after Daniel, had a smirk on his face as if the proceedings amused him. Well, I thought, they're only small boys. It's no remarkable thing if they do not know how to behave on an occasion of such solemnity.

David's way of dealing with his grief was to look for a problem that would absorb his mind. He threw himself fully into the search for a new capital, poring over maps, conferring with strategists. He fixed on a hilltop redoubt named Yebus. It was a town of some forty-five dunams—only a little larger than Hevron, but more secure and defensible. Set on a low, narrow, arrowhead-shaped spur between the deep wadi of the Kidron and the valley of the cheese makers near Hinnom, it stood right on the border between the lands of the Benyaminites and the Yudaites, and for that reason had caught his notice. It was a long-settled place, and famously impregnable. Yehoshua had tried to take it, and failed. Later, the Benyaminites and Yudaites each had tried to conquer the city, and been rebuffed.

This was not a town to fall easily, and could not be taken by one tribe alone.

The Yebusites were Knaanite people, and Hittite refugees had found welcome there when their own kingdom fell to the Sea Peoples. They had offered their skills as builders and warriors to reinforce the Yebusite defenses. Until our tribes had conquered the surrounding lands, the Yebusite king had ruled from there and made it the most important town in the hill country. Because we had not been able to take the city itself, we had come, over time, to accept this foreign enclave in our midst. We lived alongside them, trading in peace.

But now David set his eye on it. I stood by him as he waxed on about its qualities, the foremost, in his mind, being that it had no strong connection with any one of our tribes. In addition, its location on the central ridge put it out of easy reach of Plishtim raids. Though it was far from the main trade routes—the Sea Road on the coast and the King's Road to the east—it was close enough to the Mountain Spine Road, which connected it to Hevron and Shechem. While the current town huddled on a single spur of the Yudean hills, there was room to expand the settlement in several directions. Furthermore, it had one great asset: a secure water supply, from an elaborately fortified year-round spring, the Gihon.

David ran through all these concrete advantages. And then, as he often did, he set aside the practical. The pragmatist was gone, replaced by the poet and mystic. "This is a sacred place, Natan. Melchizedek ruled there, and he was both king and priest. A king should be more than a war leader . . ."

I could see it through his eyes, the rational and the romantic arguments, both. My concern was that we were picking an unnecessary fight with a people who were not our enemies, when we still had adversaries aplenty at our heels. "Are you sure you wish to stir that hive?" I asked. "For if we try, and fail, we will have made an enemy right in the heart of our territories, and at a time when we can ill afford it."

"Do you ask me this as Natan, or as . . . as . . ." David never seemed to find a name for that nameless voice inside me.

"I speak only as myself."

"Then have faith. I will not do this lightly. But a town like that— with a secure spring and excellent fortifications, and right on the border of Yudah and Israel—I could scour the Land and not find another. Such a city we could make there, Natan . . ." And he went on, building it in his mind, until some pressing matter called for his attention, and he had to turn reluctantly aside.

Discreetly, David sent around to find any traders who knew the place, or slaves who had been in service there, and had them questioned closely about every aspect of the town, its layout, its defenses, and the habits of its people. Because relations had been peaceful for so long, there were many who knew the town quite well, and were pleased to offer their small share of information in return for the king's favor.

Sometimes, if the informants were especially knowledgeable, David would see them himself, after administering a stern oath that they not disclose the meeting. I was there for each of these briefings. I think he hoped I might have a vision to tell him how best to frame his assault. But nothing came to me, and sometimes my mind drifted as David delved into tedious details as to how and where livestock was housed, or how exactly the watches on the gates were staffed and timed, and how the fields in the valley floor beyond the walls were irrigated. Seraiah the scribe was also present, noting everything that was said. What I did not know was that every scrap of information was being compiled into a kind of master plan of the city. By the time the year turned again, David was satisfied that he had a full accounting. When, finally, he unrolled the skins that Seraiah had worked on, Yebus lay there before us.

It was a dispiriting sight. David's informants had described, in detail, the might of the town's defenses. The walls looked to be unbreachable: powerful fortifications of undressed stone that stood five

cubits thick. Nor would a siege be practical. The Yebusites had enjoyed excellent harvests, according to our sources, and their strategic
stores of grain and fodder stood full. As for water, the spring was
ingeniously defended.

"Well, it has to be," David mused, running a finger over the marks
that showed the spring and its defenses. "It stands outside the walls—
as it must, low as it sits there, at the foot of the hill. If they'd brought
the wall down to encircle it, they would have laid the lower town open
to an attack from above." So the city walls stopped some seventy-
five cubits short of the spring. In peacetime, this was no problem.
The water gate stood open and citizens came and went with their
waterskins or tall clay vessels. For wartime, the Yebusites had constructed a defensive rampart that ran out to a high tower that overlooked the spring. The rampart offered a measure of cover to water
fetchers; from there, the archers on the tower could defend them from
attack.

The logical direction of attack was from the north. The mountain, Har Moriah, was unoccupied and overlooked the city. From the
south, troops would have to negotiate the steep sides of the Wadi
Kidron even before they reached the formidable town walls. David
was well advanced planning a massive attack from the north, even
though he conceded that it would be costly. But all those plans proved
unnecessary.

I was in a dead sleep when a servant came to rouse me, saying
David wanted me urgently in his chamber. It was the middle of the
night as I made my way through the silent halls. The servant, yawn-
ing, led me past the night guards. David was sitting opposite a richly
dressed young stranger. Yoav stood behind him, looking grim and
bilious. The detailed drawings of Yebus lay unrolled on the table.

No introductions were made. "Tell him," David said tersely. "Tell
him what you just told us." The young man ran a finger along the
parchment, between the spring and the town walls, measuring what I
guessed to be a distance of some fifty cubits. He inscribed a sharp

turn westward for thirty or forty cubits farther. He tapped his finger on the parchment, turned his hand upward and shrugged. I had time to notice that it was a soft hand, unblemished: this young man was neither laborer nor warrior.

Then all at once the carefully drawn lines, etched with such precision, smudged and ran. The ink, wet, traveled in a dark smear across the pale parchment.

"Why do you deface it?" I cried, outraged to see Seraiah's work so carelessly despoiled. But then I saw that the liquid was not ink, but water. The temperature dropped. I hugged myself against the damp chill. As my eye followed the dark line, moving like a stain now across the drawing, I felt myself pulled down into its shadow. I could hear the water, the steady trickle of a stream finding its way through stone. I was underground, below the soil, into the bedrock, in a deep crevice that was steadily filling. I felt the water rising past my thighs, up to my chest. As the stream fed the hidden basin, it brimmed. Then the pressure of the rising liquid forced its way into a spout in the rock and came gushing upward, outward, tumbling with sudden turbulence through the earth and into the air. Gihon. *Giha.* The word meant rush of water. I was above ground again, beside the Gihon spring, the mighty walls of Yebus looming before me. I watched the water pulse its way out of the earth. Time passed as the hidden crevice emptied itself and the force of the flow lessened.

Touch the tzinnor *and the town will fall. Wait for the water. When it abates, advance.*

The air warmed again. David grasped my shoulders and steered me into his own chair. The map on the table was unsullied, the lines still crisply drawn.

"How did he know?" The young man's face was pale, his eyes wide. "How did he know about the *tzinnor?* Only the king and a handful of his most trusted servants know this."

David's voice was gently mocking. "I assumed one seer would recognize another. Natan, this is Zadok, priest of Araunah, the ruler of

Yebus. He says he has had a vision that I will take the town, and he has come to negotiate terms for its people."

I could not answer, so ill did I feel. I signaled for a basin and staggered into the corner to make use of it. David sent a servant for cool cloths and wiped my face himself. Though I was still addled, with one foot in my fading vision and one in the king's chamber, I noted that Zadok's eyes were wide.

When I could speak, I turned to him. "You come with terms for surrender?"

Yoav gave his rough bark of a laugh. "Araunah? Surrender? By no means. He thinks his priest here has come to put a spell on us. He is threatening to turn us all blind and lame if we dare attempt to breach his walls."

"But we don't need to breach his walls," I said.

"What?" said Yoav sharply.

"Go on," said David.

"We will take the town from inside. A small party. Climbers. They will enter through one of the irrigation pipes that lie in the Wadi Kidron."

"That's what you meant when you said 'Touch the *tzinnor*'?"

"Is that what I said? I don't know what I said. But what I saw was the water, how it runs from under the city, through the rock, to a spring. . . . I saw a tunnel that has been cut in the rock, from the spring to a shaft. Climb the shaft, and you reach another tunnel. This one runs right under the walls. It's how the city gets its water during siege. We thought the spring was defended from the fortifications above, but it's better than that. They don't have to go outside the walls at all. They have diverted the water to a pool inside the walls, for use in wartime." I turned to Zadok. "Is that not so?"

Zadok looked stricken. He had hoped to bargain this information for a high price. Now I had given it to David for free. He might have been reflecting on the well-known fact that kings generally do not look kindly on the betrayers of other kings.

Yoav was pacing. "So one need only climb the shaft . . ."

"Only?" said Zadok, finding his voice. "It's a vertical climb, half again as tall as this building. The walls are slick."

"We'd be fully armed," David mused. "If anyone inside gets wind of us, all they need do is drop a rock on our head and it's over. Bad odds. A job for the brave or very desperate."

Yoav stepped forward, and reached out to clasp David's arm. "Someone like you were, King, the day you offered to fight the giant of Gath. You spared my life after Avner. Let me do this, in recompense." The two men stood eye to eye for a long moment. Then David nodded. "So be it," he said.

It was the season of reaping. The season when kings go out to war. David marched, in force, to Har Moriah, to the north of the city. It was the first time Israel and Yudah had taken to the field as one army, and it was an impressive display. David had ordered a night march. When the sun rose, the people of Yebus looked up toward a hilltop dense with archers, spearmen, slings.

At daybreak, Araunah played what he thought was his best tactic. Up onto the massive walls shambled a sad army of the deformed, the lame, the blind, the leprous. It was a sight to fill a heart with dread. A taunt, and an attempt at dark magic. Foot soldiers on the eve of battle are notoriously superstitious. Our men believe that to kill an accursed person—one afflicted by illness and disfigurement—is to invite the same curse down upon oneself. In that way, Araunah reasoned, these unfortunates were an effective defensive line. Even the blind and the lame can defeat an army that is afraid to shoot them. And behind that unhappy vanguard, he arrayed his true army, the archers and the pots of oil.

As the Yebusites looked north, I was already south of their walls, with Yoav and the small, handpicked force drawn from the elite warriors known throughout the army as David's Mighty Men. I was their guide, using the details of my vision to lead the way to the *tzinnor*. Even in the dark, it was easy. I felt pulled to the place as if by a line of force. When we found it, we flung ourselves to the ground and covered ourselves with leaves and boughs so that no sentry on the guard tower could see us as the sun rose. We would have to wait for the water, as my prophecy had advised. In this season, the spring was most active, gushing forth five or six times a day in massive surges that could last for more than an hour. Only just after it abated would it be safe for us to crawl through the pipe, enter the tunnels and attempt to climb the shaft in the short time it took the underground pool to recharge. If we missed our timing, we risked being caught in a narrows during an onrush of turbulent water. We would be trapped and drowned.

Waiting was difficult. I could smell Yoav's sweat. My own muscles twitched and ached with effort to be still. From the other side of the city we could hear the clash of spear butt on shield and the cries of the armies, taunting each other. We knew that a second, flanking unit was also on the move. David's best fighters were circling from the west, to be ready to rush the Water Gate if our mission succeeded. A third force, mostly retirees and civilians outfitted to look like fighters, was moving to the east, their only role to confuse Araunah.

At last, I heard another, more welcome sound . . . of water forcing its way through earth. The stream, which had been flowing steadily, gave forth a massive arc of water, a surging pulse, followed by another, and another, for almost a full hour. As soon as we were sure the spate was over, we moved. Yoav went first, fast and low, positioning himself where he could see the Yebusite archers pacing the parapet on the tower above us. He was in a crouch, his own arrow nocked, ready to shoot if one of the guards caught sight of him. Fervently, we hoped that would not happen. We did not want to draw eyes to the western wall. Once Yoav was in position, he waited for the archer to turn, then gave a sign. Avishai crawled forward, as swift as a lizard, flattening himself to enter the muddy pipe. I went next.

The distance through the pipe was not long, but the rough rock tore at my greaves, so that my forearms and shins were raw and bleeding. I inched forward as fast as my strength would allow. The pipe was not of uniform size, and when it suddenly narrowed, I had to discipline my mind not to give way to panic. The water, between surges, was just a few inches of gently flowing stream. But I had to push away images of myself, pinned in the dark, unable to go forward or back as the stream swelled again into a mighty throb of water. It did not help that Avishai, ahead of me, was slighter in build, and might be able to negotiate a girdle of rock where I might be entrapped. I gulped the air when finally the pipe opened into the tunnel, and unfurled myself to stand upright. The tunnel was mostly living rock, a natural fissure, widened only where necessary by hammer and chisel. We felt our way along cool, moist stone, moving toward the telltale shaft of light that indicated the place of ascent.

It was a dispiriting sight—sheer curved walls of slick wet stone rising vertical from the man-made pool that was Yebus's wartime water store. We did not speak, unsure if the tunnel above was guarded near the shaft, or only, as we hoped, at the tunnel entrance. Zadok had maintained that only a small, elite unit was entrusted with the secret of the pool, just men sufficient to provide a discreet guard in peacetime and to fetch the water during war. Our hope was that those few had been called to duty on the eastern walls.

Avishai pointed up into the dark. High above us, in the ceiling of the cavern, there was a ring of iron set into the rock. In wartime, when the pool was in use, a rope threaded through this ring, so that a large waterskin could be lowered to draw from the pool. Our plan for scaling the shaft relied on that ring. I hoped it was firmly set. Avishai had a length of strong, slender rope wound around his person. I helped him unspool it as we waited for the rest of the men. By the time Yoav, bringing up the rear, joined us, Avishai had the rope furled on the edge of the pool, and had attached the sturdy string, which he had sewn into one end, to the shaft of an arrow. He passed it silently to Ira of Tekoa, who was the best archer in the army. Ira nocked the arrow to his bow, aimed, took a deep breath, exhaled and let the arrow fly. It fell a hairbreadth short, so we had to retrieve it and try again. On the second attempt, it soared straight and true, carrying the rope after it. We all of us grasped the other end as Yoav began the ascent, hand over hand, his strong torso quivering with the burden of his own weight. When he was level with the rim of the shaft, he swung his body, using his weight like a pendulum, until he could reach out and grasp for the rim. On the first try, he missed his grip, and flew back out over the drop, his arm flailing. On the second try, he was able to grasp an outcrop of stone for a moment, but his grip was not firm enough, and again he swung out over the drop, swearing under his breath. Finally, on the third try, he strained to keep hold of the rim, and flung himself onto the ledge, where he lay for a moment, gasping like a beached fish. Then we heard him scrambling to affix the rope, so that it dangled over the edge, allowing the rest of us an easier ascent, able to brace our feet against the slick wall as we pulled ourselves up, hand over hand.

I said "easier," but I struggled to inch my way up the slippery rock face, my hands rubbed raw and my muscles quivering with the effort. I was shaking like a jellyfish when I finally made the lip of the basin and Avishai's strong arms drew me safely over the edge. Luckily, depleted as I was, I had little to do with the rest of that day's work. Yoav's fighters surprised the two tunnel guards and dispatched them with short swords, swiftly, with no more than a grunt issuing forth as their last mortal utterance. When we came out into the light, we ran to the foot of the wall where the archers held the water gate. Their backs were turned, all their attention fixed beyond the walls to where David's vanguard maneuvered, just out of range of their arrows. Ira and Shem, our two best archers, nocked arrows and took aim, thinking to shoot the guards as they stood. But Yoav, too honorable to shoot a man in the back, called up to them, so that they turned and were facing their doom as the arrows pierced them. Ira took his man through the eye. He crumpled in place and dropped out of sight below the crenellations. Shem struck his through the throat. He scrabbled vainly at the arrow through his neck and staggered forward until he reached the low parapet and fell. He landed in a crash of armor and a thud of broken flesh right at my feet, a red mist rising. I stepped through it and ran to help work the winches that drew back the big gates. David's vanguard surged through, surprising the Yebusites from the rear as the main army then swarmed the walls. The town was ours by sunset.

It was the first time I saw the pearly moon rise over these walls, where the rough-hewn siege ladders leaned all askew in the aftermath of the battle, some rungs splintered under the rush of the ascent. David stood on the ramparts, bathed in starlight. He was leaning on the walls, his arms outstretched on either side of him, the blood and dirt of the fighting crusted on his skin. The night wind lifted his sweat-dampened hair. His face was smeared with grime and flecked with blood, but it was radiant. He turned to me, smiling. "Here, it begins," he said.

I thought of him a few years earlier, prone in the ashes of Ziklag with his outlaw band about to mutiny. If that was the lowest pit of his existence, then this moment, on the ramparts of the city he had made his own, might mark the summit. I stood there, and breathed in the night air, and tried to take in every detail.

From below us in the town came the sounds of soldiers carousing, their wine-drenched voices rising in tuneless victory songs. While there was weeping and keening from the houses of the fallen, there were no screams, no shrill cries of pain and fear. David had ordered restraint, and his army was obeying him. There would be no rapes this night, no wanton killings. He had already renamed the town. It was Ir David now—the City of David. It was our home, the heart of our nation, the seat of his kingship. He intended to bind up the wounds of the defeated, not lay them open. All who surrendered had been allowed to go to their homes, Knaanite and Hittite alike. He had spared even the life of Araunah, allowing him to retire from the city, unarmed and under guard, and go to his farmhouse on the mountain above the town.

I wish I could write that this night marked an end to the bloodshed. It did not. As soon as word of our victory reached the Plishtim cities on the coastal plain, they mobilized their several armies and marched on us, thinking to attack before David's power in the new capital could be consolidated. I had a vision—debilitating, painful—exhorting him to go out and meet them on the plain. So that is what we did, fighting and routing their armies piecemeal before they could join forces and come at us as one. Even after that, they remained a thorn in our side, refusing to quit the harassment of our settlements in the Shefala. But over the years, we pushed them back, and farther back, until all that was left of once mighty Philistia was a handful of shrunken towns that could barely support the fighters to guard their walls. By the end of it, many of their best men came to us, begging David to hire them into his service. We have a unit of their mercenaries who fight for us now.

There were other victories. I have no wish to relive each of those battles, when we marched out of Ir David to subdue Moav, or Edom, or the Ammonites. But even though I wish to forget those years, I cannot. In dreams, the images come to me. Muwat says I sometimes cry out, in nightmares from which I cannot wake. Other times, I do wake, my heart racing and the sweat standing cold on my brow. On those nights, the dark is full of the cries of the dying and my only relief comes with the rising sun.

Whatever it takes. What was necessary. Ten violent years, and then, at last, our vassal states stretched from the border of Mitzrayim to the edge of the Two Rivers. Finally, we were notorious enough to give our enemies pause. They looked at the heavy cost of warring against us, and came suing for peace. The plunder from the defeated—their gold shields, their horses—enriched us. Treaty seekers offered gifts of gold, of alabaster—fine vessels such as we had not seen. There were cups of chased metal and swords inlaid with ivories. We were no longer a collection of impoverished herders and farmers, but a people whose trade thrived and whose friendship was bid for and highly prized.

David drew to him everyone who could help in this making and mending. He did not care about tribe of origin, or even if one was Ivrim. Our high priest, Aviathar, the only survivor of Shaul's massacre at Nov, was given to understand that he would share ritual duties with the Yebusite Zadok, and that devotions and sacrifices would retain any elements of their style of worship that did not conflict with our own. Yoav was allowed to fulfill his ambition, to be general of the army of Israel, but David brought up one of Avner's promising young lieutenants, Benaiah, to command the growing corps of foreign recruits and mercenaries. David was impressed, in particular, with the men who came to us from across the sea, from an ancient island kingdom where youths trained for war by vaulting bulls. This was a dangerous sport, requiring great athleticism, speed and courage. It was from among these strong and graceful young foreigners that David selected his handpicked bodyguard. This proved wise, as it showed no favoritism to the men of Yudah or of Benyamin.

As the wars dwindled to skirmishes and our strength grew, David was able to spend less time with military commanders and more with the engineers and overseers who were fanning out through the land, digging cisterns, making roads, fortifying, connecting and generally making a nation out of our scattered people.

It was a time when any man could seek and find justice. I think that David's own experiences as an outlaw, a falsely accused man, had made him resolve to deal justly with his subjects now that he had the power to do so. In those years, he never tired of hearing suits, and would listen for hours to all sides of a grievance, taking pleasure in teasing out the threads of a dispute and weighing all the evidence laid before him. Any who felt dissatisfied by the decisions of the elders at their own town gates could appeal their matters to David himself, and know they would be fairly heard.

He composed some of his best music at this time, training choirs to praise the Name in musical rites that drew great crowds to worship. He would join with the choirs at such times, his soaring voice carrying the melody, enriching the harmony, his face lifted up to the heavens and lit by the ecstasy of his ever-renewing bond with the divine. As word spread, musicians and singers—men and women both—flocked to his service. You could not walk the lanes without hearing delightful sounds issuing from nearly every casement: lutenists and flute players, singers and drummers. The life of the city moved to the rhythms and melodies of an ever-changing musical score.

There was, as well, the percussion of the building trades. The hectoring scrape of massive ashlars across the ramps. The tolling of iron hammers ringing on reluctant stone. The roar of forges, burning all night to make good the day's wounded tools.

King Hiram of Tyre sent David cedarwood—the fragrant, prized timber of the northern forests—and craftsmen skilled in stone dressing to build for him this fine house. David chose the site, high on the spur, even though at the time it stood outside the wall of the city. This was a bold move that showed his confidence and his vision. Ir David, he declared, was to be double the size of Yebus. He would fill in the gully and push the city west, to the very top of Har Moriah. And there, he said, he would build a shrine for our ark, and bring it home at last to the city at the very heart of the Land. As soon as the first stage of his palace was complete, he gave the order that this be done.

When word came that the ark was within a day's march, we did not sleep, but went to the Gihon spring to purify ourselves. We dressed afterward in fine linen garments that David had ordered for the purpose. These were simple tunics that resembled priestly robes, yet were made more plainly, with no dyes, borders or adornment. David would wear no purple cloth, no symbols of his kingship, when he went to greet the ark. In its presence, we were all of us servants.

We waited at the city gates as the ark approached. It was *sohorhim*, the hour of light, when the outriders came into view, cresting the Mount of Olives. The olive trees had turned their leaves so that the bright undersides shimmered. David gave a great sigh of longing,

almost a groan. And then, in a wincing flash of brightness, the sunlight caught the gilded wingtips of the cherubim atop the ark itself.
The people cheered. David gave the sign, and the choirs he had assembled burst into song. Cymbals, systrums, flutes, lyres, drums—every
musician the city possessed—and there were hundreds—had been
called to raise a joyful noise to the heavens. Soon, the procession was
in the valley, the curtain that shielded the ark rippling in the warm
wind. We could hear the voices of the singing men and women, chant-
ing the words David had composed for the occasion:

> Give praise, proclaim his Name,
> Proclaim his marvels to the nations,
> Sing to him, sing praise to him . . .

David, standing just in front of me, could not keep still. He held his
arms out from his sides, his fingers stretching down to the earth,
quivering as if some great energy were passing up and through them.
He was breathing fast and deep. Suddenly, he raised his chin, and gave
a cry—like a paean, but higher, sweeter—rich notes that filled every
heart with gladness. Then he was loping down the hill, as wild as a
boy, as ardent as a lover, sprinting toward the ark. When he reached
it, he cast himself down in full prostration, his arms stretched out as
if in the widest embrace. It was a lover's moment, between him and
the Name, the great One who had blessed him, kept him and brought
him to this moment. I knew how he prayed: I had felt its ardency.
Now all his people felt it. I could hear the sighs and the cries all
around me, as the power of it moved and stirred the crowd. When
David rose to his feet, he did so as if lifted by strong and tender arms.
Then he began to dance.

 Such a dance I had never seen, and will not see again. Writhing,
stamping, leaping, his face lit with ecstasy, leading the way before the
ark in its procession toward the city gates. The crowds surged to fall
in behind him, the cheers and the swell of music deafening. We all of

us were caught in the power of his dance, filling the streets with a swarm of prancing, joyful bodies.

After a time, I could not keep up. My lungs were starved for breath, my chest burned, my feet were raw and bruised from the abrading stones. Yet David leaped ahead, whirling in the air. The light linen of his tunic flew aside, revealing the long line of hard muscle that ran from hip to thigh. He had recently turned forty, but his limbs remained lean and strong, traced over with the fine white puckers of scar tissue from old wounds. He did not care that he exposed himself. He was far away, lost in the dance. There was no regard for kingly dignity, for manly self-mastery. This was naked joy, uncontained, abandoned. He had let go of self. He was a bright flare, a blur of stamping, springing, whirling animal energy. I realized then that what I witnessed was pure worship—beautiful—and I let go of my own inhibitions and danced on, catching the gladness that flew from him like sparks.

He had ordered a pavilion built atop Har Moriah. Cloths of the finest weave billowed from gleaming copper stanchions. He danced the ark into the pavilion, and then bowed out before the high priest, who made his lonely way to the recesses of the inner curtained enclave where he alone, purified in stringent ritual, might enter. There was incense and the fragrance of cedarwood from the sacrificial fires, and the sharp, delicious scent of the burned offerings. David turned, such a smile of pure delight upon his face, so that a well of feeling brimmed up in me—and I think in all of us who stood close to him. Any reservations or misgivings about the acts that had brought us to this day seemed to melt like the fat on the altar of sacrifice, to rise up like vapor and blow away.

He clapped me on the shoulder—his hand was hot, heavy—and we turned toward the palace. He had arranged distributions of honey cakes and fine loaves to all the people, and as he passed through the crowd they reached out to kiss his hand or the hem of his tunic. There was so much laughter, and yet my cheeks were wet with tears. A smiling servant held the door for us, and David turned and waved to the cheering crowd before we stepped into the cool interior. I was hot and spent, yet he flared with energy, and though his chest rose and fell, gulping great breaths, and though he was misted all over with a fine sweat, the scent of him was as sweet and fresh as mown hay. His face shone and his flesh gleamed. I did not want the moment to end, so I walked with him, the laughter still on our lips. When we reached the foot of the staircase that led to his apartments, we saw Mikhal on the landing above, seated in the window recess. Here, I thought, glad-hearted. Here is the moment of reconciliation. She's waiting for him, ready at last.

"Did you see?" His voice—his beautiful voice—rang high and light. He bounded up the stairs toward her, his arms open for an embrace. She stood, but instead of stepping toward him, she drew back, her face pinched in a frown of revulsion. He, lost in his own joy, did not mark it. He reached out and grasped her. She pushed him off with a violent shove. He was unprepared for it, and lost his footing. He would have fallen on the steps had I not been behind him to extend a steadying hand.

She spoke then, her voice low and intimate. "Didn't the king of Israel do himself honor today?" She tossed her head, her eyes narrowed. "Exposing himself before the slave girls of his subjects like a whore."

David's head snapped back as if she had slapped him. The light in his face turned ashen, his joyful expression erased.

"It was before the Name," he said plaintively. Then he gathered himself and raised his voice.

"It was before the Name, who chose me"—he thumped his chest—"*me*, instead of your father and all your family. Who appointed *me* ruler over his people Israel!" He took a step toward her, menacing. Even though I felt myself shrinking under his gathering rage, I reached out and laid a warning hand on him. I thought at that moment he might strike her dead.

He shook me off. "I *will* dance before the Name, and 'dishonor' myself even more, and be low in my own esteem." He brought his face close to hers, and dropped his voice to an insinuating whisper. "But among the slave girls you speak of, I will be honored!"

He pushed her aside. He walked on, holding himself stiffly, his demeanor now unmistakably regal. She stood on the landing, staring after him. A slight tremor shivered through her body. Our eyes met. Hers were blank, empty. For years, she had nursed that serpent of anger, coiled tight inside her, eating everything else away. Now, at last, she had unleashed it. It was gone, and had left no spark behind. I turned and followed the king. As I closed the door to his private apartment he did not even turn. "I never want to look at her face again. See to it."

"Shall I send her back to Palti?" I should not have asked. I knew it the minute the words were out. I should have just acted. But the words could not be unsaid.

"Never! She remains *my* wife. Mine." He thumped his chest, but his hand was shaking. "I have given her every chance. For years I've put up with her coldness, spent time with her, even though there was nothing in it for me. Not a kind word or a soft look, much less the chance to make a child, even though she knew how much I wanted it, and she must have known it would be in her interest. She could have been mother of my heir. So be it. I'm done with her. But here she will stay until she dies. Have her put away in some dark corner, and warn her, upon her life, to keep out of my way."

That encounter upon the stairs reverberated for many months following. In the midst of his triumph, in his moment of most intense joy, Mikhal had succeeded in rupturing his heart. She had torn an opening, and hatred flooded into it. Hatred and memory. Mikhal's insult recalled to him an earlier slight, delivered by her elder sister Merav. I do not think David had wasted an instant pining over Merav until that moment. Merav, who had objected when Shaul, in his first infatuation with David, had promised her to him in marriage. David had preferred Mikhal—flattered by her affection, attracted by her resemblance to Yonatan. But now, in the base mood brought about by Mikhal, he chose to recall this older insult.

This bitterness spread like a stain on those golden months of making and building. He became obsessed with Merav, and sent to know how many sons she had with her husband Adriel. When he learned that there were five boys, he began to fret over it. The boys were young, even the eldest barely fighting age. But I could see him counting it over, figuring how long he might have before one of them could pose a plausible alternative, if elements of discontent in the Israelite north should ever coalesce and begin to cast about for a descendant of Shaul to raise up against him.

Of course, we had one such descendant with us, eating every day at the king's own table. David had kept faith with his promise to Yonatan, that he would be guardian of his house. Unfortunately—or, maybe, fortunately, since there could be no rivalry with the king's own sons—Yonatan's "house" consisted of just one living boy, a poor lad sorely afflicted with club feet, who could not walk unassisted. David was unfailingly kind to the boy. And why should he not be, since such a one could never pose the slightest threat to his kingship.

To Merav, he had made no oath and owed no kindness. Whenever he had too much to drink, he would fall to cursing both women, Mikhal and Merav. I would try to divert him, stating the plain fact that neither woman was anything to him. It was on such occasions that I missed Avigail. She, perhaps, might have found the way to convince David that such old and minor slights—a young girl's foolishness; a bitter woman's insult—were not worth the time of a powerful monarch, who should be attending to greater matters, such as his treaties and his borders. I tried to tell him this, and sometimes, for a time, it seemed he listened.

But my arguments came back to haunt me not long after, when a delegation of Givonites came to negotiate their treaty. With David and his clan, they said, they had no issue. But from Shaul's tribe, a blood debt was outstanding. Shaul had tried to exterminate them, in violation of ancient oaths.

Somehow, by indirection, David led the Givonite delegation to think about Shaul's grandsons. I was at the audience, and I sensed his manipulation, but I did not at first grasp where it was leading. He pretended he had let slip the fact that the five boys lived and thrived on a thinly defended rural estate, and switched the subject to other matters. But later, at meat, he somehow brought the conversation back to blood debts, and their gravity, and the long tradition among our tribes that allows for satisfaction without reprisal. I saw the leader of the Givonite delegation exchange glances with his associates. I looked at the king. Fox, I thought. He will get the Givonites to do his work, and not for any blood debt. Merely a debt owed to his vanity and wounded pride. I will speak to him later, I thought. I will get him to make clear to these men that the family of Shaul is under his protection. But as I readied myself to confront him on the matter, I decided against it. It was not certain what the Givonites would do, with his tacit sanction or without it. And if these heirs were not removed, and they grew up and later became a threat, David would have to kill them himself, which would bring opprobrium. I decided to let the matter rest, and accept the outcome.

So the Givonites hunted down Merav's boys. They carried them off to Givon, where they executed them horribly, impaled side by side on a mountaintop.

When word came of the manner of the deaths, I felt ill, disgusted at myself for not acting to try to prevent these killings. David feigned dismay. When he did so in public, I let it pass. But when, in a private moment, he began to tell me how saddened he was, I could not let him go on.

"You can tell the world that," I said quietly. "Indeed, you *must* tell the world that," I said. "But I know how you brought this to pass, and I know why you did—*all* the reasons, political and personal." I stopped there. I was on unsteady ground. "I did not counsel you against it, and so I may not condemn you for it. Yet these youths were innocent. I think you would do well to make some public act that separates you from it."

He took my advice; indeed, he embraced it, and made a great business of it. He dispatched a party to retrieve the boys' remains. At the same time, he sent an honor guard to Yavesh, to disinter the remains of Shaul and his sons. He had them all buried together, with great ceremony, in Shaul's father's tomb in the land of the Benyaminites. There, he wept once again, most sincerely, for the loss of Yonatan and the memory of Shaul as he had once been. On the outside, all of it seemed well done. But turn over the leaf, and a canker stained it. He did not send for Merav, nor did he send to her to offer condolences. The rot was there, for those who wished to see it. For myself, I fashioned it as one more necessary thing, done to secure the kingship and build the Land. But I never sent to inquire what became of Merav. I imagine her, blank-eyed like Mikhal, doing long, bitter penance for insulting a youth who became a king, living out her empty days in grief and loneliness.

My days, by contrast, were never empty. My life took its measure from the pace that David set, and in those years, it was a demanding one. I was busy in his service, high in his confidence. Over time, as I have said, we were less and less at war, and I was glad of that. In the lengthening intervals between campaigns, I served as counselor in his handpicked inner circle, and when I was not needed at his side, I spent my time in conversation with the delegates who came to us from other lands, trying to learn from them what I could, gleanings that might serve the king in the future in ways that were not yet clear.

And so we went on, until the skirmish with the Plishtim, about which I have written, when David faltered for a moment and Avishai stepped in to save his life. In fear and in love, the decision was made that he should no longer lead the army in the field. Like all who cared for him, I was glad of it. But as I have set down, I was blind, and did not foresee either the evil or the good that this decision would beget. When I began to write this chronicle at that time, I knew it for a turning point in David's life. But I did not then know that we stood on the very brink of a crisis that would rend his soul and alter his destiny.

I will never forget the day—the stifling, drowsy day—when my eyes first opened to the truth.

XII

I'd often thought that if an enemy wanted to spy on David, it would be a simple business. One did not need to penetrate his secret councils or insinuate a man into his bodyguard. All one needed was a pair of ears and access to the royal precincts. Just to eavesdrop upon his singing was to develop an accurate idea of his state of mind. I have heard people say of a musician that he poured his heart and soul out. In most cases this is exaggeration. Not so in the case of David.

Since his reckless dalliance with the wife of Uriah, I had noticed a distinct brightening in the nature of his musical selections. When the choirs of singing men and women would come in, after meat, he would ask them for songs of celebration, or victory anthems. His own compositions of that time were mighty things that reflected the building of the city, constructed of solid, symmetrical sounds, perfect fifths stacked one atop the other like the confident edifices of a powerful and joyous king.

The year had advanced swiftly from the mild days of planting. The full heat of the ripening season was upon us like a millstone, crushing the juice out of everybody. In a gesture that had won him much love from the people, David had instructed the foremen to rest the laborers in the heat of the day. He said this edict was to honor the memory of our ancestors, who had toiled in the furnace heat of Mitzrayim. Those who could—the high officials, the more senior of the king's servants—also took advantage of the noonday hush and ceased their own work for an hour or two. A stillness would fall over the private quarters of the palace as the lucky ones took their rest.

Unlike the others, I welcomed the heat. It brought to mind the hot afternoons of my childhood in Ein Gedi. I liked to walk in the garden at that still hour, listening to the low buzz of the bees, enjoying the sharp scent of the dry, fallen cedar needles and the wild zatar that fingered its way between the cracks of the paving stones. From the king's rooms, the notes of the harp drifted. He was composing, playing through passages, repeating some measures, changing a note here and there. I sat on a bench and rested my back against the warm wall, closing my eyes and letting the music caress my ears. I must have fallen into a doze. I was in some vague, happy dream or reverie. But into that dream crept a note of unease. I shook off sleep, and became aware that the music had changed. David was working with strange intervals. I listened more closely. Not fifths now. Tritones. Uncanny sounds that robbed the music of its power to delight. I became aware of the stone at my back, its roughness. I shifted my weight to relieve the sting of a jutting edge of rock. The sun's glare stabbed my eyes, a blade of pain. My sight blurred. I raised my hands to my ears, trying to shut out the dissonance. And then I was on my feet.

As soon as he saw me in the doorway, his hands fell from the strings. He righted the harp and stood. With a gesture, he dismissed the courtiers who had been his audience. As they left the room, his eyes, haunted, scanned my face.

"So you know." It was a statement, not a question. His voice was low. "I suppose you've always known. You warned me I would be found out. And now, as always, events prove you."

He turned and paced, picking up an alabaster vase and turning it in his hands, examining it so that he would not have to meet my eye.

"How did you learn that the wife of Uriah is pregnant?" I demanded. "Have you seen her?"

"Of course not. I told you I would have nothing to do with her after that night, and I've kept to that. This morning, she sent her maidservant to the open audience. She was wearing the jewel I gave to her mistress, so I would know who she was. I contrived a word in private. What can I do, Natan? It is as you said. This was not well done, to take a man's wife who fights for me—and bravely—while I sit here at home, at my leisure. The army will take it ill. I don't want an enemy in Uriah, especially not now, when the battle goes in our favor, and largely because of Uriah's own valor, and the discipline of his men."

"There is your answer," I said. I could see only one way out. Base and dishonorable, but the only way to protect the king. "Send for Uriah. Offer him leave, as a reward for his good service. She can't be far along with this child." I counted it in my mind. "Not yet even two months? If he lies with her soon enough, then the child can be passed off as his own." I did not add that the child would be a *mamzer*. Nothing could change that. And David, of all people, knew what this deception would mean.

"Think you so?" His brow creased, considering. "I suppose it might serve. You know, of course, that officers take an oath to be continent during a campaign. But if she were my wife, and I away for two months . . . Uriah won't be the first to break that oath. I told you she was beautiful. I'd give a lot to see her myself, what the bloom of a pregnancy might do to . . ."

I suppose he saw my look of censure for he did not complete the sentence. He strode to the door and told the servant waiting outside to fetch a royal messenger. When he turned back to me, the creases on his brow were gone.

Rabbah, in the hills across the Yarden, was no very great distance for a messenger well mounted, and Uriah presented himself in the audience hall four mornings later. David greeted him warmly. Even I, knowing what I knew, found it a flawless performance. He questioned Uriah about the disposition of troops and the battle tactics. Uriah's account did not offer much in the way of useful elaboration on the daily reports of the runners, who were fully briefed by Yoav. But

David also offered Uriah commendations for his part in the suppression of the Ammonites, and made much of him in the hall. After a decent interval, he dismissed him kindly. As Uriah saluted and turned, David added, as if as an afterthought: "Go down to your home and bathe your feet. You have had a long road, and a weary one."

At my suggestion, he sent my Hittite servant Muwat after him, carrying delicacies from the royal larder. Uriah had many Hittites in his household staff and Muwat was friendly with some of them. I had instructed him to linger in the kitchen, on the pretext of waiting to return the royal dishes. It was a good chance to listen an ear to the kitchen gossip, and learn what the household had to say, if anything, about their mistress and her condition.

I was therefore taken aback to find Muwat waiting in my rooms as soon as I returned from the audience hall.

"What's this?" I said. "Why are you not at Uriah's house?"

"He didn't go there. He's in the officers' barracks. He distributed the king's food and wine to them. I think he means to sleep there . . ."

Of course, I thought to myself: the king *would* have to cuckold the only upright man in the army. Uriah intended to keep his vow. He wouldn't even risk laying eyes on his lovely wife. I turned on my heel and went back to the audience hall.

When I whispered the news to David, he cursed. He threw a light mantle over his shoulders and went himself to the barracks. I followed. He entered, and greeted the men with his usual soldierly banter. It was no uncommon thing for the king to be there, and although everyone stood as he entered, after an easy word they went back to their dice games and their wine cups as he made the rounds, speaking by name with this officer and then another until he came to Uriah, and feigned surprise to see him there. "You just came from a long journey—why didn't you go down to your house?"

Uriah stood to greet the king, smiling. He was a handsome man, tall and swarthy, with very fine white teeth and thick dark hair worn in Hittite braids. "The men of Yudah and the men of Israel are camped in the open on the hard ground. My general Yoav has no comfort this night. How, then, can I go home and eat and drink and sleep with my wife?"

David had no choice but to compliment him on his fortitude. They shared a few pleasantries, then David said, "Take at least another day here, resting. Then I will send you back to your brothers in the field."

The next night, David invited Uriah to a feast in his honor. He sat him on his own couch and plied him relentlessly with unwatered wine. I could see that Uriah was reluctant, at first, to drink so much, but he could scarcely refuse the king's many toasts. Soon enough, the quantity of drink played fool with his restraint, and he downed cup after cup until it was plain that he was inebriated. At a very late hour, he stumbled out, once again attended by Muwat. Once again, however, even drunk, he refused to walk down to his house, and passed out on a mat in the barracks.

In the morning, when he came to the audience hall to take his leave of the king, David showed no trace of his displeasure. He charged Uriah with orders for Yoav, and as he pressed the rolled, sealed hide into Uriah's hand, he covered it with his own, and embraced him. Then he raised his voice to the assembly: "For there is no man in my army in whom I have more trust. Truly, Uriah is the very model of a soldier—a man of duty, discipline, courage and loyalty. Go with my blessing, and bring us the victory!"

What is he going to do now, I asked myself as I fretted and paced, waiting for him to call for me, to ask for advice, to work out a new plan. I dreaded the call, because I had nothing to offer him. It would be a matter of weeks—a month, two at the most—and the pregnancy would be patent. Uriah would know the child was not his, and what then?

When David did call for me, others were present. I would wait impatiently through the discussion of minor suits and civic projects, expecting David to ask me to stay when the others were dismissed.

But he gave no indication that he wanted me, even though I lingered behind until it became conspicuous and, no sign having been given, I had to withdraw.

A week passed in this way. On the eighth day, I was sitting fretfully through morning audience when Yoav's messenger arrived to deliver the latest news from the front lines. The king called him forward as soon as he saw him, and commanded him to speak.

"My lord, the men of Rabbah sallied out against us into the open; we drove them back to the very gate of their city. But the archers on the wall were in range by then. Six officers fell."

David struck the arms of his chair and jumped to his feet. "Six? What was Yoav thinking, to send them within range of the archers on the wall?"

"My lord, the sally threatened our positions. He had to drive them back." The messenger paused a beat, and looked down at the floor. "Your general Yoav said to be sure to report that your brave servant Uriah the Hittite is among the fallen."

David fell back on his great chair and covered his face with his hand. I had seen it done better. I thought then, as I stood there, of all the times I had witnessed him mourn over deaths of great benefit to him. The butchery of Shaul. The murders of Avner and Ish Boshet. The impaled sons of Merav. I had witnessed him rend his clothes even for deaths, like my father's, that he had done with his own hand. I had seen him tear his garment so many times it was a sudden wonder to me that he had an intact tunic to lay upon his back.

I recalled Uriah as I'd last seen him, here in this hall. I recalled a rolled, sealed hide. Uriah's hand, reaching to take it from the hand of the king. As the pain pierced my brow, I saw that same hide, unrolled on the rough-hewn log that served as a table in Yoav's tent at Rabbah. I saw Yoav's face in the candlelight, frowning as he strove to make out the writing. The hand was crude, not the work of a trained scribe. As Yoav grasped the meaning, his face registered shock, and then disgust. He crumpled the hide under his fist and swept it to the ground.

Place Uriah in the front line where the fighting is most fierce, then have the men fall back and leave him undefended.

Words that the king could not entrust even to his loyal scribe, Seraiah. Not battle orders. A death warrant, written by the king himself, delivered by the hand of the convicted. And Yoav, alive on the king's sufferance since the murder of Avner, had no choice but to give the order. I see Uriah's face as it registers what is being asked of him. A questioning look crosses his creased brow. He repeats the order, to make sure Yoav is clear about what he has asked. Yoav, on edge, masks his self-disgust in a show of anger, and barks his commands tersely. Uriah bows his head, salutes, and exits the tent. An hour later, he is at the walls, his shield arm raised against the hail of arrows raining down upon him.

The vision faded. Through the thinning images I saw that David still sat as if stricken, his face covered. There were sighs and expressions of regret running in murmurs around the hall. Uriah was a well-liked man, an admired officer.

David rubbed his hands over his face and stood up. He walked toward the messenger, who flinched. One does not want to bring bad news to a king. But David laid his hands on the messenger's shoulders and held him in his gaze. "Take Yoav this message: Do not be distressed by this matter. The sword always takes its toll. Press your attack on the city and destroy it." He looked around the hall and raised his voice. "So will these fine soldiers be avenged!"

Everyone in the hall gave a great cry then, and chants of victory filled their mouths. I did not join them. My mouth tasted of vomit.

Whatever it takes. What was necessary. But this—the killing of Uriah, and the good men who fell beside him—these deaths had not been necessary to gain a kingdom or to secure it. These deaths had not been necessary to anything other than David's own ungirt appetite. It was simple abuse of power.

I turned on my heel and left the audience hall. I did not stop at the cedar doors, or even at the courtyard gate. The guards there must have read my face, for they scrambled to open the way before me. I walked through the town, returning no greetings or salutes, and strode out through the Dung Gate, past the threshing floor, where women were at work tossing the ripe grain. The chaff blew into my eyes, stung my cheeks. I staggered on, unseeing, into the olive groves. When the trees concealed me, I raised my face to the burning sky. What had I done with my life, to give it into the service of this evil?

I had seen myself as a man in the hand of the Name—serving the king chosen to lead his people in this Land. But what kind of god could will this baseness, this treachery? What kind of nation could rise under such a leader? If David was a man after this god's own heart, as my inner voice had told me often and again, what kind of black-hearted deity held me in his grip?

I grasped a hank of my hair and pulled it out by the bloody roots. Then I bent and gathered a handful of the dry yellow soil and smeared it on my throbbing scalp. I looked up and located the hot white sun, then turned south and west, toward the Valley of Salt. I walked until my legs turned to jelly, then I flung myself down under the flimsy protection of a thorn bush, and waited to die.

I wept until there was no water in my body left to spare for tears. I stopped sweating. At first, thirst was an itch, then it became an ache. My mouth became sticky, then dry, like dead leaves. My skin shriveled and aged before my eyes. There was a burning pain in my calves. Visions came: thick, swift, relentless. There was no rest from them, nowhere to turn away. At night, they spun and swirled out of the star-encrusted sky. By day, they were shadows on the sheer faces of cliffs, murmurs in the hot breath of the wind.

I dreamed that a passing herdsman dribbled water onto my parched lips, and in the dark I awoke to find a full waterskin lying by my hand. I had strength enough to set my lips to the mouth of it and drink. I walked on then. Walked till my sandals broke and the knife-sharp rocks bit my soles. My burned skin shed itself in silver sheets, my flesh sagged on the frame of my bones. I drank from muddy seeps; I ate insects and worms. Some days, I walked in a press of muttering, shrieking ghosts. The butchered Moavites writhed once again on the ground, the shrieking horses stumbled. The Plishtim soldier whose neck I had crushed rose up and stood before me, holding his head upon his shoulders with his two bloody hands. On those days I was sure I was in the grip of madness. But then the crowds would depart from me, turning their backs, spinning away in a hundred different directions. Then came the others, who were not ghosts but people who yet walked quick upon the earth. I saw them not as they were but as they would be. They did not see me—indeed, at times they walked right through me, engaged in acts or conversations of which I was not part. I understood that I was being shown the future: shards of what would come to be. Often, I cried out for the pain of it. But other times, I was comforted, because I saw, for an instant, the pattern of the whole.

And then, one night, I woke from a restless sleep to find the world alight with the cold radiance of the full moon. I had been in the desert a full month. I was a hollowed-out gourd, as light as air. It was over. I had been shown all that I needed to see. I knew what I needed to do. The painful future stretched out before me. David would have the throne, the crown, the line of descendants that the Name had promised him. But for the rest of his life, he would be scalded by the consequences of his choices. My task would be twofold: to stand up to him, and to stand by him. To awaken his conscience, and to salve the pain this would cause him. To help him to endure through the hard days and years that lay ahead of him.

My shadow leaped out before me, as huge as a giant. With a vast effort, I put one foot before the other, and began the long walk home.

XIII

"**Y**ou look like a stream of camel piss! I can see right through you!" He put his hard, muscled arms around my shoulders to embrace me, and I winced. He drew back. He held me at arm's length and looked me up and down. "I'm afraid you'll snap in half! What have you done to yourself? They told me you were called into the desert by one of your visions. I'm glad you've been called back—while there's still something left of you!" He took me by the arm, solicitous, as if I were an invalid. "Natan will take some food and drink in my quarters. Bring wine and roast goat—no, wait. Not goat. Too rich, after such a long fast. You need to go slowly, build up your strength. Bring bread and laban, zait and zatar—and some of those good red grapes from Ammon."

All the way to his quarters, the words spilled from his lips. He was alight, joyful. Even his steps seemed to bounce, as if he were dancing through his life. "So much has happened while you were gone. You know Yoav called me to Rabbah? Yes! They wanted me—the army did—to finish off the Ammonites and take the royal city. Yoav had done all the hard work of course. He captured the water supply, so it was only a matter of time . . . but the thing is, Natan, the army—my army—they wanted me back. They wanted me to lead them to victory. They wanted it to be won in my name. I wish you'd been there when we took the crown off the head of their idol and placed it on my head. I'll tell you—I wasn't prepared for it." He gave a great, joyful bark of laughter. "It weighed a talent! Pure gold, and the gemstones . . . I'll have them bring it so you can look, later . . .

"We've filled the grain stores and the treasury. Can't count how many mule trains crossed the Yarden. We had to build floating platforms. Everyone who fought is rich now. And the families of the fallen, too. Slaves . . . we've got the workforce now for every kind of project. Not just the people of Rabbah—all the Ammonite towns fell, once word got out. I spared their lives, even though they'd resisted. Did you hear about that? It was well done—helped get the others to surrender. You've never seen people so happy to be enslaved. They were expecting us to burn them alive and throw their infants on the sword. Well, why wouldn't they? They'd heard about the Moavites. But that was necessary. This time, I saw we could do differently. We've set them to brick making, and the skilled ones are doing ironmongery for us—axes, threshing boards. We will see some changes now. We'll double the size of this city as I dreamed we would, but in half the time. We'll make it a wonder. I have ideas, Natan. I've missed you! There's so much I want your advice on. . . . Look, look at this . . ." He drew me by the hand and pulled me across the room and into an alcove. A low table had been set up there, and upon it was a model for a building such as I had never seen . . . a great work such as they say our ancestors fashioned for the pharaohs. The model was unfinished. It had been made with pieces that could be picked up and moved around, so as to try different effects. David did this as he spoke, taking fluted columns and setting them down in pairs, or in triplets, all the time talking, talking . . .

"I thought, how is it that I live in this fine palace while the ark of the Name rests in a tent? We must house it in a temple, don't you see, Natan . . . the finest materials . . . the most majestic walls . . ." He whirled around the table, rearranging the elements. He was so lost in the joy of creation that he did not notice I was still, silent.

Only when the food came in did he snap out of his grandiose planning. We sat before the trays, and he pressed me to eat, but only took a few grapes for himself. He had one in his hand, turning it between thumb and forefinger.

"And, you know, I have a new wife. The widow of my officer Uriah." He shot me a swift glance. I kept my face a mask. "Her name—I don't think you knew it, before. It's Batsheva. She's . . ." A flush had crept up from his neck—his fair skin had always been swift to the blush. Now it was on fire. "I've never had anyone like her, Natan. Ahinoam—I honor her, of course. How not, since she's the mother of my firstborn. And you know I'll always love Avigail. How I miss her! You loved her, too, I know that . . . the two of you, my wisest advisers . . . Maacah is beautiful, but this one . . . Maacah was a state marriage, and with Avigail I always felt like a boy. Batsheva makes me feel like a man." I bit my tongue, trying to hold back a gust of revulsion. Did he really think I needed to hear this? I looked down, struggling to maintain a neutral expression. I must not have succeeded, for he put his hand on my arm. "Look. I know it wasn't well done. And you were right to be against it. But it *is* done. In any case, the child that gave us so much worry. It will be born midwinter."

I said nothing. After a moment's awkward silence, he turned to chattering again about his projects and his plans. Then, out of nowhere:

"So, I am doing all the talking. Tell me what happened to you. Did you see anything interesting out there, alone all that time?"

"Oh, many things," I said. "Things that will be of use to you, no doubt, when the time is right. But I wasn't always alone." I thought of the crowds, the voices. "There was one man, victim of a grave injustice. I wanted to get your opinion on what should be done for him."

"Tell me!" He leaned forward, attentive. He loved to play the judge.

"He was very poor. He had this one little ewe lamb—that was all. No flocks. He raised this lamb in his own hut, with his children. It would share his morsel of bread, even drink from his cup. You've never seen affection like that, between a man and a beast. He'd carry it around, nestled right up to his chest."

"Did he so?" His face had softened. He had entered into the story wholeheartedly. "I did that once, when I was a shepherd, with an orphan ewe. Got very attached. I know what that's like. Go on."

"Then, one day, the richest man in the village, who has

everything—flocks, herds—he gets a visitor, and instead of slaughtering one of his own beasts, he steals that poor man's little ewe, slaughters it, and serves it to his guest."

David threw aside the grape stalk in his hand. "That man deserves to die! Tell me his name! I'll see to it that he pays for that lamb four times over, because he was greedy and had no pity."

"His name?" I said quietly. "You really want to know who he is, that greedy, pitiless man? That man who had everything?"

"As the Name lives, so I do."

"That man is you."

He stood up, knocking the tray so that the grapes fell and rolled across the flagstones.

I stood, too, crushing the grapes under my feet. The red pulp oozed, like wounded flesh. I walked up to him until we were eye to eye. He returned my gaze, insolent. He intends to brazen this out, I thought. He thinks I'm chastising him for adultery. He doesn't realize I know about the murder.

I spoke in a low voice. "You. Given everything. You are a hundred-fold more guilty than the rich man you just condemned. You took more than a man's wife from him. You took his very life." His face changed in a second with the realization that I knew the full extent of his crimes.

I turned abruptly away and strode across the room to the alcove. I looked at the model pieces, the forest of towering columns, the sumptuously scrolled capitals. The arrogance of it nauseated me. I swept my hand across the table, knocking the pieces to the floor and grinding them under my heel. When I spoke again, it was not in my own voice, but the other one. This time, however, I could hear my own words. There was no blinding pain, just coldness as the brutal judgment sprang from my lips.

"The God of Israel says this: *You will never build the temple. You are stained body and soul from your bloodshed and your butchery. Therefore, that great and holy task is not for you. I anointed you king of Israel. I rescued you from the hand of Shaul. I gave you Israel and Yudah. If that were not enough, I would give you twice as much and more. Why, then, have you flouted my commandments? You put Uriah to the sword. You took his wife in adultery. Then know you this: The sword will never depart from your house. I will make a calamity against you within your own house. I will take your wives and give them to another man before your very eyes and he will sleep with your wives under this very sun. You acted in the dark, but this I will make happen in the broad light of day, in the sight of all Israel!"*

There was a silence in the room so complete I could hear the hushed footfalls of a servant's bare feet in the passageways and the clop of a donkey's hooves passing in the street below. David stood motionless, flushed. His eyes glittered. His fists clenched at his side. He raised them, balled, the muscles of his forearms jumping. He will kill me now, I thought. Then he raised his hands to his head and dragged at his hair.

"I stand guilty before the Name."

He dropped to his knees and bowed his head, covering it with his arms as if to fend off a blow. His body shook. He wept. I put my two hands out and pushed his arms away gently. I rested my two hands in the soft thicket of his hair. I felt a wave of love and pity for him as the knowledge of his future pain surged through me.

I thought of Moshe, speaking to our ancestors after he transmitted the law to them. "I have set both before you, the blessing and the curse," he said. "Life and death. Therefore, choose life."

David's time of choice was behind him now, irrevocably. He would know both blessing and curse, each in the fullest possible measure. Everything had happened to him. Everything would happen to him. Every human joy. Every human sorrow. *Pay four times over,* he had said. In his own words. And so it would come to pass. For the one life he had taken, four of those he loved would be swept away from him in violent ruin.

"Listen to me." The voice was my own. I placed my hand under his chin and raised his wet face. "These things I have foretold—they are not all of them to happen to you yet. You will go on, and become renowned, and do great things and take joy in them. Later, when you are old, you will pay in full. For now, this: the first price you will pay. The baby you will have—this *mamzer* you have made—he will not live. Prepare for that. The rest, put out of your mind. Be glad that the Name has remitted your sin and let you live to atone it."

And atone he did. He gave himself fully to the penitent life, fasting, praying, confessing his wickedness and execrating himself in public. He became a better man in the small matters of his days, an even better, wiser king in the greater matters of state. As confession of his misdeeds made the crimes public knowledge, so also did word of my prophecy spread out, first through the city and then across the Land. Our people, who had once taken comfort in Natan's oracle, now spoke instead, in hushed voices, of Natan's curse. If people had been wary of me before, now their aversion became extreme. Common folk would cross the street to avoid me; women would draw their mantles across their faces and make the sign against the evil eye.

Only David still sought me out, heaping me with honors and attention. I was the first to hear his song of lamentation and prayerful contrition. For days, weeks, it was the only song that he would sing. I believe it was one of the finest he ever composed.

> *Purge me with hyssop till I am pure;*
> *wash me till I am whiter than snow . . .*
> *Hide your face from my sins;*
> *blot out all my iniquities.*
> *Fashion a pure heart for me . . .*
> *Save me from bloodguilt . . .*
> *You do not want me to bring sacrifices;*
> *You do not desire burnt offerings;*
> *You desire the sacrifice of a sorrowful spirit;*
> *You will not despise*
> *a crushed and contrite heart.*

So he sang. And so, I suppose, he believed. And yet, as I had told him, Yah did demand a sacrifice of him. Bloodguilt demanded a blood price.

XIV

In winter, a few days after the child was born, the king sent for me. I stopped short at the door. Batsheva was there, the child nestled sleepily against her breast. I had not expected that.

She had her head down, her back half turned to me. But even from that partial view, I could see that she was, as David had said, a striking woman: creamy skin, a glossy fall of obsidian hair, which she wore unbound and uncovered. Even in her loose robe it was possible to discern long, slender legs, a supple rounding of hips, and generous breasts, against which the baby lay, his thick shock of hair bearing fiery witness to his paternity. When David presented her she looked up, and I took a step backward. Her eyes were unexpected: a luminous blue. Also shocking: despite her tall, full figure, the face that gazed up at me was the face of a child. She was very young.

Awkwardly, not knowing how else to greet her, I asked how she did.

Her voice, when she answered, was the breathy voice of a shy girl, barely audible. "Very well, I thank you. Far better than I have a right." She gave a swift smile, very brief. But it was as if the sun had come out. A man might do a lot, I thought, to win that smile.

David cleared his throat. "It's her first, you know. She never had one with . . . him. The midwives said they'd never seen a first come so easily. And I know it's not just words. Ahinoam, Avigail, Maacah, Hagit, Eglah, Avital . . ." He counted them off on his fingers, the wives who had borne him children. "All of them, the first time, long labors. Days, sometimes. But Batsheva . . ." He looked at her and his face softened. "She turned to me at dawn and said she felt the first pain"—so she shared his bed, even in late pregnancy—"and by noon-time they handed me my son." He reached down for the boy. She settled the infant into his large hands, where the baby—a good size for a newborn—suddenly looked rather small. Batsheva's eyes locked with David's for an instant, in the uncomplicated bliss of new parent-hood. But then she bit her bottom lip, and his face darkened.

"We—I—asked you to come because I wanted you to see him." He held out the infant. "See how healthy he is. I—we—we wonder if what . . . you've said, at times, that these prophecies of yours don't always lend themselves to straightforward interpretation. That you see a part, maybe, but not the whole."

"Yes." I nodded. "That was how it used to be." Before the desert visions made everything clear to me.

"What I am asking—what we are asking—is this: Is it certain this boy will die? Is there any room, in what you saw, what you were shown, to give us hope?"

I looked from one to the other of them. Their eyes—dark amber, deep blue—were trained on me like archers' eyes, taking aim at some truth they imagined I held in my heart. I studied the baby in David's hands. Pink-skinned, perfect, his small fists punching the air. I closed my eyes. His arms fell flaccid, spilling out of David's grip. The tiny fists uncurled, the fingers limp, motionless. His skin gray as mortar. Crusts of dried mucus sealed his nostrils, eyelids.

"No hope."

Batsheva gave a cry and raised her fist to her mouth. David sucked in a breath and clutched the infant to his heart.

"You will not have long to wait. It will be soon."

The fever rose the following night. It burned him alive for six days. All through that time, David fasted, lying out in the open, on the cold winter ground.

Courtiers, those who cared for him, came to me, begging me to go to him, to tell him to eat and to take shelter, lest he, too, sicken and die. I did not go, knowing it was fruitless. Yoav did try to reason with him, as did Zadok and Aviathar. But he would not listen.

When the baby died on the seventh day, no one dared to bring him word, worried that he might do something mad and terrible, so great had been his grief during the illness. They were standing there, off at a distance from where he lay, debating it, when I arrived. I don't know if he overheard, or whether my presence was enough to open his eyes to the truth.

He ran a dry tongue over cracked lips. "Is the child dead?" he rasped.

"Yes."

He took a deep breath, and before he had exhaled he was on his feet. "Draw me a bath!" His servants looked at one another, confused. "Now!" he said, brushing the dirt off himself and walking toward the bathhouse. They scurried after him. After bathing, he called for oils to anoint himself, put on fresh linens and went to the tent of the ark, where he prostrated himself. Then he came back to his house and called for Batsheva, I suppose to console her. Later, he ordered a large meal, to which he invited his close counselors.

Yoav sat across from him, clearly perplexed. Finally, he blurted it out, in his blunt soldier's way. "I don't understand you," he said. "When the child was alive you fasted and wept. Now he's dead, you dry your eyes and feast." David put down his chicken leg and wiped his mouth. He spoke with the weary air of a man obliged to explain the obvious. "When the child was alive, I thought, Who knows? The Name might have pity on me, so I fasted and prayed that my son might live. Now he's dead, why should I fast? Can fasting bring him back again?" His eyes filled. "I shall go to him, but he shall never come back to me."

He sent then to have his six living children brought before him, to bring him comfort. The boys were Amnon, Avshalom, Adoniyah, Shefatiah and Yitraam, and his only daughter, full sister to Avshalom, Tamar. I rose and left the room before they arrived. I could not look at them.

I decided, that night, to leave David's household. I knew too much of what was coming to remain there. I asked if I might take rooms outside the palace, and be at his service at need. So he gave me this house across the wadi, nestled in its old groves of olives and almond. He wanted to raze it and build me something grander, with dressed stone and cedar left over from the materials the king of Tyre had sent him. But I said no. As soon as I walked into these plain rooms, I knew that no new house could suit me better. I knew that the large shutters would keep the rooms cool in the heat of summer and let the sun spill in to warm the whitewashed walls in winter. When Muwat flung open the shutters for the first time, the sun flared on the pink flagstones, worn to a soft sheen by generations of feet. It splashed upward, so that I blinked in the glare. When I opened my eyes, I saw him; dark-haired, bright-eyed, the beautiful boy with the grave, thoughtful face. The promise. The reason.

It was the vision of a moment, but I knew, as certainly as I have ever known, that it was a true vision, and that he would come to this house and stand there, in the window. I have no child of my own flesh, called out of the void by love, or pride, or desire. But I saw that I would have a child of the spirit, mine in heart and soul. That I would serve him, as I served his father, until he grew so great in wisdom that he would not need my counsel, and I could live out my waning days in peace, free from the visions and the pain that attended them.

And I knew I would do it right here, in this house, as I have. As I do.

XV

In the month of olive harvest, it was common enough to see strangers on the paths of this mount, carrying staves to strike the boughs
and coarse cloth to catch the ripe fruit. I was sitting on the terrace,
the outer gate open. The shifting light as the clouds passed across the
valley, the silvering of the olives at the noon hour, the glare of the sun
on the stones of the city and its changing profile as the work of building went forward—all of this gave me pleasure.

I had a scroll open on the table in front of me, a work of history
from Mitzrayim. Since my time among the Plishtim, I had become
interested in our neighbors and their gods. But the glyphs of Mitzrayim are difficult, their meanings various and dependent on context.
The hot sun on my back and the low hum of the bees were making
me too drowsy for the effort needed to follow the text.

I noticed two women climbing the path toward my house. I took
them for harvesters, since the trees on the terraces above my house
were heavy with fruit. But as they drew nearer I saw that they carried
neither stave nor burlap.

The path dwindled to a goat track beyond my house; mine was the
last dwelling. I could not think they intended to come to me. There
was no call for women of the town to seek me out. Most of them, in
truth, would go an hour's walk out of their way to avoid me. Except
for Muwat, who handled my simple needs, I lived entirely alone. The
press of people around David, with whom I still spent a good part of

my time, was more human company than I craved. I retreated to my house for solitude, and few around the king lamented my absence. I knew well enough that most people sighed with relief when I left the room.

Still, the women approached. I let the scroll close on itself. Their mantles were plain, undyed homespun, drawn down modestly over their brows. They walked easily even though the way becomes steep near to my house, so I took them to be young women. Only as they drew close did I notice that the leather of their sandals was finely worked.

Muwat had gone to the city market, so I had no choice but to greet them myself. Wearily, I pushed myself up from the table and walked to the open gate to ask their business.

And then the taller one addressed me by name, and I knew that breathy, girlish voice, even though I had heard it only once. Like a dissonant chord, her presence struck an uneasy note. Royal women did not leave the city unguarded, dressed in homespun. I mouthed some rote greeting and ushered her inside. She spoke softly to her serving woman, who nodded and remained on the bench in the garden.

Inside the house, she walked to the window, tossing off her borrowed mantle and letting it fall unregarded to the floor. Underneath she wore a fine linen robe, dyed a pale sky blue, subtly embroidered around the hem and sleeves with a thread of darker blue—the color of her eyes—and belted with silver filigree. Her black hair was caught in a thick twist down her back, tied round by a fine silver fillet.

How dare she come here in this way—duplicitous, disguised—clearly without the knowledge of the king. I waited for her to turn or speak, but she did neither.

"I do not think you came all this way to admire the view," I said coldly.

She turned then. She wore the cringing face of someone who awaits a blow.

"Indeed, Natan, I hardly know why I came." Her lip trembled, and there was a catch in her voice. "I have no cause to expect kindness from you . . . of all people." Her eyes brimmed and tears spilled down her cheeks. She made no move to wipe them away.

"Sit down," I said. The room was sparsely furnished—I preferred it that way—but there was a good couch from the palace that David had sent me as a gift. She took an uncertain step and sat, her spine still very erect even though her shoulders shook. Her entire face—her lovely face—was wet now, and still her eyes welled and overflowed.

"What's happened?" I said, less harshly. "Why have you come to me?"

"I'm carrying another child."

This was unsurprising news. It was well-known that in the second year of their marriage, the king's ardor toward Batsheva had not waned. Muwat reported the chamber servants' gossip: Batsheva was with the king on every night except for the time of the month when she was forbidden, which was when David did his duty by his several other wives.

"Is that so grievous a thing?" I asked. "It's natural, that you think of the last time. But this is different. This infant will not be victim of divine wrath. You need not fear."

"I don't fear divine wrath," she said.

"But you are trembling."

"I fear you, Natan. And I fear the king."

I laughed. "Why would *you* fear the king?"

"Why would I *not* fear him?" She looked up, her face suddenly hard. "Do you think I did not fear, dragged from my home in the dark, to be debauched and discarded?"

I regarded her coldly. Easy enough to cry rape, when you are the one who has invited the seduction. Still, I turned away from that fierce gaze, fingering the writing implements on my table as I replied. "And I suppose there was no private place inside your house where you might have bathed, instead of the rooftop directly overlooked by the king's terrace." My voice dripped with sarcasm. "Of course, you didn't realize. You had no idea you would be seen and admired, invited to his bed. A bored girl with an absent husband; you never entertained the idea that it would be diverting, to be desired by a king."

"How could you think . . ." Her voice was low and furious. "'*In-vited*'?" Her full lips compressed into an ungenerous line. "For someone who sees so much, you are so blind! I went up onto that roof *seeking* privacy. Except for my one maid, Uriah's house servants were all of them male. Most were ex-soldiers, young men in his service who had been injured in some way. He took them in and gave them work. You think it was easy, to be in that house and feel their eyes on me, and my husband far away? I needed to do my ritual purification, and I could not clear my thoughts for the prayers when I feared that at any moment I might be spied upon. The roof, the dark—it was the only privacy I had. Or so I thought . . ."

She stared at me, defiantly. And then she dropped her gaze. "Don't think I haven't flayed myself for my mistake. Every day, every single day, I ask myself why I went up there. Do you have any idea what he was like, that night? He used me like some—receptacle. The bruises on my breasts took a month to fade. I was afraid Uriah would come home on leave and see the marks."

I thought back to that spring, as David's troops mustered without him for the first time, and I had been called to the side of an angry king who had put even Yoav in fear. I recalled my own fear, as I waited for my audience with him that morning. And we were men who had known David, and loved him, almost all our lives. I looked at Batsheva and suddenly I felt as I had throughout that long night after I'd returned from Beit Lehem, when I sat up waiting for some stillborn vision. I knew now why I felt so ill that night. All through that vigil, he had been raping her. And I had let myself call it a seduction. As I looked at her now, I was shamed by my own thoughts. In a way, I, too, had violated her.

"When he bundled me out—tossing me a jewel, as if I were a whore requiring payment—it was over for him, but not for me. I lived every day in fear, knowing my life hung by a spider's thread, waiting for word of my dishonor to reach Uriah—Uriah, a man for whom honor was everything." She lifted her chin. Her eyes fixed on some distant point. "Have you ever seen a woman stoned to death, Natan? I have. My father made me watch when I was a girl, so I would know what became of faithless wives. And when my monthly signs didn't come, I thought about that woman, the sound of her moans, her mashed flesh, her shattered bone. . . . At the end of it, she had no face . . ." She drew a hand across her eyes, as if to wipe out the image. When she spoke again, her voice was a whisper. "And now, I'm guilty for this, too; that all I thought about in those weeks was myself. It was Uriah I should have feared for. I know that now. But how could I think that David would kill him? Who does that, to a loyal and innocent man? And then my son—my baby, my blameless little boy . . ." Her shoulders heaved in another sob. "He suffered, Natan. The fever burned him alive. And I have to stay with the man who caused all this. Sleep in his bed. Try to pretend that he's not a monster . . ."

"The king is *not* a monster. He has failings, as all men do. He did wrong. He has acknowledged it before the people. He repents it. How many kings have the humility to do that? He prays for forgiveness every day. He strives, every day, to be a better man. You must see—"

"I can't see! And neither can you, Natan. You, because you choose to look away from the truth. You let your love for him blind you. But I can't see anything except what he has taken from me. My child. My husband. My own body. Everything, except my life. Because he can. He can do whatever he wants. You are the only one he fears."

"No. Not me. He fears the Name."

"And you speak for the Name. I am hanging on to this scrap of breath that is my life, Natan. Hanging on to give it to my child." Beads of sweat pearled her brow. She was very pale.

"I'll get you some water," I said, and went out to the garden. I leaned my forehead against the rough wall of the spring house until the stone grazed my skin. I stood there a long time, castigating myself. I had thought this matter of Uriah was done and over. Now here it was again, with yet another, deeper layer to its evil. A trickle of blood ran down my face. I licked my lips and tasted iron. I stepped back from the wall and fingered the graze. Batsheva's maidservant was standing nearby, staring at me. She reached out and took the pitcher from my hand and bent to fill it.

When she was done I let her pour the cool water into my cupped hands. I washed the blood from my forehead. Then I took the pitcher from her and went back inside. Batsheva was lying on the couch, her face pressed into the pillow. I filled a goblet and set it down on the low table beside her. Her breath was ragged. I sat in the chair by the window and waited. Presently, she pushed herself upright and reached for the water.

"Did you love him? Uriah."

She paused, considering, her head tilted on her long, slender neck. "I wasn't thinking about love. No one talked of that. I wasn't raised to expect it. I was a child when my father promised me, and I was sent to Uriah's bed soon after I bled the first time. He was a good match. That's what my father said, and I was raised not to question what my father said. I was proud, to be known as the wife of Uriah. He never mistreated me. I mourn his death. Is that love?"

It was my turn to shrug. "How would I know?"

"How would you?"

We sat in silence. Outside, the sun dipped, throwing long shadows across the glossy flagstones. I gazed at the white veins tracing through the pink stone, and all I could see was flesh and gristle; flayed skin and torn sinew.

"You haven't told me why you came here. Why you took this risk."

"I came to ask . . . to see if you would . . . Natan, I need to know what you see. For this child I'm carrying." She placed her long fingers protectively over her belly. The light caught the sapphire that gleamed on her hand. "You said the other one was payment of the blood debt. But what about this one? Will it live?"

I stood up and opened my hands. "It doesn't work like that. I cannot . . ." And then I saw her face—lovely, even now, blotched and red-eyed with weeping. How could I leave her in this pain? In recompense for my misjudgments, I owed her hope, at least.

"I can say that, since I saw so clearly the other death, yet I see nothing for this—"

And then he was there, a beautiful dark-haired little boy, standing by the window, turning to me, his face full of laughter. I had seen him before, the first time I entered this house. Then I had known him for David's son. Now I understood that he was the child of Batsheva, the shapling growing within her.

He had a young eaglet on his wrist, and as he spoke, it walked up his arm and rubbed its head against his face. He turned away, and when he looked back again he was older, a smiling young man, a gold circlet on his brow. There were maps on the table, and he bent over them, pointing at something, then he raised his eyes in a question. The vision dissolved, and I could see through him, to the window beyond. The same tall, arched window, its big wooden shutters thrown open to the view. But the view itself was utterly changed. Where groves should be, houses stood. The city spilled down into the valley and lapped at the very foot of this hill. Far away, on Har Moriah, the sun glinted on the golden capitals of a great white temple . . .

It was my turn to sway. I staggered to the couch and sat down heavily, reaching blindly for the goblet. It was empty. She took it from my shaking hands and filled it, then held it to my lips so that I could drink. I reached a shaking hand tentatively toward her belly. I closed my eyes, and felt the power surge through me.

"He will be king, Batsheva."

She gasped and brought her fist to her mouth. "But how? How can that be? All those brothers . . . Amnon, almost a man already, and Avshalom, Adoniyah . . . and then all the younger ones . . ." I saw her tally them in her mind.

"I know." I could not reveal what else I knew: the desert visions of fratricide, treason, betrayal. "I can't say how this will be, but take comfort. This boy you carry will live and thrive. I have seen him, crowned."

She got up, pacing. "But how—I don't—it will have to be different, between me and the king. If my son is to sit on the throne, I will need to—"

Her mind was racing. I had meant to bring her comfort, and all I had done was set her into turmoil.

"Batsheva," I said. I moved toward her and set my hands on her shoulders, forcing her to stand still. Her darting eyes scanned my face. "Let this unfold as it must. Be content to know your son will live. Leave the rest where it belongs. No need to run toward it. It will come to us, soon enough."

XVI

That day, I ceased to serve a king and began, instead, to serve a kingdom. Since my time in the desert, I understood that David's fate was out of my hands. He would have to live through the punishments he had earned, and nothing I could say or do for him could remove that burden. But neither was I Shmuel, withdrawing my love and guidance. As the Name still loved David, so did I, and I would be there at his side, to offer what solace I could, to make sure he made wise decisions despite the self-inflicted pain he had to suffer, and so to make sure the kingdom was protected and kept whole until Batsheva's son became king.

To do so, I understood that I would have to secure a place at the young prince's side. This would be delicate, as I had always gone out of my way to avoid any dealings with David's children. At first, it had been the normal disregard of a young man toward any infant not his own. I thought of children as women's business—nothing to do with me. Later, as the princes grew and the older ones began to attend on David at audiences and feasts, I noticed only that they were handsome and spoiled. Daniel, the second born, the son of Avigail, was the only one who carried out his minor duties—cup bearer, page—with any seriousness or dignity. But when Daniel died, it left the eldest, Amnon, as the unchallenged and feckless leader of a wild and headstrong band, fractious with one another and contemptuous toward everyone else.

Even in the ordinary course of things, David's heirs would have been fawned upon and flattered to a dangerous degree, with only their father in a position to set limits. But because David had received no love from his own father, he was determined to lavish it upon his sons. He poured it out with a wastrel's abandon, unwilling to exact any price or place any conditions. And as he did not restrain them, neither did the world. So I viewed them, I suppose, as spoiled nuisances. Then I went to the desert, and saw what they would become. After, I could not look them in the face, and made every excuse I could think of to evade their company. Now, suddenly, I would have to reverse myself.

I expected that at some point David would confide in me regarding Batsheva's condition, and I had carefully prepared what I proposed to say. But a month passed, then two, and nothing was said. David continued his public atonement in the matter of Uriah, and I suppose he felt uneasy raising with me anything connected with that business. I saw that I would have to change that, and make it clear that I now accepted his marriage and its issue. When I saw Batsheva, it was from a distance, walking with her women in the courtyard, or listening to music in the hall, and I could not tell if her condition was evident or not. But I had to think that her pregnancy must be patent by that time to David who, according to Muwat's informants, continued to lie with her almost every night.

Finally, I decided that if he would not speak, I would. I was in his private quarters with Yoav and some others of his inner circle. Earlier, there had been music and wine and much boisterous talk. This had waned now that the hour had grown late. Yoav had fallen asleep in his chair. I saw that David stifled a yawn. He made to rise, intending, I suppose, to dismiss us and retire. Before he could do so, I laid a hand on his arm. He gave another yawn and gazed at me sleepily.

"What now? It's late, and you have that goat track to navigate in the dark. Can't it wait till morning?"

I lowered my voice so that only he could hear me. "Why do you say nothing of the child Batsheva carries?"

He squirmed in his chair, suddenly quite awake.

"How do you know?" he said sharply.

I turned a hand and gave a slight shrug. "How not?"

"But you have said you don't see personal matters . . ."

Yoav stirred. I gestured to David to lower his voice. I dropped my own to a whisper. "I don't see personal matters that are without consequence. This . . . has consequence."

"How so?" He looked alarmed. "You said the boy who died was payment of the blood debt. How is this one . . ."

I raised my hand. "Not in that way. I see nothing ill for this child."

"Then what?"

I had the words all prepared, well rehearsed.

"Your sons. Yoav has had the training of the eldest—Amnon, Avshalom and Adoniyah—as his armor bearers; Aviathar has the younger boys, Yitraam and Shefatiah, as his acolytes. But Yoav and Aviathar have sons of their own. I have no sons. It's hard, to reach such an age as I am and have no one. No son to teach, no one to guide. You do not need another general, another priest. But whichever of your older sons becomes king, he will need someone like me, who can stand by him and speak truth. If I have served you, if I have been of value, this boy . . ."

He raised a hand and interrupted me. "You are saying that this child Batsheva carries will be a prophet? You have seen this?"

I was going to lie and say yes, I had seen it. I could not tell him the truth. To do so would raise alarm about the fates of his older sons— matters of which I could not speak. To serve him, I now had to mislead him. I had practiced how I would deceive him by describing a false vision. I intended to use a part of what I *had* seen—the city, grown great, spreading out across the seven hills, the shining temple columns, rising stone by stone on Har Moriah. But I thought to people the vision with a king, standing in shadow, his face unseen, his back toward me, listening raptly to his younger brother, whose boyish face was aflame with divine power . . .

But those lies died on my lips. "No," I said, "I have not seen it." I felt a great upwelling of emotion. I had not, until that moment, felt the lack of a son. But now, having fabricated it, I did feel it—a great void, a sense of loss. Nothing I could have feigned would have moved David more. He stood, raised me from my chair and embraced me. "If the child is a boy, then he will be in your charge. I appoint you, Natan, to be his teacher."

XVII

You could say he found his own way to me. That is how it would have seemed, to any who did not know better. A psalmist might fashion it otherwise. Such a one would say he was carried to me on the wings of an eagle.

There had been a great storm in the night, lashing rains and high winds such as we rarely see in these hills. In the morning, the winds had died, but the rain continued to fall steadily, filling the dry wadis till they brimmed, spilling between the rocks in swift freshets. It was a day to be spent indoors, by the fire with the shutters closed. Not a day to expect guests.

Muwat, who was cleaning my armor—which was, happily, tarnished from disuse—flinched in surprise at the heavy rapping on the outer gate. He flung a shawl over his head and went out.

The boy did not wait to be announced, but burst in, wet through, his attendant—a tall, thin Mitzrayimite—hunched sodden and miserable behind him. He did not offer an introduction or a greeting, but simply held out his two cupped hands and parted his thumbs to show me the egg cradled carefully in his palms.

"I found this. Just at the bottom of that cliff-footed ridge, over there to the east, where the elah trees grow." His wet face was flushed, the blue eyes—deep blue like his mother's—sparkling with excitement and urgency. "My mother says you know almost everything—she told me you are to be my teacher when I'm old enough. I'm five now—I'll be six in the month of vine pruning, and my mother says I'm to come to you then. But I told Hophra we had to come today, because I want to know what to do with this. I would have climbed up and put it back in the nest, but Hophra wouldn't let me. He said the rock is too slippery in the rain. I think it must be an eagle's egg. It was a very big nest—you could just make out the edge of it."

"It *is* an eagle's nest," I said, struggling to retain my composure. I had awaited this day for a long time. Now my head was light with joy and excitement. I took a deep breath, trying to sound calm. "There is a pair that returns to that ridge every year. Come here, where it's warm, get dry and we'll decide what to do about this egg."

He stood patiently while Hophra toweled off his rain-slicked hair. He politely accepted a bowl of warmed broth, then we sat by the fire and I read to him from a scroll that gave an account of the ways of eagles. "Since we can't be sure when this egg was laid, we don't know when it will hatch," I said. "Also, it may have been addled in the fall. But since we can't return it to the nest, the best thing you can do is build something like a nest—soft and warm. Then wait. If it does hatch, and you feed it, it will attach itself to you. It will be yours, if you want it."

"I do!" he said, his face lit with pleasure. But then he frowned. "I can't take it home. My older brothers, they're not very nice to animals. Especially if they see that it's something I care about. They'll smash it on the stones, just for sport."

"Then leave it here. You can come every day, if you like, and see how it does."

"I would like that, very much, if they'll let me."

"I'm sure they will let you. But I will speak to them, if you think it will help."

And so it began. Without ceremony, without even an introduction, he became part of my life. Indeed, he became its whole purpose. Every day, I looked forward to the sound of his small, enthusiastic fist knocking on the outer door. I had to discipline myself not to wait for him, staring out the window, watching the path like some lovesick swain. She had named him Shlomo, from the word for peace, *shalom*, but also from the word that in some uses means "replacement," because he was the child she hoped would bring consolation after bereavement.

I grew to adore that intense little face, the way his brow would crinkle before he asked a question. And such questions, from the mouth of a child. "All streams flow into the sea," he said. "Yet the sea is never full. How is that?" Or, "The sun rises and the sun sets, and glides back to where it rises. How does it make that journey?" These were the questions of a curious intelligence and I did my best to answer them, drawing on scrolls from Mitzrayim and the teachings of astronomers from Ur. But sometimes his face would crease and the question would be one so profound that one could hardly credit that it issued from the mind of a small boy. "Men are born and they die, but the earth remains forever. Why, then, do we set such store on our short lives? Can they matter so much as we think they do?" In such cases, I blundered on as best I could, praying for inspiration, terrified that a weak answer or, worse, a platitude would shake his trust and draw him away from me. But that did not happen. To my joy, he seemed to look forward to our time together as much as I did.

The egg he had rescued hatched—as I knew it would, since I had seen the eaglet in the vision. It was a ball of dandelion fluff with a vociferous call and a tremendous appetite. Shlomo was immensely tender and patient with it, shredding the flesh of river fish, feeding it strand by strand, laughing when he couldn't keep pace with the hatchling's noisy demands. The bird's growth was so rapid it seemed to change appearance every day.

"You know the eagle is called king of the sky," I said. "Why do you think that's so?" We talked about the eagle's keen eyes, and how a king also must be visionary, looking beyond the surface of things; how its speed and strength surpassed other birds, just as a king must hope to surpass his subjects. We talked about its ability to find prey, and how a king also must be a provider for his people.

And then, unexpectedly: "An eagle is ruthless and takes whatever he wants," he said. "Kings do that, too." He ran a finger gently over the eaglet's downy head. It closed its eyes and stretched its neck with pleasure. "My brother Amnon told me that my father took my mother that way."

I regarded him gravely. His small brow was drawn tight and his face had a haunted look.

"Your brother should know better than to speak of such things," I said.

"Oh, he'll say anything. And not just to me. It gives him joy, to upset people. He's always goading Adoniyah, and he *hates* Avshalom. The only one he's nice to is Tamar—well, everyone's nice to her, she's kind. But Avshalom—he's Tamar's full brother, you know, they have the same mother, Maacah. Anyway, Avshalom hates Amnon to be with Tamar. He told her serving women that Amnon's not allowed to see her in private anymore. There was a big fight about it."

I closed my eyes and drew a deep breath. I felt the blood draining from my face.

"Are you all right? Should I tell Hophra to bring you something? Should I get Muwat?"

"No," I said, forcing a smile. "It's nothing. Just a headache. It will pass."

It was natural, of course, for Shlomo to speak of his brothers. I told myself that I would have to harden myself to it. Still, the words went through me like spears and I had to struggle to keep my composure and focus on our lesson.

Shlomo, of course, wasn't the only source of gossip about the older princes. In the city, it was hard to escape whispers of their outrages— which were numerous—and their enmities, which were life threatening. They had grown like wild thorns, tearing at everything they touched.

David, who so often saw so clearly, who weighed men to a fine grain, was utterly blind to the failings of the men he begat. I had been by his side often enough through the boys' youth when word came to him that one or other of the princes had abused his slave, insulted an elder or mistreated his mount. David would laugh and shrug it off, and mock the complainant, inferring that he lacked the canniness or the authority to deal with childish pranks. Then it would be seen, in subtle ways, that the king's affection for such a person had waned. He would be seated at the rear of the hall at feasts, or perhaps no invitation to the feast would be forthcoming. Courtiers who cared for their position noted this. Soon enough, the boys' outrages went unremarked and unpunished. By the time they were nearing manhood, what had been mischief had become malevolence.

If the seed was unpromising, and the proper husbandry missing, then the ground also was to blame for their ungirt growth. These older boys were the children of the red years, suckled into first awareness as David was consolidating his power. In those days, cruelty was a constant.

Amnon was thirteen, and serving as Yoav's armor bearer, when we measured out the Moavites and slew them by the span. I remember his face—still then the soft-cheeked face of a boy, not yet firmed into maturity. In that stinking field, rancid with fear-sweat and excrement, amid the screams of the dying and the pleas of the condemned, he was laughing. Laughing at a Moavite, prodding him with his foot as he lay on the ground, curled up like a snail, trying to shrink his body so as to evade the deadly quota. "That one!" he called out. "Don't miss him—he's within the measure."

Yoav, who was doing the killing with pale face and compressed lips, glared at him. Like all honorable warriors, killing in hot battle was one thing, butchering unarmed prisoners quite another. I could see that he was about to reprove the boy. But the rebuke died on his lips. Even he, the boy's kinsman and his general, had learned that Amnon was above chastisement.

It did not help that they were good-looking children, all of them products of beautiful mothers. Amnon had the dark, sloe-eyed sensuousness of Ahinoam transformed, in male form, into a solid build, with sleepy, thick-lashed eyes and a full-lipped mouth. Avshalom, on the other hand, had his mother's flawless, regal beauty, but instead of her pale coloring he had his father's vivid radiance. He was tall and slender, with a thick fall of glossy red-gold hair, of which he was rather vain. Adoniyah, son of Hagit, Avital's boy Shefatiah and Eglah's son Yitraam looked the most like brothers, sharing a dark-haired, olive-skinned attractiveness. The Hevron princes, as these youths born in that city were collectively known, attended morning audience from the time they turned thirteen. David hoped that they would acquire some understanding of statecraft. They were an impressive sight, ranged behind their father's throne. To those who did not know their nature, it seemed that David was fortunate to have such fine-looking offspring.

It became clear soon enough that all the older boys had inherited their father's sexual appetite, and were precocious, but Amnon was insatiable. Whores and slaves, boys, girls—he had them all, his urges indiscriminate. It was unsafe for a serving girl to pass him in the hallway. He would throw her, face against the wall, and take her in a moment's spasm, or he would indulge in days-long orgies organized by his reprobate cousin Yonadav. David's only answer to any of this was to give the older boys their own households, where they could pursue dissolute behavior out of his direct line of sight.

I was exceedingly glad when they moved out of the palace and I did not have to risk encountering them at every turn. Shlomo seemed pleased, too. He became noticeably less tense and excitable in his manner, more willing to make use of the abundance of scrolls in the king's library on the days when the weather was unfavorable. But on fine days, Shlomo preferred to be outside. Most mornings, we would meet at my house, and then walk, his eagle, fledged, swooping away to hunt, and then returning to perch nearby and feast on her prey. Shlomo loved the natural world and was fiercely curious as to the ways of even the smallest insect. He would run on ahead of me up the slopes and screes, then turn and pause on a flat piece of rock, spinning around with his arms out, embracing the world. "My eye never has enough of seeing nor my ears enough of hearing," he exclaimed one day, and I drew him close and hugged him, caught up in this small boy's lust for life, his joy in the world and everything in it. Nothing that lived was beneath his notice. We made a great study of ants, for example, and I found that atop his fascination for the habits of the tiny creatures, he had an appetite for moral instruction and philosophical reasoning.

I was sitting perched on a rock while he, prone in the dirt, watched an ants' nest, fascinated by the size of the burdens the tiny creatures carried, their tenacity to surmount any obstacle. After an hour or so, he turned his bright face to me. "They don't have any overseers, or generals giving orders, and yet they do their work. Do you suppose it might be possible for a nation to be like that, everyone working willingly for the common good?"

"Most successful nations have been built on the backs of slaves and forced labor," I said, considering. I took nothing he said lightly, because he seemed so hungry for answers.

"But on the battlefield I have seen men sacrifice themselves for one another. A leader who inspires people can get them to give more than they know they have. But there are few such leaders. But why only on the battlefield?" he interjected. "All wars end, and then that which was broken must be remade. It's a waste, I think. All our best men strive to be captains and generals, because their leaders reward those skills. But perhaps there are other skills, other men, who can think of ways *not* to fight. Perthaps a real leader would find those men, and train them, just like an army trains . . ." He trailed off, thoughtful. I sat there, breathless, forcing myself to credit that such thoughts could issue from the mind of a mere boy. But then I gathered myself, and led him to what followed: a consideration of the leaders in our own history.

It was natural, from there, to turn to the leaders in our own history. Of Moshe, the reluctant insurgent, and Yehoshua, the brilliant warrior. Of the judges who ruled with wisdom and forbearance in the years when our people were suspicious of kings. Shlomo, with his ability to piece together shards of this discussion and that one, advanced the supposition that our reluctance to be ruled by a king had come about because of our long suffering under the pharaohs, and had waned as memories of enslavement faded. It was a wise insight, and it led on naturally to a study of Ramses, the great builder, ruthless enough to order the slaying of the children of his Ivrim slaves. Shlomo plunged wholeheartedly into the grief of our ancestors, imagining their powerlessness as their baby boys were seized and murdered. But then he surprised me by switching his perspective, struggling to see the matter through Pharaoh's eyes. "If you are king, you must act against what threatens your people. Ramses feared the Ivrim would grow numerous and rebel. Of course, that was because he mistreated them. It's obvious what he should have done. Mitzrayim is a rich country. He could have afforded to treat them fairly. If men work hard, they should be rewarded, even if they *are* slaves. Then they have less cause to rebel. That's what I meant, before, about finding ways *not* to have war and break everything to pieces. Imagine how rich Mitzrayim would be now if we'd never left, if Ramses had made us part of his nation. If I were king, I'd . . ." He trailed off, lifting his chin and staring ahead. "But I won't be king, of course."

Then he turned to me and the words came out in a rush. "I don't think Amnon will be a good king. He hates the ordinary people. He doesn't care about them at all. He's half asleep at the public audiences and he barely ever bothers to go to Father's councils. But Avshalom is always there, when he's allowed to be. I think my father wishes Avshalom were the eldest. Amnon scares you into doing what he wants. Avshalom's smarter. He makes you think he likes you, even if he doesn't, not really . . ." He stopped abruptly. He must have noticed the pained expression on my face, and misconstrued it. "Of course, I wouldn't say these things to anyone else. Just to you. I can say anything to you, can't I? Like I do with my mother."

I needed to tread carefully. "Has she spoken to you, of who will be king after . . . after . . ." I found I couldn't bring myself to say the words.

"Just one time. She said that not every king passes his throne to the eldest son."

"That's true," I said. "We don't have a long tradition of kingship, as some other nations do. If your father lives long enough, the time will come when he will decide who will succeed him, and it will need to be someone the people will accept. But that decision could be years off. He's still a vigorous man."

He tilted his head and looked at me, his eyes widening. I didn't have to spell it out. Even as a child, he could catch an inference. I could see him turning the thought over in his mind.

"It's early to speak of this. Put it out of your mind, for now," I said. "For now, you are doing the best thing, soaking up learning and wisdom. If you like, I will speak to the king about letting you go to the minor councils. You never know, he may allow it, young as you are. For now, it's time to practice your reading." I tapped a finger on the papyrus I'd brought from the palace library. "Although it isn't the power it was in Ramses' time, Mitzrayim is still an important nation for us. Your father was wise to make peace there. Whoever is king after him will need to keep that peace. Did you know the Mitzrayimites call their writing 'god signs'? They understand that words have power . . ." We turned our attention to deciphering the glyphs, and he, delighted and puzzled, threw himself fully into this new challenge.

XVIII

"**D**id you hear that Amnon is ill? My father is worried. He even went to his house, and he hardly ever goes there." Shlomo, pushing his stylus into the wax tablet, hadn't looked up as he tossed out the information.

I was standing behind him, watching to see that he formed his letters correctly. As he spoke, the clay goblet I'd been holding slipped from my hand and shattered on the flagstones.

Shlomo turned and looked at me, puzzled. "It's probably just a flux. A lot of people get them this time of year . . ."

"Yes, of course," I said, trying to suppress the sickness rising in my throat. Muwat heard the goblet fall and came in with a broom, ready to sweep up the shards. He checked in the doorway. He had been with me long enough to know the signs. I made a small reassuring motion with my hand. I did not wish him to speak of it in front of Shlomo. I knew what was coming.

With difficulty, I managed to choke out a few words. "That's enough for today. You've worked well. Let's take it up again to-morrow."

"But I haven't finished . . ."

Muwat set down his broom and moved to the table, taking the stylus from Shlomo's hand and gathering up the tablet and the scrolls. "The master needs to rest now."

Shlomo looked as if he were about to protest his eviction, but then he saw my face, gray and beaded with sweat. "I'm sorry, I see you're unwell. I hope you don't have what Amnon has. It's not about him, is it? That upset you? I didn't think you'd care. Anyway, I'm sure he'll be fine. My sister Tamar is going to his house today, to make some of her sweet-cakes. They're very good, you know. She always makes them for us as special treats when we're sick. Amnon said it's all he feels like eating . . ."

As soon as Shlomo was out the door, Muwat helped me to the couch. He closed the shutters and fetched cold cloths for my burning fore-head and a bowl for the contents of my stomach.

The stabbing pain and nausea came, as they must. But with them, unfamiliar, was the swelling of my tongue, the closing of my throat. This was the first of the visions I was not to speak aloud. I could not warn. All I could do was bear mute witness, whether I would or no.

I lay supine, sucking for breath, as the afternoon waned and dusk gathered. I was on the couch in my own house, but I could see Am-non, naked on his bed, his dark-lashed eyes half closed in sleepy sensuality, his hand rhythmically stroking the column of his blue-veined cock. Amnon, accustomed to having his every carnal urge sat-isfied, no matter how base or bizarre. In Amnon's world, where everything was available, the unattainable had a wild allure. For months, he had been obsessed with the one young female body in the kingdom that was denied to him.

It had been impossible for him to get near her. In the palace, she was shut up in the women's quarters with her mother, Maacah, who guarded her like a bitch with a whelp. At feasts and ceremonies, or even at intimate family gatherings, Avshalom watched over her every move. Tamar, just turned sixteen, was David's only daughter. It was understood that she would be used, and very soon, in some important piece of statecraft. That she would be a queen was unquestioned; the interesting question was which of our allies David would honor with the match.

The vision shifted. I saw David, in the women's garden, admiring a piece of Tamar's needlework as a ruby-throated bird thrummed and flitted between them. He handed the piece back to Tamar, who smiled shyly up at him. She was a beautiful girl, pale like her mother, with rose-gold hair and skin so fine it was almost translucent. She flushed, pleased by her father's attention. She was happy to be singled out, asked to bring comfort to her important half-brother. For a girl so closely kept, it was an occasion anytime she was permitted to leave the women's quarters. She was excited to be allowed to go out into the city. I saw her with her maidservant, choosing a gown. The one she picked was silk, dyed in bright verticals of color, with the high neckline and long sleeves that preserve a virgin's modesty.

I smelled wood smoke, and the delicious aroma of baking. The vision shifted again: Tamar at Amnon's house, her delicate hands kneading viscous date honey into a supple, pine-nut-studded dough. The cakes sizzled as she slipped them onto the hot metal pan. Amnon groaned. He is, he says, too ill to sit up any longer in the reception hall. He must retire to his bedchamber. He needs quiet. He must have some peace. His young sister's gentle presence is all his ravaged nerves can bear.

He rose from his couch with difficulty and made his way unsteadily to his inner room, as Tamar followed with her cakes. It was quite a performance. Amnon's cousin Yonadav, propped against the door, smirked in appreciation. Amnon was playing the role Yonadav had scripted for him. This entire evening's sham was his idea. The eldest son of David's brother Shammah, Yonadav was as dissolute as his father. Raised in privilege as a nephew of the king, he learned early to cloak his nature with a courtier's ingratiating manner. As a boy, he attached himself, leechlike, to Amnon, putting up with casual slights and open cruelties until he had become an indispensable henchman, abettor, pander. He made a close study of every family tie in the king's complex household. He knew that David loved his sons with a blinding and unconditional fervor. Therefore, he deduced that if

Amnon feigned illness, David would do whatever he could to see to his son's comfort. And on no lesser authority than the king's command could Tamar be extracted from the women's precinct. Now, as the dismissed servants withdraw, he is the last to take his leave. But as he goes, he smiles at Amnon and makes a swift, indecent gesture. Amnon's eyes crease with amusement. Tamar, arranging the golden cakes, does not see.

She offers the cakes—hot, fragrant—to her brother. Amnon sweeps them to the floor and pulls her down upon the bed. At first, she's merely indignant. Sheltered, protected from knowledge of her family's darker acts, she is as innocent of evil as a child of her times can be. Of Amnon's depravity, she knows nothing. Even Avshalom, who hates Amnon and would delight in smearing his name, has felt it necessary to shield her. So she thinks her older half-brother is playing some strange, rough, unwelcome game.

Only when he throws her on her back and pushes her robe up does she panic and thrash, trying to get free. But he's astride her now, and so much bigger, so much stronger. She's a quick-witted girl. Knowing she can't fight him off, she tries to reason with him. As his hands push between her thighs she pleads. How can he do this thing to her? How can he do it to himself? He'll be shamed and ruined, just as surely as she will.

He is not hearing her. His jaw is slack with desire. He forces her legs apart. Panicking, she tries a desperate gambit: Ask David, she cries. Ask him for dispensation so that they can marry. "He'll change the law if he knows how you feel; he will not refuse you. When has he ever refused you?" But her voice is thin and shrill. He silences her with his mouth, the bristles of his beard grazing her face. There's an aching pressure between her legs. She squirms and flails, trying to resist. It's no good. A searing pain, the tear of flesh. A few hard thrusts and it's over: a spasm, a shudder and he falls off her, panting. She rolls away from him, curling in on herself like a dying insect. Her mind is a blur of hurt and shame. She's keening, retching. But he's not done.

After a few minutes, he reaches out and wraps her hair in his fist, dragging her head back. He pushes her knees down, flips her onto her face and rubs himself against her, trying to get hard. His fingers probe inside her—slippery now with her blood and his seed. He rubs this on himself, but it's no good. Angry, he pulls her onto her back, glares into her sobbing face. He hits her, open-handed first, then with a closed fist. There is a noise inside her head, a grinding of cartilage against bone. Blood pours from her crushed nose. She spits out a tooth. He takes hold of her head and grinds her face into his groin. She's a limp sac of pain. She can't fight him anymore. She has nothing left to fight for. She takes his cock into her bloody mouth and gags as it fills her throat.

By morning, there is nothing he has not done to her. His final act is to push her onto the floor. A hard stream of hot liquid showers her head. She opens her stinging eyes. He is standing over her, shaking the last drips of urine from the tip of his cock.

"Get out."

She looks up, shakes her head, clasps at the bedpost. "Don't. Please. I'm begging you. Don't send me out into the street." Her voice is distorted by the blood congesting her shattered nose. "If you shame me like that, it will be worse than what you've already done." Amnon steps over her, walks to the door and calls his servant. A single, brutal command: "Get *that* out of here."

She's on her knees in the narrow lane outside Amnon's house as the door bar slams into place behind her. She tugs at her crushed robe. The silk gives easily. She rips away the virgin's sleeves. On the pale flesh of her upper arm, bruises are already purpling. She grabs handfuls of dirt, rubbing them into her bloody, urine-soaked hair.

The city is waking. In the gray light, a boy comes out to empty a night jar; a girl sets off to fetch water. Their early morning faces crease at the sight of the injured girl, but no one moves to help her. They know very well whose house this is. They have seen such outrages before. Then a woman notices the purple silk of the torn and bloodstained robe. Her eyes widen. Tamar speaks to her, asking the way to the house of her brother, Avshalom. As Tamar struggles to her feet and limps away, the whispers run before her: the king's daughter. Her own half-brother. By the time she reaches Avshalom's house, her bright future is a smear of despair.

I lay impotent, drool stringing from my mouth. As Tamar's sobs faded, my ears rang until, after a time, I could hear the ordinary, early morning sounds of my own house seeping through the noise of vision—the grind of the well chain on stone as Muwat fetched water, the songbirds and the cockerels greeting the sun. I sat up, dizzy and ill, and spoke aloud, to test my voice, and see if the hours of enforced silence were over for me. A strangled cry issued forth. Muwat, coming in with the water, rushed to my side to see if I was well.

I managed to say the word "broth," and as Muwat went to see to it, a few lingering filaments of vision flickered. Avshalom, scanning his sister's broken face, her bruised arms. I could feel the rage licking up inside him. As her full brother, her violated honor stained his own. I felt his mind, reaching toward the hot satisfaction of swift revenge. But then I sensed struggle, and a hard-won self-mastery. He realized that Amnon, who judged others by the measure of his own ungirt passions, would be armored against some act of blind anger, some ill-considered violent outburst. Indeed, such a thing might even be what he hoped for. In such a circumstance, in self-defense, Amnon could kill Avshalom, his chief rival for the throne, and if the knife he grabbed were poison-tipped, who would think to inquire? I felt Avshalom's resolve: the only answer he would give Amnon was silence. He commanded Tamar: Say nothing of this. Then Muwat arrived with my broth, and the threads of vision frayed to wisps and dispersed. I took the cup and struggled to take a sip.

Avshalom expected his father to act. It was natural enough that he should have looked to David for justice, both as father and as king. As a father, David doted on his only daughter. As king, he had every right to be incensed. The state marriage for Tamar, so long anticipated, was now out of the question, and heavy laws had been trampled upon—this, by the crown prince, who was meant to uphold the laws.

Yet David did nothing. If he raged at Amnon, it happened in private. As days passed, it became clear that there would be no public consequences. No punishment. Avshalom, resolute, reacted to this with a steely silence. Only Maacah spoke up.

The daughter of one king, the favored wife of another, she was used to being heard. The day after the rape, she begged to see her husband. As she had her own fine house outside the palace, it was usual for him to come to her. But he did not appear that day, or the one following, sending to say that he was sorry, but grave matters consumed his every moment, and that he would attend on her as soon as he had liberty. I suppose he wanted to wait until her first spate of emotion had ebbed. If so, he misjudged her.

Muwat, who was friendly with Maacah's principal maidservant, gave me an account of their confrontation. The king arrived at her house on the third day after the rape to find Maacah still prostrate and devastated. He drew a chair, the maidservant reported, and sat down by her couch, taking her hand, offering comfort. When she composed herself enough to speak, she asked what arrangements he had made for the execution of Amnon.

The king recoiled. "Are you mad?" he said. "Execute my first-born son?"

"Then what punishment do you propose?" asked Maacah, her voice strained.

The king stood and turned away from her, pacing. When at last he spoke, it was in a low tone, as if interrogating himself. "Will punishment of Amnon restore Tamar's honor? No, it will not do that. Will it fix her disfigured face? No, it will not do that, either. If I punish my son, will it remake my daughter into the fit bride of a king, or indeed the bride of any person of state significance? No, those plans must be set aside now. What good, then, to tear my family apart over this miserable business? Enough that my daughter is ruined. Why also ruin my son and heir? It's not too late. He can change. He's only in his twenties. I was still making mistakes—grave mistakes—at a much greater age than that."

Maacah struggled to her feet, her mouth open. "How can you?" She moved unsteadily toward him. "You cannot propose to leave this rape, this act of incest, unanswered? This crime, for which the punishment is death . . ."

David raised a hand. "Not so. This . . . thing . . . took place within the walls of the city. The law says the woman in such a case must cry out. Yet no witness has come forth to say Tamar cried out . . ."

"It's you who is mad! What witness would dare accuse your brute of a son? Have you seen her? The bruises on her body, her shattered nose, her missing tooth. You think she did not cry out? Are you saying—you cannot be saying—you cannot think she invited this abomination?"

David opened his hands. "I do not say so. But some might." Maacah flew at him then, pummeling him in the chest, shrieking. The servant, although she had not been dismissed, withdrew to the anteroom at that point, afraid. She could hear the king, repeating his wife's name, trying to calm her rage.

"Maacah," he said. "Think. You cannot want the details of this matter trumpeted about in the hall. Yes, I know; word of the attack is unfortunately abroad in the city. But the less we feed the gossip, the better for everyone. Tamar included. You must see that."

"I see no such thing! I see weakness, cowardice. You are no fit father if you do not—"

"That's enough!" David raised his voice. "I will see to it that Tamar is escorted to Avshalom's farm—it's a beautiful property, I chose it myself, years ago, in the mountains of Baal-hazor. She can retire there quietly. I'll see to it she has a household, servants, all that she needs. We will close the door on this, and move on."

He left then, passing the servant in the anteroom without even noticing her, smoothing the front of his tunic where Maacah had gripped the fabric.

When Muwat told me all of this, I thanked him, and then asked that he leave me. I needed to think. This decision of the king's was wrong, undoubtedly. I knew what its consequences would be. But my mouth was stoppered. I would have to join the chorus of deafening silence. Or so I thought.

XIX

"Maacah has asked that you come to her," said Batsheva unex-pectedly. "She knows that I see you. I'm sure I do not have to tell you what it concerns."

I tilted my face to the golden sunlight and closed my eyes with a sigh. "No," I said. "You do not." It was only two months since the rape of Tamar. Amnon, after a brief absence from morning audience, was back in his usual place at the king's side, where Avshalom point-edly ignored him. David tried to cover the rupture between them with strained attempts at good humor. To foreign visitors and rural sup-plicants, no doubt the scene looked unremarkable. But like a harp string whose tuning key is forced a turn or two past proper pitch, tempers were pulled to their limits. When I visited the hall, I could feel it there, always: an unbearable tension.

"It wouldn't be fruitful," I said. "I can't give her what she wants."

Batsheva chose a ripe fig from the silver dish on the table between us. "Nonetheless, it would oblige me if you would see her." I looked away as her full lips closed on the luscious fig. Even after so many years of continence, it was hard, sometimes, to be so close to a woman as sensual as Batsheva. I don't know if she was aware of the effect she sometimes had; certainly I tried with every fiber to conceal it. As she finished the fig, she dabbed at her lips with a square of linen. "It's not easy with Maacah," she confided. "Our relations are, I could say, correct—but it sits ill with her that David gives me precedence. She's the only one of us born royal—except of course for Mikhal, but she, as you know, is not . . ." She let the thought trail away. "In any case, Maacah feels any slight, and would be my enemy if I did not take great care to prevent it."

I had barely seen the two women together. Little by little, I had detached myself from the daily business of the court. There was no purpose in my being there, as the Name had ordained David's penance, and had sealed my lips from counseling him in any way concerning it. For one whose work has been to speak, the enforced silence came hard, and the thrumming strain between the elder princes exhausted me. It was easier for me to remain at home, counting each waxing moon, teaching Shlomo and waiting for events to unfold as I knew they must.

I made exceptions, of course—I didn't want my absence to become patent enough to be remarked upon. I served the king as an ordinary adviser, giving opinions on daily matters when they did not touch on what my desert visions had disclosed. Once each week, I would visit Batsheva. We sat on her private terrace. In the courtyard below, Shlomo trained his she-eagle. Batsheva's newborn slept in a basket at her side, shaded by the fronds of a palm. They had named the new prince Natan. I was honored. David had taken to heart what I had said to him about being childless, and this, along with a free hand in Shlomo's instruction, was my ample recompense.

Shlomo's bird had grown enormous—her wingspan more than three cubits, her glare fierce and her strength lethal.

She soared above us all, riding a high thermal. Shlomo gave a single, piercing whistle. She drew herself immediately into a stoop, plummeting toward him. In unison, Batsheva and I gasped. Yet the great bird landed on his slender gloved hand as light and docile as a dove. Shlomo looked up, basking in our smiles of approval.

It still sometimes surprised me, this comfortable friendship between Batsheva and me. We were, of course, united by a passionate devotion to her boy and bound by the shared secret of his destiny. I started meeting with her as any pedagogue might, to discuss my pupil's progress. And at first, Shlomo was all we did discuss. In truth, each of us could have talked contentedly for hours on that one subject and not tired of it. But as she came to know me, her fear receded, and she began to reveal more of herself. She possessed a quick mind and a sharp intuition. There was also a pragmatic resilience that had allowed her, once she ceased to be consumed by fear for her son, to begin to repair the rotten foundations of her marriage. She was wise enough to know that her own relationship with the king would color his dealings with her son, and that if she had to set aside certain unsavory facts and bitter memories in order to further that, then she would do so. In hints and allusions, she had let me see that this was her object. When I looked at her now, I no longer saw a haunted girl but a mature and confident woman, secure in her precedence with the king.

"It's been very difficult, between David and Maacah, these last several weeks. Of course, in her grief, she first asked him for the prescribed penalty. Anyone could have told her that was a mistake. A public execution?" Batsheva gave a little half-laugh, signaling disdain. "You know what the king is like when it comes to his sons. I don't say he wasn't angry with Amnon. Of course he was. He was enraged. He blamed himself. He said his own lust and incontinence had set a poor example for his sons. He prayed, constantly, for Tamar, for Amnon, asking the Name to soften Amnon's heart and set his feet on a righteous path. But again, you know what he's like. Feelings and prayers are one thing, action another. He's stubborn about what he wants to see and what he doesn't. He didn't even say good-bye to Tamar, you know, before she left in the caravan to Avshalom's farm at Baal-hazor. That poor girl. She asked to see him, begged for it. But he put her off, on one pretext or another. Couldn't even bring himself to say farewell. Just cut her off, and you know how he used to dote on her. I'm sure it's because he couldn't bear to witness her disfigurement, to face the evidence of what Amnon did. It's as if as long as he doesn't see it, it can't be. He became enraged with Maacah then, because she'd suggested executing Amnon. He dismissed her and wouldn't see her. I do not think he has seen her still. She came to me, finally, and asked me to intercede with him—it cost her a lot, I think, to seek my help."

"And did you help her?"

"Oh, yes. I tried. I feel for her—and for her daughter."

"Of course you do," I said. "You, of all people, know what it is to—"

She cut me off. "Don't, please. I don't think of it anymore. It's not fruitful. No one of us can change the past, least of all someone like me, who had no power to alter the events even as they were happening." She closed her eyes for a moment and tilted her lovely head back, a grimace of remembered pain passing across her brow. "But now," she said, leaning forward, "I *do* have some power, and I have some choices. And I choose to look ahead, not back, and be as good a wife as I can be. In any case, these two"—she faltered, looking, I think, for a word that was not "rapes" or "crimes," and chose in the end to leave a blank space in her sentence—"mine and Tamar's—they are not comparable. I was not a virgin. He was not my brother."

I inclined my head. "As you say."

Shlomo had sent the eagle airborne again, and her eyes traced its graceful swerves across the sky. "He's using you as a shield—I suppose you know that?"

"How so?"

"He says that if the Name wanted Amnon punished, he would have heard of it from you before now."

I winced. Of course he would take my silence as assent. How could he know the real cause? "Well," I said, "if it will please you for me to see her, that is enough reason to do it."

She smiled. "Good, then, I will arrange for her to join us next time you come to me."

I barely knew Maacah. Her father, Talmai, the king of Geshur, was the first leader on our borders to seek peace with us, and David was glad to secure the north and seal the treaty with the marriage, especially once he saw the princess. He set her up in a queenly state, as befit her rank, with her own house and her familiar Geshurite attendants. I saw her, therefore, only when she came to the palace for high state functions, and I never had occasion to speak to her directly. It was remarked that David spent a good deal of time at the house of Maacah, especially in the early years of the marriage, when their children were young. Avshalom and Tamar had always seemed to occupy an especially high place in his affections.

We met in Batsheva's rooms. Maacah declined to sit, which meant that I could not do so, either. She held herself as straight as a spar, her head very erect and her long neck collared with beads of polished ebony. Her silken gown also was black. She stood with her fingers laced in front of her.

"They say you are the king's conscience." Her voice was as thick as cream, with the strong accents of her northern childhood. I inclined my head. I had no better answer.

"All those years ago, when my father told me he had made this match for me, I was afraid. I did not want to leave behind my people and my gods, familiar gods that I knew by name, that I could see and touch and worship in the high places. I was afraid of your god, this god whose name I may not even say, whose image I may not even see. But my father said it would be all right, for though this Name had no face, it had a voice, and spoke through a prophet, who was fearless, and told the king if he did good or ill."

Her gaze, as she said this, was lacerating. It could have etched a stela. I found myself looking away from her, studying the floor mosaic.

"But now I know this is not true. You say that your Name gave you laws, which you keep in your ark and proclaim as holy. And now one of those laws, one of the heaviest of those laws, has been broken. Yet the king does nothing, and the Voice of the Name is silent. How can this be?"

"I know that you—" I was stammering, my words stalled in my mouth. The Voice of the Name, she called me, yet my own voice was a rasp, a broken reed, rattling helplessly in the breeze. I reached for water, and tried to speak again. But my tongue would not shape itself to the words that formed in my mind. Then I felt the stab of pain, the blackness descending. And new words filled my mouth and issued forth, loud and resonant. *Who are you to question the Name's anointed? Justice comes when I ordain it, on the hot wind and the raging tide, when the mountains tremble and the earth opens to swallow all who offend me.* I had raised both my arms and stepped toward Maacah. I stood towering over her. She folded in on herself, reeling away. As the fit passed, I dropped my arms and stepped back, pressing the heels of my hands into my eyes to stop the blinding pain.

Batsheva had never heard me speak as a prophet before, and her eyes were wide. She looked between Maacah and me, unsure what to do. I was doubled up with pain by then, so she moved tentatively toward me, signaling to her attendant, who was cowering. "Bring Natan a chair!" she cried. "Can you not see he is ill?" Maacah, her face white, tottered toward the door, urgent to get away from me. "Maacah," I said gently, and my voice was my own again. She halted and turned. Her bearing was not regal now, but cringing and fearful.

"What I said. It means that the crime against Tamar *will* be punished, but it is not in David's hands." She looked at me blankly. I lifted my hands in a gesture of helplessness. I could not speak more plainly. *Pay him back four times over,* so David had said, in his own harsh judgment of the man who stole the ewe lamb. "The king, too, is awaiting punishment. The matters are linked. I can say no more. But you will have your justice. Just not yet. Take comfort in that, if you can."

XX

The barley ripened and was harvested twice in that time of waiting. I gave myself over in those two years to what shards of happiness I could unearth when I pushed dread of the future away. There were some golden days, when the work of making and mending went on, when music filled the king's halls, and when the city seemed bathed in a kind of radiance.

We made many new alliances at that time, and fought no wars. A few border skirmishes, merely, put down with little loss of life. Because of this, Shlomo was allowed to follow his own inclinations in a fashion that would not have been possible for the Hevron princes raised in time of war. Shlomo showed little interest in the business of killing. He was lithe and quick handed with a sword, accurate with a bow, and got through his necessary lessons with good grace and efficient dispatch, and did not seek to push his skills past a necessary level of proficiency.

But if soldiering did not interest him, the soldiers themselves were another matter. He loved to sit with the men and draw out their firsthand stories of past campaigns. After, he would come to me and ask all kinds of questions about the larger matters at stake in the battles they'd described. He was fascinated by strategy and was able to grasp how an engagement had looked from the point of view of the common fighter as well as from the vantage of the commanders. Even taciturn Yoav opened up under the youth's polite yet persistent need to know every detail—why he had used this tactic in a particular campaign and not in another, what qualities he looked for in promoting a man from the ranks, when to sit down in a siege and when to press an attack. I would find the two of them deep in these discussions, a sand map drawn in the dust at their feet. Later, Shlomo would come to me with some detail of a battle that he had learned from Yoav, and we would compare it with what was known of famous battles in the past. When he found that this or that king or general had used similar tactics, he would derive immense satisfaction. "Everything that happened has already happened, if you look hard enough and far enough back in time," he opined one day. "With enough study, one should be able to have the means at hand to win any battle and outwit any foe. It seems to me that there is nothing new under the sun." But then he paused, and looked out across the groves to the city beyond. "What would be new, of course, would be an end to all this fighting. That would be a good time to be alive."

Before very long, the boy's agile mind outstripped my own, and with David's permission I called on specialists to tutor him. We engaged distinguished magi from the east and learned Ethiops from the south. Architects from Tyre and Mitzrayim, poets and bards from the islands of the Sea People, astronomers from the Two Rivers, snake charmers, horse tamers, even wise women and herbalists—whatever it took to feed his insatiable intellectual appetite.

At my urging, David allowed him to take his place beside his older brothers in the hall of audience a full three years earlier than any other had been given such a privilege. Toward the closing of his tenth year, in that sudden way that male children sometimes will, between the waxing and waning of a single moon, he began to transform from boy to man. Out of rounded softness, a strong face emerged, cheekbones high and fine like his mother's, framed by a defined brow and a severe jawline. It was an arresting face, not perhaps as classically handsome as Avshalom's, but lit by an intelligent gaze. He had been an elegant child and seemed to be slipping gracefully into his larger frame.

He would come to me after he had attended David, avid to discuss his father's judgments, turning every matter this way and that, revisiting what had been said, recasting the arguments that had been brought before the king so as to put them more persuasively. He never shrank from his own well-founded opinion, but he would become wistful if he reached a different conclusion from his father as to how a matter should have been judged.

And within a year or two, those instances increased. There was a shadow on those sunlit days: David was beginning to show his age. A moment of inattention here, an inability to recall a fact there. Sometimes, a drawn look around the mouth and eyes, or listlessness when audiences dragged on too long. David's voice—his beautiful voice—became hoarse when he was fatigued. His skin, too, had lost its healthy glow and taken on a dry, papery sallowness. Most obvious of all the changes: his hair—that bright, thick mane—had begun to fade and thin.

All this was plain enough to me, who had known him so long, and to Shlomo, because he was preternaturally observant. But it took Yoav, as blunt as ever, to put it in words. "He's starting to look like a cur with mange," he remarked to me, leaning across the table at the feast of the new moon. I'd seen it, too; David had raked his hand absently through his hair, and a tangle of strands had come away in his fingers.

I shrugged. "He's not young; you can't expect him to keep his hair forever."

Yoav cut me off. "It's not about hair. There's something wrong with him. He's tired all the time. He—who never needed rest. And look at him—wearing that heavy cloak, in this weather."

As he spoke I saw David rise in his place to give the salutation. It was the sign for the feast to end. We all stood, the benches scraping across the stone flags. But Avshalom stepped forward and raised a hand. "Father, if I may, before you retire. . . . As you know, it's shearing season at the lands you granted to me in Baal-hazor. We expect a record wool clip this year, and I have promised my people a feast. It's beautiful there in this season, and I would be honored for you to see my improvements to the farm, to see what I've done with your generous gift. Will you do me the honor of feasting with me? You—and my brothers." He turned then, and bowed to Amnon. "All my brothers."

Everyone in the hall drew a breath. It was the first time Avshalom had exchanged so much as a look with Amnon in two long years. Amnon, who had been drinking heavily, did not have the wit to arrange his face. He stared at Avshalom, slack-jawed.

David glanced from one to the other of his sons, beaming. He rose and stepped down from the dais, walking toward Avshalom with his arms open for an embrace. He held him close for a long moment, and when he drew back, there was a look of such love in his eyes that I had to glance away from the intimacy of it.

"Avshalom, my son." His voice was quavering with emotion. "My son, Avshalom." He raised a hand to his eyes, struggling to compose himself. "It pleases me that you have been diligent in improving the lands I gave you. But it pleases me even more that you make this invitation." He turned and let his gaze rest on Amnon for a few moments. "But I have affairs to attend to, and I can't travel unless half the court comes with me. I do not want to tax your resources with such a crowd."

"Father, it would not tax me at all. We have tents, the weather is mild—"

David raised a hand. "You go with your brothers—" He glanced again at Amnon. "All your brothers. Have a young man's party. It will be better so, without the burden of a king and his retinue and all that must attend it."

The king left the hall, and the feast broke up then, unevenly, as feasts always do. Those still engrossed in their wine-fueled conversations stood in little clots here and there, making a final point, sharing a last joke, while the bored, the weary and the trysting lovers, relieved to be released, made quick exits toward their longed-for beds. Only two sat unmoving in their places. One was Amnon. His face was like a wax tablet, written, erased, rewritten. You could read everything

there: fear, then relief; confusion, then anger. You could see him working it through: Sincere act of reconciliation? One-upmanship in the
battle for their father's regard? Deadly trap? If the latter, how to escape
it, now that the king had given his permission—indeed, his full-
hearted blessing—on the invitation. I saw Yonadav making his way
across the hall to Amnon—he had been seated with his father, Shammah, several tables distant. He bent down, and spoke into Amnon's
ear. Amnon turned to him, remonstrating, but Yonadav masked the
moment with a boisterous laugh, clasping Amnon's hand as he raised
it to expostulate, drawing him up off the bench and into his chest in
a backslapping show of good humor. It was well done, and Amnon
had presence of mind enough to yield to it. As they passed my table
on the way out of the hall, Amnon held his lips in a rictus that could
pass for a smile.

But I sat there, stricken. Even as my eyes followed Amnon across the
room, I was in Baal-hazor. The sun eased up over an undulant horizon
bright with the haze of new grasses. The sheep moved in a corona of
morning light, the edges of their heavy fleeces as bright as filaments of
gold. Behind them, the high ridges of the Golan marched north to distant mountains still dusted with snow. The fine large house, sheltered
in the broad hammock of the valley, was already awake. In the still air,
threads of wood smoke curled lazily upward from the tannurs. Out in
the fields, crews hauled on ropes, raising large goat hair tents, and serving women bustled about, laying down bright carpets. A mule driver
urged his pair, laden with firewood, up a last incline, to where the spit
turners were setting up their tripods over fresh-dug pits.

From the house, a slight figure emerged, crossing the courtyard to
collect ewers of fresh goat's milk. Halfway across, she stopped, and
tilted her face upward, to receive the warm spring sun. Her veil slipped
back, and light glinted in her red-gold hair. Her eyes were closed, her
mouth curled in a private smile.

She stood there for a moment, rocking slightly. Then her eyes
opened, and their expression was fierce. I saw her lips move. A single
word: "Soon."

XXI

The princes left severally for the feast, the older with their own retinues, the younger in a caravan together with their attendants. Shlomo traveled with the younger princes, excited, as any boy would be, at the prospect of a party. I saw him off, pretending to share in his joy. But I knew that the boy who returned would be much changed. When I saw him again, ten days later, there was a drawn look about his eyes, a new gravity and steadiness. As teacher and pupil, we did not usually embrace, but that day, I opened my arms to him, and he stepped forward and let me enfold him.

It was cold, for that season, so I had asked Muwat to lay a small fire. Shlomo sat on his heels in front of the hearth and stared at the flames as he spoke of all he had witnessed. "One of the worst things," he said, "was that it started out as such a wonderful festival. The best, I think, that I have ever been to. It wasn't like the festivals in the city, with professional singers and all the expensive food and wine and the important people separate from the ordinary folk. This was everyone all together—big landowners and simple herdsmen, trained musicians that Avshalom had brought from the city, and local people playing instruments they'd made themselves. There were prizes for the shearers, and donkey races. Storytellers. Dancing. Children running everywhere. Avshalom had thought of everything. Even the little princes had entertainments. My brother Natan was there with his nursemaid, giggling and running wild with the shepherd boys. And the food—good, simple—warm bread and juicy lamb off the spit to wrap in it. And wine, of course. Rivers of wine. Everyone was in such high spirits. We could not have been more unready when it happened."

His face had lightened for a moment, but now it resumed the pinched expression he'd worn ever since he fled from Baal-hazor; the haunted look of a boy who has witnessed fratricide. I had been obliged to witness it, too, lying stricken and swollen tongued here in my own house. But I let him speak of it, because it seemed to me to be a good thing for him to give it voice.

I had watched, in a vision, as Avshalom welcomed Amnon and treated him as an honored guest, plying him with the best cuts of lamb, endless drink and, at night, willing country girls to share his tent. At first, Amnon was reserved, suspicious of his brother's intentions. But by the third day of the feast he had relaxed into the belief that the reconciliation was genuine. By afternoon, he was very drunk. The killers moved then, as pitiless as a wolf pack. Three held him down as another three stabbed him.

"Adoniyah was drunk, too," Shlomo said. "That's why he panicked, I think. He yelled out that Avshalom's brutes were going to kill us all, and then he and Shefatiah and Yitraam and the others all ran to where we'd left the mules hobbled. I saw Yitraam scoop up Natan and put him on the mule in front of him. Adoniyah was yelling, ordering everyone to split up so that Avshalom wouldn't be able to get us all."

"But you did not run."

"No. I knew it was only about Amnon. And once I saw that Natan was looked after . . . In any case, I was holding Tamar, who was sobbing. Avshalom had brought her into the tent just before the attack. She was heavily veiled, but I knew it must be her. Because I'd really missed her, you know, and one of the reasons I wanted to go to Baal-hazor was to see her again. I'd been watching for her, asking everyone where she was. I'd begun to think that because Amnon was there, she wouldn't come out to the feast, and I was disappointed about that, and wondering if I should ask Avshalom for leave to visit her in private. Then, when I saw her, I was so glad, and I got up right away to greet her. I'd just made my way through the press of people in the tent, but before I could even get a word out, Avshalom shouted to Amnon, where he was reclining in the place of honor. Amnon turned to him. Amnon was smiling—I'll always remember that. Avshalom signed to Tamar, and she threw off her veil. I don't think Amnon even recognized her. His face didn't change—he was still grinning away. I suppose after so much heavy drinking he was pretty thick witted. But that was the signal for Avshalom's men, who were all dressed up as if they were guests. They grabbed Amnon. I think he did recognize her then, at the last moment, as the knives went into him. When they stabbed him, she just crumpled up. She was crying and shaking, so I held her, and she clung to me. Everything else was a blur of screaming and yelling and people running, tripping over one another, tables falling . . . Then Avshalom grabbed Tamar by the hand and pulled her away from me. He had a mule saddled for her and packhorses ready. They were on the road for Geshur while Amnon lay there with the blood still pulsing out of him.

"It fell to me to see his body wrapped and put on a bier, and I organized his men to bring him back here. Then I went and got my own mule and followed on behind."

I had seen this, too. His grave young face a calm center in the turmoil. I saw him take charge, cool in the panic, a boy commanding the attention of grown men, stepping through the blood to do what was necessary for his brother. Not one person questioned his authority. He stood there, gesturing for this and that person to fetch water and washing cloths, winding sheets and a stretcher. When the body was tended and wrapped, he called for bearers. He walked behind them, somber and dignified. Others took their cue from him, set aside their panic and formed up behind him in an orderly procession. I saw all this, and as he moved across the field other visions crowded my sight: I saw him as a man, a tall king, leading ever grander processions, the sun glinting off the circlet of gold on his brow, igniting the bright crimson, the deep purple, in the rich brocades of his robes.

After that vision, while I was still heavy and in pain, I dragged myself off the couch, and had Muwat help me bathe and dress in my court robe, and get me on a donkey like an old man who couldn't walk the distance to the city gate. David was at audience when I entered the hall. He hadn't heard anything yet from Baal-hazor. I took my place, and did my best to return his smile of greeting. It had been a week or more since I'd last attended him there, and he seemed touchingly pleased to see me. Yoav was in the midst of a lengthy report on border matters. I let my eye travel around the room. The crowd seemed quite depleted without the princes and their retinues. Then I noticed Yonadav at the edge of the crowd, and wondered at it. He was Amnon's constant attendant. They were inseparable. Why had he not been at Baal-hazor?

I had my answer when the first dusty refugee from the feast came bursting into the hall, borne on a hectic tide of panicked rumor. Amid cries and shouts and rending of garments, the dire words passed from mouth to mouth: All the princes dead. Avshalom had sprung a trap and massacred every last one of his brothers.

As the words reached David, his face collapsed, then his body followed. He seemed to slide from the great throne to the stone floor, a ragged keening issuing from the mouth that had for so many years uttered only sounds of sweetness or sonorous power. I pushed my way through to him. The crowd around him parted for me. I knelt beside him, taking his head into my lap. I wanted to tell him it wasn't true, but my mouth was still sealed and no words would come. From the corner of my eye I saw that Yonadav also was fighting his way forward through the chaos. The soldiers, unsure of his intent, blocked his path, holding him back from the king. I raised a hand to Yoav, signaling to let him through. Yoav grabbed him by the neck of his tunic and propelled him to the king's side.

He knelt down next to me and bent over so that he was almost shouting in David's ear. "My king! Don't believe that they have slain all the young men, all your sons. Amnon alone is dead." David's eyes, dark wet pools, scanned Yonadav's face, confused, hungry to believe in this lesser evil, unable to do so. His hand shot out and grabbed my arm, like a claw. "Is it true, what he says?" he rasped. I couldn't form any words, but I tried to reassure him with every gesture of my body. I felt him go flaccid in my arms. Time slowed, an agony of waiting. And then the watchers on the walls sent word: Adoniyah was approaching, Yitraam following a short distance behind.

"See?" said Yonadav. "The king's sons come, as your servant said, so it is."

Yoav glared at him, and then grabbed him up, pulling him onto his toes so that they stood eye to eye. "How do you know this, you snake? What else do you know?"

There was a stir by the door then, and Yoav turned, without relaxing his grip on Yonadav. Adoniyah had reached the hall, and David struggled to his feet, his wet face slack with relief, his arms outstretched to receive his son. The crowd shuffled as Adoniyah pushed through to his father, clinging to him, weeping.

I slipped away then. I did not need to wait for the other sons to straggle home and be welcomed by their father, or to see Shlomo deliver to David the butchered corpse of Amnon. I knew that David's relief and joy for the spared sons would turn to grief and mourning for the murdered one. And after that, loneliness and a corrosive longing for the one escaped into exile.

I knew, also, that the people who spoke of Natan's curse believed that they had seen it enacted. He had lost his infant son. Tamar, his only daughter, had been raped and beaten. Now his eldest was dead. The king had been paid back for his sin with regard to Uriah, had he not? Accordingly, after a period of mourning for Amnon (during which, to be honest, no one but David and Ahinoam truly mourned), a relieved and even festive mood took hold of the city. Most of the court and many of the common people were glad to be rid of the erratic, dangerous young prince. Only I knew the true weight left in the balance. A fourfold retribution, so David had decreed. And that judgment had not yet been fulfilled.

XXII

Maacah sent for me as soon as the official mourning period for Amnon had passed. I had never been to her house, but I knew it for the fine dwelling beside the palace, in the street where only David's highest courtiers were permitted to live. It had a splendid terrace, with a view second only to the king's, across the Wadi Kidron to the ranks of purple hills receding into an azure sky. When a servant showed me out onto this terrace, I was so struck by the view that I did not at first notice Yoav, seated in a shady corner, his ropy legs stretched out in front of him. I startled when he addressed me, and he laughed. "Didn't expect to see me, Prophet?" he said. "So you don't know everything, after all."

"I never said I did, as you well know," I replied, but I kept my tone light and returned his smile. "Perhaps you would like to enlighten me on a few things."

"You mean, what are we both doing here? It's a good question. I—"

At that moment Maacah swept onto the terrace. She wasn't dressed in black anymore, but wore a shimmering gown of lavender, with the lightest of white veils draped loosely over her hair. Yoav had risen to his feet as she arrived, but she signaled for him to sit and waved me to a chair beside her own.

"So you knew about this." Her voice was flat, affectless. "You knew my son would kill him."

"Yes," I said. "I knew." I paused a beat. "Did you?"

"Of course I did not know!" Her long fingers gripped the arms of her chair. "You think I would have sanctioned this, knowing it would lead to his exile? That worthless scum, Amnon. I would spit on his corpse. He has stolen the thrones out from beneath *both* my children now." She got up abruptly, and paced the terrace. She did not walk like a royal lady, but strode, like a man. The silk of her robe squeaked in complaint. "And I—I am deprived of my children, and of the king my husband's favor. He won't even see me. I suppose he blames me, as you do. Thinks me complicit. Fools. I did not come here, leave my home and my gods, to raise an outlaw son and a dishonored daughter. Well, if he blames me, I blame him. He should not have left this in Avshalom's hands. He had two years to watch my son's twisted heart hardening. How could he have been so blind as to think Avshalom could forgive, could reconcile? And now even the king my father is placed at risk. He took Avshalom in—he could hardly refuse sanctuary to his flesh and blood. But he wants no rift with David. He—"

"There won't be one." Yoav's gruff voice cut across her. "David is glad Avshalom is safe. He has sent to your father to say so."

She turned, relief and surprise on her face. "He has? How do you know this?"

"My brother Avishai took the message. The king would not entrust it to a common messenger. Though he must be seen to follow the law in this matter, it pains him. You know better than anyone how much he loves that young man your son. You only have to look at him. He's sick with missing him. He's not eating. Natan, I think you should see him. See if you can talk some sense into him. Or at least bring him some comfort."

Comfort, I thought. What comfort could I offer? What comfort had I ever offered him? The visions of promised greatness had led him only to bloody deeds and a self-regard that made him think he was above the law. And since then, what? Dire threats. Curses. Silence. I could not speak to him in the voice of the Name, but perhaps Yoav was right. Perhaps I could offer him, at least, the comfort and counsel of a friend.

"I will go," I said.

"When you do so," said Maacah, "will you speak to him for me? Will you tell him the truth, that I neither knew of nor endorsed this thing. He listens to you. To both of you. That is why I asked you to come here. I'm not young anymore. I have nothing here in this city, without my children, without my husband's regard. I want his good opinion, and I want my children. If anyone has sway with him, it is you two." She looked down at her hands and dropped her voice. "I was not raised to beg. But I'm begging you."

"Will you do it?" Yoav asked, as soon as we were in the street.

"Oh, yes. I will put her case to him, but I won't counsel him regarding it."

"Why not?"

"Because if I did, I would have to say that I think it better if Avshalom remains in Geshur."

"What? You mean you don't want him to be king?"

"What I want is not at issue. But since you ask, I believe he would make a very poor king."

"Well, I think you're wrong there. I think he's decisive and strategic. Look at how he took this revenge. Two years, he waited. That shows a lack of impulsiveness. Then there's the excellent planning, the flawless execution. Ruthless, yes. But sometimes a king needs to be ruthless in order to do what's right for his people. Tamar was his to protect; his own honor was befouled. He acted like a man. It was necessary."

How many times had I heard David justify killing with those same three words? The echo made me shiver. Yoav went on: "He's less of a brute than Amnon was, and much more intelligent. In any case, we need him. He's the right age, and he has the right mix of experience so that in a few more years . . . and we might only have a few, the way the king is." He gave me a considering glance. "It's Shlomo, isn't it? You want to put your own little acolyte on the throne." He snorted. "So pure you are, but in the end you're after power, just like the rest of us."

I waved a hand. It didn't matter what motives he ascribed to me, and in any case, I could not explain it to him. "The succession is not for me to determine. In any case, the line of candidates is still very long, even without the two eldest, before we arrive at Shlomo. He's still a boy, after all. He's only twelve."

"Well, so long as you see that. And I don't stand against Shlomo, you shouldn't think I do. He's a bright one, there's no doubt of that. I've known grown men—experienced fighters—with less strategic sense than that boy has. But he is, as you say, a boy still. If you are thinking to be a kingmaker in that direction, you'd better see to David. The way he's been lately, he might not last till that whelp grows claws and teeth long enough to fight his way past his littermates."

We were nearing the palace gate, and I needed to turn the subject before we were overheard discussing such delicate matters. So I raised an issue that had been puzzling me. "Where is your cousin, Shammah's son Yonadav? I thought it odd that he knew so much about the killing. I gathered you also thought so."

"That ass-licking little shit." Yoav hawked up a gob of spittle and deposited it on the roadside. "This whole affair rests on his scrawny shoulders. It was Yonadav who pandered Tamar to Amnon like a trussed fowl. And then, when Avshalom did his little act with the olive branch, Yonadav saw how David liked it, and he thought Avshalom might be on the rise. So he switched sides. That's another thing about Avshalom—he'll take help where it's offered. Doesn't hold grudges. Can be a useful quality in a king. So Avshalom used Yonadav, that turncoat, to lure Amnon. Yonadav was party to the assassination, I'm certain of it. I had him roughed up a bit, but he's tougher than he looks. Even Avishai couldn't get him to confess to it."

"Where is he now?"

"He's in Beit Lehem, at Shammah's house. I told him I don't want to see him in the city anymore."

"What did Shammah say to that?"

Yoav laughed. "Quite a bit. All of it in cusswords, that foul-mouthed old graybeard. But I told him it was Beit Lehem for Yonadav, or the road to Geshur along with the other murderers, and that I couldn't guarantee his safety on that road." He smiled. I could tell he'd enjoyed putting Shammah in his place. But then his face turned grave. "Seriously, Natan, apart from all this business, I'm worried. The king's not well and now the succession's uncertain. While Avshalom's in exile, Adoniyah is next in line, but I don't think he's up to it. Not sure he ever will be. He's less wild than the older two, but I've seen no real substance there. If there's any kind of threat to the king while all this is unresolved . . . well, I don't like it. I'm going to Hevron myself, to make sure none of Shaul's old faction is getting any notions. I hope you can do something for the king. I think you might be the only one who can."

XXIII

Can a man grow old like the turning of leaf, blazing bright one day, dried and dull the next? So it seemed with David. He received me in his private room, where we had met so often before. In all my recollections of such meetings, he was a blur of fervent energy, the keen center of every conversation, the source of generous gesture, insight, wit. Now he reclined on the low couch, a sheepskin cloak pulled over him even though the day was fine and still. There was a silver charger on the table by his couch. Grapes, apricots, figs. Bread, soft cheese, olives. None of it had been touched. His fast had sapped his vitality. His eyes, large in his shrunken face, always so expressive, now expressed nothing but pain. His face—his beautiful face—was sunken and scored with lines, the hollows beneath his cheekbones scooped out as if a sculptor had driven his thumbs too deeply into the clay.

"You can't go on like this," I said.

His face flickered into the shadow of a smile. "Is that my prophet speaking to me again, at long last?"

I shook my head. "That voice has been silenced, for now. But you don't need a prophet to tell you to eat. I'm speaking as your subject, who cares for you. As, I hope, your friend. You can't starve yourself."

He gave a whispery laugh. "It's remarkable, how very many things there are that a king may not do."

"You are a man, also. Subject to a man's needs. You should eat something."

"I should eat something. I should do many things I have not done, and I should not have done many of the things that I have done. My heart, Natan, is as hollow as a gourd. If I am a man, as you say, then I deserve to be ranked with the lowest of men. Is not one of a man's most basic duties to raise his children, keep them safe, bring them to an honorable manhood? What good, to forge a kingdom, to win wars, to build this city, and then to fail at this most basic task—a task the most wretched herdsman in his hut can manage to do. And what have I raised? What kind of a man must I be judged, who has brought forth rapists and murderers? What kind of man begets such sons?"

"You have many sons. Not just these two. You mourn Amnon. No one blames you for that. A man may mourn his fallen son. Even though death *was* the penalty for his act against his sister, had he been punished by your justice rather than by his brother's hand, still you would have a right to mourn him. As for Avshalom, he is safe in his exile, under the protection of his grandfather. You should comfort yourself with that."

"Should I? Should I so? How, when all I can think of is my longing for him, for my son Avshalom. Two years I had him by me in the hall of audience, and all that concerned me was that he hated his older brother. Now I know that he hated me also, because I didn't act. . . . And now I have lost him . . ." His sunken eyes brimmed then, and he turned away from me. After a moment he raised a hand and gestured for me to leave.

Sunlight poured through the high windows and spilled across the floor. I pretended I had not seen his signal and walked to the tall doors that opened to his private terrace. I stepped out into the bright, still day. The stone of the balustrade was warm to the touch. I looked up, and saw what I had hoped to see . . . the she-eagle, hovering on some elusive current of air that my skin could not feel. I dropped my eyes and searched among the palms and olives in the lower garden. There he was, poised in concentration. He was wearing white, gleaming in the strong sunlight.

I went back inside and approached David's couch. I laid a hand on his shoulder and felt bone. "Come outside with me," I said. "I want to show you something." At first, he made no sign that he had heard, but then—why, I don't know—he gave a deep sigh and swung his legs to the floor. He took the arm I held out to him, and we walked together onto the terrace. I pointed up at the bird, and down to the garden. Just then Shlomo became aware of us and turned his head. His face broke into a smile just like his mother's. He raised his hand in a salute, and David returned it. Then Shlomo gave a series of shrill whistles. The eagle drew into a stoop, but instead of returning to Shlomo's wrist, she wheeled and came to us, landing on the balustrade before us in a brute beating of massive wings. She turned her indifferent eyes, bright gold, on David, and he returned her stare, transfixed.

"There is beauty and power there," I said softly. "And I don't speak only of the bird." I gestured to the bright, intense face smiling up at us. "I speak of the boy—the young man—who has mastered this bird. I speak of your son. A son of whom you *can* be proud. Your sins have consequences, but the Name has not forsaken you, King."

David turned to me, color returning to his face. "Send for the boy. Tell him I would eat with him. Send me my son."

And so it began. Shlomo, at twelve, became a salve upon his father's wounded heart, the beloved companion and the joy of his old age.

But affection was one thing, royal succession another. No one accounted a twelve-year-old in that reckoning. Adoniyah, next in age to Avshalom, seemed to be the presumed heir. But Adoniyah did not have Avshalom's presence, intelligence or political skills. Nor did he have the same place in his father's regard. David had always seen himself in Avshalom, and why wouldn't he? Avshalom had the same quicksilver nature, the same physical gifts, the same ability to attract a following. It was not just David who lamented his exile. David made no move to name his heir, and it seemed his own mind remained unsettled on the subject.

As the months passed, memories of the murder faded. It became clear that a faction had emerged, ready to say that Avshalom had acted within his rights, and that he should be allowed to return from exile. I asked Muwat to probe the matter, and in a very short while he was able to confirm, through his network of Hittite servants, that the partisan faction centered on Maacah's house, which did not surprise me, and that it was led by Yoav, which did.

When I confronted Yoav on the matter, he was forthright. "There's unrest in Hevron," he said. "We keep a firm fist on it, to be sure, but I think there's a real risk from there, with no settled successor, if David were to die untimely—and let's face it, at his age it wouldn't even be that untimely. They resent us, Natan. They resent paying taxes to build this city, which flourishes, while Hevron has become a backwater. They don't see the fruits of the taxes they pay, as we do. And outside the town, the farmers in Yudah are unhappy that their surplus food has to be sold at set prices to feed the standing army and the priests—who live and spend in this city, and marry from among its daughters, not their own. They know they can get more for their produce on the open market. The bald fact is the people have grown used to peace. They forget how it was, before. They don't value what David has done for us as they once did. It's not a good situation. I think Avshalom should come back, so that there's a clear heir, a man with military experience, who could be king tomorrow, if it came to it. David won't do it. He wants to. I know he does. But he bent the law to his own desires with regard to Uriah, as you were so quick to point out with your parables. He's not in a rush to be seen doing it again. You, perhaps, are the only one who could convince him. Make up another fine parable or two." He gave me an appraising look. "But you won't."

"No," I repeated calmly. "I won't."

"And I can't fathom you. Never could. Avshalom avenged a great wrong. Why do you hate him so?"

"I don't hate him for what he did," I said. *I hate him for what he will do, as will you, Yoav, in due season.* So I said in my heart. But I could not speak those words aloud. Yoav left in a foul mood, muttering about my intransigence.

A week later, I recalled that conversation when a widow from the town of Tekoa presented herself before David for a judgment. She was dressed in mourning clothes and had the spare, worn look of one who has grieved a long time. She prostrated herself, uttering words of thanks to the king for agreeing to hear her suit. David was clearly moved by her salutation, and waved for one of his servants to help her up and to bring her a chair, which was rare for a supplicant in the audience hall.

"What troubles you?" he asked kindly.

"My king, your maidservant had two sons. As brothers will do, they fell into an argument while tending the fields, and came to blows, with no one there to stop them. One of them struck the other and killed him, and then all the men of my clan insisted that I hand over the killer to be put to death." She began to weep, but with great composure continued speaking through her tears. "My lord, I know the law ordains this, but my son did not mean to kill his brother. He's all I have left. They would quench the last ember remaining to me, and leave my dead husband without name or remnant on the earth." She buried her face in her hands.

The king was clearly moved. "Go home," he said gently. "I will issue an order that your son be spared. If anyone says anything to you, have him brought to me and he will never trouble you again."

She raised her wet face, blinking. "You will restrain the blood avenger, so that my son will not be killed?"

"As the Name lives, not a hair of your son will fall to the ground." David gestured that the matter was closed, and a guard stepped forward to escort the widow out.

"Please let your maidservant say another word to my lord the king."

"Speak on," said David, a little surprised.

"Your majesty is as wise as an angel, and has given me this judgment. Yet he does not bring back his own banished one. We must all die. We are like water that is poured out on the ground and cannot be gathered up."

"Who are you speaking for?" David demanded sharply. The

widow, rattled perhaps by the change of tone in his voice, gave a frightened glance in the direction of Yoav, who, I noticed, was sweating. The king saw the glance, and glared at Yoav.

The widow—if widow she was—stammered as she replied. "Your maidservant thought, Let the word of my lord the king provide comfort, for my lord the king is like an angel of God, understanding everything, good and bad."

David shifted in his chair, irritated by her obfuscation. "Do not withhold from me what I ask of you. Did Yoav put you up to this?"

She clenched her hands, which were trembling. "It is as you say. Your servant Yoav was the one who instructed me."

Yoav stepped forward and prostrated himself, ready for David's anger. There was a long silence. When David spoke, he lifted his chin and looked beyond Yoav to the courtiers and supplicants crowding the hall. "I do not pardon my son. I will not receive him back into this court. But I will end his exile." He looked down at Yoav, prone on the flagstones at his feet. "Yoav, do this thing. My son may return to the Land. I will not receive him. He may not return here to the court, but I will allow him to reside outside the city, where his mother may have comfort of him. Go and bring him back. Bring back my son Avshalom."

Yoav let out a long, relieved breath. He rose to his knees, his arms outstretched, palms upward. David pushed himself from his chair and walked forward. He reached out to Yoav, took his hands and raised him. They stood for a moment, eye to eye. Then the king embraced him. To some in the audience hall it was, I suppose, a reassuring moment. The frail king encircled and supported by the strong arms of his robust nephew. A king had taken counsel from his beloved general. He had recognized Yoav's good intentions and allowed his heart to soften in the matter of his son. You could hear an exhalation of relief and satisfaction in the crowded room. Standing behind the throne, I also sighed. But for me it was a sigh of resignation, weariness, despair.

XXIV

Avshalom returned without fanfare. David granted him some land neighboring Yoav's, with the idea that Yoav could keep an eye on him. I think that David believed the young man needed Yoav's guidance and would be glad to settle modestly for the life of a prosperous farmer. Which only demonstrated how little he knew of his son.

Avshalom did not remain quiet for long. His first act was to clear half his cropland for a barracks and training ground. He bought himself a *merkava* and surrounded himself with a princely retinue of fifty bodyguards and pages. As their leader, he appointed his cousin Amasa, the youngest son of David's sister Avigal. Yoav had been Amasa's mentor and patron, promoting him rapidly through the ranks. The move seemed to be a way to draw Yoav closer, and at the same time to underline Avshalom's royal ties. If David would not restore him to the state befitting a crown prince, Avshalom, it seemed, was willing to do it for himself. He could be found most afternoons with Amasa, exercising his men in what had once been a field of swaying barley.

The mornings, however, were another matter. Muwat told me that Avshalom made a practice of being at the city gate early in the day, when supplicants arrived from the outlying villages, hoping to have their matters heard by the king. Avshalom had taken it upon himself to greet all comers, holding a kind of informal court of his own just inside the city gates. Muwat gave an arresting account of the scene there, so early one crisp morning I borrowed one of his shawls, threw it over my head and went to the gate square, to mingle with the crowd and see for myself. Sure enough, Avshalom arrived soon after, mounted on a glossy mule, surrounded by a retinue of good-looking young men; tall, hard-bodied youths who carried themselves with the confident bearing of soldiers.

Some handsome men prefer to surround themselves with plain or homely attendants, but Avshalom clearly had enough confidence in his own physical perfection to be unconcerned by comparisons. It was clear that he had not spent his exile idling, but in hard training. He blazed with good health, from the shining fall of his long hair to the sun-bronzed gleam of his well-muscled limbs. His vibrancy brought David before me—David as he had been in his prime, not enfeebled as he now was. The traveling supplicants, I thought, also would draw such a contrast. Having been welcomed to the city by this radiant figure, how would they not be disappointed when finally they came face-to-face with their aging king?

I loitered in the shadowed colonnade at the edge of the square, close enough to observe, yet far back enough to blend into the morning bustle. Avshalom could not have been more personable. He seemed to have a wide acquaintance among the city folk, greeting many by name and asking after their families. But his main focus was on the steady stream of visitors who entered the gate. He moved unhurriedly from one to the next, extending his greetings, endlessly patient with those who wished to pour out the details of their suit. He would lock eyes with each person, sometimes placing a hand lightly on their shoulder or arm, creating a sense of fellow feeling, nodding, frowning, smiling, as the substance of the conversation required. It was very well done. Very well done, and entirely devious. Day by day, man by man, hand clasp by hand clasp, Avshalom was building his faction. The merkava, the attendants, gave him the trappings of royal power, the ruler that you follow. The daily encounters at the gate brought him down to the level of everyman, the leader whom you love. I had no doubt that each of these travelers would go home to his village and tell his neighbors how David the king had disappointed them, that he seemed wan and distracted and suddenly old. But his son, ah, now, that handsome, princely fellow who took the time to listen—there was a man to watch. Avshalom was deft, I had to credit him.

Yoav, so anxious to return this heir to his father's bosom. Might as well have brought the king an asp. I wondered how he now saw things, and resolved to find out. I was so lost in thought that I neglected to take Muwat's shawl off my head as I approached his gate, and the gatekeeper barked rudely as he demanded my business. Any other day, I would have been amused by the stricken look on his face when I threw off the shawl.

He was still muttering apologies as the gate clanked shut behind me. Yoav interrupted a meeting with his unit commanders as soon as a servant brought him word that I was waiting for him.

"You've been to the gate?" he asked, direct as always. "He's not wasting any time, is he?"

"It's quite a performance," I said.

"Quite. It's not what I expected. I thought he'd be content to bide his time, as he did with that other business. He's been at me to get him invited back to court."

"Have you broached it with David?"

"No, and I don't intend to, either. I'm out on a thin branch already with this one. I did tell David about the antics at the gate, and do you know how he reacted? With pleasure. He's always been blind about his sons. You know that. Now he says he's glad that Avshalom is winning the hearts of the people. He says he's proud of him."

As Yoav spoke, my thoughts traveled to my interview, so many years earlier, with Mikhal. She had described her father Shaul's growing jealousy of David, the young upstart winning the people's hearts. Now David himself was being usurped in the people's affections, and yet what had driven Shaul deeper into madness had not caused David a moment's concern. The difference, I suppose, was that because of Shmuel, Shaul knew he had lost the love of the Name. As distant and unhelpful as I had been forced to be in recent years, David knew I was with him, and through me, he still felt the touch of the divine hand upon his kingship.

"I believe that if I did ask him to receive Avshalom," Yoav said, "he might very well say yes. And to be honest, now that I see that young man at work, I'm not sure that's a good thing. I'm beginning to understand you better, Natan. I don't trust him, either."

"Does he know that?"

"I don't think so. Although he might be starting to sweat over it a bit. I've ignored his last two messages."

"Have you so? He won't like that."

He grinned. "I am sure of it."

"Do you have someone close to him?" If Yoav could be direct, I decided, so could I. He gave me a piercing glance, but then he barked his foxlike laugh. "You know I do," he said.

"Amasa?"

He lifted his chin in acknowledgment. "Amasa. And others."

A week later, Avshalom set fire to Yoav's barley field. Yoav pulled me aside in the palace hallway to tell me about it. "Total loss, that field."

"Did Amasa not warn you?"

"He swears he didn't know. He was the one Avshalom sent to bring me the message that this was just a warning. He intended to burn all my fields if I didn't come to see him."

"And did you go?" I thought I'd seen Yoav in every mood—violent rage, deep fear for his life, lit up, variously, with battle fervor and victory toasts. But I'd never seen him look sheepish until that moment.

"Of course I did," he grumbled. "I can't set up openly against him. If I did, it wouldn't stop with my fields. He's a power, that young man. It's clear enough. David's the only one who could've dealt with him, but I think it's too late now, even for that."

"So? What did he want?"

"What he's wanted all along. To see his father, to be received at court. To worm his way back into the succession. He was as cool as could be when I got there. Apologized for the field. Offered to compensate me for the lost grain. Said I'd left him no choice—no other way to get my attention. I'm going to do it, Natan. Because you can be sure it will happen, one day. David wants it, in his heart. So I might as well keep in credit and not make an enemy there. I'm going to ask David to receive him."

"Do what you have to," I said. "I will not speak against it."

So Yoav put Avshalom's request to David, who had been waiting for any slight pretext to see this son he loved. Still, David held himself aloof at their first meeting. When Avshalom rushed forward to kiss him, he turned his head and did not offer an embrace. To cover the moment, Avshalom offered the supplicant's ceremonial kiss, touching his lips to David's shoulder, making it seem as if this respectful stranger's greeting had been all he'd intended. I am not sure why David withheld himself from full reconciliation, as it was abundantly clear how much he desired to clasp his son in his arms. In any case, the return of Avshalom breathed new vigor into him. He ate more, and gained back some of his lost weight, and started to look stronger.

Shlomo, who had become such a solace to his father, was pushed aside as soon as Avshalom returned to court. "It's as if he doesn't see me," he confided wistfully one afternoon, as we walked in the almond groves behind my house. "He never sends for me anymore. Avshalom's the only one he wants. Adoniyah is angry about it. His pride is hurt, and he lets it show. Which is stupid, I think. The king doesn't like it, and it just makes Avshalom look better by comparison. Me, it's not about pride. I just miss talking to my father. There's so much to learn from him. But Avshalom doesn't seem to see that. He doesn't even pretend to be interested in anything David has to say. It's all just flattery with him, and empty words. Anyway, maybe I'll be called on again, once Avshalom goes to Hevron."

"Hevron?" I swallowed. "When?" I had not expected this so soon.

"For the feast of the new moon. He says he promised, when he was in exile in Geshur, that he would sacrifice in his birth city. He said it would be good for relations with Yudah as well. The king hasn't been there in an age—Avshalom said his going would be a way to show that the family remembers their kin. So the king told him to go in peace. He's taking his companions, and has invited others from the city who also want to make pilgrimage to their family graves. It will be a large party, I think. They leave at first light."

XXV

It is one thing to know what is to come. It is another thing to confront it. Go in peace, the king had said to Avshalom. But he went, of course, for war.

I had expected more patience from him. The same cold patience he had used against Amnon. Had Avshalom bided his time, played upon the king's great love for him, power would have flowed gradually into his hands. In a year, maybe two at most, he would have been king in all but name. By then, it would have taken only a small push to unseat David and claim the throne. But Avshalom couldn't wait.

Some two hundred set out with him to Hevron. I do not say that all of them were conspirators. Many, no doubt, joined with him in good faith. It was a long tradition to sacrifice in the old hallows of Giloh. Some went with Avshalom in reverence, some simply looking to enjoy the feasting that accompanied such rites, some, no doubt, thinking to ingratiate themselves with the young prince who stood once again so high in his father's love. I do not know which share of them were traitors at heart, and which share found themselves caught up in events that they could not have foreseen. But witting or not, those two hundred were the seed corn of Avshalom's rebellion.

As the throng made its way south on the Hevron road, others, deep in the conspiracy, fanned out north and west across the country, to every town and hamlet where Avshalom had done a favor or settled a suit to a plaintiff's benefit. These spies and agents of Avshalom's were charged with measuring his support as well as the depth of dis-satisfaction with the king. In Hevron, he waited for their reports. Then he tallied his supporters and decided he had what he needed to make his move. At the feast of the sacrifice, when everyone was well fed and in good humor, when the wine had flowed just enough, but not too much, Avshalom stood up and made his claim. At first, some were confused, but the men of his cohort raised a loud cheer, and soon half the hillside had joined it. In the midst of the cries, Avshalom ordered that the shofars sound, proclaiming him king.

With the blowing of those horns, my long silence ended. At last, at long last, my tongue loosened. I was free to speak again. We were in the audience hall when I cried out to the king, telling him that the loyalty of the men of the Land had been stolen by his son.

It is something that, after all the time that had elapsed since I had offered vision or prophecy, he listened to me at once, even on a matter so grave. As I began to speak, he turned to me, his face full of wonder to hear that voice again. Then, as the meaning of my words came clear to him, there was a moment—very brief—when pain contorted his features. But he did not let himself dwell on betrayal by the son he loved so well. He put those emotions quickly away and began barking orders. If I was once again his prophet, then he was once again my king—decisive, determined—a leader to follow. He called for Yoav, Avishai and Benaiah, who commanded his personal bodyguard. I stopped Yoav and pulled him aside as he entered the audience hall. "How did you not know of this? What of Amasa?"

"Amasa is a traitor. I know that now."

"The others? You said you had others."

Yoav shook my hand off his wrist and pushed past me. "You're asking *me* this?" he hissed. "You're the prophet. Why did you not know?"

David's first words showed how strategically he was thinking. "I can't stay here," he said. When Yoav made to interrupt, proclaiming that the city had the best defenses, he raised a hand and silenced him.

"I will not have Avshalom put this city to the sword. It's me he must kill, not the people of this city. He knows that. So, I will not stand my ground here, but lead him away. Let him think we've fled in fear. I will go like a humiliated penitent, barefoot and weeping. Let him think me weak. Let him pursue me to some place where we can set a trap and close it upon him." He called for maps and soon had devised a plan. He sent runners ahead, secretly, to three of his staunchest supporters across the Yarden River, in the well-fortified town of Mahanaim. This stronghold was to be our secret destination and the staging point from which to spring our trap.

Although we went out dressed as mourners and penitents, David had weapons and armor hidden under straw bales in the wains that followed behind us. We would move fast and travel light, just as we had in the days when Shaul pursued us. As we were about to pass through the city gates, I noted that the barracks of the Plishtim mercenaries were abandoned. I saw David looking up at the blank windows, resignation on his face. "They've gone back to Gath," he said. "I can't blame them." But as we passed through the gates, Yoav raised his hand and halted the column. There was an army of six hundred in ranks, armed and arrayed for battle. Ittai, the Gittite captain, stepped forward and saluted. David was visibly moved. "Why should your men join in this? The new king will pay for your services, I am certain of it. I have no call on you to ask you to follow me into this uncertain fight. Go back to your barracks. I release you from your service with honor."

Ittai shook his head. "As my lord the king lives, wherever you are, there I will be, I and my men, whether for death or life."

David reached out a hand to Ittai and clasped his forearm. His eyes were wet. "You are resolved in this? All of you?"

"All of us, my lord king."

"Then march by," David said. He was too overcome to say more.

We had crossed the Wadi Kidron when a messenger rode up the ranks, bringing the king word that Zadok and Aviathar were following with the ark in a long, doleful procession, with all their sons. David raked a hand through his hair and shook his head. "I don't want this," he said. "I need to move at speed, and I need Avshalom to think I leave a broken man, not a fighter with the ark as his rallying point."

"You'll have to send them back," I said. He nodded, and halted the march until the priests could make their way forward to him. He spoke to them in the sorrowful, humble tones of a man unsure of his destiny. "Take the ark back to the city," he said. "If I find favor with the Name, he will bring me back and let me see it in its rightful place. And if the Name should say 'I no longer have use for you,' then I am ready for that. But the ark belongs in the city, not in the wilderness. Those days are past. So go, with all your sons, and replace it in the tabernacle where it belongs."

We marched on, barefoot and with covered heads, as David had directed, climbing the Mount of Olives until we paused to rest at the summit. Along the way, dozens of people came out of their homes, greeting us weeping. Many handed over dates and parched corn, whatever supplies they had in their stores, to sustain us on our journey. Only one—a member of Shaul's clan—came running at the king, throwing stones and hurling insults. "Get out, get out, you criminal!" he yelled. "So you are requited for your crimes against Shaul!"

Avishai, always quick to anger, was at the king's side in an instant, putting himself in the way of the stones, his sword drawn and his short knife in his other hand. "Why let that dead dog abuse you?" he snarled. "Let me go over and cut off his head!"

David laid a hand on Avishai, restraining him. "What has this to do with you? If my own son, my own issue, seeks to kill me, why wouldn't Shaul's kinsman do the same?" He turned and walked on, allowing the Benyaminite to follow beside him, flinging dirt and insults.

I smiled grimly to myself as I trudged beside him, feeling the sting as an occasional pebble missed its mark and bit into my flesh. I knew that David wanted word of this humiliation to get back to Avshalom. David knew he would take it as further evidence of his father's defeated state of mind.

Finally we reached the shores of the Yarden, where David said we would rest for the night. As we set up a makeshift camp, an old man approached the pickets, asking to see the king. At first, I didn't recognize him. Like us, he was wearing rent garments and ashes. It took me a moment to place him as Hushai, who had been part of Shaul's court and had advised David when he first joined the royal retinue after the battle at Wadi Elah. He was a sage old man whose wisdom David valued. He had served in David's court for a time, until he grew too old and retired to his lands on the western slope of the mountain. David greeted him warmly, and drew him aside for a private word. "I need to be frank with you, Hushai. I'm touched and honored that you come to me. But if you march on with us, you will be a burden, at your age. We need to move fast and rest little."

Hushai's face fell. David reached out a hand. "I do not say you may not serve me. I have a grave charge for you, if you are willing. Go to the city. Lay your services at the feet of Avshalom when he comes. Tell him you saw me, weak and broken, tell him that the Plishtim mercenaries have deserted and that I have only my core of seasoned fighters at my side. Say you stand ready to serve him, as you once served me. Then send word to Zadok and Aviathar of all you see and hear. They can dispatch their sons to bring me word of Avshalom's plans. We will trap him, and put an end to this young man's mad folly."

Hushai embraced the king and set off willingly to the city. As it happened, he arrived just as Avshalom's forces entered the gates, unopposed. Most of the citizens stayed indoors but many greeted him, cheering.

Hushai, summoning all his strength, forced his way to the front of the column and presented himself to Avshalom, crying out, "Long live the king!"

Avshalom threw up a hand, halting his procession. "What's this? Hushai? Is this your loyalty to your old friend my father?"

"Not at all!" Hushai cried. "I am for the one whom the Name and all the men of Israel have chosen, and I will stay with him. Whom should I serve, if not David's son? As I was in your father's service, so am I now in yours."

Only a man as vain as Avshalom, perhaps, would have accepted this switch of allegiance so unthinkingly. But so he did, and so Hushai was at his side to send us word of what happened next. As soon as he entered the palace, Avshalom called for the chief eunuch.

"Bring Batsheva to me."

"My lord, Batsheva and her sons left with David."

Avshalom's brow furrowed. He had not expected that. "Which of my father's wives is here, then?"

The eunuch kept his eyes on the floor, his face beaded with sweat. "Your mother, my lord. None other. The king ordered all his wives— saving my lord's mother—to take refuge outside the city. Only the concubines remain here."

Avshalom's face was cold and still. "How many?"

"My lord, I am not—"

"How many?"

The eunuch cleared his throat. "Ten, my lord."

"Very well. Pitch a tent on the roof, leave the sides open. Bring the ten. I will lie with them tonight."

"My lord? In the sight of the city? The king's concubines?"

"As you say. The king's concubines. And am I not the king?"

I do not know how many of those young women Avshalom raped that night. Hushai had too much decency to bear witness, and David never spoke of it. But even one would have been enough to make the point: what had been David's was now his son's.

Whatever the extent of Avshalom's debauchery, as soon as he was done with it, he called his war council together. Amasa, his general, and Ahitophel, his chief counselor, advised a night march, to come upon David weary and unprepared. Hushai, wanting to win time for David to reach Mahanaim, shook his head and spoke up stridently. "The men who still follow your father are few, maybe, but they are courageous soldiers. The king will not be with them this night, be sure of it. He will have found some bolt hole to hide in, as broken as he is. If you send your men tonight, Yoav and his brother Avishai, those blood-soaked sons of Zeruiah, will have a trap to spring, be sure of it." He turned to Amasa. "You know your cousins. You know how they can fight when cornered. And if you lose men—even a few—and yet don't make an end to David, word of it will shake confidence in your uprising. Wait, gather your forces from Dan to Beersheva, call up a great army and lead it yourself. We'll descend on him then as thick as the dew."

Avshalom gazed from Hushai to Ahitophel, weighing the matter. "Hushai, I think, is right in this. Call the muster. We will wait, and march out in strength." He gave an exaggerated yawn and raised his fist in a lewd gesture toward the roof terrace. "In any case, I've done enough to secure my kingdom for one night."

Within an hour, Hushai had sent word to the high priests, who entrusted their sons Yonatan and Ahimaaz with the message for the king, disclosing Avshalom's plans.

As they made their uncertain and dangerous way, eluding Avshalom's forces and hiding from his supporters, David retired to his tent to attempt to get some rest. But within the hour, I knew that rest eluded him. I could hear harp music, and the sound of his voice, singing with something close to its old sweetness and power:

> Many are saying of me,
> "Yah will not deliver him."
> But you are a shield around me,
> my glory, the one who lifts my head high.
> I call out to Yah,
> and he answers me from his holy mountain

I lie down and sleep;
I wake again, because Yah sustains me. . . .

Fear and faith, but faith the stronger. The words washed over me, and I took comfort. He was still singing when I drifted into a restorative slumber.

Yonatan and Ahimaaz reached our camp just before daybreak. David, awake and alert, smiled grimly as he heard of Hushai's success. Then we moved as we had when we were all much younger men— those outlaw years had taught us the meaning of nimbleness. By the time the sun was fully up, every man in the king's army had safely crossed the Yarden. It was no easy thing. The water was swift and bracingly cold, born out of the snows of high Ha Hermon. When I had made my own difficult crossing, I stopped for a moment on the far shore to wring out my tunic and catch my breath. I looked back, and took heart from the sight. Foreigners and natives of the Land, working together as brothers, those who were strong swimmers supporting those who clung for dear life to the ropes we'd strung from bank to bank. David's army—this polyglot, mongrel force, forged out of loyalty and love.

The leaders of Mahanaim, all devoted to David, sent wains to collect us, and an honor guard to bring David into the city, where sanctuary and supplies awaited us. The result: our army was well fed, rested and ready for combat by the time Avshalom's forces set out in pursuit.

David divided his forces into three companies, one led by Yoav, one by Avishai and one by Ittai. Initially, he intended also to lead out a force of his own, but his generals prevailed on him. They pointed out that since his death was Avshalom's chief object, once it became known which company he led, it would become the focus of all the fighting. David misliked this, but he saw the reason in their argument and agreed to stay back in the town and direct the fighting from there.

As the troops mustered outside the town walls, Shlomo came to his father and begged to be allowed to join the fighting. David placed his hands on Shlomo's shoulders and looked down at his son's bright, intense face. He smiled. "I did not take you for a warrior. Natan says that your interests do not lie in that direction."

"This is different," Shlomo said. "I want to fight for you, Father. I do know how. You can ask Avishai—"

David drew the boy into his arms and held him close for a moment. Shlomo had not yet grown into his full height—his father still stood a head taller.

"It is not fit that brother takes up arms against brother," David said. "And in any case, you are just thirteen years old."

Shlomo gently extricated himself and stepped backward. He fixed his father with a direct, unfaltering gaze. "And how old were you when you slew the giant of Gath?"

David gave a sigh and smiled slightly. "Older." But his face had softened. He glanced over his shoulder, to where I stood behind him. I gave a slight nod. Shlomo needed to do this; the common desire of any boy who feels his approaching manhood. Beyond that, he needed to do it so that the troops would remember he had fought. Since I knew his future, I also knew there could be no grave danger for him. David looked to me to confirm that.

"Go, then," David said. "Go with Yoav. Assist his arms bearers. But see the armorer first. You're not going to battle in a tunic."

As Shlomo sprinted off to the armory, David signaled to me. "You know he will be safe." It was not a question. "But go with him, in any case. It will ease my mind to know you are beside him." As I strapped on my greaves, I was glad to find the leather oiled and pliant, and was thankful to Muwat, who had kept my gear in good repair through the years when I had happily had no need of it. I had not thought to go into battle again.

As the watchers sent word that Avshalom's forces were nearing the Yarden, David called his generals together. After some stirring words of thanks for their loyalty and service, he looked down at his hands and gave a deep sigh. "What I am now going to say will not sit well with some of you." He gave a sharp glance at Yoav and Avishai. "Nevertheless, I will speak my heart. Deal gently with my boy Avshalom, for my sake. Pass the word to your troops to take him alive." Ittai kept his face impassive. Avishai scowled. But Yoav could barely contain himself. His face turned a mottled purple with the effort it cost him to contain his disgust.

The battle, when it came, took place in the forest of Efraim on the east bank of the Yarden. Anticipating this, Yoav had arranged for a force to close behind Avshalom's army after it crossed the river so as to cut off a retreat and force them forward into the difficult terrain of the eastern shore. I would like to write that it was a masterpiece of strategy, in which Avshalom's vainglorious folly was ended with little loss of life. Unfortunately, that didn't happen. The battle was a bloodbath, notable for the confusion imposed by the dense forest, low scrub and rocky outcrops, which impeded movement and coordination—ours, as well as theirs. A great slaughter took place, of which they say that the forest devoured more troops than the sword. There were some terrible deaths. A brushfire, set to drive a unit out of the woods into open ground, got out of control when the winds changed direction unexpectedly. The ensuing blaze engulfed more than a hundred men—our soldiers among them. When we found the bodies they were blackened husks. Others, who fell wounded, were eaten alive where they lay by the lions and wild boars that inhabited the forest.

It was Yoav's way to lead from the front, and so we moved with him through a day as bloody as any I had experienced. Shlomo fought proficiently, and with courage, but I saw none of his father's warrior zeal, no zest for killing, no bloodlust. He demonstrated his courage when another young armor bearer fell wounded in open ground, exposed to the enemy archers. It was Shlomo who ran forward into the rain of arrows to drag the youth to safety.

As it sometimes happens, in midafternoon there came a lull in the fighting. I found myself in the tight knot of fighters around Yoav. He was bent over, hands on his knees, catching his breath, when one of his captains from a separate unit burst out of the underbrush, calling out that he had a message for the general.

Though I couldn't recall his name, I knew him for one of Yoav's chief captains. Sweat stained, bloody, he gasped out word that he'd just left Avshalom, hanging in a tree.

"How is this?" Yoav snapped.

"We prevailed against his bodyguard—hard fighting, many dead. When he saw that his best men had fallen—killed or injured, all—he fled for his life. He thought he'd give us the slip by driving his mule into a dense grove of elah trees. He was pushing his mount—booting it bloody. It was tossing its head and shying. He couldn't bring it under control at all." As he spoke I could feel the mule's resistance to Avshalom's cruel boots digging into her bruised sides, and his hard hand, wrenching the bit in her mouth. I felt the pounding of the beast's generous heart, pressed beyond endurance. I was seeing as she saw, in great wide arcs on either side, but nothing at all straight in front of me. I felt her raw fear of the shifting light and shadow as she plunged forward into the trees. The assault of scent was overwhelming—the stink of blood, the fear stench coming from the man on my back. For a moment, I ceased to be Natan, standing in the clearing, but became the mule herself. Avshalom's sharp heel once again bit into my side. I bucked. Avshalom leaned forward to clutch for my mane, but as he did so, I reared, throwing his head back, right into the twisted bough of the elah tree. The two halves of the branch had grown one over and around the other like crossed legs, formed over years in just such a way that one part gave way as the prince's head cracked against it, opening just enough to entrap his neck, snapping back in a second to pin him in a timber noose, a living gallows. I shied sideways underneath him, freeing myself from his tormenting weight, then I plunged forward, leaving him dangling helplessly, suspended between heaven and earth. The vision ended. I saw and smelled once again as a man, through my own eyes and nostrils.

"Hanging?" barked Yoav. "Is the whoreson dead, then?"

"No, sir. He's alive still, over yonder, caught up in the boughs of that high tree—you can just make out the crown of it from here," he said, raising a quivering arm. I could see the tree he pointed to—wide, graceful, its oblate leaves quivering and shimmering in the slanting light.

Yoav grabbed up the bridle and slung his leg over his own mule. "You witnessed this, and you didn't kill him? I'd have owed you ten shekels of silver and a belt."

"Even for a thousand shekels, I wouldn't raise my hand against the king's son. We know the king's orders. If I disobeyed them, would you have stood by me against his anger?"

Yoav gave no answer. He turned his mule toward one of his arms bearers and grabbed up three darts from the boy's pouch. Then he urged his mule toward the thicket. Shlomo scrambled to his mount also and galloped after him. Yoav's other attendants followed his lead.

Avshalom must have heard the crash of us, coming toward him through the trees. Yoav halted his mule and gazed up, his craggy, weathered features softening into a smirk of satisfaction. Shlomo drew up behind him, his face drawn. Avshalom's eyes, bloodshot and bugging out of his breath-starved face, widened in fear. He tried to strangle out a cry but nothing issued from his purpling lips. He struggled anew to free himself, pulling at the boughs with all his strength, peeling his hands raw with the vain effort to pry the branches apart. But the pressure on his throat, starving him of air, soon depleted him. All he could do was use his failing strength to grip the boughs and support his weight, heaving himself up every moment or so to allow a shallow wisp of breath to reach his chest. His arms trembled with strain. His long hair enspooled itself in the twigs like yarn around a spindle.

Had Yoav waited—even a few minutes—Avshalom would surely have expired of suffocation. But as Avshalom had been impatient for power, so now Yoav was impatient for justice. He took the three darts, which he held in his left fist, and urged his mule forward. He took one dart in his right hand. "This," he cried, plunging the dart into Avshalom's chest, "is for betraying your father. This"—as he sank the second dart—"is for stealing his throne. And this," he said, as he rammed home the last dart, "is for playing me for a fool."

Avshalom's body sagged, the handsome face transformed into a purpling grotesque, his swollen tongue hanging slack from his mouth. Yoav's arms bearers, crying out in relief and bloodlust, swarmed forward and grabbed at the body, wrenching it out of the forked boughs, dragging it to the dirt. Half of Avshalom's hair dangled from the branches, torn, the bloody shreds of scalp still attached. Only Shlomo stood back, his eyes blank and his lips compressed. When the youths stepped back from the corpse, only then did he move forward. He bent down and picked up a stone in each hand. For a moment it seemed he meant to further desecrate his brother's body. Instead, he knelt, and placed the stones reverently. Then he rose and scanned the ground for more. The other youths looked to Yoav, confused. He lifted his chin and folded his arms. "Do it," he said. "Help him." Yoav turned away and rode back to the main part of his army, where he ordered the sounding of horns in the series of blasts that signaled victory. As the failing sun fingered through the treetops, the only other sound was the scuffling of feet in the leaves and the chink of stones settling upon Avshalom's shattered body, as his cairn rose high around him. When it was done, Shlomo threw dirt on his hair and tore his tunic. But as he said the words of the prayer for the dead, his eyes were dry and his voice steady.

Shlomo and I turned back toward Mahanaim, to be with David. I knew that we could not outrun the news of Avshalom's death, so we did not force our pace, resting the footsore, battle-weary mules that carried us. As we rode, the shofar calls carried from one unit to another, echoing all around us through the smoky air. As they heard the high, exultant blasts, Avshalom's forces scattered and fled, knowing that their uprising had failed. Yoav sent out orders: Let them cross the river. There would be no more killings. No pursuit.

XXVI

Well before Shlomo and I reached the gates of Mahanaim, a sentry on the tower called down to David that he saw a man running, alone.

David sprang up. "If he is alone, he has tidings in his mouth." He raised a hand to shade his eyes, scanning the distance for a sight of the messenger. As soon as he could make him out, he left his place at the gate and ran forward to meet him.

As he closed the distance between them, the messenger cried out, "All is well! Praised be the Name, who has delivered up the men who raised their hand against the king."

"Is my boy Avshalom safe?" David cried out to him.

"Let my king know that the Name has vindicated you from all who rebelled against you!"

"Is my boy Avshalom safe?" David demanded again, his voice quavering.

Because he was a foreigner, perhaps, the messenger did not know how his next words would be received. His voice was joyful. "May the enemies of the king and all who rose against you to do you harm fare like that young man!"

The king turned away, blindly pushing off all who rushed to bring him comfort. He staggered back to the gateway, braying like a beaten donkey. It was Batsheva who told me all this, when I rode in with Shlomo. Her face lit for a moment when she saw Shlomo unharmed, but a hollow-eyed look of anguish and concern soon clouded her features. "He's inconsolable," she said. We walked to his rooms. He was prone on the couch in the inner chamber and would not admit us. Through the door, I could make out the rasping words, repeated over and over again: "My son, Avshalom. Oh, my son, my son Avshalom! If only I had died instead of you! Oh, Avshalom, my son, my son!"

On the other side of that door, I felt a great sigh shudder through me. David did not, could not know it, but with this last loss, his punishment, the fourfold retribution that he himself had decreed, was at last completed. The nameless infant. Tamar. Amnon. Avshalom. This would be the last great mourning of his long life, and the most bitter of them all.

Yet it came hard, to the battle-weary troops filing back into the city. They expected to be greeted with singing women and celebration. Instead, they had to creep into a town where a funereal silence prevailed.

When Yoav arrived to the mute palace, he became inflamed with rage. He barged into the antechamber where I sat with Shlomo and Batsheva, and pushed past the attendants who tried to bar his way. "I will see the king, for whom I have just won the victory."

I did not try to hold him back, but followed him, and almost got hit in the face by the heavy door as he slammed it in his anger. I put out my boot at the last minute to wedge the door open, and sidled in behind him. The king lay with his face to the wall, a shawl cast over his head. Yoav stood over the king, his arms folded and his legs apart. Yoav's face worked. He could hardly choke his words out, so intense was his anger:

"What sort of act is this?"

The king rolled onto his side, took the cover off his face for a moment, glanced up at Yoav with wet, blank eyes, and then threw himself back onto his face, moaning.

"Do you even know what you are doing?" Yoav's voice rose. "You have humiliated all your followers. All of us who this day saved your life. And the lives of your sons, and the lives of your wives and concubines. You show love for those who hate you and hate for those who love you. For today you have made it clear that the officers and men mean nothing to you. If Avshalom were alive today and the rest of us dead, would you like that better? You would! Fool, you would prefer it!"

David didn't move. Yoav kicked the pallet, hard.

"Get up! Come outside, and speak a kind word to your loyal followers! For I swear, if you don't get up and get out there and give these men the love that is due to them, not a single one of us will be here in the morning."

Slowly, the king raised a hand and drew the shawl off his haggard face. He fixed his gaze on Yoav. It was the blankest, coldest look I have ever seen. He got to his feet. Deliberately, he walked to the ewer, poured water into the bowl and splashed his face. When Batsheva came in, and moved to help him, he pushed her gently away. He dragged his hands through his damp hair and drew himself up to his full height. He took a breath, and without looking back at Yoav, he spoke in a low, dead voice. "I will do as you say, and set aside my mourning, even if I do not set aside my grief." His voice caught for a moment on that last word, but he took another breath and composed himself. "Send word to Amasa. He is my flesh and blood just as much as you are. But you killed my son, and he served him. I will have him, therefore, to command my army. Not you. You"—he turned, and leveled a killing glare at Yoav—"are relieved."

David walked out, holding himself very erect. I could see the lines of strain in his face, the effort each step cost him. He went to the gateway and called for his troops. And there he stood, for hour after hour, as the men filed by, taking time with each man who wanted a word with him. He did not hide his pain from them. He didn't have to. Unlike Yoav, the common soldiers did not blame him for his excessive grief. They knew him. They knew his flaws. Indeed, I think they loved him all the more because he was flawed, as they were, and did not hide his passionate, blemished nature.

I did not go down with him, but stayed behind in the bedchamber with Yoav. I watched the high color of his anger drain away until he was the pale gray of mortar. I made a sign to clear the room and poured a cup of wine. I had to place it in his hand and curl his fingers around the stem of the goblet.

As soon as we were alone, the door closed, I spoke to him in a low voice. "This is not what it seems to be," I said. "Don't take it to heart."

Yoav snapped out of his stunned trance and glared at me. "'Don't take it to heart'? Are you entirely witless? I have been relieved of my command—I, who saved his wretched life a dozen times, who have followed him, murdered for him. . . . 'Don't take it to heart' when he replaces me with that traitor?"

"You must see that it's a ploy," I said. "He needs Amasa to bring the insurgents back to his side. He can't return to the city if half the people are cowering, afraid of his wrath because they cheered for his traitor son. And he must also win back those who still are against him, willing to rise up for the next man who can rally Shaul's loyalists. He has always been a fox, you know that. He's using his grief for his son and his anger at you as a shield to hide his true intentions. He needs Amasa. For now. But not for long. Be patient. Bide your time. Eat your pride. When the kingdom is knit back into whole cloth, then you can avenge this slight. Think on it. You will see I'm right. You're not your brothers. You're not reckless like Asahel and Avishai. You never have been. The making of this kingdom is your work as much as the king's. So don't throw it away in a moment's rage, no matter how justified."

Yoav drained the cup and banged it down on the table. "You talk and you talk. And I never know what to make of your words. Do you *know* these things? Or are you playing me for some other purpose? If he's a fox, what are you? Snake? Rat? You say you serve him, and yet you've let him walk into every kind of misery and disaster. I never know where I am with you. What you say could be solid gold or not worth a pitcher of piss. How's a normal man to fathom you? I don't even *know* you, after all these many years."

I opened my hands at my sides. "All you say is true," I said. "I am a breath, no more than the ever-turning wind. I can only ask you to believe that I serve the kingdom. This kingdom that you have done so much to make. You will do now what you must. But think on what I have said." Then I left him there and went to find Shlomo. It was important to bring him with me, to stand behind the king, so that we would be there if he turned to look for us.

XXVII

David seemed to take some sustenance from the outpouring of love that he felt from his fighters as they came to him one by one at the gate. In any case, he came to himself sufficiently to make the shrewd judgments that were required of him at that delicate time. We sat down in Mahanaim to bury the dead, mourn the fallen and bind the wounds of the injured. During that time, David sent emissaries to the city and to the provinces, offering pardons and allaying the fears of the rebels who had expected retribution. The elevation of Amasa served him well there. But Amasa wasn't half the general—or the man—that Yoav was, and I felt in my bones that David must know that. One sign that he did: he redivided the army and distributed command. He left Ittai in full charge of his loyal Plishtim. Benaiah still had command of the other foreign forces including the king's bodyguard. But most tellingly, Avishai retained command of his own company and was given his brother's units also. So Amasa's direct control of the forces was severely constrained.

The return to Ir David was accompanied by much celebration. We returned in a very different manner than we had left. David was escorted home by a contingent that included representatives of all the regions and tribes. There was music, of course, and dancing. All who came to the hall of audience seeking reconciliation were granted it. Even the life of Shimei, the kinsman of Shaul who had stoned David during his flight from the city, was spared. Avishai protested, of course, begging the king to let him dispatch the man, but the king rebuked him and said he would show mercy. By extending forgiveness even to such a one, David made sure that his message was clear. He was back on the throne as the king of all Israel.

Which is not to say there was peace in the waning years of his reign. Our strife-prone people are quick to fan grievance, to take sides and to foment revolt. But David's hand was steady in those final years, his judgments cool and measured. It was as if the shortening length of his days and the toll of his illness made him more aware of the limits to his strength. And having less, he spent more wisely. By paying attention to small grievances, he acted to make sure they did not fester into major enmities. If the underlying demand was reasonable, the older David was more likely to accede to it. But conversely, the older David was less likely to overlook any small act that presaged rebellion. If news came to his ears that someone was fomenting schism, that man would be eliminated with dispatch.

During the months after the return to the city, David drew Adoniyah close, thinking to test his mettle now that he was no longer thoroughly overshadowed by his fierce older brothers. It was clear that Adoniyah expected this, and he preened under the king's attention. But it became painfully clear that Adoniyah's abilities were modest, his nature incurious and his understanding limited. In a very short while, David became impatient with this, and stopped including him in the most important councils, finding it easier to get things done with those who knew his mind.

Rather than seeing this as a slight, Adoniyah took it as license to resume his dissipated occupations. He did make a stab of emulating Avshalom, if not in ability, then in excess, providing himself with merkavot and horses, hiring outrunners, and generally assuming the trappings of a young man who expects to be king. David, typically, only shrugged indulgently at the folly of it when it was brought to his notice.

Avshalom had gained much from his mother—the sense of

destiny that derived from her lineage, and the polish and entitlement that came with being the son of a favorite wife herself born royal. Adoniyah had none of these advantages. His own mother, Hagit, had been one of the minor political marriages of the precarious early years in Hevron. She was never a favorite. Once David got a son on her, his interest waned. The king rarely sent for her and, as a boy will, Adoniyah keenly felt the slight. It was, I think, a bitter little seed that he watered over time with envy.

Avshalom had possessed other qualities Adoniyah lacked, in addition to the advantage of his birth. Avshalom had been willing to do the work of winning men's hearts, and had an inborn understanding of what it took to do that. Adoniyah had no such qualities. Vain and feckless, he cultivated only such people who were sycophants and opportunists. There were always plenty of those, ready to fawn on a young man who stands in line for a crown. Some of Avshalom's followers fell into Adoniyah's circle, seeking the superficial glamour it offered. None of this was surprising.

What did surprise me was Yoav. It became clear, in a very short time, that Yoav had become Adoniyah's chief supporter. Yoav blamed me for his estrangement from the king. So he was not inclined to support Shlomo, seeing him as my creature, no matter what his merits. I suppose he transferred his loyalty to the one among David's sons he deemed likeliest, in return for that loyalty, to restore him to his accustomed full command. I began to take note, and to be on guard when I perceived this.

I made sure to let David know of it. I was well aware that he would never again love Yoav. But I sensed that he missed his abilities. And I also sensed he was looking for a way to be rid of Amasa. It was in the midst of a trivial attempt at insurgency among a Benyaminite faction that Yoav found his moment, and David allowed him to seize it. A disgruntled Benyaminite named Sheva had tried to rally supporters and David, acting at the first sign of dissent, dispatched Amasa to deal with it. When Amasa blundered and let Sheva and his rebellious faction give him the slip, David turned to Avishai to take command of the pursuit and set matters to rights. Yoav rode out with his brother. They caught up with Amasa's troops by the great stone of Givon. Yoav dismounted to greet Amasa, coming up to him as he might have approached one of his brothers, drawing him close with his right arm. Amasa never saw the unsheathed knife in his left hand.

It was a reprise of the killing of Avner. But this time, David did not mourn or curse. The king chose to see the matter as Yoav exacting an overzealous punishment for Amasa's dereliction of duty. It helped that Yoav went on to make an end of that rebel without damage to the town in which the scoundrel had taken refuge. In a gesture that recalled Avigail to me, a woman of the town bravely came out to Yoav and begged him to spare her community. Yoav agreed. If they surrendered Sheva, he said, there would be no fighting. That night, a party of townsfolk cornered Sheva, cut off his head, and threw it over the wall to Yoav.

David made public his gladness that the town had been spared and praised Yoav for his management of the incident, using it as the occasion to give Yoav back his place at the head of the armies. But it was not the full command he had once enjoyed. David left in place the division of authority that he had created under Amasa, which meant that Yoav had no direct command of Ittai's forces or, more significantly, Benaiah's. This chafed at Yoav. It proved that the wall raised by the killing of Avshalom still stood between him and David. In some measure Yoav continued to blame me for that, as if I could somehow have forestalled the events that had caused this estrangement. For myself, I did not care. Yoav and I had never liked each other, not from that first moment in the hallway of my father's house. At best, we had been civil, and managed to work together for the same ends. But now those ends diverged.

XXVIII

I have been allowed to see many things. But one thing I had not seen. I did not know David's end. I had imagined it, many times. How not? When Shaul chased us through the dry hills, or the Plishtim arrows darkened the sky above our heads, or the scalding oil, intended for him, showered from the ramparts to splatter and blister my own shoulders, death had been a breath away. When I stood between him and his own enraged, grief-maddened warriors, or we struggled for our footing in the rushing waters of the Yarden, the shadow of death lay heavy upon him. Everything in our entwined lives had prepared me to witness a violent death. But a silent, stalking death, creeping in on the footpads of age and illness: that, I had not foreseen.

I could never have conjured a vision of David as he finally became: a husk of a man, shivering under a mountain of bedclothes. Because he had been so strong, the illness was slow to truly claim him. But at seventy, he finally seemed spent. His body lost all capacity to warm itself. The constant shivering was like a wracking palsy that exhausted him until he could not rise from his bed. And his mind, also exhausted, seemed to wander, so that it was hard to get him to attend to matters that required his word.

As his condition grew worse, Batsheva defied all household protocol to remain at his side, night and day, seeing to his comfort in any way she could. I think everyone, with the possible exception of the dazed and baffled king, knew exactly why she was there. But if her motive was to buy time for Shlomo, David benefited greatly from the ardency of her care.

Adoniyah, still the presumptive heir to the throne, tried his best to thwart her in this. It was not fitting, he claimed, for the king's wife to be ever present. Even in his depleted state, the king received his ministers and his generals when he was able to do so; these men should not have to wait about in an anteroom, kicking their heels, while a mere woman decreed who might come in or when they must go out.

Adoniyah had never liked Batsheva, jealous of her place in the king's affections while his own mother remained unloved. But he played his hand too soon, when David still had the strength to resist him. David ignored Adoniyah's protests and instructed his body-guard, under command of Benaiah, to admit Batsheva without restric-tion, and to rely on her word as to which others might come or go. Unsurprisingly, Shlomo was often in attendance, whereas when Adoniyah or any others among the princes tried to see their father, it often happened that he was sleeping.

Although David had showed little outward concern, I think the knowledge of the tacit alliance between Adoniyah and the unforgiven Yoav weighed heavily on his mind. And Adoniyah's behavior, when he was admitted to see his father, did not help his cause. Each time, he looked his father over with a kind of hunger in his face, as a greedy man might examine a fatling lamb, anxious for the day of slaughter. He did not tap his foot, but one had the sense that he wished to, so impatient was he for this death. David, as frail as he was, sensed this, and was curt with Adoniyah, feigning greater fatigue than he in fact felt, so as to have the young man gone in the shortest pos-sible time.

Batsheva, during these days, wore herself to a nub ensuring the best possible care for David. She searched out healers and herbalists, anyone who could bring a moment of ease. The best of these proved to be a young woman from Shunem, barely more than a girl, who had a prodigious knowledge of plants. This, so she said, had been passed down from mother to daughter in her family over many generations. She knew how to infuse warmed oils with peppercorns, mustard seeds and other heat-giving plants, and applied these unguents with slow, soothing strokes, pressing and releasing David's poor wasted flesh as she hummed low incantations in some forgotten, ancient tongue. She ordered bowls of steaming water, constantly replenished, that she infused with crushed aromatics. These gave the bedchamber a clean and wholesome scent, recalling the honey fragrances of springtime meadows and the bracing tang of cut hay in fresh-mown fields. Whether it was the herbs, the healing touch (she was skillful, and seemed to know every sinew of the body) or merely the presence of a lovely young girl (she also was very beautiful), David seemed to rally from these treatments. And so, at Batsheva's insistence, the girl, Avishag, became David's chief nurse and most constant servant. I noticed that Adoniyah had no issues with *her* presence in the room when he came to visit his father. In fact, his eyes were more often on her, as she organized and prepared her remedies, than on his father.

Shlomo, for his part, brought a different kind of healing. His presence seemed to raise David's spirits, and he took comfort in having the youth stay by him. Sometimes, when he had the energy, he would compose. Shlomo would sound the notes of the melody on the harp strings as David directed him, and write down the words. Although the king no longer had the breath to sing, some of these psalms live on as his finest. Shlomo would bring the notes and lyrics direct from David's chamber to the singing men and women to learn, so that David could hear the psalm he had composed performed for him. David seemed to take pleasure in it, and it delighted Shlomo to be useful in this way.

"You have to hear this one," Shlomo said. He still liked to come to my house when we were not with the king. It was not a matter of lessons anymore; he had no need of them. But to my joy, he seemed to crave my company, and sought it out whenever he had an hour's liberty. He had been with the king earlier in the morning and wanted to share with me the new composition they had worked on together. "Listen, it's lovely—" He hummed the melody, following the lines he'd inscribed.

"*He who rules justly is like the first light of daybreak, a cloudless clime, sunbeams after showers, fingering forth the green of the earth . . .*' And then there's this bit, a little further on . . . '*Will he not cause my success to blossom and my every desire to bloom? But the wicked shall be raked aside like thorns . . .*' I love that—'raked aside'—you feel the carelessness of the gesture, the violence of divine indifference. I wish I had a voice like his, so I could sing it for him myself. I think I will ask that young singer who came to us from the Yezreel—you know the one? He's got the purest tones I've heard, saving the king's own, of course—I wish I could—"

He broke off there, and looked up in surprise as Muwat burst into the room, breathing hard and dropping his market bundle on the flagstones.

"What is it?" I said sharply, starting up from my bench. "Is it the king?" Muwat shook his head, wincing, pressing a hand against a stitch in his side.

"No. They say the king's condition is unchanged. It's not the king. It's Adoniyah. The whole market is abuzz. He's placed vast orders. He's giving a feast, this day, at Enrogel." I knew the place—a pleasant spring in the Wadi Kidron, just southeast of the city walls and set in a wide meadow where a large crowd could assemble for major sacrifices and ceremonies. "I could barely find a loaf or a hen for sale, all the food and livestock—oxen, sheep, fatlings—being prepared and sent off. They say that all the princes are invited—"

"All the princes?" I interrupted sharply. "You?" I said, turning to Shlomo.

"Of course not! I would have told you if he'd—"

"That's what I thought. Who else do they say?"

"The king's courtiers from the tribe of Yudah—not the

Benyaminites, they are not included, or so the rumors say, anyway—
and Yoav, and Aviathar the priest is to perform the sacrifices."

"Is that so? And yet I am not invited, nor Shlomo here, and not
Benaiah, either, I'll be bound." I turned to Shlomo, who was standing
now, wide-eyed. I put my hands on his shoulders—he was almost as
tall as me, suddenly—and I felt the power surging through me, painful and raw, as if I'd grasped a naked flame. He felt it, too. His large
eyes widened and a deep flush of excitement colored his ivory skin.

"It's time," I said. "Are you ready?"

He didn't answer me in words, but the high carriage of his head
and the set of his shoulders gave me my reply.

At the palace, I did not need to ask for Batsheva. She was waiting for
us in the anteroom, and as soon as we entered she sent the guards out.

"This is it, isn't it? Adoniyah is going to declare himself king today."

"He will—he may be doing so even now. And if he does this, the
next thing he will do is kill you, and your son."

"No!" said Shlomo, enfolding his mother in a protective embrace.

"Let her go," I said. "Go in there, Batsheva, and tell the king to put
Shlomo on the throne. Remind him that he made you this promise,
when his sin caused your first son to die."

She stared at me, her eyes very wide, her face pale. "But he made
me no such promise," she whispered.

I turned my hand, brushing away her concern. "Say it. I will support you."

"I can't," she said, her voice catching. "It isn't true."

"You will. If you love your son. You will do what is necessary."

I heard the words come out of my mouth. David's words. *What is
necessary.* How often had I despised those words—the utilitarian will-
ingness they signified, that anything may be done in the quest for power.
Now I, too, was after power, and I, too, would do what was necessary
to secure it. "Go in," I said to Batsheva. "I will come in after you and
tell him that it must be."

"Must be? You mean you know it will be?"

Did I? At this moment, I was no longer sure what I truly knew. I had seen Shlomo crowned, the city grown great, the glory of the temple on the hill. But of how that would happen, and if it would begin today, I had no certainty. I did not share this doubt with her. At this moment, I needed her to believe in me. "I have said it. Now go."

I gave her a few moments, and then I came in behind her. She was kneeling by David's bed, his spare, trembling hand clutched in her own. "The eyes of all Israel look this way," she whispered. "Tell them who shall succeed you on the throne. Otherwise—" Her voice caught. "Otherwise, when you lie down with your fathers, Adoniyah will have us put to death."

I came up then, and bowed low, as I had not done in some years. "Did you say that Adoniyah was to succeed you as king? Because right now, at the sacrificial feast, with Yoav's army behind him and your priest Aviathar in front of him, they are claiming your throne. Listen, and you will probably soon hear the shouting. If you have decreed this, without telling me, your servant, then I will say no more."

"I decreed no such thing, as you well know," he rasped. His face creased with strain. He struggled to sit upright. He was gasping for breath, his skin mottled. The girl Avishag hurried to assist him, supporting him into a position that eased his breathing, then running her hands across his brow and temples. He shrugged her off. "Batsheva!" he said, his voice clear. "As the Lord lives, who has rescued me from every trouble, I swear that your son, Shlomo, will succeed me as king, and sit on my throne this very day."

Batsheva bowed her head and kissed his mottled hand. "May you live," she said, her voice breaking.

"Summon me the priest Zadok, and Benaiah."

I had already asked Muwat to fetch them, and they were waiting outside. "Get me to the chair," David commanded. "Bring me my cloak." David let Avishag and me help him to his high-backed, carved chair. Batsheva draped his purple cloak around him, arranging the folds so as to hide his tremors. When Zadok and Benaiah entered,

David intended that they should see a king, not an invalid. I registered the surprise in their faces. Benaiah, who had a daily audience at which the king, at times, was often too weak to raise his head, checked at the door in surprise to see David looking more like himself. I could read real gladness in his face at the change. But when Benaiah and Zadok began their greetings and well wishes, David cut them off abruptly.

"Take my loyal soldiers, and have my son Shlomo ride on my own mule, and bring him down to Gihon. Zadok, Natan, you two will anoint him there, king over all Israel. When that is done, sound every shofar, and proclaim 'Long live the king.' Then march up after him, and let him sit on my throne. For I say to you here: He shall succeed me as king; today I designate him ruler over Israel and Yudah."

As soon as Benaiah and Zadok left the room, David slumped in the chair. We helped him to the bed, where he fell into the pillows, spent. Avishag busied herself with her herbs, crushing a handful of leaves into boiling water so that a sharp, refreshing scent filled the chamber.

I knelt beside David and whispered in his ear: all that I had seen and had not been able to say, the vision of the great kingdom that would arise under his son's rule, its grandeur and magnificence. The judgments he would render that would make his name a byword for wisdom and good governance through the centuries. "And there will be peace, at last," I said. "What you started, what you bought with so much blood, that will be over finally. He will finish it. And then, all the days of his rule, the people of the Land will dwell in safety, each under his own vine and his own fig tree."

David closed his eyes and smiled. But then he gripped my hand. "And the temple?" he rasped.

"The temple!" I built it for him there, dressed stone by dressed stone, the carved cedars inscribed with gourds and calyxes, the solid gold overlay gleaming within the holy of holies. Every detail of my vision I set out for him, and I think, by the end of it, he saw what I had seen. He lay back, breathing easier. After a little, a frown creased his brow. "He'll have to kill them. Yoav, for certain. Adoniyah, probably. Others . . ."

I laid a hand on his forehead. "Not now. You do not need to think of this today. I promise you, you will have time. Because of what you do today, you will have time to sit with him, to tell him how to be a king. To show him what he needs to do, to tell him what will be . . ." I swallowed, as if to choke back the word, but it came out, as it must ". . . necessary." But this time, what was necessary also would be what was just. David sighed. "It won't be easy for him."

"Not at first," I agreed. "But you will live to see with your own eyes the beginning of the greatness you have created."

"With your help, Natan. With your help." He put his trembling hand on my head, and gave me his blessing. I felt a surge of power pass through him into me, and I knew that the Name was still with him, animating his soul, even as his body failed.

There was a knock on the door then, Benaiah's aide telling me that all were assembled. "They wait only for you, to start out for the Gihon spring."

I clasped David's hand, feeling the bones move under the loose flesh. "Rest now," I said. "Rest, and listen. May what you hear make you glad." I stood, and signed to Batsheva. She came and knelt in my place, running her hand tenderly through the strands of David's faded hair.

Outside, a crowd was already gathering, word running in whispers and cries through the streets of the city. The king's bodyguard had formed up in ranks, the sunlight flaring off their polished armor and their bright painted shields, their banners snapping in the light breeze. Zadok was there, in his priestly robes, his acolyte holding aloft the great chased horn of sacred oil that resided in the tent of the ark. In the midst of it all, Shlomo, clad in brilliant white linen, gleamed. He was already mounted on David's mule. They had caparisoned her richly in ceremonial cloths and combed her mane till it rippled. She held her proud head high.

We took our places, Zadok on one side of Shlomo and I on the other. Benaiah gave the order and we marched, the soldiers' feet on the stones beating a celebratory tattoo. By the time we reached Gihon, the crowd was enormous. I looked up at the high walls that surrounded the pool of the spring. People stood four and five deep on the ramparts.

Shlomo dismounted, and I led him to the spring. "Behold," I cried, "Shlomo, son of David, whom the king himself chose this day, by the will of the Name, to succeed him, and sit upon his throne, so that he can see with his own eyes the new king, and may the Name exalt him and make him even more renowned."

Then Zadok stepped forward, and when he raised the horn, a deep hush fell on the crowd. He tilted the vessel, letting the holy oil fall in a sinuous golden thread from the mouth of the horn to the glossy head bowed before him.

Then Shlomo stood, his face, ecstatic, lifted up to the sunshine. The silence erupted. A cry went up, "Long live the king!" And then the shofars sounded, echoing off the walls until it seemed as if the whole city, even its earth, stone and mortar, cried out in joy.

Over in Enrogel, Yoav paused, a juicy lamb shank halfway to his mouth. He turned his head sharply in the direction of the clamor. "Why is the city in such an uproar?" There were flutes now joining in the mix, cymbals and drums, and cheers turning to voices raised in song, as the anointed king made his way back up through the streets to the throne room. Yoav threw down his uneaten meat and pushed his way through the crowd to Adoniyah, who was also on his feet, staring blankly back toward the city.

There, in the palace, in the king's bedchamber, David heaved himself upright as he heard the cries of acclamation, the blasts of the shofars. He reached for Batsheva, drew her close and kissed her. Then he lay back on the soft bank of pillows that Avishag had arranged to cradle his wasted body. As sometimes happened, there was a moment of respite from the storm of tremors. The ague stilled. David lay quietly, listening.

This is what he heard: All the musicians he had brought to the city. All the singing men and women. All the children who had grown up with instruments in their hands and songs on their lips. His own music. His gift to the people now returned to him in magnificent abundance. He had made of his city an accidental choir, an unintended orchestra. The surge of sound rose and swelled. Then, for a long moment, all the notes came together, all the music of the heavens and the earth, combining at last into one sustained, sublime, entirely glorious chord.

Afterword

David is the first man in literature whose story is told in detail from early childhood to extreme old age. Some scholars have called this biography the oldest piece of history writing, predating Herodotus by at least half a millennium. Outside of the pages of the Bible, however, David has left little trace. A single engraving uncovered at Tel Dan mentions his house. Some buildings of the Second Iron Age period might have been associated with a leader of his stature. But I tend to agree with Duff Cooper, who concluded that David must have actually existed, for no people would invent such a flawed figure for a national hero.

Of the innumerable studies and analyses of David, my personal favorites are Robert Pinksy's classic monograph *The Life of David* (Schocken) and David Wolpe's recent study, *David: The Divided Heart* (Yale). Both of these arresting accounts accept David's character in all its dazzling contradictions rather than feeling the necessity, common in other biographies, of all-out veneration or execration.

I relied heavily on three other reference works: *The Jewish Study Bible* (Oxford), *City of David: The Story of Ancient Jerusalem* by Ahron Horovitz (Lambda) and *Life in Biblical Israel* by Philip J. King and Lawrence E. Stager.

My rabbi, Caryn Broitman, offered many valuable insights. I am grateful to Richard North Patterson and Bob Tyler of the Cohen Group for introducing me to Dr. Joseph Draznin, who gave me the benefit of his strategic thinking as to how David and Yoav might have managed their assault on Yebus.

My younger son, Bizu Horwitz, was a marvelous research assistant during our trip to Israel, playing the agile young David to my weary Shaul as he sprinted ahead of me up rocky hills behind Ein Gedi.

I am blessed with remarkable publishing teams, especially in the United States and Australia, and I would like to especially thank Paul Slovak, editor extraordinaire, and my agent and friend Kris Dahl.

I'm thankful to my early readers Darleen Bungey, Elinor and Tony Horwitz, Christine Farmer and Laure Sudreau-Rippe. But most especially, as always, the incomparable and indispensable Graham Thorburn.

In 2005, my nine-year-old son made the unusual decision to learn the harp, which started me reflecting on that other long-ago boy-harpist. At his bar mitzvah five years later, he played an arrangement of Leonard Cohen's classic "Hallelujah." So it is to Nathaniel that I owe both the inspiration for this book and the idea for its title.

West Tisbury, March 2015

KITTIM
[CYPRUS]

The Kingdom
of
DAVID
c. 1000 B.C.E.

Th

map by Laura Hartman Maestro ©2015

• Bubastis

• Memphis

MITZRAYIM
[EGYPT]

Lake
Moeris

Nile River

Conjectural Boundary
of the Kingdom of David =

0   25   50   75 miles
0   40   80   120 kilometers